Real Love From A Real One

MISS JENESEQUA

Contents

Miss Jenesequa

Sex Ain't Better Than Love: A Complete Novel
Down For My Baller: A Complete Novel
Bad For My Thug 1 & 2 & 3
The Thug & The Kingpin's Daughter 1 & 2
Loving My Miami Boss 1 & 2 & 3
Giving All My Love To A Brooklyn Street King 1 & 2
He's A Savage But He Loves Me Like No Other 1 & 2 & 3
Bad For My Gangsta: A Complete Novel
The Purest Love for The Coldest Thug 1 & 2 & 3
The Purest Love for The Coldest Thug: A Christmas Novella
My Hood King Gave Me A Love Like No Other 1 & 2 & 3
My Bad Boy Gave Me A Love Like No Other: A Complete
Novella
The Thug That Secured Her Heart 1 & 2 & 3
She Softened Up The Hood In Him 1 & 2 & 3 & 4
You're Mine: Chosen By A Miami King: A Complete Novel
A Love That Melted A Capo's Cold Heart: A Complete Novel
Real Love From A Real One

She's a go-getter who walks to the beat of her own drum, ready to ride for her sisters whenever and wherever, and taken by a man who would rather she play housewife than CEO.

He's an undisputed king in his city, a man that commands the attention of any room he walks into, and unconcerned with matters of the heart.

Thyri Wright and Killian Miller are next on Cupid's hit list. And one thing about Cupid's arrow? It never misses its target. Once Thyri and Killian's worlds collide, nothing will be the same ever again.

Chapter One

"You're married?" Loud laughter filled the room. "You must be joking."

If a random stranger had told her yesterday that this would be the scene playing out in front of her today, Thyri would've straight up laughed in their face.

"I'm not, Tru." Thyri's sister, Tanai, the one that had decided to drop the biggest bomb on their lives this afternoon, lifted her left ring finger. The pretty diamond rock sitting on her espresso brown skin sparkled brightly. "I'm really married."

If a random stranger had told her yesterday that her sister would be sitting opposite her today, flashing a ring that looked like it cost a damn fortune, Thyri would've laughed the entire place down. Because that had to be a joke, right? There was no way that her sister had gotten hitched to some unknown man without having her two sisters by her side. There was absolutely no way! It had to be a joke.

This was no joke though and as Thyri's eyes dropped back

down to the invitation she held in her palms, she was well aware of how unfunny this situation was.

The gold, elegant font clearly read:

Thyri Wright,
Please join us to celebrate the new union of Mr. & Mrs. Miller.
Kason & Tanai Miller were married in a private ceremony on July
14th and would love to have your presence at their reception.

"You leave us for six months and pop back up as someone's wife." Truth laughed once again. It was clear however from her dry laughter that she wasn't finding any of this funny. "Wow. I'd rather this be one big joke after all."

Tanai was silent but the guilty look growing in her deep-set eyes said everything she failed to say.

She knew how bad it looked. Leaving her triplets and their company behind had been a selfish thing to do but she'd needed the space. She needed time to do her own thing. Did she know that in the six months that would pass she would return a married woman? *No.* But what she did know was that she'd found her soulmate. A man that loved her for her, flaws and all. The man she planned to spend the rest of her life with and push out all the babies he wanted.

"You leave us all alone, to deal with all our clients and don't even give us the courtesy of a damn phone call during your time away but you have the audacity to show up here after all these months and act like everything is sweet. Like we're just supposed to drop everything and be there for you at this wack ass reception. The same way you were there for us, huh?"

"Truth..." Thyri gently called out to her, hoping that she could get her to calm down because it was clear by her harsh tone and hardened face that she was getting riled up.

"No, I don't wanna hear it, Ri." Truth shook her head dismissively at Thyri before glaring at Tanai who sat on the other end of the sofa she currently sat on. "How do you think Dad would feel knowing that you not only left us - the one thing he made us all vow to never do - but you also got married without us being present? Huh? How do you think he would feel, Tanai?"

"I'm... I'm sorry, Tru... I didn't plan for things to happen that way but it did and I'm sorr—"

"Fuck your sorry," Truth snapped. "You weren't sorry when you left us, claiming that you needed a break to... what was that sorry ass excuse she used again, Ri?"

Truth rubbed her right hand on her chin as she pretended to be deep in thought.

"Oh yeah I remember. You claimed you needed a break..." Truth lifted up air quotes as she said the words, "to find yourself." Truth released a callous chuckle. "And you most definitely weren't sorry when you let this Kason mothafucka put a ring on your finger without even introducing him to your family. Your *real* family. Not this new fake ass family you've got now that you're married to this nigga that I know for a fact you don't even know that damn well."

"Truth, that's enough."

Truth's face scrunched up with anger at Thyri's attempt to get her to chill.

"No, she needs to hear how the fuck I feel about her bullshit ass marri—"

"I said that's enough," Thyri ordered, cutting Truth off in a tone that was stern enough to make her go quiet. "Enough."

Thyri's eyes darted from sister to sister. One was clearly filled with anger and her chest now heaving up and down showed that it had no intentions of going away just yet. The second was filled with shame as her head was lowered, making her lap her only view right now.

"Tanai."

The call of her name made her look up and stare into her sister's loving eyes.

"I'm not gonna lie and act like you didn't hurt us when you left us because you did. But I understand why you did it. All our lives all we've known is this." Thyri pointed at the large space around them. "Daddy left us this place and it's all we've ever done. Keeping this place thriving the best we can and making him proud."

The Wright triplets were the proud owners of The Wright Way LLC, a successful cleaning company that had been passed down to them from their late father. He'd built the company from the ground up and the office they were in now had been his office that they'd expanded. They'd made it so that they each had their own individual desk area by each wall of the room and their own seating area where they were all seated now.

They were triplets but non-identical and had been raised by their father who they'd sadly lost three years ago to a brain aneurysm. Their mother had died two weeks after giving birth to the sisters due to a rare condition - amniotic fluid embolism – which triggered her heart and lungs to collapse. So unfortunately the girls had never met their mother.

The Wright sisters had been dealt a hard hand in life a couple times but the sisters came out stronger each time. Despite no longer having both their parents in their lives, they were doing well for themselves and thanks to their late father, they had a successful company that was providing them with a healthy income and a trusted team of workers.

"Now look... Truth has every right to feel the way she does towards you but what she will always feel, no matter how hard she tries to fight it, is love. We will always love you no matter what. And we're glad that you've found someone who makes you happy, Tanai. That's all we could ever want for you. As for the reception, you can count me there. I wouldn't miss it for the world."

"Thank you, sis. That really means everything coming from you," Tanai replied, sending a warm smile Thyri's way, which she returned.

Tanai slowly looked over at Truth to see that she wasn't looking at either of them. Her sight was set on the teal wall behind Thyri's head, her expression still annoyed from before.

"And I know I have a lot of making up to do in order to repair our relationship. Truth... Truth, please look at me."

Not wanting to give in easily, Truth remained looking at the wall for a few seconds but when she felt a soft hand hold hers, she looked down to see Tanai's hand. Then she looked over at Tanai to see that she'd shifted down the sofa to be closer to her.

"I really am sorry and I promise to make things right. My time away from you both made me realize how much I love running Dad's company with my sisters. It's what I'm good at the most and I have so many new ideas that I really want to share with you guys. I missed you both terribly and I really hope you can find it in your heart to forgive me for being such a fool. I never should've left you both and I'm sorry I didn't call. Those lousy texts I sent weren't good enough, I know. I just didn't know how to pick up the phone and talk to you both after what I'd done... I wasn't even sure if you'd want to see me again. I'm so sorry. Please forgive me, Truth."

Truth was silent as she stared into the eyes of her sister but her hardened face was softening more and more with each passing moment.

"Please, Tru?" Tanai lifted her sister's hand and gently shook it. "Forgive me?"

Truth's silence remained for a few more seconds before she said, "Buy me a new car and I might consider it."

Tanai giggled and her sisters followed suit, giggling happily.

"Y'all are laughing now but I'm dead ass," Truth commented between her laughter before stopping to say, "I'm sorry for calling your marriage bullshit... Anger got the best of me there."

"Apology accepted, sis." Tanai moved even closer to her sister so they could embrace and Thyri smiled at the sight of them hugging. It was a sight she'd truly missed seeing.

"You're right to feel some type of way about it though," Tanai announced after their hug was done. "Kason and I haven't been together that long but I feel like I've known him my entire life."

"Where did you even meet him?" Truth questioned, wanting to know everything about her sister and her new husband.

"How did he propose?" Thyri asked, also wanting to know everything. "And where was this private ceremony?"

They couldn't help it. This was their sister that had gotten married without their knowledge and now that the news was out, they wanted to know every single detail.

Without hesitating, Tanai told them everything. How she met Kason outside the gym she went to, located in downtown Atlanta and how he wanted her number and wasn't letting her leave him without it. How he'd called her that same night to take her out on a date and feeling smitten by him, she decided to take him up on his offer. She thought he'd be the one to pick her up but he'd told her to meet him there. Not thinking too deeply into it, Tanai met him at the restaurant and to her surprise he'd arrived dressed casual.

"The man still looked fine as hell so I didn't care about the sweats and hoodie."

The date seemed to be flowing well. He told her to order whatever she wanted and she did. They got to know each other

6

better over their delicious meal, sides, and drinks. Everything seemed to be going just right until Tanai was suddenly taken by surprise.

"Tell me why we get to the end of this date and this nigga tells me he forgot his wallet."

Both Thyri and Truth's eyes grew large.

"What the hell, man?" Thyri frowned.

"You sure you married the right man, sis?" Truth asked, looking her sister up and down suspiciously.

Tanai stifled a laugh and nodded before continuing. She went on to say how she paid for the meal and chalked up the situation to him genuinely forgetting his wallet. That was until she got outside and saw the car he was driving. Its bumper was falling off, it had scratches all over its paint job and one window was missing and had been replaced with duct tape. You would think that seeing all that and the fact that he'd forgotten his "wallet" would make Tanai flee from this man but when he asked her out on a second date, she said yes.

"Oh my God, my sister has married a bum!" Truth cried out, suddenly dropping down to her knees. "Lord, why, whyyyyyyy!"

Now Tanai couldn't hold back any of her laughter and she watched as Truth cried out to God and Thyri jumped into the empty space next to her and started shaking her incessantly.

"Can the real Tanai Wright please come out! Whoever's taken over my sister, your ass needs to get the fuck gone, now!" Thyri yelled as she shook Tanai's shoulders.

"Both of you please stopppp... I can't breathe!" Tanai's uncontrollable giggles filled the room at her sisters' antics. "Just let me finish the story. I promise you it's good."

Thyri and Truth decided to listen and stop acting out at the potential fact that their sister had married a bum. Tanai went onto explain the second date and how they went for another meal.

Again, Kason forgot his wallet and this time Tanai decided to confront him about it.

She told him how she didn't appreciate the lies and if he couldn't afford to keep taking her out, then he shouldn't force himself to do something that he clearly couldn't do at the moment. He was already aware of the cleaning company she owned with her sisters as it had come up during their conversations so he knew she didn't need him for his cash but what she would need was some honesty about his financial situation. He'd already said on their first date that he worked for a security company but didn't go into detail about what he did at the company. Tanai figured he would open up eventually but now that he was using the "I forgot my wallet" excuse again, she was starting to realize that there was a deeper reason as to why he wasn't going into detail about his job.

The "I forgot my wallet" trick was old and downplayed. She was a grown ass woman and wasn't here for the games. She liked him a lot and admitted that to him but she didn't want him to feel like dating her was something he had to do. She would rather he get himself in order and then maybe one day soon when he had gotten himself together, they could resume dating.

After she spoke her mind, Kason didn't say a word. He just simply nodded which Tanai found odd but she took it as him having nothing to counter what she'd said. In her mind, he was agreeing with what she'd said about getting himself in order and their dating stage had come to an end. And just as the waiter passed their table, Tanai told him that she was ready to pay the bill. However, the waiter told her that it had already been taken care of. She asked, "By who?"

Kason answered with, "By me."

It was then that she was led out the restaurant by Kason, who refused to answer any of her questions just yet. She saw a parked

Rolls Royce outside the restaurant and her confusion only heightened when Kason led her to the car's backseat that had an unknown man sitting in the driver's seat ahead. She soon learned the man to be Kason's driver.

Once inside, Kason told her everything. How he'd been testing her and though it angered her to hear him say what he'd been doing, she understood once he told her about his previous bad experiences with women. Since she didn't know who he was when they first met and the weight his first name carried in the city, he wanted to make sure that she was really legit. That's why he'd tested her by not telling her his full name, dressed casually for their date with no jewelry on, pretended to forget his wallet and shown up with a busted ass car that he'd gotten from his brother's car shop.

Instead of having the angry reaction that women who were only after his funds would usually have, she had the opposite. Encouraging him to get his financial situation in order first before trying to court her, she'd rather he sort out his pockets and make sure he was good first before trying to impress her. He respected that too much and knew that he wasn't letting her out of his sight after tonight.

That same night, Kason took her out the country on his private jet and he'd made it clear that he wanted her. Her and *only* her. Tanai already being smitten by him long before finding out about his wealth, wanted him just as bad.

So it began.

He jetted her from country to country in his private jet and spared no expense when it came to treating her right. Anything she needed he took care of. Her clothes, her food, her happiness - all taken care of without her having to say a word. Kason Miller was a man who knew who and what he wanted and Tanai was exactly that.

9

Five months later after their trips around the world, he'd proposed on a private island in Grenada and that same night, they'd gotten married.

"I didn't even realize the first day we'd met, that I'd met him outside his luxury gym. I thought it was my first day meeting him but he'd seen me many times before, coming in and doing my thing at the gym. He was just waiting for the right moment to ask me out. All this time I'd been going to his gym and didn't even know. The KMG? That stands for Kason Miller. And he owns a tech company... Shield."

"Oh. My. God." Truth's bottom lip dropped wide open. "No. Fucking. Way."

Thyri was speechless. All she could do was look at her sister with wide eyes.

Shield was the security system company that the women used in their office. It was also used all over the country by millions and used all over the world.

The Miller Sisters had no idea that Kason was the CEO of Shield because they hadn't cared to know or find out. All they knew was that Shield was a popular security tech brand and the brand that guarded their office. Truth's mind drifted to a memory of last week when she'd caught a glimpse of a news ticker on CNN about Shield's financials.

"Isn't that company worth over a billion doll..." Tanai started nodding and Truth gasped, quickly covering her mouth.

The more Thyri stared at her sister, the more she realized that though Tanai remained her sweet, kindhearted sister, she'd become a new woman now that she was the wife of a billionaire. There was an aura about her that was different, more high class and even the clothes she donned today showed that.

She wore a white blazer pant suit set that gave very much rich bitch energy with the Tom Ford padlock heels on her feet. The white Kelly Birkin that she'd left on the other end of the sofa only added to the rich bitch energy including her diamond earrings and matching diamond tennis necklace. There was also a diamond encrusted Patek Philippe watch that was secured around her left wrist.

Now don't get it twisted... The Wright sisters had a lot of coin thanks to their father leaving them behind a six figure empire that was well on its way to being seven but the coin that Tanai Wright currently exuded? It was well past seven, eight and even nine figures.

"Tanai Wright, you've won," Truth voiced. "There is no *how we met* story that could ever top yours, girl. You've won."

Tanai chuckled before sighing happily.

"I never in a million years thought I would ever meet a man like him... he's rich yes but he's so good to me. He's everything I could've ever needed and more. He said from the second he laid eyes on me, he knew that I was his wife. Now here I am..." Her eyes dropped to her ring. "His wife."

"You deserve this and so much more, Nai." Thyri wrapped her arms around her sister, pulling her in close. "He better treat you right or he'll have us to answer to. I don't care how rich he is, I'll break his face if need be."

"And that Rolls Royce and however many cars he has will all be smashed to pieces," Truth chimed in as she neared her sister, wrapping her arms around her as well.

Tanai chuckled at their jokingly threatening manner towards her husband, glad to know that no matter what they always had her back.

Both Thyri and Truth rested their heads against Tanai's shoulder while they hugged. The Wright sisters all looked down at Tanai's oval shaped diamond ring that seemed to be shining brighter and brighter with each look they gave it.

"I can't wait for this reception now," Truth spoke up moments later. "I hope his family's nice."

"...I hope they are too," Tanai responded and her response was enough to make Truth and Thyri look over at her with surprise.

"You haven't met them yet?" Thyri questioned.

Tanai shook her head from side to side.

"It all happened so fast and since we've been back, he wanted me focused on picking out our house and working with our reception planner. I'll be meeting his brothers later on today, his mother and father tomorrow but as for the rest of his family... I'll be meeting them at the reception for the first time." Tanai sighed. "That's why I'd really appreciate it if you were both by my side when I do."

Both Thyri and Truth nodded.

"We'll be there," Thyri promised, knowing that she meant it.

They would be supporting their sister no matter what and hoped to God that Kason's family didn't disrespect her because if they did, they'd be getting disrespected right back. Thyri didn't care who they were and how much money they had, no one was about to treat her sister horribly.

"And there's no way in hell that I'm about to miss meeting the man who bagged up my sister so quick," Truth added.

"He wouldn't miss meeting both of y'all, either," Tanai voiced which made her sisters send pleased looks her way. "Which is why he's outside in the car waiting for me to give him the green light."

"What?" Thyri's lips curled into a small smile.

"I didn't want to ambush you guys by bringing him up with me," Tanai explained, reaching for their hands, and squeezing tight. "I knew it was best that I came to see you alone and tell you the news. I also knew I had to apologize for my absence out of your lives and I didn't want to force him in your face if you weren't really feeling me."

"Well we're feeling you, hoe! Go get his ass!" Truth exclaimed, snatching her hand out of Tanai's grasp and pointing to the door. "I was gonna beat his ass at the reception *and* bust the windows out his car for marrying you without our permission but I guess my lucky ass can do it all now."

"Truth!" Thyri shook her head and chuckled at her sister's playful threat. "Guess we're beating his ass together cause you know damn well you can't take him on by yourself with your short self."

"Can too." Truth stuck her tongue out at her sister.

Alright, alright, no beating up my man, please and thank you." Tanai giggled lightly. "Let me go get him."

Tanai got up from her seat, leaving her sister's side and grabbed her Birkin.

"I'll be five minutes," she said, reaching into her bag for her iPhone.

Both Thyri and Truth nodded and watched her slip out the room. The girls started squealing with delight, playfully pushing each other and seconds later Truth started running up and down their office space, wailing her hands up in the air like a madwoman that had just set herself free from a mental asylum.

"Tru, if you don't stop playing around!" Thyri's laughter couldn't be contained as she watched her sister running up and down.

Truth ignored her, continuing to do her thing until the sound of footsteps nearing their office door caught her attention minutes later, making her stop messing around and race back to her seat next to her sister. She quickly fixed up her clothes and hair, straightening them out and sitting up straight with one leg crossed over the other. By the time the door's handle started turning, Thyri and Truth's heads were facing the door.

The door was pulled open and Tanai's pretty face appeared

with a friendly smile. Her arm was stretched out behind her as she held onto the hand of the man who owned her heart.

"Ri, Tru... I'd like you to meet my husband... Kason Miller."

Tanai stepped into the room and right behind her was her husband.

Kason Miller was no eyesore. His tall frame towered behind his wife. He had low cut hair with light curls spiraling out his scalp, small yet bold, chestnut eyes that sat below thick brows, a light beard that covered the lower half of his face and full, pink lips.

He was clad in a white button down shirt, matching Tanai's pant suit and gray slacks covered his long legs with a silver Hermes belt around his waist. From the way his shirt framed his physique, you could tell he was in good athletic shape and the arms of his shirt had been rolled up slightly, giving a sneak peek of the tats inked into his smooth beige skin. A silver chain hung around his neck, a matching silver stud in each ear and a shiny silver watch locked around his wrist.

To put it simply, this man was fine as hell and The Wright sisters could clearly see how their sister had become smitten with this man regardless of how much money he had in the bank.

They'd stepped into the room looking like a damn power couple and Thyri and Truth were truly enthralled by the sight of them together. Tanai led him deeper into the room, walking towards the seating area where Thyri and Truth sat.

"Thyri, Truth, it's a pleasure to finally meet you both," his deep baritone sounded into the room. "I see beauty clearly runs in the family. Got me feeling like Shrek up in here being around the three of y'all."

"Oh wow, he's a charmer I see," Truth spoke up, feeling her cheeks warm at his compliment.

"Still keen on beating my man up, sis?" Tanai questioned

Truth with a smirk, coming to stand a short distance away from where Thyri and Truth sat.

"You snake." Truth sent a shocked look her way. "You were supposed to keep that between us, heifer."

Kason chuckled.

"My bad for not having you both by your sister's side when I made her my wife and not seeking permission before I did so. I deserve that beat down for sure but before you try to beat my ass, how about you take me up on my offer of making it up to the both of you with a trip to the island I married your beautiful sister on someday soon?"

"I like him already, sis," Truth announced, getting up from her seat and rushing over to the newlyweds. "Throw in a new car too and you can forget all about me planning to bust the windows out your Rolls."

"Truth!"

"Kiddingggg," Truth replied to Tanai's playful yell of her name.

Thyri had gotten out her seat too and was now walking over to Tanai and her new husband. Thyri hadn't said a word yet and it had Tanai slightly on edge because out of the three sisters, Thyri was the mother figure. She was not only the triplet that had come out first, but she was also the triplet who always settled their disagreements and the one that always held the highest and most important voice. Whatever she said went and Tanai hoped to God that she wasn't about to show her disapproval towards Kason.

Thyri came to stand next to Truth. There was a short gap between the sisters and the married pair. Thyri's eyes darted up and down, carefully taking Kason in with a straight face. An awkward silence quickly formed and Tanai felt her stomach begin to knot at Thyri's lack of words. But her worry was short-lived.

"I'm liking the sound of that trip but a free membership to your bougie ass gym sounds even better."

"Deal," Kason agreed, grinning wide at Thyri, and extending his hand out for her to shake which she did.

"Welcome to the family, Kay Billy," Truth announced, making both Tanai and Thyri throw her a strange look. "What? He's a billionaire right? Only right I nickname him Billyyyy!"

"You're crazy, you know that?" Thyri shook her head at her sister. "You ain't even known the man long and you're already nicknaming him and shit."

"Kay Billy works just fine," Kason stated, a hearty chuckle escaping him. "It's got quite a ring to it. Don't you think, baby?"

Tanai nodded at him, smiling at the interaction between him and her sisters.

Thyri and Truth took turns in giving him a friendly embrace, both feeling like tiny ants in his arms as they each hugged him.

Thyri was glad that Kason seemed so friendly and hoped that the rest of his family were the same. Their reception was next weekend and as much as she was looking forward to meeting the rest of The Millers, Thyri still had her guard up. If any of them wanted to try to disrespect Tanai, Thyri would be defending her sister no matter what and didn't care who felt her wrath. Anyone could get it. Even Kason if he didn't treat her sister right in the long run so if he knew what was best for him, he wouldn't mess things up. If he did, Thyri Wright would be coming for him and Truth Wright would be right beside her, ready to make him pay.

Chapter Two

"This has to be a joke." Kadiri shook his head as he stared down at the invitation he held. "Ain't no way this ain't a joke."

Killian's eyes were fixed on his invitation too. His eyes constantly shifting from his brother's name to the word 'married.' A word he never in a million years would have thought his younger brother would become this damn soon.

Killian Miller,
Please join us to celebrate the new union of Mr. & Mrs. Miller.
Kason & Tanai Miller were married in a private ceremony on July 14th and would love to have your presence at their reception.

"It's not a joke," a mellow voice spoke up. "We're really married."

Killian's gaze lifted from the invitation to the owner of the voice that had just spoken up.

She had thick brows that sat above chocolate brown eyes that were fringed with long eyelashes. Her oval shaped face was coated with flawless looking espresso brown skin. Skin that seemed to be glowing more and more with each passing second. Her jet black hair was split into a middle part, flowing past her shoulders, and stopping at the middle of her back. The woman that now carried the Miller last name was a beauty and anyone denying it was a fool.

"Blink twice if you need to be saved, sweetheart."

Killian almost cracked a smile at Kadiri's comment but he suppressed it. He wasn't in the mood to smile because this moment wasn't a smile worthy moment. This right here was a mouth wide open worthy moment.

"'Cause ain't no way in hell, you over here married to his goofy ass out of freewill."

Kason lifted his freehand towards his brother and extended his middle finger at him.

"Sonny... be nice."

But the call of his nickname and the order for him to act appropriately made Kason drop his rude gesture and turn to his wife, sending an apologetic smile her way. He leaned into her, kissing her cheek before turning back to his brothers.

"*Sonny?* What kind of a silly ass nickname is that?" Kadiri let out a loud chuckle. "Aye, you letting her call you that shit, for real, bruh?" Kadiri's laughter continued before he turned to his older brother who sat to the left of him. "Kill, you hear that shit? Sonny? Now I know for sure that this shit must be a joke."

"Why is it that everything seems to be a fucking joke to you?" Kason snapped. "I'm here to tell the both of you about my marriage and you're over here cracking stupid jokes and you, Killian, you ain't said a damn word."

Killian's eyes narrowed at his younger brother.

"And here I thought my own flesh and blood would be happy for me."

"Oh I'm happy alright," Kadiri announced with a smug grin. "Happy your ass is about to get beat by momma once she finds out that you eloped because I know for a fact you haven't told her yet."

Kason didn't say a word. He just gave his brother a blank look before his eyes fell on his wife who sat on a chair around the conference table. He was standing behind her chair but had an arm around the back of it. She was too busy staring over at Kadiri and Killian who sat on the opposite end of the table but Kason noticed the apprehensive look she wore.

"You see if he'd told her..." Kadiri stared directly at Tanai as he spoke. "You wouldn't be here right now with us. You'd be too busy trying to nurse his wounds from the beatdown our momma would've given him."

"I'm sure she can't get that angry," Tanai replied. "If we just explain to her how we fell in love I'm sure she'll understand."

"And just by that response, I know for a fact you haven't met my momma cause you clearly don't know her the way I do." Kadiri shook his head. "None of us have gotten married yet and in her mind when we do, she's throwing each of us a big ass wedding that's gonna wake the entire city up. So for Kason to have gotten married without her being present... it's about to be world war three up in this bitch."

"Don't listen to him, baby. He's exaggerating," Kason told Tanai, rubbing a hand over her back as he looked down at her. "She's going to understand. I promise. I'll make her understand."

Tanai's apprehensive look still remained and even when Kason placed a kiss to her forehead, trying to ease her mind, the apprehension showed no signs of going away. That was until a new voice spoke up.

"She'll have no reason but to understand because the two of you are now one. There's nothing she can do or say to change the fact that you're husband and wife. You're now Kason's wife which makes you his family and ours too," Killian stated. "We've got your back, Tanai. Believe that."

Killian's statement was enough to ease Tanai's worry and make her crack a small smile.

"We've got her back?" Kadiri frowned at his older brother's words. "No offence, sweetheart, but we hardly know your ass. How do we know you're not just here to run off with our brother's coins?"

"'Cause I've got my own coin," Tanai fired back. "I've got my own company alongside my sisters. A *very* successful company. I don't need his coin. Never did and never will."

"But it's here for you anyway," Kason told her, squeezing her shoulder and glad that she'd had a quick comeback for Kadiri. In this Miller family, you couldn't be weak and you needed to be able to have a sharp tongue so you could handle your own. Kason was glad that Tanai was beginning to handle her own just fine.

"So you signed a prenup then?" Kadiri asked.

Kason quickly shook his head.

"She didn't sign anything. I never drafted one up and I don't plan to."

Kadiri's eyes bulged at Kason's revelation.

"What the... Man, I never thought the day that you lost your damn mind would finally come but it's definitely come. Wow."

"He hasn't lost his mind, Kadiri," Tanai said. "He's in love. *We're* in love and he knows that if anything was to happen between us, I don't want a dime from him. I'll be leaving the same way I came. With me, myself, and I. If the three of you want me to sign a document proving that then I'll do it. But believe me when I say, I'm in love with your brother because of the way he makes me feel.... the way he makes me smile every day without fail... the way he knows when something's wrong with me without me even saying a word... when I look at him, I know that everything's going to be okay. He's my peace and happiness all in one and the only person I want to spend the rest of my life with."

How could anyone argue with that?

Kadiri had nothing to comeback at her with and he was finally understanding just how in love these two really were. Even the way his brother looked at her, he'd never seen Kason look at any woman like this before. Like he would risk losing everything he owned in the world for her alone.

"You don't need to sign anything to prove to us how much you love our brother, Tanai," Killian spoke up seconds later. "The only person you need to prove anything to is him. He's your husband and he's the one you're going to be coming home to every night, not us."

Tanai nodded but Killian wasn't done.

"You're part of the family now but please don't mistake my kindness for weakness, baby girl. I've got your back but if you even think about messing around and trying to come for everything my brother's worked hard to build, you'll be answering to me and I can tell you now for a fact, I don't play about my family. Don't get yourself hurt by playing with the wrong one because I promise you, I'll end up being the right one to put you in your place."

After speaking, Killian got up from his seat and pushed his chair back.

"I look forward to your reception next weekend," he said, picking up his invitation. "Now if you'll excuse me, I have a meeting to get to."

"And that's my cue to get the hell out of here too." Kadiri got up from his seat. "Y'all gon' have an open bar at the reception, right?"

Kason nodded and Kadiri grinned.

"Well you can definitely count my ass there, *Sonny.*" Kadiri's

21

reference to the nickname that Tanai had called Kason earlier almost made Kason flip him the bird again but he decided against it. He would let Kadiri have his fun for now.

Kadiri smirked as he grabbed his invitation from the walnut wood table before making his way towards the exit behind Killian who had already made it halfway to the door. By the time they were out the room, Tanai's shoulders slouched and she sighed deeply.

"They hate me."

"No, no, no..." Kason reached for both her hands, lifting each to his lips and kissing the back of them. "They don't, Nugget."

Tanai looked up at him, feeling her heart warm at his sweet gesture and his use of the cute nickname he'd coined just for her. *Nugget.* It was somewhat silly but she found it so cute whenever he called her it. She was his Nugget and no one else's. He started pulling her up out of her seat and before she knew it, she'd been lifted to sit on top of the conference table while Kason came to stand in the middle of her open thighs that hung off the desk.

"They don't." He rubbed his nose against hers which made her instantly smile. "Yes they can be quite cold... and annoying, Lord knows how I've put up with Kadiri's annoying ass all these years, but they don't hate you, baby. If anything, they hate me for keeping your pretty ass away from them all these months. I'm known to go ghost when I get overwhelmed with business and shit, so it wasn't a shock that I left the city to go hopping from country to country. But they never expected me to pop back up with a whole ass wife and now that it's happened I know that they feel some type of way about me keeping you a secret. We're quite close so for me to keep this under wraps, it's definitely got them salty deep down."

While Kason had been talking, Tanai lifted her hand to his face, rubbing his soft skin and stroking on his beard in that affectionate way he loved the most. He puckered his lips, turning his head slightly to kiss the inside of her hand.

"I've got a lot of making up to do with them..." Kason leaned closer to her, pressing his lips to the side of her neck. "The same way you've got a lot to do with your sisters."

"My sisters who I think might love you more than they love me."

Kason chuckled, kissing her skin, and inhaling her wonderful aroma. That peach and vanilla scent of hers always drove him wild and today was no different.

"Rightfully so... I'm fucking amazing."

Tanai pulled back so his lips were no longer on her skin, throwing him a side eye.

"What?" He flashed her a sexy grin. "You know I'm right."

"Cocky, huh?"

"Ain't that why you love me, Nugget?" he asked, moving closer towards her once again and pecking her flesh. "Hmm? Because I'm so amazing?"

"No, you're not that amazing..." Tanai giggled as his kisses turned into licks. "Sonny! Stop being nasty..." She moaned when his licks turned into sucks and his strong arms circled her waist, pulling her deeper into him.

"Sonny... we could get caught."

"By... who? The boss?" He started kissing up her throat again, landing on the back of her ear before whispering, "You forget who owns the building? Baby, I am the boss."

The way he'd affirmed his boss status made her body tingle and every inch of her craved him now more than ever.

They were currently in the conference room of his company's building. It was where he'd asked his brothers to come meet him and his new wife. It was also where they'd been for the past hour as Kason explained his new status as a married man to a woman he'd felt like he'd known his whole life. And where Killian and Kadiri had been personally handed their invites to their upcoming reception.

"And the boss wants to have his sexy wife right here, right now on this table."

Tanai's hands found their way to the back of his neck and as he looked down at her, she was one hundred percent ready for him to have his way with her. How could she resist those enchanting eyes of his that always knew how to lure her in and that face... baby, that face she could never get tired of seeing over her as he pushed past her walls. These walls that now belonged to him.

"Well... the boss better hurry up and have his way with his wife or she might just beat him to the punch and turn him into her little bitch."

Kason chuckled before suddenly sinking his teeth into her neck, making her whimper. He released her, soothing his bite with soft kisses.

"You and that mouth, Tanai Miller."

"Mmh, ain't that why you love me, Kason Miller?"

One last chuckle escaped him before he straightened back up, gave her a lustful stare then crashed his lips to hers. Both their hands moved over each other's bodies, quickly trying to take their clothes off. Desperate to join their bodies as one and bring each other to the greatest of climaxes right on top of this table. If anyone interrupted them, well they could simply enjoy the show because no one was about to stop this married couple who had become addicted to one another, from enjoying each other for the next hour.

We still on for tomorrow, girl?

Send.

Thyri dropped her phone to the nearby counter, her eyes darting over to her shrimp. She reached for her wooden spoon, using it to stir the sizzling pan and flipping a few shrimp over.

Ding!

She focused back on her phone to see her new message.

Yes, love. 6pm.

Dayana.

Thyri lifted her phone, pressed on the message, and began typing.

Thyri: *Can't wait to see you!*

Thyri: *It's been too damn long since you hooked your girl up.*

Thyri: *Excited to see this new spot you've been working at too.*

She pressed send then locked her phone and her attention went back to her cooking.

Just as she turned off the stove seconds later, her phone went off once again. Thinking it was Dayana, Thyri reached for her phone but when *his* name popped up, she let out a harsh breath and dropped her phone. She tried to act like she hadn't read his three new texts but she definitely had and now she couldn't get them out of her head.

I won't be able to make Tanai's reception.

Still caught up with work outta town.

Be back soon.

Thyri decided that the best thing for her to do would be to shake off thoughts of him. He wasn't who she wanted to think about right now. Who she wanted to think about was her sister, Tanai, and her new marriage.

As Thyri prepared her shrimp tacos, she couldn't help but smile as she remembered how happy her sister looked today. Just seeing that smile on her face whenever she looked at Kason was enough to melt Thyri's heart. He was making her happy, that was evident to see and Thyri was glad her sister had found a love made just for her.

Thyri was especially glad that Tanai was back in her and Truth's lives. Things just hadn't been the same without her and Thyri had missed having her around. The Wright triplets couldn't be triplets without the three of them present and now that Tanai was back, the gang was restored. She was back where she belonged and Thyri was looking forward to getting their relationship back on the mend. Today at their office made Thyri realize that despite Tanai's six month departure, Tanai had fit back in with her sisters like she hadn't even left. That was the power of their bond and now that she was back, they could work on bettering that bond, making it ten times stronger than before.

Minutes later, Thyri sat on her sofa with "My Wife & Kids" reruns playing on her mounted flat screen while she ate her shrimp tacos. Despite it not being Taco Tuesday, Thyri had been craving the delicacy badly all day and knew from the minute she walked through the door that she would be making it.

Ding!

Her phone lit up on the center table and she leaned forward to grab it.

Yo? You don't see me texting you?

Ding!

Answer me Thyri.

Reluctantly she unlocked her phone and replied with: *I see you.*

Chosen: *So why the hell ain't you answering me?*

Chosen: *What the hell has gotten into you today?*

Her face hardened at his texts but she wasn't in an arguing mood so she decided to keep things short and sweet.

Thyri: *Nothing.*

Thyri: *Busy.*

Chosen: *A'ight.*
Chosen: *Like I said, I'll be back soon baby.*
Chosen: *Love you.*
Thyri: *Same x*

Thyri placed her phone on do not disturb, locked it then slammed it down to the coffee table ahead. Her pulse racing due to the fact that he thought *be back soon* was supposed to make everything okay. As if *be back soon* was supposed to make her feel happy. She hated when he took his business trips out of town because he became this unreachable person who could only be spoken to when he initiated contact. He would never call, only send short texts, never telling her when exactly he was returning only that he would be back soon. He took one every month and you would think Thyri would be used to his uncommunicative nature but she wasn't.

How was she supposed to be okay with her man being a complete ghost with her for several days then suddenly popping up like everything was okay?

It was what it was though. She knew what type of man she was with. The type that loved his money and business more than anything in the world and she'd grown accustomed to it. Did she like it? *Hell no.* But it didn't matter how many times she voiced her dislike, he was a man who walked to beat of his own drum. There was nothing she could do or say to stop him from being about his money.

You could say that that was one of the reasons why she'd first fell for him. He was about his hustle just like she was and didn't play games when it came to his career. However, unlike her, Chosen didn't know how to keep a healthy balance between his personal life and business. He could only focus on one at a time and if his mind was on one, then the other was completely forgotten about until his brain decided to remind him about it.

He had his flaws but what man didn't? There wasn't a single man in this world who was perfect but Jesus. However, Thyri knew that regardless of Chosen's flaws, it didn't change her feelings for him.

Thyri sighed, reaching for her phone once again and clicking on her phone's screen.

Chosen: *Same?*

Chosen: *Really Ri?*

Chosen: *That's cold and you know it.*

Indeed she did and it was why her conscience made her pick up the phone and make amends.

Thyri: *I love you too.*

Chosen: *That's more like it.*

Chosen: *You know I'm out here working for us. For our future together.*

Chosen: *I promise I'll be back soon, baby.*

There was nothing else left to be said. He would be back whenever he was ready to be back and she would have no choice but to be his loyal girl awaiting his return.

Chapter Three

"I don't know how you stand it though... all that poking into your skin. It hurts."

"I kinda like the pain, Tru."

"Of course you do, you weirdo." Thyri's lips lifted into a smile. "I hate pain, just like any normal person... Alana, momma's almost done. I'ma need you to stay still for me so I can finish making you look ten times prettier than you already are. You wanna look prettier don't you?"

"Yes, Mommy."

Thyri's smile grew bigger once she heard a cute little voice come on the line.

"So stay still for me, baby, okay?"

"Okay."

"Tell my princess I said hi," Thyri chimed in while turning left onto the next road.

"Your auntie RiRi says hi, baby."

"Auntie RiRi! Auntie RiRi! Auntie RiRi!"

"See now you got my baby all excited." Truth chuckled. "Keep still, Lana, please... you almost there, Ri?"

"Yup." Thyri's eyes went to her mounted phone that had Google Maps open, giving her the GPS navigation to her desired destination. The journey's time now read five minutes and she was glad to know that it wouldn't be long till she was where she needed to be.

"Alrightie. I'll speak to you later. Enjoy your pain session, freak."

"I will," Thyri replied with a light chuckle. "Speak to you later. Tell my baby I said bye."

"I will. Love you."

"Love you more, sis. Bye."

Thyri pressed the 'end call' button on her Lamborghini's phone screen. Once the line cut off, Thyri focused solely on driving, trailing behind a red Volvo. Five minutes later and her destination appeared up ahead, on the left.

At first Thyri thought that her destination was part of the strip mall she could see ahead but as she entered the parking lot, she quickly realized that it wasn't actually a strip mall, it was one large building with a center sign that read 'House of Hayes.'

Thyri parked her car in the available spot in front of the shop before cutting off the engine and grabbing her Louis Vuitton backpack from the passenger seat. She then made her way out her car, locking it behind her and walking up to the front entrance of House of Hayes.

As soon as she stepped in, eyes were on her and she found those hazel eyes behind the front glass desk a short distance away from the entrance.

"Hi, can I help you?" the hazel eyed woman greeted her.

"Hi... yes, I have a six o'clock appointment with Dayana."

The woman's eyes dropped to the silver iMac sitting in front of her and she examined her screen closely before nodding.

"Thyri, right?" she asked with a friendly smile.

Thyri nodded, sending a smile back the woman's way.

"Have a seat just over there, love." Thyri's eyes followed hers and two wine velvet couches were situated to the far left. "Dayana should be here soon. I'll call her now and let her know you've arrived early."

"Okay, thank you."

Thyri nodded and started making her way over to the seating area. Once in her seat, she took in her environment, noticing how modern and clean the front area of the shop looked. The receptionist's desk and the seating area was the only area you could see at the front of the shop. Behind the receptionist's desk was a graffiti wall with the House of Hayes logo. To the right of the receptionist's desk, there was a walkway that Thyri realized led to the tattoo artists' studios.

Thyri placed her backpack on her lap and unzipped it to bring out her phone.

D, I'm here. Early as per usual lol.

Send.

She knew the receptionist planned to call Dayana but Thyri had no problems sending her friend an extra heads up about her arrival.

The time was five-forty p.m. and her appointment with Dayana was at six p.m. She'd arrived early out of habit, something that her father had instilled in her from a very young age. Even after all these years, you could still count on Thyri to show up early to a commitment.

Your new place is niceeeee, she typed before pressing send.

See you soon boo, was her last text.

Dayana was Thyri's good friend of five years. They'd met

through Instagram when Thyri messaged her to enquire about her availability to do her first tattoo. She'd found one of Dayana's designs on her explore page and been stalking her page for days before finally plucking up the courage to hit her up. Once Dayana provided her with her availability and they set a date, the girls met at Dayana's private studio in the outskirts of Atlanta.

Doing her first tattoo with Dayana proved to be one of the best decisions Thyri had ever made because they got on very well and Thyri loved how at ease Dayana made her feel while she tattooed her. They decided to exchange numbers and keep in touch. Five years later and not only had Dayana tattooed almost all the designs on Thyri's body, but they'd also become really great friends.

When Dayana first started tattooing, she'd rented out studio space and used the space as her place of work to tattoo her clients. Her work she'd promoted on social media and through word of mouth. This year however, Dayana had decided that she wanted to become part of a tattoo shop. Tattooing independently had been fun and all but it got lonely and sometimes boring. Being part of a shop would not only provide her with a family but exposure that would bring in new clientele and more money. She'd moved into House of Hayes about a week ago and Thyri already feeling the urge to get a new tattoo was excited to be able to come down to her friend's new location.

Now here she was. In House of Hayes.

I wonder who Hayes is, Thyri thought to herself as her sight set back on the graffiti wall behind the receptionist's desk. She noticed how the receptionist started shaking her head as she placed the phone down.

"I don't know why but she's not picking up, honey... I'll try again in a few minutes, maybe she's busy driving or something."

Thyri nodded in agreement and decided it was best she killed some time by checking over work emails from new potential clients and scrolling through Instagram.

The minutes began to pass and before Thyri knew it, six-fifteen p.m. had come and Dayana? Nowhere to be found. She'd tried calling her a few minutes ago and just like the receptionist, who Thyri now knew was called Cleo, had said earlier, Dayana wasn't picking up the phone.

Girl... where you at?

Send.

Thyri looked up from her phone, her eyes landing on Cleo who gave her a small smile.

"Let me try calling her again and see if she'll pick up this time," Cleo said, reaching for the phone.

Thyri watched her call Dayana's number once again but the sound of footsteps was heard, making Thyri lose focus on Cleo and turn in the direction of said footsteps. Only to suddenly wish she hadn't.

"I don't wanna hear it, Kadiri..."

Lord have mercy on me.

"You need to be nice. She's his wife, which makes her family. *Our* family."

Lord please, please, please, have mercy on me.

Walking down the corridor towards her was a man. No scratch that. This wasn't just a man. *No.* This person right here had to be a king. From his voice to his face to his walk, Thyri was entranced. He wasn't even talking to her but each word he spoke captured her attention.

"I don't wanna hear that shit. You be nice or I'll make you be nice. The choice is yours."

Please Lord.

Thyri was internally begging for mercy because she was sure that The Lord had to be punishing her. He had to be because what else was the reason as to why this man had been placed into her presence with no warning?

"I'd love to see you try, kid." He chuckled, holding Thyri captive with his eyes and his chuckle made heat curl down her spine. "You must've forgotten about the last time you tried to beat me up with your weak ass..."

He was tall. Too damn tall it seemed and despite the building's high ceilings, Thyri was low-key convinced that he could touch the ceiling if he wanted to. As he walked down the corridor there was a certain aura in his stride... a certain je ne sais quoi that had Thyri unable to take her eyes off him. But she knew she had to look away especially since the man was staring at her just as hard while engrossed in his phone call. And most importantly, she was a taken woman that had no business staring at another man for this long.

Thyri's focus went back on Cleo who still had the phone to her ear as she waited for Dayana's line to pick up.

Even with her gaze off him, Thyri couldn't forget those attractive eyes, that healthy looking beard and the way those juicy, pink lips moved every time he uttered a word.

The handsome stranger emerged from the corridor and moved towards the front desk. Thyri felt his eyes on her until he arrived opposite Cleo. Sensing his stare was no longer on her, Thyri looked back over at him. She now stared at the back of his low cut hair and she was able to see the way Cleo's eyes lit up as he stood in front of her.

He had his phone glued to his ear with one hand while the other reached into the back pocket of his jeans, pulling out a small, folded piece of paper. The hand that held his phone was tatted and despite the fact that she couldn't see the design up close, she knew that against his golden honey skin, it was a work of art.

"No, I was honest with her. You made fun of her nickname for him and used their choice of an open bar as the basis of your attendance."

Thyri watched as he placed the paper on the desk in front of Cleo and she reached for it, grinning wide and nodding as he mouthed words to her that Thyri couldn't make out since his back faced her.

"She knows she has my support but you on the other hand..."

He turned back around and his eyes met Thyri's one last time, making her heart skip several beats. She hadn't expected him to turn around so quickly and she'd wanted her gaze to be anywhere but on him when he did. However, now he'd caught her and their eyes locked one last time before he looked away and made his way back down the corridor. Heat formed in the center of her chest as she watched him walk away but as quickly as that warmth formed, it dissipated when Cleo spoke up.

"She's still not picking up." Cleo shook her head with a frown as she placed the phone down to its holder. "I'm really sorry about this, Thyri."

"Don't apologize, it's not your fault," Thyri replied. "This is really unlike her to not be picking up her phone... especially not my calls."

Thyri took one last look at her phone, reading the last text she'd sent to Dayana.

Girl, seriously, you've got me worried. Are you okay?

At this point, Thyri wasn't even concerned about the tattoo or Dayana being over twenty minutes late. She was more concerned about the fact that her friend wasn't responding to any of her messages. She just wanted to know if she was okay.

"When was the last time you spoke to her?"

"Yesterd—"

Thyri's eyes fell to her ringing phone and the caller ID made relief spread through her body.

"This is her now," Thyri said to Cleo before picking up her phone.

"D, are you okay?" Thyri now had her phone sealed to her left ear as she listened intently to her friend on the other side. "I've been calling you... Oh, damn... I didn't realize you were coming back today, I thought you were already back... No, no, no that's okay, another time for sure... Well, I'm glad you're okay... Yeah, sure... Alrightie... Please let me know when your flight lands... Okay, see you later, girl. Bye."

Thyri ended the call and looked over at Cleo to see her carefully watching her.

"Is she okay?"

Thyri nodded in response.

"Yeah, she's fine." Thyri stood to her feet and neared the front desk. "Her flight back from her parents got delayed and her phone died. She's waiting to board her flight now and won't be back in the city for another five hours."

"Awww, that's a shame," Cleo stated, looking up as Thyri now stood at the other side of her desk. "I was looking forward to seeing your new tattoo."

Thyri gave her a small smile before replying, "So was I. But it's okay. We'll just reschedule once she's back."

"Sure thing, honey... unless you wanna try a different artist? We have a few in their studios right now and the rest on call if there's a particular artist you want."

"Oh..." Thyri found her thoughts getting sidetracked once those footsteps that were quickly becoming familiar were heard again, coming down the corridor towards her. Only this time she forced herself to not look in that direction.

"You can see all their work via their online portfolios which are available on here." Cleo reached to the side of her work area for an iPad Air which she lifted and gently shook in Thyri's direction. "The choice is yours."

"Umm... I think I'm okay. I don't wanna be an inconvenience to anyone."

"You wouldn't be an inconvenience," that deep voice she'd heard just moments ago melted into her ears. "What did you want tatted?"

Thyri slowly turned around and looked over at him standing a short distance away in the corridor with his hands nested into his pockets.

"My sternum," she said and watched as he looked at her like she'd suddenly grown two heads. "Is that a problem?"

"You sure you can handle that?"

She nodded but that wasn't enough to convince him.

"That area is all bone, sweetheart, and I definitely don't want you crying in my studio like a baby once you realize you can't handle the pain."

Thyri frowned, feeling some type of way about his lack of confidence in her.

"I'm sure I can handle it," she replied with her head held high. "Besides, I never agreed to you tatting me so you don't need to worry about me."

She tore her eyes away from him, focusing back on Cleo who had been watching the entire interaction between her boss and Thyri.

"I definitely want to see just how much you can handle the pain so I do need to worry about you," he voiced but Thyri decided to ignore him and put her attention back on Cleo.

"You said there's a few artists available, right?"

Cleo shook her head 'yes' at Thyri.

Initially Thyri had been all for coming another time once she'd rescheduled with Dayana but the handsome, skeptical, and slightly rude stranger had made her feel some type of way. She was getting that sternum tattoo and she was getting it today.

I'll show him who can't handle pain.

"Who would you recommend as the best?"

"Well..." A small smile grew on Cleo's lips as her line of sight drifted behind Thyri's head. "He's standing right behind you."

Thyri internally groaned. That wasn't the answer she'd wanted to hear even though she had a feeling it was coming.

"What about the person who owns this place?" She pushed, not wanting to give in to the stranger behind her. "Is he or she in and available to do my tatt?"

"Yes I'm in and I'll gladly do your tatt," his voice sounded and Thyri went dead silent. "We can head to my studio once you finally stop acting like I won't be tatting you today."

Ugh... I should've known he owned this place.

She turned around to look at him. That fine ass face of his was revealed to her once again. His dark brown orbs swept up and down her body and she felt a little rush of butterflies in her stomach but suppressed them as best as she could.

"I'm good."

He smirked at her nonchalant response and crossed his arms over his chest. Thyri was unable to help the way heat stirred in her core at the movement of his large muscular arms. Both were inked with tattoos and both looked like they would fit perfectly around her waist as he held her tigh—

"You mad cause I called you out on not being able to handle the tatt, huh?"

"No," Thyri lied, a shadow of dismay crossing her face.

His smirk grew.

"Okay so come and prove me wrong, beautiful."

Beautiful.

Just hearing that one word come out from his mouth had Thyri's heart racing and those butterflies took motion inside her stomach once again. She didn't like all the ways this stranger was affecting her.

"I wanna see you handle the pain," he added. "Trust and believe I won't fuck up your skin. Cleo's already told you who the best artist is up in here and I don't hire liars. I'll take care of you. I promise."

For some strange reason, Thyri believed he would. Confidence was wrapped in his tone and the words he'd spoken suddenly made her feel at ease.

You don't even know this man, Ri. He didn't have faith in you getting your tattoo in the first place. Are you sure you want him tatting you?

He started walking down the corridor but Thyri didn't follow. She was conflicted. One part of her wanted to be far away from the man that initially didn't have faith in her getting her sternum tatted and another part of her wanted to be as close to him as possible, letting him take care of her.

Upon realizing she wasn't walking behind him, Killian stopped and looked over his shoulder to say, "Come on, Thyri, I ain't got all day to be waiting on your pretty ass. Let's go."

Like a moth to a flame, Thyri was awakened and she made a beeline for the corridor, ready to have his hands on her. She didn't even care to ask him how he already knew her name. The only thing on her mind was wanting to be taken care of by him. Anything else just didn't matter.

Chapter Four

God... she's breathtaking.

Killian couldn't take his eyes off her. Who could blame him? The woman that he'd had the pleasure of being acquainted with this evening was a beauty who had his undivided attention. Even while he'd been on the phone to his younger brother, all Killian could see and think about were those innocent looking eyes that were tempting him more and more with each passing second to say something to her. He didn't know what to say but when he'd overheard her current predicament with his newest hired artist having flight issues, he'd found his window of opportunity.

Now that he had her time for the rest of today, Killian was filled with fresh energy. All day he'd been dealing with clients but something about this client who hadn't actually been his in the first place, had him feeling different.

He'd seen her name this morning on the list of clients that were coming into the shop today. As CEO of House of Hayes, Killian was always emailed a list of all the people that his artists were tattooing each day of the week and he would always check it so he could know how many people would be coming through to the shop. He liked staying on top of shit and despite having a manager who handled the day to day activities of the shop, Killian still enjoyed knowing what was going on.

He'd led the way to his studio, opened the door for her and watched her come in with an intrigued look. Her eyes started darting across the space, inspecting and admiring everything she could see. He wasn't surprised to see her fascination. His studio space was his mini oasis, basically his second home and he'd decorated it so that all his recent artwork was each framed and neatly arranged on the four white walls around them. He also had incense burning in one of his favorite scents, sandalwood, providing the space with a rich, exotic aroma.

He saw her eyes find the tattoo chair in the center of the medium sized space and he told her to take a seat which she quickly did. He followed her to the center, unable to help his line of gaze dropping down her back to her heart shaped butt. It was small but it looked like the perfect size on her slim frame and he'd be lying if he said he hadn't already thought about being able to hold it in his palms.

Once she was seated on the leather chair, Killian took his seat on the nearby swivel chair and kept his eyes focused on her. She hadn't said a word yet and from the way she gently bounced her left knee, Killian could tell she was nervous.

He would also be lying if he said that he didn't like the fact that he made her nervous. To be the sole reason as to why her heart was most likely racing right now and her body heat rising - Killian loved every single second of it.

He decided to use the silence that had formed between them to let his eyes linger over her face some more. And what a face it was.

He could see it so much better now that he was seated quite close to her, not too close but close enough. She rocked a side parted pixie bob that did wonders for her alluring facial features. Killian wasn't one to usually go for women with short hair but there was something about this hairstyle on this espresso brown baddie that he found irresistible. Her oval face housed thick arched brows, deep-set chocolate brown eyes that were fringed with short yet cute lashes and bow shaped lips. Lips that looked as soft as butter. Lips that he wouldn't mind feeling against his. There was something familiar about her face, like he'd seen it somewhere before but he was certain that he hadn't because if he had then they would've already met as Killian wouldn't have been able to walk past her without saying something.

"So are we just going to sit here in silence and stare at each other all day, Hayes?"

Hearing her call him by his middle name made his body sizzle and the extension between his thighs became more rigid.

"You tell me," he replied, crossing his arms across his chest. "You're the one whose been quiet as a ghost since I brought you in here. You scared of me or something?"

"No..."

"You sure?" Killian leaned back in his seat, watching as a small smile tugged on her lips. "I'm one big mothafucka with an even bigger appetite. You ain't scared I might eat you?"

Thyri's laughter suddenly poured into the studio.

"Eat me?"

"Yeah." Killian smiled as she giggled. "You look like you taste good."

Heat stained her cheeks at his comment and she let out one final giggle before coming to a stop. She had no idea what to say to his flirty words and quite frankly, it'd thrown her off guard. The image of his head between her thighs popped into her head but she quickly shook it away.

Get a hold of yourself, Ri.

"Ignore my corny ass." He chuckled at her silence. "You ready to tell me what you want done?"

Thyri nodded, pulling out her phone from her jacket but the second she held it out in front of her, Killian shook his head with displeasure.

"Uh-uh. Describe it to me."

"I'm not good at describing things," she admitted.

"I'm sure that's a lie, Thyri," he replied.

"It's not... I'm crap at it."

"Try for me."

She lightly sighed, placing her phone to her lap as she watched him.

"Okay, well... what I want is..."

She began to describe her desired design. Taking her time since she wasn't the best at being descriptive. While she talked, her eyes were stuck on his dark brown irises, unable to pull away.

Jesus, this man is too damn fine.

Her eyes caressed his face as she kept talking about her tattoo. His golden honey complexion looked smooth as silk with hardly any blemishes in sight. He had low cut hair with a tapered fade on the sides and a round face that housed features that Thyri was sure she could stare at forever. From those almond shaped eyes to that full face beard and that thick moustache that lined perfectly around his plump lips, Killian Miller was a ten out of ten in the looks department. Ten was even too small in Thyri's eyes. Trying to deny her attraction to this man would be stupid because of the way her body came to attention the more she stared at him.

He was clad in a gray fitted t-shirt with black cargo pants and black Yeezy 350's on his feet. A diamond stud was locked in each ear, a silver AP on his left wrist and three silver chains hung from his neck.

About five minutes later, she'd successfully described the artwork she wanted.

"See that wasn't so hard was it?" He smiled and something about him smiling made her smile twice as hard.

Thyri observed him turn away to the nearby drawers on his left, pulling out his required tools and placing them on his silver tray. She'd told him what she wanted but a part of her didn't have faith in her words being descriptive enough.

What if I didn't explain my design well enough and confused him?

"Are you sure you don't want to see my pictures? I'm sure they'd make much better sense than I did."

"Nope."

"But Hayes..."

Killian stopped grabbing his items and turned to look at her.

"What'd I tell you earlier?"

She started racking her brain, trying to figure out what it was that he'd said that was so important. There were a lot of things that he'd said today, things that had stirred her soul in ways she hadn't expected.

"That I'd take care of you," he reminded her, seriousness cradled in his handsome face. "So I'ma need you to trust that I will. A'ight?"

"A'ight," she copied him, causing a grin to form on his lips at her trying to sound like him. She'd put on a deep voice, trying to match his own.

She's beautiful and funny... my type of woman.

Killian resumed grabbing his equipment and setting up. By the time he was finished, he turned to Thyri to see that she'd taken off her leather jacket and had relaxed on the chair. It was nice to see that she'd gotten comfortable but what was even more nice for Killian to see was the fact that she'd come dressed in a halter neck top that showcased her toned chest and under boob area.

Damn.

He hadn't noticed it before because she'd had her jacket covering her frame, shielding what she had underneath. But now he could see it all and he didn't want to stop staring at how well the color khaki complimented her brown skin and how well her plentiful sized breasts sat up in the garment. He knew he had to look away though because he didn't want to come across as a creep.

He reached into his drawer for body tape. Despite turning away from her, that changed nothing about the fact that her body had become ingrained in his mind. He'd managed to spot her left sleeve of tattoos, a mandala design of some sort, her belly button piercing and a small tattoo on her left wrist. He couldn't help but wonder how many other tattoos she possessed but as quickly as the thought popped into his head, he pushed it out because of the heat rushing more and more to his center.

"So I'll be stepping out the room so you can take your top off, put the tape on and..."

Shit.

By now Killian had turned over to Thyri again only for him to freeze at her new exposed state.

"Shit..." He turned his back to her, not wanting her to feel uncomfortable by his stare on her naked upper half. "My bad, I didn't know you were already stripping."

She'd sat up to remove the tie from the back of her neck, causing the material to drop to her lap and her breasts to free themselves. They were full, round and suited her frame well. And he couldn't forget about the two silver bars in each of her nipples that he'd spotted.

"No need to apologize," she voiced. "I know what I signed up for. There's no way I can get a sternum tattoo and not show off my girls."

That she was right about.

"You don't need to step out, Hayes."

"You sure?"

"Positive."

Killian turned and handed the tape over to her, making sure to keep his gaze on her eyes alone. Their hands touched slightly as she reached for it and the connection caused fire to spread through her.

While she covered her nipples with the tape, Killian hung her jacket and backpack up on the clothing rack in the corner of the room. He then sanitized his hands and placed his gloves on, followed by his glasses which Thyri found cute on him.

Since he was a freehand artist, he didn't use stencils unless he was doing really small tattoos and even then he still didn't like using them. Freehand was what he was best at because it was how he'd taught himself to tattoo at the age of fifteen, something Thyri was greatly impressed by when he told her.

Killian started off with sanitizing and cleaning her skin with green soap, using a disposable razor to remove any fine hairs before cleaning her skin one last time. He then grabbed a thin body marker and began drawing her design on her skin. He was extra gentle with her, taking his time with each piece of the design. When the drawing was complete, Killian asked her if she wanted to see it and she said no, telling him that she trusted him.

He then got her to lay down on the tattoo chair that he lowered for her and provided her with a pillow to support her head and neck while she lay.

Scribz Riley, a black British artist that Killian had asked Alexa to play, filled the space with his melodic vocals.

Said you don't believe in love
Old nigga messed you up
Check for you, then I spend a cheque on you
Now that I'm next to you

Killian hadn't been lying when he said that the sternum was one of the most painful areas to get tatted on because Thyri felt the tension as soon as he pressed the needle into her skin. Her whole body tensed up and Killian immediately sensed her discomfort.

"Just breathe, Thyri. You've got this. You told my ass you could handle it, right?"

She nodded.

"So handle it, baby."

Thyri was unable to help the way her heart jumped every time he called her something other than her name. Just hearing him call her name was enough to make her hot but him calling her baby? Beautiful? Now that was enough to make her wet. Even his voice was enough to make her wet and now more than ever Thyri wanted to hear more of him.

"How long have you owned your shop?"

"Thirteen years."

"No way."

Killian looked up from her skin briefly and flashed her a grin. Those teeth of his were pearly white, straight, and natural looking. Thyri loved the fact that he was clearly a man who knew how to handle his personal hygiene well.

His eyes dropped back down to her skin and he continued inking her flesh. As he inked, he would pause every few moments to rub Vaseline into her skin and wipe it down with a clean cloth.

"So you were born and raised in Atlanta?"

"Yup," he confirmed. "And I'm guessing by that pretty accent of yours that you were born here too?"

"Yeah... been here all my life."

"You sound unhappy about that."

"...I'm glad to be from here but I really wanna get out and see the world."

Shock marred Killian's face and he looked over at her as he asked, "You've never been out the city?"

Thyri shook her head 'no'.

"Damn... that's no good," he stated. "Why? You broke or something? Spent all your coins on that LV backpack, huh?"

"No..." She smirked at the light joke he'd made in reference to her designer bag that he'd hung up earlier. "I've just been really busy."

"You can't be that busy to not catch a break and see the world. No one's ever too busy to make time for what they really want."

"That's what I thought but I've been running my late father's company alongside my sisters for the past three years nonstop... a break to go see the world just hasn't been on my horizon. I know it's not healthy to be working nonstop but all I've ever wanted is to make my father proud, strengthen his company and..." Thyri tensed when she felt slices of pain run across her ribs from the exact spot where he was currently tattooing. She inhaled deeply and exhaled, embracing the pain as best as she could. "Sorry, I'm going off on a tangent right now."

"Why you apologizing?" His brows furrowed as he rubbed jelly over her skin.

"'Cause I'm probably boring you with my life story."

"Did I say that shit?"

"No but... I know I am."

"Nah, you ain't so stop assuming shit that ain't true. I like hearing you talk, Thyri." She blushed at his comment. "Don't ever apologize for sharing your truth either. That's the number one thing you'll always have in this life. Don't be afraid to share it. You got that?"

She nodded as he stared deeply at her.

"Now finish telling me about making your Dad proud."

Thyri did exactly that. Telling Killian all about her efforts in running her father's cleaning company and improving it over the years. He admired her hustle and her strength in taking over her father's work but he didn't admire the fact that she hadn't had a real break in the last three years. She'd come straight out of college with a 4.0 GPA, lost her father five days after her graduation and taken over his business.

"From the sound of things, you've definitely been making your father proud as he watches over you and your sisters. But I'm sure he wouldn't like the fact that you've been doing all this hard work and haven't had the time to fully enjoy the fruits of your labor. I'm sure he wouldn't have wanted you to stay stuck in the A your whole life. The world's your oyster and you deserve to see everything it has to offer."

Thyri was quiet, taking in his words and undoubtedly agreeing with him.

"Besides a beauty like you deserves to see all the beautiful things in this world."

"Thank you, Hayes."

"No need to thank me on what's true. Just promise me you'll make the time to go enjoy yourself out the country sometime soon."

"I promise."

His eyes raised to hers and he threw a strict look her way.

"Don't lie to me, Thyri."

She giggled at how serious he was being with her all of a sudden.

"I promise." She nodded, trying to reassure him. "I will. I'll even email you the flight confirmation and everything."

"Sounds like a plan," he replied, liking the sound of being able to stay in contact with her after today. "Don't forget your hotel confirmation too."

"Aye, aye, captain."

Now it was his turn to laugh. After her words, they fell into a comfortable silence with only Scribz Riley playing in the background, singing all about how he used to wear his heart on his sleeve. It wasn't long till Thyri found the desire to hear more from Killian once again. She enjoyed the sound of his voice and enjoyed the conversation they'd been having so far.

"I know I didn't say anything when I first came in... but your artwork?" She started looking at the canvas filled walls surrounding them. "They're amazing."

Killian was unable to stop the smile forming on his lips.

"Appreciate you, baby."

"Have you always wanted to be a tattoo artist?"

"Originally no... I wanted to be an astronaut."

"What?" Her eyes widened. "Really?"

He let out a light chuckle and Thyri's surprise began to fade from her face.

"You liar."

"I'm just fucking with you," he said. "I ain't have a clue what I wanted to be. But I always knew I loved drawing and painting... then I discovered tattoos by the age of fifteen and the rest was pretty much history."

He went on to explain how he started perfecting his drawing skills, creating his own portfolio of work and pretty much stuck with it. When his parents realized that their son was a creative, both of them were caught off guard but out of the love they had for him, they warmed up to the idea and let him study art classes. Once it was time to apply for colleges, Killian got accepted into the top three art schools in the country. He decided to go to Yale but dropped out because he hated the course. He found it too restrictive and just didn't feel like he fit in enough. So he came back to Atlanta, made plans to open up his tattoo shop and started doing his passion full time at the age of twenty. Now at the age of thirty three he was living out his dream.

"I'm glad you followed your heart, Hayes."

"So am I. It's allowed me to do what I love and leave my mark on so many people."

Like your pretty ass, he thought to himself as he rubbed ink away from her skin.

About an hour later, Thyri now stood in front of the large mirror in Killian's studio, looking at the new design on her sternum.

It was a lotus flower with extended arches under both her breasts and chains dangling off the main flower and arches. The lotus had been drawn extremely well, shaded perfectly, and looked very realistic on her melanin rich skin. To put it simply, it was a pretty tattoo. Too pretty in her eyes and she couldn't believe that it now sat on her skin forever.

"Oh my God... Hayes. This is amazing... oh my God."

She couldn't believe it. He'd freehanded the entire design and not once asked to see the pictures she'd brought for reference and somehow he'd managed to create a design one hundred times better than any design she could've showed him.

"Thank you, thank you, thank you!"

A smile took possession of his lips at her happiness.

"You welcome. I guess you trusted me after all, huh?"

She nodded, still admiring her new tattoo in the mirror that they both stood in front of. She looked up at his reflection behind hers.

"Best decision I've made this year," she told him.

"Don't gas me up, Thyri."

"I'm being serious." Her smile strengthened as she stared at him in the mirror. "Best. Decision. Ever."

She slowly turned to face him, stood up on her tippy toes and placed a kiss to his cheek. The gesture had him feeling weak all of a sudden. It was as if from one simple kiss, this woman had made him become a feen for her. Willing to do whatever she asked of him, whenever she asked it. He already knew he was attracted to her from the second he laid eyes on her but he'd suppressed his want for her during the time they'd spent together. Only now he was done fighting his feelings. Yeah they'd just met but it changed nothing for Killian.

I want her.

Their eyes remained locked and no further words were exchanged between them. Nothing needed to be said. He knew she could see the lust burning in his eyes because he could see it just as bad in hers.

Killian lifted both his hands to her shoulders, sliding his palms down her soft skin, refusing to take his eyes off her while he stroked her arms.

She inched nearer to him, not too close but close enough for him to register that she welcomed his touch. The more his large hands rubbed her skin, the more her breaths quickened and the more her most intimate spot throbbed.

He started lowering his head towards hers and that's when she remembered that her attraction to this talented artist changed nothing about her current status as a taken woman.

"Hayes..."

His lips stopped right in front of hers, leaving the smallest distance between their faces. He refused to break eye contact and gave her a look that seemed to ask her, *What do you need to say, Thyri? Tell me.*

But she was losing all focus especially with how close he was. She could smell his manly scent and God, did it smell good. Warm amber, sandalwood and hints of vanilla filled her nostrils. Thyri had never been more grateful for those three scents until now.

"Hayes... I..."

He moved his lips forward and just when Thyri thought he was about to kiss her, he moved his lips over to her right ear, causing her heart to drop.

"Stop being shy and say what you want to say to me," he whispered into her ear.

His order was clear and her being entranced by his handsome face, his orgasmic voice and his irresistible scent made her have no choice but to obey his command.

"I have a boyfriend."

"I know."

He knows?

Thyri blinked rapidly, watching as he straightened up, took his hands off her body, and looked down at her carefully.

"How did you kno—"

"Doesn't take a rocket scientist to figure out that a woman like you is taken. You're intelligent, independent and you already know how I feel about that face."

Her cheeks warmed at his compliment. She remained silent but her mind raced with thoughts about this man who'd managed to figure out her relationship status without her having to say a word. This man who she was attracted to from the second she laid eyes on him.

"I've never been shy about what I want in this life and I want you, Thyri. Every part of you." Thyri's nipples hardened under the tape shielding them. "And I know you want me too. We only just

met today but we both know that you can feel the connection we have already."

He told no lies. She'd felt it from the very second she'd laid eyes on him.

"So when you finally realize that that nigga ain't good enough for you and ain't gonna do shit for you, I'll be here. Ready and waiting for you. Ready to show you just how good you deserve to be treated."

She was not only speechless but her breath hitched in her throat, causing her to be breathless for a few seconds until she remembered to breathe again. She opened up her mouth to talk but he beat her to the punch.

"Let's get a couple photos done then I'll get you wrapped up."

After his words, he left her in front of the mirror and she observed him walking away, still stuck on what he'd said. Still stuck on the fact that he'd been dead right.

She wanted him too but she knew deep down she couldn't have him. She belonged to someone else so her having another man that wasn't hers, just couldn't work. And she knew from the moment she stepped out of House of Hayes, she could never come back here again.

Chapter Five

R*i, you home from your tattoo?*
Thyri stared down at her bright screen and started typing.

Yeah, she sent, unable to stop the memories of hours ago from popping into her head. Unable to stop the reminders of his gentle touch on her body, his sexy voice, and those words... that promise he'd made about being ready to show her everything she deserved.

I still can't believe he said that.

Ding!

Truth: *Good.*

Truth: *I bet that shit hurt.*

Truth: *Can't wait to see it though.*

Thyri smiled as she remembered his initial lack of faith in her and then how he'd encouraged her while she'd been in pain during the tattoo process. She was sure that because of him she'd handled the pain well.

Truth: *Nai, you okay? Are you still with Kay Billy and his parents?*

Thyri: *Oh yeah, you were meeting them today.*

Thyri: *How's it going, sis? Have they gone home yet?*

Tanai's response didn't come in right away and that caused Thyri's thoughts to drift back to the man she'd spent the evening with.

After he'd taken photos of her tattoo and wrapped it up with a protective film, he told her all she needed to know about the aftercare of her tattoo. He also handed her a leaflet with everything he'd said so she wouldn't forget it and a House of Hayes care kit with all the lotion, oil, and soap she needed to take care of her tattoo for the next month.

When it came to her finally leaving, Thyri felt her mood plummet and she tried to convince herself that she didn't understand why when that was far from the truth. She knew exactly why she was feeling the way she was but she didn't want to admit it to herself right now. Her mind knew the truth though and because of that truth, she couldn't stop thinking about their last few moments together.

Killian handed over her jacket and LV backpack before heading over to the exit and opening his studio door for her.

"Bye, Hayes. Thank you once again for the tattoo."

He nodded without saying a word but just as she walked towards the doorway, he decided to speak up.

"I wasn't playing about what I said, Thyri. Don't forget that."

Now it was her turn to be silent and their eyes connected one last time before Thyri walked out his studio and headed back to the front reception area.

House of Hayes didn't take cash payments. When she'd booked her tattoo with Dayana she'd done it through an online booking system that required her to put down a booking fee that would be part of her final tattoo fee. The front receptionist, Cleo, told her that the remaining payment would be taken from her debit card in the next twenty four hours and once Cleo had said all that needed to be said, Thyri said her goodbyes and walked out the shop.

While walking to her car, Thyri's mood refused to lighten up and as she sat in front of the steering wheel, she realized one thing:

She didn't want to leave him.

Thyri sighed, lightly shaking her head at her own thoughts.

How crazy am I? I don't even know him and here I am, still thinking about him, still wanting to be in his compan—

Ding!

Her thoughts were interrupted by a new text message and she was lowkey glad because all this thinking about the stranger that had tattooed her was making her feel silly.

Tanai: *His father is great.*

Tanai: *A really sweet man.*

Truth: *And his mom?*

Tanai: *She's not here.*

Thyri: *Why?*

Truth: *Why?*

Tanai's response didn't come in right away and Thyri's face began to harden.

Thyri: *Did she not show up?*

Tanai: *No.*

Truth: *Wait what?*

Truth: *She didn't show up?*

Tanai: *She didn't show up.*

Truth: *What the hell?*

Truth: *Did Kason already tell her about your marriage?*

Tanai: *Yeah... he told them the news without me this morning, just to break the ice.*

Tanai: *Only his father showed up to our house a few hours ago.*

Tanai: *I don't think she's coming to the reception either.*

Truth: *Is she crazy?*

Thyri: *What did Kason say?*

Tanai: *That he'll talk to her.*

Tanai: *And I shouldn't worry.*

Tanai: *But how am I supposed to not worry about my husband's mother not liking me?*

Tanai: *She hates me and she hasn't even met me yet.*

Truth: *Fuck her.*

Thyri: *Tru.*

Truth: *Nah, fuck her for real!*

Truth: *What kind of a mother doesn't even show up for her son?*

Truth: *She's crazy.*

Thyri: *I don't think she doesn't like you.*

Thyri: *Seems like she might be hurt about you and him eloping.*

Thyri: *Which she has every right to be because that's her son after all.*

Thyri: *You haven't spoken to her at all? Not even over the phone?*

Tanai: *No.*

Tanai: *I just wish she'd show up and I could explain everything in person.*

Thyri: *I'm sure Kason's explained it all, Nai.*

Thyri: *I can't believe I'm saying this but just give her some time to come around.*

Thyri: *I'm sure Kason can get her to come to the reception.*

Tanai: *I don't even wanna go anymore.*

Tanai: *I think I'm gonna tell Kason to cancel it.*

Thyri: *No!*

Truth: *Hell no!*

Truth: *You're not cancelling it because of her.*

Truth: *We are celebrating your new marriage.*

Truth: *Fuck anybody else who doesn't like it.*

Thyri: *We are definitely celebrating your new marriage.*

Thyri: *It's been a minute since the three of us turned up together too.*

Thyri: *Please stop worrying about her for now, Nai. I know it's easier said than done but please just focus on all the positives.*

Thyri: *You met his brothers yesterday, right? And you said that went okay?*

Tanai: *I think they hate me too but his oldest brother Killian seems to not hate me the most.*

Tanai: *Kadiri definitely doesn't like my ass.*

Truth: *Well Kadiri better watch his ass before I fuck him up.*

Tanai: *I don't regret eloping with Sonny but... I just wish we did things a bit differently.*

Tanai: *We weren't thinking. We were just so ready to get married.*

Thyri: *You're in love. There's no crime in that.*

Thyri: *Please stop worrying, love. I'm sure everything is going to be just fine.*

Thyri: *And you know no matter what, we've always got your back.*

Truth: *Yeah stop worrying, Nai. We've got you always.*

Truth: *Your reception is going to be fire and I'm about to get you so drunk.*

Tanai sent two laughing emojis into the chat.

Tanai: *Tru, you said I can see Alana after preschool tomorrow?*

Truth: *Yup.*

Truth: *The little monster will be done at 3.*

Thyri: *Don't call my princess a monster.*

Truth: *Well FYI your princess threw a huge tantrum last night because she didn't want to go to sleep.*

Truth: *So yeah she is a little monster who sadly has me wrapped around her finger.*

Thyri: *Leave my baby aloneeee.*

Tanai: *Can't wait to see her. It's been too long.*

Truth: *She can't wait to see you either. She's missed you so much.*

Truth was the only Wright sister who had a child. She'd had her daughter three years ago and could honestly say she was the best thing in her life. Alana Capri Wright was the spitting image of her mother. She was basically her mother's mini me and there wasn't anything Truth wouldn't do for her baby.

Thyri: *Don't forget our meeting tomorrow with Theresa at 1.*

Tanai: *Yup x*

Truth: *Got it.*

Tomorrow afternoon, the Wright sisters had a meeting with their head cleaner who managed all the other cleaners working for their company and helped them manage the company whenever they needed her to. Theresa was not only their manager but she was their mother figure, someone they'd known since they were little girls. She'd been quite close with their father and been by his side when he started building his cleaning company from the ground up. They swore up and down that they were just friends but the Wright sisters knew how fond they were of each other over the years. It was just a shame that their father was now gone before he and Theresa could admit their true feelings to each other.

After texting her sisters, Thyri decided to get ready for bed. It was quite late and all she wanted to do was sleep. She had a busy day ahead of her tomorrow and needed all the sleep she could get.

Once in her bathroom, she stripped out of her lounge wear and started taking the protective film off her tattoo so she could wash it and moisturize it as she'd been told to.

After taking the film off her body she stood in front of the mirror and saw how red it was with small blood and ink oozing from the area. She knew this to be normal though since she'd been told what to expect after taking off the protective film. She then wrapped her hair up, placed it in a shower cap, stepped into her walk in shower and closed the door behind her.

While the warm water cascaded down her skin, she found herself closing her eyes and giving into the mental images of the one man that she couldn't stop thinking about. As soon as those dark brown orbs came into mind followed by that heavenly face of his, Thyri was unable to stop the shiver that ran down her spine and the longing whisper that told her one thing:

You know you want him.

Without hesitating, Thyri let her hand travel between her soft thighs and she spread them further apart while resting her back against the shower's glass.

It doesn't matter that I want him. I'm in a relationship. I can't have him and I'm never going to see him again. So let me just have this moment and never think about him again.

In Thyri's mind, she could give into the pleasure that her body wanted to feel while he remained ingrained in her head and then forget all about him once she'd rode her waves of pleasure. She was sure that after tonight, he would no longer dominate her thoughts.

"I love Momma to death but man does she know how to drive me crazy."

"Oh believe me I know," Killian tittered. "God ain't give us a Nigerian mother for no reason."

"He definitely didn't... but I just wish she'd listen to me. I don't know why she's convinced that Tanai is after my money, *our* money. That's not the case at all."

Killian went silent.

"That's not the case, Kill. Trust me."

"I'm not gonna act like I don't have my reservations about the woman because you hardly know her ass."

"I know enough."

"But not everything," Killian affirmed. "I support you with almost all the decisions you've made so far in your life but Kay... this one's different. You're married to a woman that your family don't even know, most of them haven't met her yet and you expect us all to just welcome her in with open arms? Come on, bro, you're smarter than that."

Kason let out a heavy breath.

"I love her."

"I know you do," Killian replied. "I saw that look in your eyes yesterday. You'd do anything for her."

"In a heartbeat."

"So be prepared to stand by her when our family don't accept her initially."

Kason groaned before saying, "I just wish everyone would understand that I'm grown, in love and made a decision to marry the girl of my dreams without any interference."

"With time they'll come around, I'm sure." Killian dropped his pencil and looked out the glass to ceiling windows showcasing the stunning night view of the city. "Look... I'll talk to momma and I'll make sure she's at the reception."

"You can't guarantee that, Kill. I know she always listens to you but this time's different."

"When have I ever shown you that you can't count on me?"

That was a question that Kason couldn't find a solid answer for because there wasn't one. He could always count on his older brother to come through for him.

"You haven't."

"Exactly so trust and believe that I'll have momma at your crib on Saturday."

"A'ight," Kason agreed. "Thank you, bro."

"You welcome." Killian lifted his pencil and focused back on his drawing on the desk below him. "You looking forward to Saturday?"

"Yeah, I can't wait to turn up with my baby... and the family of course."

"I bet."

There was a brief silence between the brothers until Kason spoke up again moments later.

"Kill?"

"Yeah?"

"What do you think of her? Like honestly, keep it real with me. What do you think of her?"

Killian paused his artwork once again and started rummaging his brain to find the words he wanted to say.

"Honestly... I like her. She's not afraid to speak her mind and she loves you. I know I was a lil' hard on her yesterday but she's got to understand that I won't tolerate any bullshit whatsoever if it ever comes down to you two getting a divorce."

"Damn, bro, you ain't got no faith in us, huh?"

"That's not what I'm saying. I just don't need her getting her rocks off on the idea that she can walk away with one hundred times more than she came with if she ever decided to leave you. But I feel like you wouldn't let her ass go even if she tried." Killian chuckled. "Knowing you, you'd probably try to handcuff her ass to your bed if she ever tried to leave."

"She's stuck with me till death and she knows that shit."

The corners of Killian's mouth curled upwards as he said, "Oh I bet she does."

"Believe me we're in this for the long run, Kill. I don't want any other woman in this life but her."

"Good to know."

Killian placed his pencil back to the paper and began finishing the last touches of his piece.

"I'ma catch up with you later, bro. Thanks again for keeping it real with me."

"You know I've got you always," Killian reminded him. "Later, kid."

Once their call was over, Killian reached for his phone in the far corner of the table and unlocked it to head to Apple Music. Just as he clicked on Anderson.Paak's *Malibu* album, the banner of an email notification popped up and he clicked it while his AirPods played Anderson's first track.

The email's title read **Tanai Kristen Wright** and it had no words written in the main body of the email but a PDF file was attached at the bottom. Killian clicked on it and began to skim read over the document that contained all the information he'd wanted to know about his brother's new wife.

Of course he respected his brother's new union but he'd be a fool to not have his guard up and not have Tanai investigated. As soon as Kason had introduced Tanai to him, Killian had immediately made a mental note to hit up his personal P.I. who would give him a full rundown in the next twenty four hours of Tanai's life, family, and friends. If there was anything that she was hiding, anything at all, Killian wanted to know exactly what it was.

From what he could see so far, she'd lost her father three years ago, was a triplet and owned a cleaning company, The Wright Way LLC, alongside her sisters Truth Wright and Thyri Wright...

What the...

Killian did a double take, trying to make sure that his mind wasn't playing tricks on him. Trying to make sure that he hadn't tricked himself into thinking that he was seeing the name of the beauty he'd met today. But this was no trick. The name Thyri

Wright sat on the white page clear as day and he couldn't stop the flush of adrenaline that tingled through his body.

Fuck.

Now it was making sense to him as to why her face looked so familiar! He'd met Tanai yesterday and Thyri today and although they weren't identical triplets, they definitely had a resemblance.

He'd told Miss Thyri Wright that he wanted her without even asking for her phone number, email, or address. Not that he needed any of those things as she'd made a booking online through his shop's website so all her personal information had been stored when she'd filled out her form. But he wasn't planning on getting her info from his website because in his mind, their paths would cross again eventually and he would get everything he needed directly from her. However, what he hadn't expected was for their paths to cross so damn quickly.

His eyes fell to his drawing and his heart warmed at the sketch portrait he'd almost completed. The portrait of the one woman he couldn't get out of his head.

Her.

Since leaving her, he'd managed to memorize every feature she owned and had put his pen to paper to create a realistic and stunning piece of artwork that captured the essence of her beauty. He couldn't stop staring into those gorgeous eyes of hers, those eyes that he was going to be able to see in person again very soon.

Now that he knew that their lives were connected due to their siblings falling in love, Killian's determination had skyrocketed. There wasn't a single doubt in his mind that she was going to be his.

Chapter Six

"Hmm... That's funny."

"What's funny?"

Thyri turned and her eyes met the curious ones of her sister.

"I haven't been charged for my tatt."

Her head dropped and she stared down at her checking account's recent transactions. All she could see was the withdrawal she'd made out of an ATM yesterday to pay for some gas and the money she'd spent at Target this morning before heading to work.

It was while she'd been browsing her social media that Thyri suddenly remembered Cleo telling her four days ago that her fee for her tattoo would be taken from her card in the next twenty four hours. Today was Saturday and it was only now that Thyri had realized that she hadn't been charged for her sternum tattoo.

"Well it looks like your lucky ass got a free tattoo," Truth voiced with a pleased smile. "And it's fire too. Maybe I need to get over my fears of getting one and head to Dayana's new spot. What did you say the name of the place she's based at is called again?"

The memory of Tuesday evening flew into Thyri's head, making her remember being all alone with him, as he worked his magic on her skin. Making her remember all the ways he'd had his hands on her body while he left his talented mark on her.

"House of Hayes."

How could she ever forget it... or him?

Even after that night of touching herself with only his face in mind, Thyri hadn't been able to forget him. She'd been a fool to think she could forget him so easily. He ruled her mind almost twenty-four-seven and it seemed the more she tried to fight out thoughts about him, he would come back stronger and more vivid in her head.

"I'm going to call the receptionist on Monday," Thyri said. "There must be some kind of mistake."

"You're a better woman than me, boo. 'Cause ain't no way in hell am I about to pass up on the chance to get a free tat."

Thyri locked her phone and looked out the window, focusing on the high trees that bordered the road they were on.

It's been four days and my card hasn't been charged... this doesn't seem like a mistake, Thyri. I think this has something to do with Hay—

"Hey."

Just as her head twisted back around, Thyri felt a hand grab her arm and she looked into chocolate brown eyes identical to hers.

"You okay, sis?"

Thyri nodded, placing her left hand over Truth's hand, and gently patting it.

"I'm good. Just ready to be with Tanai."

"You and me both." Truth released her grip on Thyri's arm. "I knew Alpharetta was on the outskirts but damn I ain't know it was this out."

The girls were currently being driven by an Uber driver to their sister's new house where her reception was taking place this evening. So far it had taken over thirty minutes to get from Atlanta to Alpharetta and their destination was still about ten minutes away. They'd encountered usual traffic while getting out the city to enter the next which wasn't a surprise as Atlanta's traffic was no joke.

"It's only been like thirty minutes, Tru." Thyri smirked.

"I know but you know how much I hate car journeys," Truth reminded her. "If we could've caught a flight you know I would've been down for that instead."

Thyri gave her sister one last look before her eyes found the tinted window next to her once again. She was looking out the window but not actually paying attention to anything outside. She could only pay attention to her thoughts that were telling her that Hayes had something to do with her card not being charged for her tattoo. She didn't like the thought of her not paying him for his hard work. He'd done an amazing job and she wanted him to be compensated for it.

No worries. I'll call Cleo on Monday and get this all straightened out.

Less than ten minutes later, the girls' Uber driver entered a side road and slowly pulled up to a black gate that was a short distance ahead. Just as their driver rolled down his window to press the intercom's button, the gates slid open, granting them automatic entry.

Thyri and Truth kept their eyes sealed on the view ahead. A view that quickly had their mouths parting wide. Both of them remained speechless as their driver drove on the long winding driveway leading to the breathtaking home up ahead.

It was a grand two story home that sat on an eight acre lot. Its exterior had been painted white and the house was surrounded by a freshly mown lawn and healthy looking trees of different sizes and species. The sisters also spotted a long row of expensive looking cars parked outside the house. It wasn't until the driver brought the car to a halt that the girls snapped out of the trance they were in.

"Is here okay, ladies?"

Thyri stared at the front view mirror that showcased the emerald eyes of their driver.

She nodded and replied, "Yes, thank you so much."

"Thank you," Truth said.

"You welcome. Enjoy the rest of your day, ladies."

Once they'd said their goodbyes to their driver, the girls left the car, linked arms, and followed the concrete path leading to the house's front stairs. Up ahead they could see a man in a black suit and tie, holding a silver tray of champagne glasses.

"Ri, are you seeing this house?" Truth asked her sister as they walked, trying to ensure that she wasn't dreaming. "My God..."

"I'm seeing it, babe. It's everything."

Each step they took did nothing to ease the excitement rushing through their bodies as they stared at the fifteen thousand square foot house. The closer they got, the more they could hear loud upbeat music coming from the house. They started walking up the concrete steps and the uniformed man greeted them with a welcoming smile.

"Good evening, ladies. Welcome to Mr. and Mrs. Miller's reception." The caramel skinned man extended the champagne tray towards them. "Can I interest you in some complimentary champagne?"

Before they could reply, the front door suddenly opened and Tanai's pretty face appeared from the other side.

"About time you two heifers showed up," Tanai announced, making Thyri and Truth giggle.

The sisters all started squealing with delight and rushed up to one another, circling their arms so they could form a group hug.

"You look amazing," Thyri complimented Tanai, loving everything about the way her dress sculpted her womanly figure.

She reached for Tanai's hand and twirled her, causing the sweep train of her dress to spin around her. Tanai laughed happily before coming to a stop and reaching for her sisters once again.

"Not as amazing as you two."

Truth wore a strapless ruched midi dress in a rich wine color that complimented her cocoa skin well and allowed those small curves of hers to shine. She had on black Saint Laurent Opyum heeled sandals with a matching chain strap bag. Her jewelry was simple yet elegant - gold hoop earrings and a gold chain with the initial 'A' in its center. Her hair was in a middle part and had soft loose curls.

Thyri was clad in a beige bandage dress that had a pretty sweetheart neckline and a flattering midi cut. On her white toed feet were her favorite black Bottega heels and on her shoulder hung her Balenciaga hourglass bag. A silver diamond tennis necklace graced her neck with matching earrings and bracelets on each wrist. She was no longer rocking short hair and had on one of her favorite frontal wigs in a water wave texture that perfectly framed her face.

"Shut up. We definitely don't look as good as you, Mrs. Miller."

Tanai's attire was a blush pink gown that had an off the shoulder neckline and a mermaid fit that didn't miss a single curve on her voluptuous figure. She wore a pearl choker and a pearl earring was locked in each ear. Her hair was in a half up half down hairstyle with the front part of her hair braided up while the back of her curly hair remained down.

"No but for real... you look so beautiful, Nai. Kason is one lucky man."

Tanai started blushing and smiling so hard that she was convinced that the corners of her mouth would reach her ears if they could.

"Come on, time to get you two inside." Tanai turned around to face the suited man. "Leon, I'm gonna get my sisters something stronger to drink inside. I hope you don't mind."

"No not at all, Mrs. Miller."

Tanai came to stand in the center of her sisters but before she could link arms with them and lead the way inside her new house, Truth swiped two glasses from Leon's tray, making her sisters smirk.

"Tru."

"What?" Truth took a quick sip from her first glass, giving Thyri a side eye as she'd been the one to call her name. "I'm thirsty and you know I never turn down the opportunity to drink some liquor. Especially *free* liquor."

Truth eagerly gulped down the first glass before gulping the second.

"You damn alcoholic." Tanai giggled, watching as Truth placed her empty glasses back on Leon's tray. "I guess I better make sure I get more liquor in your hands tonight."

"Oh absolutely. That's your number one priority for the rest of the night, my darling sister."

The Wright sisters laughed as they walked into the space. The first thing Thyri and Truth laid eyes on was the two story foyer's curved staircase that led upstairs. It had a balcony that overlooked the front foyer and living room.

"I'll give you the grand tour later. I promise," Tanai announced, knowing from their wide eyes that her sisters wanted a personal tour of her new house but that would have to wait 'til later. "Let me just let Sonny know you're here."

"How did you know we were here?"

"The front gate cameras," Tanai told Thyri. "I have the live feed on my phone and I spotted you two in the backseat of your Uber. And before you ask, yes I've been watching it waiting for you two to show up."

"Of course you have, you big baby." Truth snickered which made Tanai chuckle while leading her sisters deeper into her home.

The sweet sounds of Wizkid and Tems filled the space around them.

Say I wanna leave you in the mornin'
But I need you now

Tanai led her sisters through the foyer, past the living room and through two open doors that led to the backyard where there seemed to be an endless amount of faces now looking their way.

Who could blame them? Three beauties had just stepped into the backyard and anyone not looking their way would be missing out on the goddesses.

Thyri's heart rate kicked up a notch and her eyes kept darting around as they walked deeper into the yard. She couldn't focus on one person in particular as her nerves wouldn't allow her to. She soon noticed a few familiar faces and received a few waves accompanied by pleased smiles from mutual friends of her and Tanai. Her heart rate began to return to normal as she greeted the people she recognized by returning their smiles and waves.

You don't need no other body
You don't need no other body
Only you fi hold my body
Only you fi hold my body

"Sonny, baby, look who's finally here!" Tanai called out to her husband who was standing on the other side of their pool with a tall figure standing right beside him.

Oh. My. God.

The minute Thyri found eyes that she was sure she'd seen before, she was unable to look away and her heart almost stopped at the way he was looking at her.

I'm dreaming. I must be dreaming right now.

He was looking at her like he wanted to eat her up for break-fast, lunch and dinner and her cheeks suddenly burned hot.

Oh my. Oh my. Oh my. Oh my! It's him.

"Thyri, Truth!" Kason lifted his champagne flute in the air towards the girls. "It's so good to see y'all."

Kason was talking but Thyri wasn't paying attention to him or anything he'd just said. The only thing she was paying attention to was the man standing right next to him. The man that she'd been thinking about nonstop for the past four days.

Hayes.

The more their eyes remained locked, Thyri was sure that her heart was going to leap out of her chest at any given moment.

He looked too damn good for his own kind! A white button up shirt covered his upper body while his long legs were cloaked by smart navy pants. He rocked a silver iced out chain, two Cuban link bracelets on his right wrist and an expensive looking watch on his left.

Tanai left the side of her sisters to walk up to Kason who reached out for her, welcoming her into his space as they gave each other a quick closed mouth kiss.

Kason then announced, "Thyri, Truth, I'd like you to meet my older brother, Killian."

Wait... who?

76

Thyri's confusion waved through her as she gazed up at the man she knew to be called Hayes.

"Kill, these are Tanai's gorgeous sisters, Thyri and Tanai."

"Pleasure to meet you, Truth," Killian greeted her before letting his eyes wander back to the woman who he'd been looking forward to seeing for the past four days. "Thyri, I hope you've been taking care of that tatt like I told you to."

He let his gaze slowly sweep down her pretty face to that beige dress that looked like it'd been painted on her figure. The thought of him being able to paint her while she wore no cloth—

"Y'all know each other?"

Truth's query tore Killian away from his nasty thoughts.

"Yeah," Killian confirmed. "She came through to my shop a few days ago to get a tatt."

"Wow, what a small world," Tanai voiced. "Thyri, I had no idea you got a new tatt."

"I thought your name was Hayes." Truth frowned before turning to her sister. "That's what you said the owner was called, right, Ri?"

"That's his middle name," Kason explained, smirking as he kept his arm around Tanai. "Well one of the many middle names he has."

Killian simply nodded while his eyes remained fixed on Thyri.

"Hayes was the perfect fit to go along with House and ever since then it's always just stuck." He paused, remembering that he hadn't heard a word from Thyri since she'd walked up to him and Kason. And he didn't like that shit at all. "So you've been taking care of it, Thyri?"

"Yes, I have." She slowly nodded. "Just like you told me to, Killian."

His name felt smooth against her tongue, slightly cool too. She licked her lips, as if savoring its sweetness.

77

Killian.

She liked his name. As a matter of fact, she loved it and now that she knew it, she knew she could never forget it.

Hearing his actual name come out from her mouth was enough to make the swelling under Killian's pants get ten times worse than it already was.

"That's what I like to hear," he replied.

Their eyes remained locked while a brief silence formed between the group. Thyri was still surprised that the man that had been running through her mind all week was standing right in front of her now. Still looking as fine as ever.

"Baby, I'm gonna get the girls a drink and show them around the house real quick," Tanai told Kason, breaking the group's silence.

Kason nodded before moving closer to Tanai to peck her lips one last time.

"Don't leave me too long, Nugget," he whispered to her, making her cheeks flush.

The Wright sisters then left Kason and Killian so that Tanai could grab them a drink. While following Tanai to the drink station, Thyri used this opportunity to properly scan the backyard.

Tanai and Kason's backyard had been decorated in a simple yet elegant way. The trees that surrounded the yard had beautiful fairy lights hanging off them and on the other side of the yard was a long, white clothed dining table with white roses, white candles and white lace patterned placemats.

So far Thyri had spotted various uniformed waiters and waitresses, Tanai's friends, a few men she guessed had to be Kason's friends and of course she'd seen Killian. But who she hadn't seen was Kason's parents and didn't Tanai mention that Kason had two brothers?

"Jimmy, my love, I need you to hook me and my sisters up with a shot of tequila each."

"Sure thing, Mrs. Miller," Jimmy replied, the bartender in charge of getting everyone drunk tonight - Tanai's specific order.

"Nai, didn't you say that Kason had two brothers?"

Tanai turned away from Jimmy to Thyri who stood on her right.

"Yeah, he does." She nodded at Thyri. "Kadiri isn't here yet... I think he's running late."

"And what about his mother? Have you heard if she's changed her mind about coming?"

"Well..." Tanai turned back over to Jimmy who had just finished pouring out their three shots of Clase Azul accompanied with lemon wedges and salt. "Thank you, Jimmy," she said as she dipped her finger into the salt bowl. "Killian promised Kason that their mother would be here tonight."

Thyri watched as Tanai licked the back of her hand before placing salt on it. Truth then did the same. The mention of Killian made heat flood Thyri's insides.

"He did?"

Tanai nodded then reached for the first shot, passing it over to Truth.

"He did," she confirmed. "And if there's one thing I've learned about Killian, he isn't one to lie. He says things exactly how they are. Still can't believe he's the one who tatted you."

Neither can I, Thyri mused while placing salt on the back of her hand that she'd just licked.

"I mean I figured from the way you told me his name that he was fine as hell but I didn't think he was *that* fine."

Thyri's brow arched at Truth's comment.

"And how exactly did I say his name?"

"Like you wanted to thank him for how well he did your tattoo." A smirk formed on Truth's lips.

"I did thank him."

"With words," Truth reminded her. "But you were talking like you wanted to thank him in a different way... *physically.*"

Thyri's eyes bulged and her bottom lip suddenly dropped, making Truth and Tanai burst out in laughter.

"I'm a taken woman thank you very much."

"Yeah, taken by a nigga who doesn't deserve you," Truth mumbled but her sisters had definitely heard her.

Truth's comment was enough to make a weight settle on Thyri's heart and her face went blank. Not wanting to make Thyri uncomfortable by the topic of her boyfriend coming up, Tanai knew it was time to get her sisters drinking.

"Alright, alright, I think it's time we take these shots, heifers." Tanai passed the second shot over to Thyri. She then lifted the final shot glass in the air and her sisters quickly followed suit.

"Oooo, lemme make a quick toast," Truth chimed in. "To you, Tanai and your new marriage to the man of your dreams. You deserve this and so much more, sis."

"Thank you, Tru," she replied with a smile.

Thyri decided to say a few words too.

"To you, Nai. You and Kason are perfect for one another. I'm so happy for you, love."

"Thank you, Ri."

The sisters then clinked glasses, tapped the bottom of their shot glasses on the bar's countertop for good luck, licked the salt off their hands before downing their tequila in one large gulp and sucking on their lemon wedges. Their faces went funny as the liquor burned down their throats but it wasn't long till they were all smiling because of how good it felt to be drinking with one another.

"Okay, tour, then we come back for another shot!"

"Deal," Thyri and Truth agreed as they placed their empty shot glasses down to the open bar's countertop.

"Thanks once again, Jimmy! We'll be back for more."

Jimmy nodded at Tanai, grinning wide as he collected each of their empty glasses. Tanai reached for her sisters' hands and led the way through the backyard back into the main house.

Mr. and Mrs. Miller's new six bedroom home was a place that suited the word palace too well because it was truly a place fit for a king and queen. As Tanai gave her sisters the grand tour of her new abode, Thyri and Truth couldn't stop marveling at each detail. From the kitchen to Kason and Tanai's individual offices, the fireside sitting area, the main living room, the dining room, the master bedroom, the guest bedrooms, Tanai's two story closet, the custom bar room, the theatre room, the exercise room, the wine cellar, Kason's man cave, the indoor and outdoor basketball courts, the tennis court, Tanai's woman cave, the home spa, the game room, to the indoor and outdoor swimming pools, Thyri and Truth felt like they couldn't keep up. Their sister's new home was out of this world and they were delighted that this was the fortress she now called her home.

Tanai finished the tour in the outdoor living room which allowed the girls to be back where they started in the backyard.

"Nai, baby!"

The call of her name made Tanai turn in the direction of her husband's voice with a smile only for the smile to slightly weaken when she laid eyes on who stood beside her husband. Kason motioned for her to come over and having no choice but to obey her man, Tanai began stepping to where he was.

"Nai, do you need us to come with you?" Thyri asked just before Tanai had walked completely away from her and Truth.

Tanai turned and shook her head 'no', still wearing that same smile from before.

"I'll be good," she said. "Both of you go and get another shot. Save one for me too, okay? Go." Tanai motioned for them to go with a toothy smile.

Thyri and Truth watched as their sister walked away, making her way to where her husband, his father, his two brothers and his mother were gathered.

Thyri took a quick glance around the backyard and realized that during Tanai's tour, more guests had arrived. The backyard was much fuller than it had been before especially since more of Kason's family members and friends had arrived. And by the looks of the new bodies, Kason sure as hell had a lot of family and friends.

"I swear to God if anyone tries to disrespect Nai tonight... it's about to be world war three up in this bitch."

"Oh we know, missy." Thyri reached for Truth's arm and linked hers to it. "Come on let's get those shots like Nai said."

The girls made their way over to the bar where they met Jimmy, the bartender who had served them earlier. While walking to the bar, Thyri felt many eyes on her but it was the eyes of someone in particular that she could feel the strongest. However, she refused to look at him, afraid to make the fire rushing through her worse. The fire that refused to stop rushing through her because of him and all the ways he'd made her feel from the first day they'd met at his shop till now.

After taking two more tequila shots each, the sisters decided to browse the backyard and mingle with the familiar faces they recognized.

Tanai had invited a few high school friends, college friends and all their employees from their cleaning company were here. The girls began to have a blast, offering hugs and smiles to all their friends. The tequila shots they'd taken so far had them feeling very nice and the high moods they were in right now, neither sister saw themselves losing that vibe anytime soon.

"Both of y'all look amazing," Theresa, their mother figure, complimented them. "Those dresses are to die for!"

"No but you look beautiful, Mama Tee," Thyri replied, calling her by the nickname the sisters had called her since they'd first known her fifteen years ago. "You need to dress up for us more often!"

Theresa Peters was the only mother that the girls had ever known. She didn't look a day past forty and she was turning fifty five this year. She owned the clearest looking caramel skin, sepia colored eyes that pulled you in from the moment you laid eyes on her and made you want to know exactly who she was and a curvy figure that looked amazing in the lilac, tight fitting, one shoulder dress she wore tonight. It stopped right below her knees and to compliment it, she'd worn white ankle strappy heels. She was a gorgeous woman and the girls were so lucky to have her in their lives.

For several minutes, the girls spent time mingling with friends and people they considered family. Occasionally, Truth would look over to see where Tanai was and saw that she remained with Kason's immediate family. Since Tanai's back faced them, Truth couldn't see her face and that left somewhat of a bitter taste in her mouth because she couldn't see how her sister was feeling. But she was sure that Tanai had to be doing just fine meeting Kason's mother for the first time.

Ding! Ding! Ding!

Minutes later, the sound of a spoon tapping against glass was heard and every guest looked over at Kason who now stood in the center of the backyard with his arm wrapped around Tanai's waist.

83

"Tanai and I would like to thank you all for coming out tonight. It means the world to us that we could have all our family and friends with us to celebrate our new union. And although we got married behind all of y'all backs—"

"Which was totally his fault by the way," Tanai injected which made everyone laugh.

"My bad y'all... I just couldn't wait to marry her fine ass." Kason leaned into Tanai's neck and peppered her skin with kisses. Unable to help herself, Tanai began blushing and her lips curled upwards.

"Sonny, the toast," she whispered to him.

"Can wait," he whispered between his smooches. "I want my wife right now."

"Get a damn room!" Kadiri yelled out which only made more laughter erupt from every guest.

Tanai placed her hand to Kason's chest and pushed away from him so she could finish addressing their guests.

"We're sorry for eloping but we just couldn't wait. But we're so happy and blessed to have you all with us now. In the next few minutes, dinner will be served at the grand table so if everyone could take their seats that would be great. You'll find your name card on the table in front of your seat."

Everyone began to follow Tanai's instructions and made their way over to the long grand table.

Thyri and Tanai found their seats right next to each other and took their place at the table. Sitting next to Thyri on the right was Theresa and it was only on closer inspection that Thyri realized that she, Truth and Theresa were seated at the top of the table on the right side. On the left side sat Kason's family and as they each took their seats, Thyri realized that Killian sat opposite Truth which basically meant that he was sitting opposite her too. Still not giving into looking at him, Thyri set her gaze on

Kason's mom, sending a warm smile her way but she didn't return it.

What the hell?

Tension began to fill Thyri's chest but she decided to ignore Kason's mother's lack of friendliness and turned over to the head of the table where Kason was pulling out Tanai's chair for her. Her smile returned at the sight of Kason making sure Tanai got into her seat and was comfortably seated before he was. He pressed a kiss to her forehead before taking his seat.

The head of the table had two positions, one for Tanai on the right side and one for Kason on the left.

"Okay everyone, you'll be served individually by your assigned waiter or waitress." All eyes were on Kason as his baritone travelled down the long table. "Just let he or she know what you want from the menu in front of you. Anything at all that you want just let them know. Whenever you're ready to order, just press the button on the back of your name card and you'll be served."

Thyri looked down at her placemat to see a white menu with elegant gold font. Glasses of water had been placed out for everyone.

"Tanai and Kay Billy went all out I see," Truth said to her sister. "Our own personal waiters... do you see how long this table is?"

Indeed Thyri had. The table was the width of the entire backyard and then some. Every chair was filled by one of the one hundred guests present.

"That's a whole lotta waiters. But shoot, I ain't complaining at all." Truth grinned. "I'm about to order this whole damn menuuuu."

Thyri shook her head at her sister and smirked as she peered down at her menu, trying to decide on what she wanted to eat.

"Momma, Dad, Kadiri," Kason's deep baritone caught the

attention of his family. "I haven't had a chance to introduce y'all to Tanai's family yet. This is Theresa, her mother figure and these are Tanai's sisters, Thyri and Truth. Killian, you've met Thyri and Truth but not Theresa. Theresa, Thyri and Truth, this is my Mom, Temilola, my Dad, Memphis, my younger brother Kadiri and my older brother Killian. My aunties, uncles and cousins are further down the table but I'll be sure to introduce y'all properly later on."

Everyone began to exchange smiles and hellos except Kason's mother who kept silent during the greetings. She simply reached for her glass of water and sipped on it without offering anyone but her son, Kason, eye contact.

What the fuck is her problem?

Thyri was trying her hardest to hold her tongue and so far doing well but she knew deep down she wanted to address Kason's mother and her lack of communication. And she knew from the sisterly connection she shared with Truth that she wanted to speak up too. As a way to hold her off, Thyri reached under the table for Truth's hand, squeezing tight as she turned to face her, offering her a look that said, *Just stay calm, sis. For Nai.*

Truth exhaled and did exactly that, not wanting to stir up trouble on Tanai's special day. At least not before they'd gotten the chance to eat.

Thyri looked back over at her menu one last time before making a move to have her order taken. Just as she pressed the button on her name card, her eyes lifted only to land on the one person she wasn't trying to see yet.

Him.

He was giving his order to his waiter but those dark brown eyes were stuck on her. His eye contact was firm and intense, almost so intense that Thyri wasn't sure she wanted to give in. But that was a lie the minute she thought of it. Of course she wanted to give in. The hairs on her arms and on the back of her neck rose as their eye contact intensified.

All he's doing is looking at you and look how you're reacting. Get a damn grip, girl.

"Hello, Thyri. What can I get you tonight?"

It was the voice of her female waiter that made her tear away from Killian. She let out a light breath as she ratted off her order to her waitress.

Every guest ordered their various meals, sides, and drinks. The sounds of pleasant conversation with upbeat music playing in the background filled the atmosphere and it wasn't long till everyone's food had been brought out. Grace was led by Kason and just before everyone dived in, Kason's father got up from his seat and lifted his champagne glass in the air.

"Everyone I promise I'm not about to hold y'all up from feasting on your delicious meals. I just have a few, quick words to say."

The attention was now on Kason's father.

"Those of you who don't know me, I'm Kason's father, Memphis, and I just wanted to congratulate my son on his new marriage. Though it caught us all by surprise, I'm happy that my son has found his soulmate. Someone he can count on when times are hard. Tanai, it is an honor to welcome you and your family into our family. I look forward to getting to know you better. So if everyone could join me in lifting their glasses as we toast to the happy couple, To Kason and Tanai."

"To Kason and Tanai," everyone said in union, lifting their glasses and toasting.

Kason's mother had reluctantly toasted with everyone but it was clear by her stern face that she didn't actually want to toast to the happy couple. No one but Thyri and Truth had noticed her attitude and the urge to want to check her was creeping more and more within the sisters.

"Thanks, Dad. That really means a lot coming from you." Kason smiled at his father once he'd taken his seat.

"Thank you so much," Tanai replied. "I'm happy to be a part of your wonderful family too."

"Of course you're happy to be part of this family. Who wouldn't be happy to be married to a man worth over a billion dollars?"

And. There. It. Was.

There was the first snide comment of the night from Kason's mother. Words that Thyri had a strong hunch were coming and now they'd finally arrived.

"Mom," Kason called out to her, a frown settling into his face. "Don't."

"What? I'm just speaking the truth. Ain't no harm in that," his mother voiced smugly. "Of course she's happy now that she's secured the biggest paycheck of her life. Because ain't no way in hell did she marry you for love, Kay."

"Momma, stop it."

"And everyone sitting here and pretending like they don't know the truth about her character is beyond me."

"And what truth would that be?" Thyri suddenly spoke up.

Kason's mother's lips curved into a sinister smile as her eyes settled on Thyri.

"That your sister ain't nothing but a gold digger."

"Watch your mothafucking mouth before I watch it for you, old lady," Truth injected before anyone could get a word out first.

And that was all it took for all hell to break loose.

"Who the hell are you calling an old lady?"

"You, *old lady*. Keep talking shit about my sister and I'll gladly call you a whole lot more than old."

"Yo, you better watch the way you're talking to my momma," Kadiri intervened, shooting daggers Truth's way.

"And if I don't?"

"I'll fuck your big forehead ass all the way up."

"Kadiri, watch it," Kason warned.

"I'd love to see you try, Skinny Boy," Truth taunted.

"This Skinny Boy will gladly squash your potato shaped head," Kadiri replied.

"You can't do a damn thing to me so shut the hell up."

Kadiri and Truth's argument carried back and forth while Kason tried to intercede, hating the fact that his brother and sister-in-law were now bickering.

"Your sister is just as rude and bratty as I know you probably are," Kason's mother commented, looking directly at Tanai as she spoke.

"Temi, please sto—" Kason's father tried to plead with his wife but didn't get a chance to finish talking because he was cut off.

"See what you ain't about to do is disrespect my sister and then have the audacity to talk to her while also disrespecting my other sister. Shut the hell up before I walk around this table and make you shut the hell up," Thyri announced and her threat was enough to make everyone's core fill with shock.

And that meant everyone. All the guests of Kason and Tanai's reception had stopped their conversations because the altercation happening at the top of the table had captured all their attention. Especially the words that Thyri had uttered just seconds ago.

Who would have thought that such an innocent looking woman could have the prowess to make serious threats against a woman twice her age?

And Thyri wasn't done.

"Excuse me?" Temilola's eyes narrowed to slits. "What did you just say to me?"

89

"You heard every word I just said. Don't act dumb. You have no right talking to Tanai like that and you have no right judging her when you don't even fucking know her. Call her out her name one more time, I dare you. You thought my sister calling you old lady was bad? Watch what I'll call you if you even think about disrespecting Tanai again. Don't you ever disrespect my sis—"

"That's enough, Thyri."

Now it was Thyri's turn to have her core fill with shock at who had interrupted her rant. No one had expected him to talk and now that he had, everyone's attention was on him. Killian's order had jabbed Thyri like the sharp end of a stick and anger spiraled from the pit of her stomach.

"No one asked for your input," she fired at him, refusing to look his way.

"Well I'm giving it. I said that's enough."

Who the hell does he think he's talking to?

A tightness formed in Thyri's jaw and she kept her gaze on Kason's mother who was staring at her with the same amount of resentment that Thyri was currently sending her way.

"Look at me when I'm talking to you, Thyri."

It was as if a spell had suddenly been casted over her because Thyri's eyes shifted in his direction. The moment their eyes connected was the same exact moment every negative feeling in Thyri's body melted away.

"Enough," he repeated, giving Thyri one last look before his eyes travelled around the table. "All of you. That's enough. Mom, apologize."

"Over my dea—"

"I didn't ask for a story, Momma. You know what you said to Tanai was foul and false. Apologize. Now."

Temilola sighed before reluctantly obeying her son.

"I apologize."

"Her name, Momma."

"I apologize, Tanai."

"Kadiri."

The call of his name made a scowl form on Kadiri's face but he kept it gangsta by not objecting his older brother's wish and apologized to Truth.

"Truth," Killian called.

"I ain't do nothing but defend my sister," Truth said with a shrug. "I'm not apologizing for that."

"No one's asking you to apologize for defending your sister, Truth," Killian voiced. "But you will apologize for disrespecting my momma."

"Fine." Truth rolled her eyes before apologizing to Temilola like Killian had told her to.

"Thyri."

Thyri was the final person to apologize and though she'd had no plans to do so when she'd first spoken rudely to Kason's mother, the spell she was under had her ready to apologize right this instant. Killian not only had a spell over her but everyone else too and his ability to be able to quickly diffuse the situation, without raising his voice, proved to Thyri that he was a king. Everyone listened to him and respected him with no hesitation.

Thyri apologized and that was enough to bring a warm, fuzzy sensation to Killian's chest. She'd listened just like he'd told her to.

"Good. Now can we all get back to enjoying our meal and celebrating Kason and Tanai's marriage? Thank you."

After his words, everyone tucked into their meals and conversations further down the table slowly started to pick up once again. There was still a tense mood at the top of the table though and neither Kason's immediate family nor Tanai's family bothered to talk. They focused on eating and drinking.

Thyri was still left reeling at the fact that Kason's mother had called her sister a gold digger. Tanai was far from one and for Thyri to hear her be called one made her want to seriously hurt Kason's mother.

How dare she?

For such a beautiful woman, she really had such a venomous tongue. Temilola Miller had flawless beige skin, dark brown eyes, full lips, and thick, healthy looking hair that fell past her shoulders. It was her real hair too because there were no signs of it being a wig.

I hate this for Nai. Kason's mother doesn't like her and I don't think she ever will no matter what Nai does.

Thyri looked over at Tanai to see her looking down at her plate of food but not eating from it. Kason had his arm around her shoulder, whispering to her. However, whatever he was saying didn't seem to be working because Thyri soon noticed water dropping out of Tanai's eyes.

"Nai, baby, please don't..."

Kason's pleas fell on deaf ears because Tanai shrugged his arm off her body, got up from her seat and rushed away from the dining table. Without hesitating, Kason got up too, calling after Tanai. Thyri and Truth jumped out their seats also and followed their sister who was now racing towards the house.

"Nai!" the sisters called after their sister, trying to get her to stop and talk to them. If not her husband then at least she could talk to her sisters, right? But it was no use because Tanai kept running towards the house without turning back.

Once they were in the house, Thyri, Truth and Kason made their way upstairs where Tanai was currently heading.

"Your mother disrespected my sister and only apologized because Killian told her to," Truth told Kason while they each climbed the stairs. "You better tell your mother to watch the way she talks to my sister or the next time she tries to disrespect her I'm putting hands on her. I don't care how old she is."

"No one will be putting hands on anyone."

It was the sound of *his* voice that made Thyri freeze and look over the stairs to see that he too had followed Tanai into the house. He stood in the front foyer, carefully watching the three of them on the steps.

"Kay, let Thyri and Truth go up to see Tanai alone."

Kason stopped climbing upstairs and turned, only to frown at Killian.

"I need to be with her right now."

"And what she needs right now are her sisters," Killian informed him. "Let them handle this for now."

Kason deeply sighed and his shoulders dropped. He started walking downstairs, the opposite direction to where he wanted to go, but he knew that his brother was right. His wife needed her sisters with her right now.

Thyri watched as Killian patted Kason's back once Kason had reached where he stood. They both turned around to return to the backyard. She was about to start walking upstairs to follow Truth who had gone ahead of her but she caught Killian's head turning. His eyes held her prisoner for just a few seconds before he finally released her, focusing on looking ahead and heading back to the backyard with Kason.

"Killian, hold up."

A sudden surge of energy had rushed through Thyri, causing her to head downstairs towards Killian and his brother.

"Tru, go up without me," she told her sister without turning back to look at her. "I'll be there in a minute."

"Whatever you say, *Ms. I'm A Taken Lady,*" Truth said in a tone loud enough only for Thyri to hear and hurried upstairs before Thyri could even think about giving a rebuttal to her words.

Thyri observed as Killian said a few words to Kason before Kason then left his side. She stopped a short distance away from Killian, feeling her knees weaken when he decided to draw nearer to her. He didn't speak up to ask her what she wanted so Thyri knew it was best she spoke up first.

"I was gonna phone Cleo on Monday but since I'm seeing you now I figured it was best to say what I realized... I haven't been charged for my tatt yet. I think there's a problem with your payment system."

"Nah, there ain't a problem with the system." He stepped closer to her, shortening the already small gap between them. "You ain't getting charged for it so don't bother looking for the transaction anymore."

"But, Killian..." Thyri's breath hitched in her throat when he closed their gap completely and her heart wouldn't stop pounding away as his six foot four frame towered over her. His masculine aroma filled her nostrils and she couldn't get enough of how good he smelt. "I need to pay you for your hard work."

"Uh-uh." He shook his head from side to side. "I don't want mine spending her hard earned cash on anything I can handle for her."

Mine.

The word sounded too sweet coming out from his lips. And those lips? They looked too sexy moving as he said it.

"Killian, I can't not pay you." She started shaking her head but the touch of her chin made her stop moving and wetness dripped out the portal between her thighs due to his hand now on her face.

"Do you know how beautiful you look tonight?" he asked, caressing her soft chin with his fingers, and letting his sight drop down her body. Loving every part of how she looked under him. "Because I do."

All night he hadn't been able to take his eyes off her. It'd been bad enough when he couldn't stop thinking about her during the week but now that he was finally graced with her presence, he couldn't stop watching her. She was the only person he wanted to focus on and it didn't help that she was wearing a dress that looked too damn sexy on her. A dress he wished he could take off at the end of the night. That dirty thought was enough to make the bulge between his legs grow in size.

"God, the things I wish I could do to you tonight, Thyri Wright," he spoke in a low tone. A tone so low that she could've missed his words if she didn't pay close attention. Lucky for her, the only thing her mind could be bothered to attend to right now was him. Nobody else but him. "You don't even know how bad I want you..."

Her fingers began to tingle and she was hit with the sudden urge to touch him. She didn't know where she wanted to touch, all she knew was that she wanted to feel him. Any part of him would do, just as long as she could touch him.

"But I can't have you." He dropped his hand from her face. "Not until you realize what I told you about that other nigga."

Snap out of it, Thyri. You belong to someone else. All this lusting over this stranger has got to stop.

She decided to listen to herself and stepped back from him as she said, "He's not just some other nigga, Killian. He's my man that I'm in a relationship with. A man that loves me."

His lips expressed amusement as he asked, "Is that right?"

"Yes," she stressed, trying to convince him but more so trying to convince herself. "There's nothing for me to realize."

"Are you in love with him?"

His question had caught her completely off guard but nonetheless she knew she needed to answer it and prove herself to him. She wasn't sure why she felt like she had to prove anything to him but she was going to do it anyway.

"...Y-Yeah."

"You hesitated, Thyri."

"I'm in love with him and I have no plans to leave him."

"Where is he?"

Confusion stained her pretty features so he chose to add to his current question.

"Where is he tonight?" Killian's curious gaze dipped into her as he searched for an answer to a question he already knew the answer to. "Tonight's an important night. Your sister's celebrating her new marriage. Surely the man that you're in love with should be right by your side, supporting you as you support your sister."

He made a very good point. A point that Thyri now hated. Why did he always have to be right?

"He's... He's b-busy."

"Busy doing what?"

"Busy," she affirmed, ignoring his query. "But him being busy doesn't change the fact that he loves me."

Laughter dripped from Killian's lips, bringing a frown to Thyri's face.

"What's so funny?"

"The shit you just said," he said with one last chuckle that sent a shiver down her spine. "Of course him being busy doesn't change the fact that he loves you. Any man can love you but a man that's *in* love with you, will be by your side no matter what. Willing to support you whenever and wherever."

Once again Killian closed the gap between them and Thyri's mouth went moist. He reached out a hand to pull back a loose curl from her face and just that simple action had her brain turning to mush. His deep gaze on her refused to break away, making every part of her body sizzle uncontrollably.

"Ready to remind you every chance he can about how beautiful you look and how lucky he is to have you. How crazy he would be to let another nigga have the chance to steal your heart."

Killian stepped away from her, ready to head back outside. But before leaving her side completely, his dark eyes bored into hers as he said, "You're not paying for the tatt and that's final. You may have argued with my mother tonight but you're not arguing with me. I know she was wrong for what she called your sister and I'll be checking her on that shit in private but I don't ever want to see you get out of character like that again. And don't you ever threaten my mother again unless you want to see a side of me that you really won't like. I'm only gonna tell you this shit once, Thyri. Don't make me have to tell you twice."

Then he walked off, leaving her all alone with a racing heart and soaked panties.

Chapter Seven

W hat a night.

Thyri entered her apartment building and walked through the dimly lit front desk area. While she walked, all she could think about was the shit show of a night she'd just experienced with her sisters.

After Killian had said his final words and left her side, Thyri eventually recovered from the shocked state that she'd been placed in because of him and made her way upstairs to the master bedroom where she found Truth consoling a sobbing Tanai.

"I haven't done anything but fall for her son and she hates me! She called me a gold digger in front of everyone and he just expects me to sit there and play happy family. I c-can't!"

It wasn't a surprise for Thyri and Truth to see their sister in such an emotional state because out of the three of them, Tanai was the most emotional. She cried whenever she was upset, whenever she was angry and even when she was happy, tears would form in her eyes. She was the cry baby of the trio as Truth liked to call her. So the sisters weren't surprised by her crying. And because of that, they knew exactly how to handle her and make her high spirits return.

Just the mention of one of their best memories together - the day when their father had lost a bet he'd made with them and because he was the loser he had to have a full body wax - was enough to make Tanai's tears of sadness turn into tears of pure joy. It was also enough to allow Thyri to get through to Tanai and convince her to not let Kason's mother ruin a great night. This was the day of her reception and Tanai deserved to enjoy the rest of it.

Temilola had been wrong about the shit she'd called Tanai and Thyri made it her duty to remind her sister of how much of a successful go getter she'd been over the years, running their father's company and coming up with so many great ideas that had put the company in a very profitable position.

Tanai of course listened to her sister and it didn't take long for her to wipe her tears away and fix her make up. She then made her way back downstairs to finish enjoying her reception with her sisters right by her side. The mood was slightly awkward when the sisters returned to the dinner table and continued to eat their meal but once Tanai stirred up conversation with Kason's father, Memphis, the mood eased and it was like nothing had even happened just minutes prior.

Temilola didn't say much to anyone during the dinner, but Tanai didn't let her ruin the rest of her night. She focused on enjoying her meal and making conversation with Kason's father and brothers. What surprised everyone was what happened after the dinner when Temilola pulled Tanai to the side for a private conversation. A conversation that Tanai revealed to her sisters shortly after it was finished.

"She apologized again for calling me a gold digger and says she

wants to make things right by spending time with me some time soon."

"Let's hope her ass ain't plotting on how to kill you 'cause I don't mind going to jail this year for avenging your death."

"Truth!"

"What? She better not be playing any games cause I'm not here to play either. I know exactly what I'm gonna say to the cops when they pull up to her crib and find me with the gun that I used to kill her ass."

"She better not be playing any games because I won't hesitate to make sure she learns her lesson," Thyri added.

"You too, Ri? Guys come on... She hurt my feelings yes, all of our feelings but I really think she's trying to make amends with me. She's my husband's mother and I owe it to Kason to form a relationship with her."

"And no one's saying you can't," Thyri replied. "I just don't buy the whole sudden change of attitude, Nai. Just an hour ago she was calling you a gold digger. She clearly had some beliefs about you before y'all even met. I don't buy the whole nice act, I ain't even gonna lie. But let's just hope and pray she knows what's best and doesn't try to fuck with you anymore."

Though it was nice to hear that Kason's mother had realized the error of her ways, Thyri found it quite suspicious that she'd changed her tune so quickly. Just less than an hour ago she'd been hurling insults Tanai's way and now she wanted to make amends? Thyri wasn't buying it and she knew she'd be staying on high alert when it came to Temilola having any contact with Tanai.

The rest of the night ran somewhat smoothly as Thyri drank and danced the night away with her sisters. The only thing that didn't run smoothly was her ability to not make eye contact with Killian Miller.

She tried her hardest to not look in the direction of wherever he was and somewhat succeeded until somehow he managed to be in her line of sight. *Every. Single. Time.*

Whenever those captivating dark browns connected with hers, she found her insides burning up. Fire that formed both from lust and anger. When Wizkid's *Essence,* one of her favorite songs was played again by the DJ, Thyri was looking right at Killian as Tems sang all about her lover not needing nobody else but her and Thyri was reminded all about the fact that she was attracted to everything Killian embodied. It was a fact that had flames of anger shooting through her and made her tear her eyes away from him. This time she was determined to keep her line of sight far away from him.

She didn't want to look at him. Not after the way he'd warned her like he was her daddy or something. She only had one father and sadly he'd passed away so for Killian to be talking to her like he had any authority over her definitely had her feeling some type of way. But his warning was the same reason why she couldn't stop finding his gaze during the night. Only he possessed the power to make a warning sound so alluring that her panties became soaked because of him.

Thyri now stood outside her apartment door and reached into her purse for her key. She pulled out the silver metal, slid it into the black door and pushed through to enter her home.

The sound of a neo soul instrumental playing in the background greeted her as soon as she stepped through the door and from where she stood in her front foyer she could see her brightly lit living room area, telling her that she had a visitor. The aroma of spicy, sweet, and sour lamb chops and creamy mashed potatoes filled her nostrils and a smile grew on her lips as she kicked her heels off. She then sauntered across the foyer into the living room only for her to freeze when she spotted who stood on the other side of her kitchen island. His sienna brown eyes met hers and that was all it took for Thyri's cheeks to hike.

"There's my baby... wow, you look amazing, Ri."

Thyri dropped her purse to the floor and raced to the other side of the island where her man stood. She wrapped her arms around his torso and pulled him in tight, refusing to let go.

"Damn, girl. You really did miss me, huh?" He chuckled. "I missed you too, Ri."

Just as she now held him close, Chosen did the same to her and rubbed on her back while repeatedly kissing the top of her head. Thyri slowly looked up at him and began to admire the one face she'd missed for weeks.

The first day she'd ever laid eyes on Chosen Evans was the day that Thyri knew she was a taken woman. With those tender brown eyes that had a hint of hazel within them and that charming persona of his, Chosen swept Thyri off her feet two years ago and she hadn't looked back ever since. Sure they'd had their ups and downs during their time together but what couple didn't?

"I was starting to get worried that you wouldn't be coming home tonight," he announced. "And all of this would be going to waste."

Thyri looked over her shoulder and it was only now that she was able to notice the dinner laid out for her and him with a candle between the two plates.

"Cho Cho," she cooed the nickname that she'd coined for him at the beginning of their relationship. "You shouldn't have."

He smiled as she turned back to look at him and the happiness glowing in her eyes was unmissable.

"But I had too... I've been gone so long and I've missed my wifey. It's the least I could do. I still have so much making up to do after missing your sister's reception."

Her spirits soared at the thought of him doing more to

please her. Thyri's top love language was acts of service and whenever her man went out of his way for her, it was a huge turn on.

"Thank you, baby."

She leaned forward and tilted her head up to press her lips to his soft ones. Finally the two of them were able to give each other the one thing they'd been deprived of for weeks and once their tongues entwined, that was all it took for Chosen to forget all about them eating. His hands slid down Thyri's frame, landing on the small of her back and he grabbed her ass cheeks with each palm.

"Mmmh, Cho," she moaned out between their kiss before pulling away from him and sighing softly.

"What?" He planted his lips to the side of her neck, inhaling her jasmine scent. "I've missed you, Ri... I know you've missed me too."

She had. Lord knew she'd missed her man and more than ever she'd missed feeling him slide between her thighs. But that was before she'd encountered a man... no, a *king* who knew how to bring her to an orgasmic high with only his voice.

"I have but I don't want your good food to go to waste," she said, turning back over to the meal that Chosen had made. "You know how much I love your lamb chops."

"Uh-huh." He pecked her skin one last time. "I do."

Chosen straightened up and looked down at Thyri.

"A'ight, let's eat first. I wanna hear all about how Tanai's reception went. You still ain't told me who the dude she eloped with is?"

"And I promise to tell you everything right after I murder these lamp chops." Thyri gave him a quick kiss before racing to the first empty seat opposite the island.

Chosen chuckled and went to take the seat beside her. The

couple then bowed their heads, said grace together and dived into the meal that he'd prepared.

"This is bomb," Thyri commented seconds after her first bite of her lamb. "How lucky am I to have a man who cooks as well as you do?"

Chosen grinned and placed his left hand to her thigh, squeezing tight as he used his other hand to eat.

"So talk to me, beautiful. How was the reception?"

Thyri began to fill her man in on all the details of what had happened at her sister's reception. Well not all the details. She'd be the biggest fool revealing to Chosen her run in with Killian. Chosen had been a jealous lover at the start of their relationship and nothing had changed. He was still jealous as ever when it came to Thyri. She was not about to add fuel to the fire by revealing the truth about a man that had staked his claim on her, knowing fully well she belonged to someone else.

"Wait, Tanai's married to Kason Miller?"

Thyri nodded as she sipped on her glass of water. She placed the glass down to the white quartz island top and turned to face him.

"You know him?"

"Yeah something like that." Chosen shifted in his seat. "I don't know him personally but his family owns a huge stake of Atlanta's construction industry. They're responsible for the construction of a lot of buildings around the city and if they're not the ones that constructed it then they're the ones that provided the materials for another smaller company to do it. My cigar bar? The Millers constructed it before I even bought it and all the shops on the same line as it."

"Oh wow," Thyri said in a soft tone.

She didn't realize that The Millers were such an influential family in the city of Atlanta and she had no idea of their construction background. All she knew was that alongside his brothers Kason owned the biggest gym in the city, had a billion dollar tech security company and Killian owned the biggest tattoo shop in the city. Now that she was putting the pieces together it was obvious that this family had their hands in places that were bringing in a lot of revenue. And everything she'd learned so far was connecting. The Miller family constructed buildings throughout the city, owned the biggest gym that they'd created with their construction company and Kason had the security company that protected all the buildings the company created.

Wow. They're really doing big things.

"So your sister lucked up by marrying into that family. Their wealth runs deep throughout the city. She's set for life."

"Well I'm not too sure about the lucked up part... their mother called Tanai a gold digger tonight."

"What the..." Chosen's mouth fell open. "She really said that shit in front of everyone?"

"Yup," Thyri confirmed, rolling her eyes at the memory. "Almost made me get up out my seat and beat her ass."

"Not you tryna beat up a lady double your age, Thyri."

Thyri shrugged without showing a hint of emotion to what he'd just called her out on which made him titter.

"My lil' fighter." Chosen reached for her cheek and squeezed tight. She smirked and playfully squatted his hand away.

"So what happened after she called Tanai a gold digger?"

Thyri continued to tell the story of what happened at Tanai's reception. While she talked, Chosen listened and devoured the rest of his meal. When it came to Thyri explaining how apologies were passed around the table after the disagreements that happened, she was extra careful not to give Killian too much significance in the story. She didn't want Chosen getting suspicious and envious about another man's ability to get her to soften up so quickly. She simply explained that everyone felt it was necessary to let bygones be bygones in order to not ruin Tanai and Kason's special night. By the time Thyri had reached the end of her story, Chosen was finished with his meal.

"Sounds like you had an eventful night indeed, bae. You had fun in the end though?"

"Yeah," Thyri replied with an assuring smile. "Enough about little old me. How was your trip? Did the investors like your new idea?"

"Well..." Chosen reached for his napkin and gently dapped the white cloth to his lips. "They didn't like it..."

Thyri's heart suddenly dropped at his words.

"They fucking loved it."

But his next sentence was all it took for her heart to leap and she jumped out her seat to wrap her arms around him.

"Oh my God! Baby, that's amazing! Congratulations!"

He pulled her closer to him and their mouths branded together for a kiss.

"I'm so proud of you!"

"Thank you, Ri." He flashed his million dollar smile at her and pecked her lips again. "That's why I was out of town for so long. They loved the idea so much that we've already started working on the prototype. In the next few months, niggas will be able to come into my bar or shop online and get their favorite e-cigar with a speaker that connects to their phones and plays their favorite songs. Can you picture it, baby? People vibing to their songs while smoking on my cigars."

"Yes I can."

Thyri smiled as she watched him getting lost in his thoughts. Excitement sparkled in his eyes and it only made her smile harder to see how he felt about his dreams coming to fruition.

"You've accomplished so much already and to see you accomplishing more of your dreams is amazing, Cho. I'm so proud of you."

Chosen reached for Thyri's hand that was now resting on his shoulder and pulled it up to his lips, kissing the back of it as he stared at her.

"And I'm so lucky to have you by my side, Ri. You know how much you mean to me and you know how bad I want to give you the world."

She nodded.

"My new idea is only gonna make me richer and before you know it, you and I are gonna have that big wedding we've always talked about having."

Her nods continued while she reached for the side of Chosen's clean shaven face, rubbing into his pecan butter colored skin. Her smile continued to crease her face, showing no signs of fading away because of the enticing words pouring out from Chosen's full lips.

"And before you know it, I'll be bringing in so much damn money that you won't need to work anymore. You can sit back, relax and focus on pushing out our babies."

The smile had shown no signs of fading away until Chosen uttered words that felt like poisonous daggers slicing through her heart.

"Excuse me?"

Thyri snatched her hand out of Chosen's grip and removed her other hand from his shoulder.

"I don't intend to stop working, Chosen. You know that."

A frown quickly formed on his pink lips and he looked at her like she'd lost her damn mind.

"I don't want my wife working when she should be taking care of our kids. You know that."

Thyri's face tightened and she turned away from Chosen, taking her seat, and facing the kitchen.

The one topic that her and Chosen clashed on had made an appearance tonight. The one topic that they could never seem to agree on – which is why Thyri tried to avoid it as best as she could – had finally made an appearance after months of not being in their environment. This was the last thing Thyri needed to deal with after the night she'd just had. But it was now the number one thing she was going to have to deal with tonight.

"Thyri, things are changing for me. My business is growing and alongside it I'm changing too. I told you when I met you that I planned to make you my wife one day and I wasn't joking. That day is coming and when it comes I don't want my wife working. That's not something you'll ever need to do ever again. All you need to do is focus on taking care of our kids and the big ass home I'm buying for us."

Chosen's eyes stayed glued to the side of Thyri's face since she wasn't facing him. He patiently waited for her to respond. But when she didn't respond after several minutes, Chosen could no longer hold his tongue.

"Did you hear what I just said, Ri?"

What Chosen had failed to realize was that Thyri's anger was boiling through her and despite how much he thought he knew her he couldn't read through her current silence. But he was about to feel the wrath of her growing irritation towards him.

"Thyr—"

"If you think I'm about to stop doing the one thing I love just so you can have your picture perfect dream of having a slave as a housewife, you've got another thing coming."

Chosen's eyes bulged and he watched as Thyri finally turned to face him. She glared at him without blinking.

"I'm not going to quit running my father's company alongside my sisters."

Now it was his turn to glare at her.

"And I'm not going to marry a woman who refuses to put anyone but herself first."

"Fine," Thyri spat. "I guess we're not getting married then."

Chosen's heart almost stopped at her words. He gritted his teeth for control, trying to steady his breathing that was now increasing by the second.

"What did you just say?"

"I guess we're not getting married then," she calmly repeated, cutting her eyes away from him and picking up her fork to finish the last bits of her meal.

However she never got the chance to pick up said fork because within a split second, Thyri's forklifted into the air and crashed down to the other side of her kitchen with her plate of remaining food. Her plate that had now smashed to pieces and her hands tightened into fists as she remained seated in her chair.

"You really just said that bullshit to me, Thyri! Your boyfriend! Have you lost your damn mind?"

Another negative trait about Chosen? His temper. Thankfully, he'd never laid a finger on Thyri and she was glad he hadn't because Thyri was sure that if that ever happened that would be the same day she got sent to jail for murder.

"You don't want to marry me? That's the mothafucking bullshit you're trying to tell me right now?"

"I'm not having this conversation with you while you're yelling at me and throwing my shit around like a crazy person, Chosen."

She rose to her feet but the second she did was the same second that her arm was grabbed. Every muscle inside her tensed at the action.

"No, we're having this conversation. Right fucking now."

Her eyes zeroed in on his face and to see the way he'd become livid with anger was enough to make an alarm ring in her mind.

"Get off me."

"You're not going anywhere, Thyri."

"I said get off me, Chosen!" She tried to shake his tight grip off her arm. "Leave me alone!"

It was no use though because the more she tried to shake, pull, and push him away, the tighter his grip on her arm got and the tighter his hold got, the more she began to see red.

"I said leave me alone!"

Thyri lifted her free hand and smacked it hard across Chosen's face. His face turned to the side at the impact and his pecan butter skin instantly flared up red.

Without thinking twice about it, Chosen released his grip on her arm and Thyri stepped back away from him. From the way his jaw was currently twitching she knew that it was best she backed away from him.

A silence formed between them and if it wasn't for the neo soul instrumental playing in the background, Thyri was sure that the lack of words between her and Chosen would be unbearable. She took several breaths to calm herself down before deciding that she needed to cut through the growing tension.

"Look..." she exhaled deeply, scraping a hand through her hair. "I'm sorry for hitting you but you wouldn't let go..."

Chosen's head turning towards her made her pause but she continued talking despite the venomous look he'd shot her way. If looks could kill, she was certain she would be dead by now.

"...I think it's best you leave, Chosen."

When it came to their arguments, Chosen was the peacemaker. So she expected him to protest and fight her on him staying. She expected him to beg her to let him stay the night and for them to talk things out but that was the very last thing Chosen was about to do tonight. He slowly stood up from his seat and started nodding at her.

"I think it's best I leave too." He flicked the tip of his nose with his thumb. "No point in staying in the house of a woman who thinks it's okay to put her hands on me and disrespect me."

Without saying another word, Chosen left the kitchen and headed to her bedroom to get his things. Neither him nor Thyri spoke for the five minutes it took for him to grab his shit. And before she knew it, he was out the door. *Gone.* Not once did he look back and not once did she try to stop him. Not once did she try to get the man, she claimed to love, to stay. He was gone and she wasn't even upset about it. She somewhat felt relieved, like a huge weight had been lifted from her shoulders and that right there was the problem.

You say you love him but you just watched him leave without feeling the need to fight him on staying? You hit him and you didn't even try to make amends? You call that love?

Guilt struck Thyri's soul as she realized that she had a serious problem on her hands and now she was forced to ask herself the one question that Killian had asked her tonight.

Are you in love with him?

Chapter Eight

"I forgot you only know how to shoot like a little girl."

Kason lifted his fisted hand and extended his middle finger towards his younger brother, causing a fake horrified expression to appear on Kadiri's face.

"Oh I'm definitely reporting you to your CEO. You know she hates it when you're not being nice, *Sonny.*"

Kadiri chuckled as he passed the ball, he'd just bounced, over to Killian who now wore a smirk.

"Be nice, *Sonny,*" Kadiri voiced in a mellow, feminine tone. It was his version of Tanai's voice and he'd just brought up the memory of Tanai's authoritative hold over her husband. A memory that had all the brothers wanting to laugh.

"Your annoying ass," Kason commented, shaking his head lightly before an amused grin split his face into two. "Keep talking shit and I'll be sure to get my CEO to come beat your ass... better yet, I think I might just get Truth to do that. What was it she called him last night, Kill?"

"Skinny Boy," Killian spoke up, bouncing the orange ball and moving across the court.

The Miller Brothers were in Kason's indoor basketball court, enjoying a game together.

"Oh yeah that was it," Kason tittered. "I'm sure Truth would love to beat your skinny ass up."

"I'd love to see that stupid bitch try."

"Aye!" Killian's head snapped in Kadiri's direction and he froze in place with the ball tightly nested between his palms. "Watch your mouth, kid."

"What?" Kadiri's frown quickly settled into his face. "You know that's exactly what she is after she disrespected Momma last night. Was I the only one who heard what she called Mom?"

"We all heard her. She was angry which she had every right to be after what momma called Tanai. That doesn't make her a bitch, Kadi."

"Whatever man." Kadiri waved Killian off. "I don't wanna hear none of the things that were said last night by those girls ever again. I don't care if they're related to Tanai or not. Things were said that just didn't need to be fucking said."

"There were a lot of things said yesterday that shouldn't have been said... I'm just glad Momma apologized to Nai again in private," Kason said, sighing lightly. "I don't want my baby feeling uncomfortable around our family. Especially not around Mom. They're the two people I need getting along the most."

"Mom assured us that she wouldn't cause any more problems with Tanai from here on out," Killian reminded Kason of the conversation they'd had with their mother at the end of the reception. "I trust and believe she knows that you love each other regardless of all the extra wealth now available to Tanai through you. And I'm positive Mom will make the effort to get to know Tanai better over these next few months."

After Tanai and Kason's reception had been said and done, Killian got the chance to have a heart to heart with his mother and Kason had been right by his side when he'd done it. He hadn't been lying to Thyri when he said that he planned to check his mother about the things she'd said to Tanai and he did exactly that. Temilola was apologetic about the comments she'd made and promised to make an effort from here on out with Tanai. That was all Killian needed to hear and he was glad that his mother wasn't being difficult about the situation. The Nigerian in her sometimes made her stubborn as a mule but it was also the loving nature she housed that the Nigerian in her constantly brought out.

"Speaking of getting to know Tanai better... what are y'all's thoughts on coming to Calivigny island next weekend?"

Kason's query made Kadiri's brow raise.

"Wait, what? You're going to Grenada next weekend?"

"Yeah man... after the shit that went down last night, I need to make it up to my baby. I'm taking her away for the weekend and she said y'all should come through if you want. You know she wants to get to know y'all better and I'm all for it. Besides you both can have the opportunity to see the island we got married on."

Killian was silent but his thoughts weren't. He slightly bent his knees and kept his eyes on the hoop's rim as he jumped up to shoot his ball into the hoop.

Should I go? Killian asked himself. *It's been a minute since I had a real break.*

"A'ight cool," Kadiri responded, running across the court to grab the ball that had just fallen from the hoop. "I'm coming and I'm bringing Kiana too. She's been bugging me since I didn't invite her to the reception last night. Lord knows how the fuck she found out about the shit when it was a private function

115

but its whatever, I'ma bring her ass along, dick her down in Grenada and hopefully that'll be enough to make her shut the hell up."

"Pictures from last night got shared all over the damn blogs," Kason explained, running up to Kadiri who was now bouncing the ball. He began trying to steal the ball from him. "That's probably how she found out."

"I mean last night was a spectacle so I'm not really surprised. Your reception planner did her thing," Killian commented, observing as Kadiri dribbled past Kason and took his shot. "But yeah, I'll come along on your lil' trip."

"A'ight cool... You bringing anyone, Kill?"

Killian started shaking his head 'no'.

"Course his ass ain't. Y'all get onto me about being a playa but at least you've seen the girls I mess around with and you both know that I've been rocking with Kiana for a minute now. But him?" Kadiri pointed to Killian. "He's the biggest hoe here and we still don't know half of the girls he's been messing with this past month."

Laughter erupted out of Kason and Killian threw an unimpressed look his way.

"What, man?" Kason shrugged, lifting his hand to wipe away the sweat beads that had formed on his forehead. "He has got a point. We never do see the girls you mess with but I know you're definitely messing with some."

"Oh one hundred and ten percent. With all those baddies he's hired at the shop? He's definitely knocking a few ankles loose."

"FYI, I don't sleep with any of my artists," Killian retorted. "I don't care how bad they are, doesn't change the fact that I've hired them for business and nothing else."

"And what about Soraya?"

Killian's heart skipped a beat at Kadiri's mention of a woman who he'd had the pleasure of seeing face down, ass up, more times than he could count on his fingers.

"Oh yeah, his manager, right? She's not an artist."

"And they've definitely fucked," Kadiri knowingly stated. "Last time I was there she was walking around with those tight ass shorts and that booty was just looking extra fat."

Killian remained quiet and that was more than enough evidence for his brothers to realize that he had indeed messed around with the manager of his tattoo shop.

"I knew it!" A smirk sprang to Kadiri's lips. "Big K killing all the girls' hearts and pussies."

"Shut your skinny ass up," Killian piped up, no longer able to keep quiet at Kadiri's teasing remarks. "Yeah we've messed around a couple times but it's nothing deep. She knows what's up and so do I. We enjoy each other's company from time to time but that's it. That's not mine."

Mine is the girl that refuses to quit playing and realize that I'm the only man she needs in her life, he mused to himself, unable to stop his thoughts slipping to the one woman he wished he could be with every night.

"So you're definitely not bringing her along?"

"Nah... she's probably busy with some other shit," Killian told Kason.

"And you know that how?"

"I just do," Killian affirmed with a firm gaze on Kadiri before softening up his face when he realized he was starting to get worked up over nothing. Soraya wasn't important right now and he no longer wanted her to remain their topic of discussion. "Enough with all this damn talking, man, I'm eating both your asses up in this game and I ain't once seen none of y'all shoot the ball properly."

"You lil' liar," Kadiri playfully snapped, jogging towards where the ball was sitting on the court. "Watch me school both you grannies on how to shoot."

"Oh a'ight." Kason chuckled. "You tryna school us? Pigs must be flying outside."

The brothers continued their game of basketball and throwing playful insults each other's way while they played. While playing, Killian was unable to help the thought of Soraya popping into his head.

It's been a minute since you've got some and Lord knows you need it... maybe you should just invite her? We both know who you really want but she's still stuck on someone who isn't you and Kason didn't say anything about Tanai's sisters tagging along. Maybe being with Soraya for a few nights is what you need because all this simping over Thyri really ain't it man. Since when do you do that bullshit?

Killian wasn't sure what to do but what he did know, was that it was time to let the idea of being with Thyri go. After the fiasco that had gone down last night with her and his mother, it had left a sour taste in his mouth and more importantly, her telling him that she was in love with her dude that he didn't give two shits about, definitely had him feeling some type of way. It was clear that she didn't want to leave her boyfriend even though Killian knew for a fact that he wasn't the right man for her. Killian also knew that he was everything that Thyri needed in her life right now but she was too dumb to realize the truth. What good would it do for him to wait around for a woman that didn't want him?

I could've given her the world but oh mothafucking well. It is what it is.

Killian knew from this point onwards that it was best he moved on. Once him and his brothers had finished their game twenty minutes later, Killian swiped his phone from the silver bench that bordered the court and went straight to his iMessages to look for the chat he had with Soraya. He found it within seconds and entered the chat.

You free this weekend?

Send.

Within thirty seconds, her response came flying in and lit up his phone's screen.

Soraya: *Yeah.*

Soraya: *What's up?*

Killian: *You're coming to Grenada with me for the weekend.*

Soraya: *I am?*

Killian: *You are.*

Soraya: *Okay.*

Soraya: *I am.*

Chapter Nine

"Girl, I am so sorry once again about not being able to do your tatt. Killian did a good job though I'm sure."

Oh he definitely did... and he managed to fuck with my head in the process.

Thyri nodded as she stared into dark chocolate peepers belonging to her best friend.

"I really am sorry, babe."

"Stop apologizing, I told you it's fine, Day. Is your mother doing okay?"

Dayana nodded.

"She's doing good... still recovering from the accident but she's doing much better."

The main reason why Dayana hadn't been in Atlanta last week was because of her trip to see her parents in Portland. Her mother had gotten in a car accident the week before and thankfully she hadn't been seriously injured but it had definitely shaken her up which is why Dayana rushed down to Portland to see her.

"I'm glad to hear that, boo."

"But I'm back now and I miss you. When are we gonna catch up in person?" Dayana's eyes began to sparkle at the thought of seeing her bestie sooner than later. "I still owe you a tatt and besides, it's been a minute since I had a good night out. When are you free?"

"Well I'm pretty backed up with work this entire week."

"No surprise there," Dayana muttered which earned her a side eye from Thyri. "What? You know I ain't lying."

Thyri let out a harsh breath.

"I know..."

"But I get it, you're on your grind and I'll forever respect that shit. Maybe next weekend when you have some time we can have a girls night in instead of us going out. You can fill me in on all the tea happening with your sister and her new husband. She's all over the Shaderoom, Baller Alert and Hollywood Unlocked."

Thyri had heard about pictures from the reception making it onto many gossip blogs. Turns out, Kason was a pretty big deal in not just the city of Atlanta but online too because of his status as a billionaire and him being handsome didn't help the situation either.

"And I miss you, TT."

"Miss you more, Day. I promise I'll see you next weekend."

Thyri's words were all it took for Dayana's mood to soar high.

"Yayyyyyy!" She started doing a happy dance while she sat upright on her sofa, causing Thyri to giggle. "I get to see my girl, I get to see my girl! And I can fill you in on the tea with Ethan."

"You guys sorted things out?"

"Yeah... sorta."

"Sorta?" Thyri's left brow arched.

"I mean he's not going anywhere and I don't see myself going anywhere either. So yeah we've sorted things out... I guess."

"Have you guys even talked?"

"Umm..." Dayana's eyes darted away from her phone's screen and her lack of eye contact told Thyri the answer to her query.

"No you haven't talked. You've just fucked."

A sudden look of guilt passed across Dayana's face as she said, "I can't help it, TT... he's good."

"That good that you couldn't even talk about his jealousy towards you tattooing male clients?"

"*That* good," Dayana confirmed, winking, and sticking her tongue out which caused an instant laugh to slip out from Thyri's mouth. Her laughter was all it took for Dayana to start laughing too and the girls both laughed together.

"You still need to talk to him, Dayana. For real," Thyri advised moments later after their amusement eased. "He needs to know that feeling insecure about your career is stupid when he knows how you feel about him."

"I know, I know," she agreed, gently nodding. "I'll talk to him. For real this time. I promise."

"Please do."

"What about you and your nigga? How are you two doin—?"

"Auntie RiRi! Auntie RiRi! Auntie RiRi!"

The sweet voice of a girl that Thyri loved more than anything in this world came bursting into the room and Thyri looked over her shoulder to see a three year old running into her bedroom.

"Mommy said the fwood is here!" Alana came over to the side of the bed where Thyri lay and Thyri smiled at the sight of her.

"Thank you for letting me know, my love. Tell Mommy I said I'm coming now."

"Okay," Alana replied before turning around to leave the bedroom.

"Uh-uh, where's my kiss?"

A mischievous grin formed on Alana's mouth and she turned

back to her aunt, moving nearer to peck the cheek that Thyri was currently pointing to. She planted a kiss to Thyri's skin and that was all it took for Thyri's wide smile to appear.

"Why thank you, pretty lady. I'll be out in a sec, okay?"

Alana nodded and then rushed out Thyri's bedroom, leaving her alone with her phone.

"You gotta go?"

Thyri nodded at Dayana.

"But I'll be seeing you next weekend for sure."

"Oh absolutely," Dayana agreed. "See you then, girl. Love you."

"See you then and love you more, Day."

The girls ended their FaceTime call and Thyri's eyes were greeted to her Home Screen. She locked her phone and made a move to place her phone to her nearby lamp stand until the sound of her phone going off made her movement pause.

She lifted her phone back to her line of sight and joy bubbled within her when she read Chosen's name on her screen. But when she spotted the first line of his message, '*I love you to death, T, but I think we need to take a break*', her chest tightened and she unlocked her phone to read the entirety of his message.

I love you to death, T, but I think we need to take a break. It's clear that we have different priorities in life and I don't want us clashing over things that we both want. I still want to be with you and I still want to make you my wife one day but we need to take a pause on us. You need to figure out what I really want from you and figure out if you're willing to be all you need to be for me.

Instead of responding to his text, Thyri locked her phone, chucked it to the side and headed out her bedroom to join her sisters in the living room. The delicious smell of margarita pizza, pepperoni pizza, garlic bread and spicy chicken wings surrounded Thyri as soon as she stepped into the space.

"There you are," Tanai announced as she grabbed a pizza from the first open box sitting on the coffee table. "Come eat, sis."

Thyri stepped forward, inching closer to where her family sat.

"You good, Ri?"

Thyri nodded in response to Truth's question and joined her sisters and niece on the gray three seater. The Wright girls said grace then began to enjoy their Sunday meal together. It had been a minute since they'd had the chance to sit down and eat together on a Sunday and they were all glad that they were doing it now. Truth cut up Alana's pizza slice into small pieces so she would find it easier to pick it up and chew on it.

The sisters then shared casual conversation about how they were all feeling about this coming work week. The girls had an important meeting this week with their employees, to fill them in on the new cleaning products that they were launching in the next coming months.

As the owners of their late father's cleaning company, it only made sense for the girls to have their own cleaning product line. It had taken them a minute to sit down and plan all the products they wanted but they'd finally got it together. They'd managed to find a manufacturer for their own bleach, glass cleaner sprays, disinfectant sprays, antibacterial wipes, and hand sanitizers. This was just the first of many cleaning products that the girls planned to launch and hopefully next year they would be adding cleaning supplies such as mops, brooms, and dustpans to their portfolio. They were expanding and they just prayed that they were making their father proud from up above in the heavenly realm where they knew he was. Truth bringing up the weekend was what made Tanai remember what she needed to tell her sisters.

"Y'all remember when Kason offered to take you guys to see the island we got married on?"

Thyri and Truth nodded as they both chewed their last pizza slice.

"Well that day is coming on Friday," Tanai announced. "Sonny wanted to take me there for the weekend and I've decided I want you both there too. It's in Grenada and you're both going to love it. It's the vacation that you both need and it'll be a good chance for you guys to get to know Sonny better as well."

"Ain't y'all having a baecation?" Truth queried in a surprised tone. "I thought you'd want to be alone."

"We have the whole island to ourselves, sis." Tanai smiled. "Trust me if we want to be alone, we'll be alone and y'all wouldn't even notice."

"This weekend?" Thyri dropped her paper plate to her lap as she started shaking her head from side to side. "I can't. I'm spending time with Dayana this weekend."

"And I'ma be with my baby girl all weekend." Truth placed her hand to Alana's face, stroking her soft cheek. "Her father ain't picking her up this weekend since he's busy with something dumb I'm sure."

"Just bring Alana along," Tanai offered. "The island comes with a whole bunch of staff that are really nice. Whenever you feel like you need a break, she'll be with me and Sonny or if we're busy doing something then she'll be with one of the staff."

"I don't know if I feel comfortable leaving my baby with a total stranger..."

"They're not strangers, Tru. They're Sonny's employees and he'd kill them if they let anything happened to Alana. So would I."

"Hmm... just for the weekend?"

"Yeah but you're free to stay longer if you like," Tanai voiced. "I'm sure Theresa won't mind if you workaholics take a very long overdue vacation. Plus I'll hold down the fort here if you guys decide to stay longer. And Thyri? You can see Dayana any other time, she's your bestie and you've seen her how many times in your lifetime so far? This is a chance for you to take the break that you both deserve. Just please don't say no. I really want you both to come and Kason wants the both of you there too."

"Alright, alright." Truth nodded and a slow grin crinkled her mouth. "Alana and I will be there. Isn't that right, baby? You, me and Nai Nai are going on a vacation!"

Alana started cheering and that was all it took for a smile to light up her aunties' faces. A smile that receded from Thyri's lips as she began to think about the fact that she'd already said she wasn't going to Grenada.

A vacation was the last thing that Thyri was thinking about taking right now. After what had happened last night with Chosen and the text he'd sent her minutes ago, a vacation was the last thing she wanted. Annoyance and frustration rushed through her during the entire time she ate with her sisters but she'd managed to suppress it as best as she could which wasn't too hard because being around her sisters and niece always made happiness dance through her heart. Any negative emotions couldn't stand a chance. But now she was forced to think about her reality.

Her boyfriend had basically broken up with her through text message and she was left reeling at the fact that he thought that a "break" was supposed to fix everything between them. What exactly was a break supposed to do when it was clear that he was stuck in old patriarchal ways of women being in the house, serving their husbands and not being free to work on their dreams if they wanted to?

Thyri was suddenly struck with the reminder of the fact that she'd never been out the country. At her tender age of twenty five, she couldn't even say that she'd been on vacation and that right there was a joke.

You deserve this trip, Thyri. You know you do. Take it and live your best life.

"Okay..." Thyri lifted her head up high and gave her sisters a focused look. "I'm coming to Grenada too."

Chapter Ten

Tanai: *The car will pick you up outside the airport once you've landed.*

   Tanai: *See you both soon!*

Truth: *See you soon, cry baby x*

Thyri: *See you soon, sis x*

The day for Thyri, Truth and Alana to fly out of Atlanta and head to Grenada had finally arrived and the girls were over the moon at how fast the week had flown by. Their three p.m. flight was two hours away, giving the girls plenty of time to get their bags checked in, get through security, and even grab a bite to eat at one of the airport's restaurants, One Flew South.

It also gave Thyri some time to grab a free seat by her terminal and work on something she hadn't found the time to do in over a week. While Truth and Alana explored the various shops that Hartsfield–Jackson Airport had to offer, Thyri was left sitting alone. She lightly tapped her pen against her mini notepad, letting her eyes skim over the words she'd just jotted down.

I don't know what you've done to me
But you're now a part of me
Are we really meant to be?
My mind surely disagrees
But my heart won't set me free
Thoughts of you consume me daily
Shit's got me feeling so damn crazy
I know you're a complete stranger
But somehow with you I feel safer

Thyri wouldn't exactly call her writing poetry or songwriting. If that's what it was then fine but she personally didn't care for putting a particular title on her work, but she knew she loved doing it and couldn't see her life without it. She'd gone ten days without writing and she'd started to feel empty. But today she'd finally found the time to get her mental down on blank pages.

Her entire life all she'd known was going to school and following the same old routine but writing provided her the escapism that she never knew she'd needed until she'd picked up a pen to express herself. She loved being a business owner and delving into the world of hygiene with her sisters but being a creative gave her that momentum and edge to keep living as best as she could each day. More than ever she was excited to take her creativity on vacation and see what ideas she came up with. The piece she'd finished in the airport was of course about no one else but... Killian.

She wasn't lying when she said he was a part of her because not only had he left his mark on her physically with the tattoo he'd inked into her flesh, but he was also the brother in law of her sister which meant that they were connected through their siblings. They were part of the same family now, not through blood but through love.

*I just need this vacation to free my mind of him for a while...
please God.*

Thyri was begging The Creator above to free her from a man
that wasn't even hers. The man that was hers... or *used to be* hers
wasn't even an afterthought right now. She hadn't responded to
Chosen's "break" text all week and she had no plans to. And he
hadn't bothered hitting her up either. It was clear to her that he
was serious about this "break" that he wanted them to have and
Thyri wasn't going to stop him. If a break was what he wanted
then a break was what he could have. Thyri wasn't making any
promises to herself about welcoming him back into her life with
open arms though. She wasn't stupid and she knew the type of
things niggas did whenever they were on breaks with their girls.
He could go fuck the whole of Atlanta if he wanted to, Thyri
didn't give two shits. He could live his best life and she was surely
going to live hers. She had no plans to think about Chosen during
her vacation. All she wanted was space to do whatever the hell she
wanted and turn up with her sisters in Grenada.

When ten a.m. arrived, Thyri was comfortably sitting in her
first class seat and staring out the oval window beside her, in awe
as her plane prepared to take off. She took a quick glance to her
right to see Truth making sure that Alana was strapped into her
seat securely.

"Mommy, the plane is twaking off!"

"Yes, sweetheart, it is. We'll be with Nai Nai soon."

"Yayyyy!"

"Shhh, baby. There's others on this plane too. We need to use
our inside voices."

"Okay, Mommy," Alana whispered.

Thyri was glad to be going out the country for the first time
with her sister and niece right by her side. Tanai had taken an early
flight yesterday morning with Kason on his jet which she offered

to her sisters but they respectfully declined, wanting to give the newlyweds some privacy. However, Kason didn't back down on setting the girls up with their tickets to Grenada and thanks to him they were sitting in the comfort of first class.

Five hours later and their plane landed in the tropical capital of Grenada, St. George's. It was nighttime but the environment remained humid and heated. Just as Tanai had told them, a car picked them up from the airport and drove them to the boat's dock fifteen minutes away.

Once arriving at the boat's dock, the girls were helped onto the boat with their luggage by cute Caribbean sailors that had Truth wiggling her brows at Thyri, making a smile tug at Thyri's lips. It took the girls five minutes to arrive on Calivigny island and when they did, Thyri and Truth could not believe their eyes.

Calivigny island was a gem that exceeded any of the preconceptions the sisters had had about the place. The entire island looked like luxury and even the air smelt fresher. *Cleaner. Purer. Richer.* How air could smell expensive, Thyri had no clue but she knew that's what she smelt. From where they were on sea, Thyri could see a large beach house, a second house with an overhang roof and various beach cottages to the left of the island.

Oh my God... this place is breath taking.

Her thoughts told no lies because the more she admired the private island, the less oxygen travelled into her lungs. She quickly inhaled, finally remembering to breathe again.

"Tru! Ri!"

On the dock's edge stood Tanai with her husband right by her side. They were both waving as the boat came closer to the dock where they stood. Kason and Tanai were like two pees in a pod, rarely seen without one another and Thyri admired that.

Thyri let her eyes dart over to where she could see the pool area and when she spotted two manly figures coming from that direction, every muscle inside her tensed up.

No.

"Is that... oh hell nah, don't tell me that's Killian and Skinny Boy?"

No! No! No!

Thyri was silent as a ghost while Truth talked. There was nothing she could bring herself to say. And when she finally noticed the two women walking alongside Killian and Kadiri, anger churned in her chest and her breathing quickened.

Everything began to feel like a blur as Thyri was escorted off the boat with Truth and Alana by the boat's sailors. Even as Tanai hugged her, followed by Kason, Thyri's thoughts wouldn't line up. Every time she tried to align one, it tumbled down, scattering the rest. All she could see from a distance was Killian, Kadiri and the two unknown women beside them, all walking closer to the dock.

It was the woman next to Killian that had Thyri's rage strengthening inside her but she refused to show it, appearing as calm and collected as she could to everyone else. The closer the woman got, the more Thyri got a better look at her and was able to see the qualities she possessed.

Smooth cocoa brown skin... thicker than a snicker... perfect sized breasts sitting pretty in her red bikini top... flawless skin... wow.

The woman was everything and Thyri could see exactly why *he* liked her.

"Kason invited his brothers the same way I invited y'all," Tanai informed her sisters. "And he let them bring a plus one which I didn't know about until now or I would've told you to bring Chosen, Thyri." Thyri remained silent, feeling her stomach knot at the mention of Chosen. "But no worries. We're all going to get to know each other so much better. This is going to be such a fun weekend!"

Just as Tanai had finished talking, Killian, Kadiri and the two women had made it to the boat's edge where everyone stood. Introductions were said by Kason and Tanai alone because no one had bothered to speak up. Not Truth, Thyri, Killian or Kadiri and certainly not Kiana or Soraya, who immediately felt the tension between the two new arrivals and the brothers they'd accompanied.

Kadiri stared blankly at Truth while she held Alana who had fallen asleep on the drive from the airport and boat ride to the island. His curiosity grew at the young girl that she held but he pushed it away, trying to convince himself that he didn't care about Truth or anything about her life.

Truth rolled her eyes at Kadiri, in disbelief and annoyed that her vacation now involved being in the presence of a man she couldn't stand.

Thyri's eyes still hadn't left the woman standing beside Killian and Soraya noticed her gaze, offering her a small smile but Thyri let her gaze fall on Killian, shooting him a quick frosty look. Then she put her focus solely on Tanai who was excitedly yapping on about the plans for dinner tonight. Killian's face hardened at Thyri's reaction to him until a sudden realization struck him.

She's jealous.

That was all it took for his face to ease up and he felt light on his feet, like gravity had no authority over him.

She's mothafucking jealous!

It was a fact that had him fighting against the smile wanting to form on his lips. His face muscles began to ache as he kept his lips pursed together, appearing nonchalant to everyone else but deep down inside he was gassed like no other.

His eyes refused to waver from Thyri's gorgeous face and he

was hit with one big reality. He'd never stopped wanting Thyri despite convincing himself last weekend to forget all about her. Now that she was here on this island with him, he could hear his thoughts berating him for bringing along another woman that he didn't care about.

Fuck. You idiot. Knew you should've just came alone.

If he'd known that Thyri would be coming along on this trip then Soraya never would've got on the damn plane with him.

"Okay! Let's head inside so we can have dinner. I'm starving!" Tanai exclaimed, smiling wide and pulling Kason by the hand as she led the way towards the main beach house. "Thyri, Truth, wait 'til I show you your rooms! You're gonna love them!"

Her voice was drunk with happiness and Thyri was glad to see that her sister was happy because happiness was the last emotion Thyri felt right now. What was supposed to be a vacation of a lifetime had now turned into hell on earth.

She was stuck on an island with the one man she was trying to forget all about and here he was with another woman. A woman that wasn't her. The whole situation pissed Thyri off the more she thought about it. All she wanted to do was go home but that would mean breaking Tanai's heart and she wasn't about to do that. The only thing Thyri planned to do on this trip was spend time with her sisters, get to know her sister's husband better and stay away from Killian Miller.

Far away!

Chapter Eleven

"**W**hat the fuck, Nai? You didn't say anything about Kason's brothers being on vacation with us!"

Tanai remained quiet while standing in front of her sisters. Her eyes nervously darted from Thyri to Truth who both housed a cold look as they stared right back at her.

"You know I hate that nigga, Kadiri, and I'm pretty sure he hates me too which I don't give a fuck about," Truth pouted. "Why didn't you tell us they were coming?"

"...Because I knew you wouldn't want to come, Tru."

"Damn straight," she retorted. "That's still not fair. You should have told us."

Tanai's face continued to carry a guilty look and seeing the way the guilt was consuming her sister made Thyri sigh softly before speaking up.

"Okay well... we know now, Tru, and there's nothing we can do to change it. Now we can choose to be miserable for the rest of our time here or we can choose to have a good time on this gorgeous island. I don't know about you but I'm ready to have a great time on my first ever vacation. Nothing and no one else matters."

Truth was quiet for a few seconds, contemplating Thyri's words. This was not only their first vacation together as a trio, but it was also Thyri's first vacation out the country and ruining the good vibes that they all wanted this trip to be filled with would be stupid. Truth knew that Thyri was right and she'd be foolish trying to argue about the situation at hand. The Miller brothers were on this trip with them and there was nothing that Truth could do about it. It was best she just sucked it up and enjoyed her free vacation.

"Fine... you're right, there's nothing I can do to change the fact that Skinny Boy is on this trip... well actually... I coul—"

"Tru," Thyri quickly cut Truth off as she'd noticed the way her eyes had lit up, knowing that she'd thought of doing something sneaky to Kadiri. "Stop playing. He's Nai's family now which makes him our family too."

"Alright, alright." Truth lifted her hands up in surrender. "I'll leave Skinny Boy alone... let's just make this vacation the best vacation ever."

"Sounds like a great plan, sis!" Tanai yelled out before quickly placing a hand over her mouth. "Shit... I forgot about my baby sleeping."

She turned to look out the door and saw Alana laying in the center of a king sized bed on the other side of the room. She remained sleeping peacefully, not having a clue about her aunt's yelling.

"She's knocked out," Truth said, smiling as she watched her sleeping three year old. "She refused to sleep during the flight but I knew by the time we arrived she would no longer be able to fight it."

"Awww, my sweet baby," Tanai cooed with a smile, giving her

niece one last look before turning back to her sisters. "Y'all ready for dinner now?"

"Absolutely." Thyri shook her head in agreement.

The sisters then left the bathroom, each gave Alana a loving kiss on her cheek and left the bedroom to head downstairs to the main dining room.

The main beach house that everyone was staying in, looked beautiful on the outside but inside was ten times better than anything Thyri could've imagined. The residence was a masterpiece, styled in a French Colonial and Balinese way. Everyone had their own bedrooms with a balcony that showcased the incredible view of the island's white beach and crystal blue water. Their bedrooms also accompanied a luxurious looking en-suite that looked more like a spa to Thyri than an actual bathroom.

Since it was quite late, Thyri and Truth wouldn't be able to tour the island until tomorrow morning which they were fine with and eagerly looking forward to.

The girls entered the large dining room to see that Kason, his brothers and their two guests were already seated at the round table.

"Everything good, girls?"

Tanai nodded at Kason, walking over to the empty seat next to him. Thyri and Truth took the empty seats next to Tanai's seat and since Truth had reached the table first she got the middle seat between her sisters. Whereas Thyri was forced to take the seat next to Kadiri which she didn't mind. They hadn't uttered many words to each other than "Hey" and even though he'd clashed with Truth at the reception, Thyri didn't have a real issue with him.

"Great," Kason replied once the girls were all seated. "Let's eat."

He rang a silver bell and seconds later a dark brown skinned man in a white, short-sleeve popper jacket and black pants appeared. He began introducing himself to the group. He was, Elian, the head chef of the island and the man responsible for making sure they all ate good tonight.

"Tonight my team and I have prepared a special feast for you," he announced with a thick Caribbean accent. "Mr. Miller tells me that this is the first time some of you have even stepped foot in Grenada which is why it's my job to make sure you eat nothing but the best tonight."

"I'm loving the sound of that, sir," Truth blurted out. "You gon' make sure we drink nothing but the best tonight too, right?"

Elian chuckled and nodded.

"Yes, of course, Miss," he promised. "Nothing but the best to drink *and* eat tonight. I promise."

He told no lies because five minutes later, the large round table they sat around was filled with traditional Grenadian dishes and endless amounts of alcohol.

Thyri couldn't keep up. There were all types of food from fried bake and saltfish, lambi, pelau, crab back, curried goat, callaloo soap, roti, oil down, cocoupois and various bottles of expensive red wine were scattered across the table too.

With each bite she took, Thyri was transported to a whole new world. Each flavor was exquisite, satisfying her taste buds and making her crave more food until she could no longer fill her stomach up.

"You damn light weight."

Thyri faked a shocked gasp then released a loud cackle.

"I am not, Kadiri."

"You definitely are. Why those eyes suddenly gotten so low, huh?" He moved closer to her and narrowed his eyes. "Huh? Someone's tipsy ain't she?"

Thyri laughed some more and playfully pushed his shoulder. A push that made a burning sensation form in Killian's chest.

During the dinner, everyone had been enjoying their food and all the drinking they were doing had made everyone loosen up. Kadiri had asked Thyri how she was finding her meal and that coupled with the red liquor flowing through their systems was all it took for the two of them to become best buddies, chatting away like two long lost friends who had finally had the chance to release all the words they'd ever wanted to say to each other. They got to know each other better and became more comfortable with one another as they conversed. Now Kadiri was teasing Thyri about her inability to handle her liquor.

Their interaction had definitely made Killian feel some type of way as he sat opposite them. He hadn't even had the chance to hear Thyri say anything to him but here she was, being friendly as ever with his younger brother.

Another person feeling some type of way about their new connection was Kiana, the girl that Kadiri had invited along to Grenada. To see the man she loved, talking, and joking around with another woman rather than her, stung quite a bit. Especially because they'd gotten into a little argument this morning about Kadiri not inviting her to his brother's reception last weekend. It was the second argument they'd had about the reception and Kiana understood that he was trying to make things up to her by inviting her out to Grenada but it wasn't enough. She still wanted to talk about the issue at hand - Kadiri didn't even bother inviting her to one of the most important days of his brother's life and that right there was proof enough to Kiana that she wasn't as important as she thought she was in Kadiri's life. She was supposed to be his girl but he hadn't even shown her off to his family when she'd introduced him to hers.

After dinner, the group were stuffed and because of how much they'd all eaten, niggaritis came quickly for them all.

"Rest up well y'all. We've got a fun and busy day planned

tomorrow," Tanai informed them while holding Kason's hand. "See y'all in the morning."

Everyone said their goodbyes, parted ways, and Kason and Tanai made their way to the master suite on the second floor.

"You know you ain't getting any rest just yet, Nai." Tanai's heart rate sped at Kason's words. "I ain't forgotten about the teasing you did this morning, girl."

"What teasing?" she asked, staring at him innocently.

"Oh I'm about to remind you of the teasing as soon as you get through that door, Tanai Miller." He pulled her into him, causing her to stop walking and he pressed his lips to the back of her ear. "You know better than to play with your husband but don't worry I'm about to remind you and her what happens when you tease him..." His free hand travelled down the back of her yellow sun dress, sliding down her ass and gripping her pussy from the back. "You're getting slutted out for the rest of this trip and you know it."

She nodded, biting her lips as her clit now throbbed for him.

"I know," she whispered. "You know this pussy's yours so you better stretch your pussy out for the rest of this trip, Daddy."

Without hesitating, Kason let go of Tanai's hand and grabbed her waist. He threw her over his shoulder and raced to their bedroom. Making her giggle and smile at his eagerness to get them to their suite. On the other side of the villa, Killian was almost outside his door.

"Kill, are you sure you don't want me to co—"

"No," he snapped.

He stopped walking and deeply exhaled, turning around to see Soraya standing at the end of the corridor. She still had on her red bikini top and denim shorts from earlier. The color red complimented her cocoa brown complexion too well and everything

riding the jet, made Thyri's thighs heat up and immediately she'd been taken to a naughty place in her head.

I'm sure he could ride you well... if you'd let him.

She quickly pushed her voice out her head, not wanting to give into the secret desires that her most intimate part craved and had been craving since she'd first set eyes on him.

When the boys were done racing around with the jet skis, Kason called for Tanai to come ride with him and Kadiri called for Kiana to do the same. There were still some tension between Kadiri and Kiana but Kadiri was ready to squash the unnecessary beef and enjoy the rest of his vacation with no stress attached. Killian called for Soraya to come ride with him which she quickly accepted. He felt obliged to make sure she was having fun because he was the sole reason for her presence on this trip. Him feeling regretful about inviting her changed nothing about her being here so he had no choice but to deal with it.

Thyri, Truth and Alana were left on the boat alone and courtesy of the island staff, Alana was given a whole drawing kit with a blank sketchbook, crayons, and pens for her to draw to her heart's content. While she drew and colored away, Thyri and Truth relaxed, talked, and sipped on their glasses of Moët.

"Lord knows I needed this," Truth announced, laying her head against the boat's soft suede sofa, and looking up into the blue sky. "*We* needed this."

"Yes we did." Thyri let out a light exhale. "I can't believe I almost passed this up."

"Thank God you didn't," Truth said as her eyes dropped from the sky to Thyri's dark browns. "You would have regretted it big time, sis."

"I know... and now that I'm here, all I want to do is keep travelling, keep seeing the world as much as I can."

"That's such a vibe," Truth commented. "I'm all for it and you know I'd be down to come with you if you'll have me."

"Of cours—"

"Thyri."

The call of her name made her heart pound and she turned, allowing her eyes to meet the mesmerizing brown pools belonging to Killian.

"Come ride with me," he said without waiting for her to ask him what he wanted.

It was a request - more like an order actually - that had both Thyri and Truth surprised.

Thyri started shaking her head 'no' but the shaking didn't last long because of the heated gaze she was receiving from Killian as he floated on the water. Soraya was still sitting behind him as he drove closer to the yacht's swimming platform. They'd finished their ride and instead of getting off the jet ski with Soraya, Killian had another idea in mind.

"I'm not taking no for an answer so unless you want me to come get you myse—"

"She's coming," Truth spoke up on behalf of Thyri, causing Thyri to throw her a side eye. A side eye that Truth sent back her way.

"Girl, go before you make that man get on this boat and come get you himself," Truth said in a tone loud enough for only Thyri to hear.

Thyri placed her gaze back on Killian and her heart banged inside her chest at the position he'd placed her in. It didn't matter if she said no, Killian was hell bent on making sure she got on that jet ski with him, even if he had to first get off it then go get her. Just from the seriousness embedded in his eyes, Thyri knew he wasn't playing any games with her.

"Put on a life jacket and let's go," he ordered.

Feeling like she had no choice but to do what he wanted, Thyri slowly rose to her feet and sauntered over to the boat's edge where one of their sailors, Nigel, stood with a life jacket in hand for Thyri to wear.

Once she'd put it on and Soraya had docked the jet ski, Thyri boarded Killian's jet ski with Nigel's help while Killian kept the watercraft steady. Nigel also helped Thyri get secured onto the jet ski's seat straps.

"Hold him tight, Miss," Nigel instructed, causing a smile to grace Killian's lips.

Thyri didn't even have to see his face to know that he was smiling, she could just feel it. She placed her hands around Killian's body that was shielded by his life jacket. Nigel then coached her on where to put her feet while Killian turned the jet's ignition switch back on.

"Alright, all set," Nigel said and that was all it took for Killian to push the throttle and drive off away from the boat.

He began to speed and Thyri let out a yelp as her body thrusted forward, ultimately placing her much closer to Killian than she already was. Killian let out a light laugh and pushed harder against the jet's throttle, causing panic to snake through Thyri's heart.

"Killian! Slow... slow down!"

He drove away from their boat, away from his brothers and their significant others. When she realized he was going far away from the entire group and their extremely useful sailors, her worry only worsened.

"Killian, wher—"

"Relax," he ordered. "I'm not going that far."

Thyri looked out to sea, seeing that their boat was quite a distance away but not super far as she'd originally thought.

"Stop acting so scary, Thyri."

He'd started to slow down the jet and Thyri finally felt like she could breathe again.

"You're the one..." She released a deep breath. "You're the one driving like a crazy person."

Yeah, crazy for your ass, he said to himself, not having the balls to say it out loud to her.

"I'm driving the way a normal person drives a jet. Not like how your slow ass was driving earlier."

"I was not driv... Killian!"

Once again, Killian accelerated, thrusting them forward and making Thyri scream.

"Killian!"

"Alright, alright." He released a hearty chuckle as he eased off the jet's throttle. "I'll stop playing with you, Bubba."

Thyri's cheeks warmed as she came to the realization that Killian had just coined a personal nickname for her.

Bubba.

The jet ski slowed down and a short silence formed between the two until Thyri decided to break it.

"Why did you want me to ride with you, Killian?"

I don't just want her riding with me... I want her riding for me and riding me too.

"Don't be asking me questions you already know the answer to, Thyri," he replied as he cruised along the shore. "You know why."

"Do I?"

"Yes you do," he affirmed. "You and I haven't had the chance to be alone and I just couldn't stand that shit any longer."

Thyri went silent, not knowing how to respond to his bold statement. He was right about them not being alone until now and when Thyri had arrived yesterday, she'd been keen on staying far away from Killian. But after a good night's sleep and the remembrance of how this man could make her weak in the knees with just a simple order, she no longer wanted to stay away.

"I'm sorry for bringing Soraya along on this trip. If I'd known you were coming, I—"

"You don't need to apologize for bringing your girlfri—"

"She's not my girlfriend," he sternly cut her off. "You know she ain't."

So why the hell has she stayed so close to you during this trip like she is? Thyri asked herself rather than him. Yeah she'd been jealous about Soraya being on this island with Killian and still had a hint of jealousy within her but she definitely wasn't about to let him know that.

"It's whatever."

"No it ain't," Killian retorted. "Let's get one thing straight..." The engine of the jet ski was turned off and Thyri's heart skipped several beats when Killian looked over his shoulder at her. "She's not my girlfriend. Yes, we've fucked in the past but that's exactly what she is - the past."

"So the night I wasn't here yet, you didn't touch her?" Thyri asked before berating herself inside her head for having the guts to ask Killian about his sex life.

"No," he promised, staring deeper into her eyes. "I haven't touched her or anyone else since the day I met you, Thyri... there's no one else I want to touch but yo—"

"Yo, Kill!"

The shout of his name made him stop talking and reluctantly turn away from Thyri's pretty face to the face of his younger brother.

"Why the hell are you all the way out there for? Bring your ass over here so we can smoke your ass in these final races!"

Killian was about to tell Kadiri that he was good on racing but a voice stopped him from speaking up first.

"He's coming!" Thyri yelled back to Kadiri. "I need to pee anyway!"

No she doesn't. You know she's only saying that shit so she can avoid hearing you tell her how bad you want her.

"Bring your ass over here, Kill, and let the lady pee!" Kason shouted and Killian knew from both his brothers now having their attention on him, that his private time with Thyri was over.

Killian restarted the jet ski and drove back over to the boat so that Thyri could get off. That was the last thing he wanted her to do but he had no choice but to let it happen. He couldn't force her to stay on the jet ski with him forever even though that's what he low-key wanted to do.

The gang continued to enjoy their time at sea for an hour more before heading back to the main villa for lunch. Then the girls split from the boys to go onto the overhang roof of the second villa to sunbathe.

The Wright sisters had started to mingle and bond with Soraya and Kiana on this trip, much to Tanai's pleasure as she didn't want anyone feeling uncomfortable while on vacation with her and her husband. This was a trip that her husband had made happen and she wanted it to be a great experience for everyone who was here.

Thyri found Kiana to be quite sweet and she found Soraya sweet too... a little quiet but still sweet nonetheless and hadn't received any rude vibes from her... until now.

During their sunbathing, Soraya refused to look Thyri's way whenever she spoke up, refused to offer Thyri any words whenever Thyri would add to their group conversation and from the corner of her eye, Thyri was able to see the sly glares that Soraya would give her, thinking that Thyri wasn't noticing but she was.

Thyri knew that Soraya was feeling some type of way about the fact that Killian had made her ride with him on the jet ski just hours ago. But honestly, Thyri didn't care about how Soraya felt.

She didn't know the woman from Adam and had no plans to ever see her again after this vacation. She could feel some type of way all she liked, it had nothing to do with Thyri.

When nighttime came, everyone enjoyed dinner together before moving upstairs to the roof's terrace to relax while staring out into the night view of the island.

It was a therapeutic moment to say the least and the group didn't do much talking. They decided to bask in the moment of looking out into the magnificent view of Calivigny. Alana had fallen asleep on her mother's lap and it was sight that had Kadiri smitten. Just the image of the cute little girl in a tranquil sleep and Truth stroking her curly hair, had him glowing inside. He'd watched Alana on the trip so far and from what he'd seen, he figured out that she was a lively, well spoken, sweet and attentive toddler. He didn't know why but he felt the urge to want to get to know her better.

I'm tripping. I don't even know the kid and I certainly don't wanna know her mother. Dead that shit right now, nigga.

Kadiri put his attention back on Kiana, who was resting her head against his shoulder and gently caressing his right thigh. He already knew what she wanted tonight and he had every intention of giving it to her once they were in the privacy of her room.

Everyone soon decided to say their good nights before heading to their bedrooms and while on her way to her room, Thyri was hit with the urge to write something. But she didn't want to write in the confinement of her room, despite how gorgeous it was. She wanted to go outside and write on the beach.

So that's exactly what she did. While everyone was in the comfort of their rooms and getting changed for bed, she grabbed her notepad and silver pen from her luggage and headed downstairs to leave the villa.

She arrived outside minutes later, standing on the white sandy beach and feeling the cool breeze of the island swipe across her cheeks. She gazed out into the dark sea, loving her life right now before taking her seat on the lukewarm sand.

She sat with her legs crossed and her notepad on her lap while she tried to figure out the right ways to capture her love for this island in just a few sentences. She remained undisturbed, penning her thoughts to paper, and lost in her own world. She was too focused and too in tune with her own creativity to notice that someone was watching her from the balcony of his room. Around nighttime, Killian liked to enjoy a joint and tonight was no different.

He watched Thyri write and his heart melted at the sight of her getting lost in her own world. She was in her own little bubble right now and he knew it would be cruel to go downstairs and disturb her.

I wonder what she's writing...

Killian had a hunch that she was writing some sort of creative piece and the thought of him being right only brought more pleasure to his heart. If she too was a creative like him then Killian had another reason to add to the already long list of reasons as to why he knew that woman was the one for him.

He continued to observe her, seeing the way she would pause and look out into the sea, gain some inspiration before getting right back to penning her thoughts. Killian was convinced that there was no greater view than watching her create and he decided to forget about rolling his joint so he could focus on her for the rest of the night.

About an hour later, Thyri got up and sighed happily, feeling at peace with the words that had flowed through her tonight. She made her way along the beach, watching the blue water sink into the sand as it moved up and down. She then headed back to the villa and pushed open its large door once outside.

REAL LOVE FROM A REAL ONE

She entered the dimly lit front entranceway, too determined on her journey upstairs to notice who stood posted up against the wall next to the door. But she definitely noticed and felt the pull of her arm once the door shut behind her.

The same second her head whipped round was the same second she'd been pulled back and gently pushed against the front door. Her mini notepad fell from her hand at the same moment her back pressed against the large door. Killian took his place in front of her and their eyes connected.

Surprise made her silent as a shadow but desire made her as wet as a faucet right now. He loosened his grip on her arm and let both his hands stroke down her skin until he was able to reach for her hands. It was an action that she quickly welcomed by holding his hands and interlocking her fingers with his.

She knew that the moment for them to be alone again would come, she just didn't think it would come this soon. In her mind, he'd been sleeping, too deep in dream land to worry about little old her. His gaze took hold of her, searching her body up and down like a man on a mission to please. Please nobody but the haven that sat between her thighs.

She too let her eyes linger over him. He was in nothing but purple beach shorts. This was the second time she'd seen him shirtless, the first time being this afternoon prior to them all getting on jet skis. She'd watched him put his life jacket over his bare chest and just the sight of his muscles flexing as he wore the jacket was enough to make her knees feel weak. Now this second time seeing him shirtless with no one else around to watch her while she watched him had Thyri afraid for her sanity because all she could hear were the voices in her head telling her to never stop looking at him.

Why would she ever want to stop looking at this hunk of a man who stood tall and mighty in front of her with his hard rock abs on display, those long toned legs, those large, tatted arms and that even larger print in the center of his shorts. He had the word 'royalty' tatted on his right pec and Thyri had never wholeheartedly agreed with the word of a tattoo until this very moment. Royalty was exactly what he was. He was a king that exceeded any description.

Killian slowly raised their hands till they were to his face and he kissed the back of her right hand before moving over to kiss the left one. Thyri's body sizzled at the touch of his lips while his lustful gaze held her hostage. Once he was done kissing her hands, he lifted them up, pushing them over her head and suddenly pressed them against the door's space above her head. He made sure one was over the other before locking them in place with a single hand around both her wrists. He let his other hand drop to her chin, gently hoisting it up so she had no choice but to look at him.

"When we get back to Atlanta, you need to go ahead and tell that other nigga that you're mine."

Thyri's eyes widened and her inner thighs heated up.

"I watched you write on the beach tonight and all I could think about was how beautiful you looked expressing yourself... how beautiful you looked giving your all to a piece of paper. That same all that I've wanted from the second I laid eyes on you, Bubba."

Thyri was surprised to learn that he'd been watching her write. That same surprise was mixed with elation.

"I'm done wasting time with you, Thyri. We both know what this is. We both know you belong to me."

Killian leaned in closer, moving his lips to her right ear and whispering, "And we both know how bad I want to be inside you right now... right here."

The wetness that now dripped out of her flowed ten times

faster than it had already been flowing before. A whole damn flood was happening between her thighs and there was nothing she could do to stop it.

"Tell me you know," he ordered and without missing a beat, she responded.

"Yes." Her voice was barely above a whisper. "I know."

Killian straightened up and looked down at her. The lust burning in his eyes only made her attraction for this man worse. Here he stood, shirtless, smelling as great as ever and lightly fanning her skin with his fresh breaths. She'd be a fool not to be attracted to him and everything he had to offer. What she really wanted now more than ever was to feel his juicy looking lips against hers but he hadn't made the move to kiss her. A part of her wanted to initiate it first but she was too spellbound by his stare.

"You better tell him that you belong to me or I promise you, Ri... I'ma do it for you."

He then released her hands, much to her displeasure and stepped back. But before he could turn away, Thyri reached for his neck, pulled him back towards her and joined her lips to his.

Paradise.

It was the one word that came to both of their minds as their lips locked. Thyri felt her whole entire being melt once his soft lips pressed to hers. She'd been the one to initiate the kiss but he was the one in full control of their new connection.

Killian grabbed her waist with both hands, keeping her locked in place in front of him as he worked his magic on her mouth. He traced the outline of her lips using his tongue before dipping his tongue in and the more he took possession of her mouth with his tongue, the more warmth built between her thighs. Killian soon felt a hard ball tap against his tongue and the sensation strengthened his arousal.

Shit... she's got a damn tongue piercing. How the fuck I ain't notice that shit before?

Killian let one of his hands trail up her frame and once he'd reached his desired destination, he flicked a thumb against her right nipple at the same speed and momentum that his tongue lashed against hers. His skillful tongue paired with his thumb now toying with her pierced nipple was all it took to elicit a moan out of Thyri.

Killian pushed her harder against the door, released his lips from hers and pressed them to her neck. Her hands squeezed tighter on his neck to release some of the pressure building within her as a result of all the desire she felt for this man.

"Killian," she moaned out his name.

He now had both his hands cupping her large breasts, kneading them through her tank top while his lips dropped kisses all over her neck.

Killian couldn't help the way he was handling Thyri right now. All the pent up lust that he'd felt towards her was finally being let out and he had no choice but to act out on the very things he'd wanted to do to her. The very nasty things.

Once he started running the tip of his tongue over her skin and sinking his teeth into her flesh, Thyri could no longer take it. Not only was every part of her body on fire but she could no longer think straight. The only person she could see or think about was Killian.

She parted her thighs, pushing down on Killian's neck so she could push him closer to her. Killian immediately clocked onto what she was doing and released her breasts to lift her legs onto his torso. He spread her legs wide, providing the perfect access for him to do what they both desired.

Thyri quietly gasped at the hard print of his shorts pushing against her folds. Killian looked up from her neck and stared at her with hungry eyes.

"Don't gasp, Ri... this is what you wanted to feel, right?"

He began rubbing his erection onto her moist middle. Their clothes shielded their sacred parts but didn't stop either of them feeling how much they both wanted each other. The heat radiating off them both was unmissable. Killian leaned forward and sunk his teeth into her bottom lip, causing her to whimper.

"I asked you a question, Thyri," he reminded her in a tone heavy with seriousness but also desire. "You better answer it."

"Yes," she whispered, earning another grind of Killian's hips and a stronger feel of his shaft against her yoni. "That's what I..."

He continued to grind, throwing her thoughts off track, and making her mind go hazy. But she quickly reminded herself of the fact that she needed to answer him. Just like he'd told her to.

"That's what I wanted to feel."

Thyri met his grinds, thrusting her hips forward at the same time he did and rubbing her pussy against his swollen print.

"Shit."

It didn't take long for Killian to groan and that same tapping sensation that he'd felt earlier while they French kissed he could now feel while they humped.

"Thyri... what the..."

He pressed his mighty frame onto hers so that they were both pushed against the door and no longer moving.

Thyri's lips began to curve as Killian slid his fingers between their bodies, reaching down to the gap between her thighs and when she felt him press her clit, her moan was instant.

Killian watched as she reacted to his touch on her piercing. Her eyes were low, her mouth parted wide and her hands stroking the back of his neck.

Fuck... she's got her clit pierced too.

His fingers continued to caress her sensitive spot, increasing the sounds of her moans, and making her crave him one hundred times more than she already did.

"Kill... I need you inside me."

It was the one phrase that Killian didn't realize how bad he needed to hear until now. He suddenly released his fingers from her clit and reached for her throat, stopping her from reaching her first orgasm of the night. His grip was firm yet still managed to be gentle at the same time and his piercing eyes bored into her soul.

"I need you to understand something... when we do this, Thyri, there's no going back. You are mine and I am yours. Ain't no one allowed to touch or enter you the way I'm about to touch and enter you tonight."

He used his thumb to stroke the side of her neck while his tense look remained.

"And I mean that shit. No one. So please don't test my crazy, baby, because I have no problems getting my gun and emptying the entire clip out on any nigga that does not understand who you are to me."

Thyri was tongue tied. This man had a way with words that she just couldn't believe. Even as he talked about murdering a man, she was still horny for him.

"You got that?"

She nodded and finally found the right words to say.

"Yes. I got it."

"Good," he replied, leaning forward to peck her pillow soft lips. "Let's go."

Killian released Thyri from his hold against the door by lifting her legs off his torso and releasing her neck. When her feet touched the floor, he reached for her hand and pulled her away from the door. Thinking he was about to lead them to the spiral staircase leading upstairs, Thyri faced that direction until she heard the door opening.

"Killian, where are we going?"

He offered her a simple look once he'd fully opened the door.

"To the next villa," he explained, pulling her into the hard planes of his chest. "I don't want you holding out on me when I'm deep inside you for the rest of the night, Ri. I intend to hear just how I'm making you feel."

Her hand that he held, he moved toward his inner thighs and pressed it against his hard bulge, causing Thyri's breathing to hitch.

"You're getting every inch of this dick and you're not allowed to be shy or quiet once he's inside you."

He then leaned forward, pressing one last kiss to her lips while slowly moving her hand, that sat on his erection, up and down. Thyri felt her cheeks burn hot scarlet while he used her hand to stroke him and she knew from this moment onwards there was no going back. There was no undoing the hold that Killian had over her and there was no turning back from the path they'd chosen. Tonight and every night after this, she belonged to Killian Miller.

Chapter Twelve

Thyri's heart wouldn't stop racing. She took in and released out several deep breaths in the hopes that they would slow down her racing heart but they did nothing. Her heart refused to relax and she gripped the edge of the king sized bed she sat upon. She let her eyes wander around the room, admiring the elegant master suite that she'd stepped into just minutes ago.

Chocolate, cream, white and gold were the colors that surrounded her and every piece of furniture looked like it'd been perfectly crafted to reside in this room. It was a large sized room with a bed at the back of the room where she currently sat, a seating area on the right with a TV that lifted out from the floor and a dining area on the left for guests to enjoy a meal in the comfort of their room.

This room was stunning just like all the other rooms that Thyri had seen on this island and the fact that Thyri knew she was going to get her back blown in this very room tonight made her nerv—

The room's door suddenly opened and Thyri's private thoughts were pushed to the back of her mind. Her attention was on the figure who now stood in the middle of the doorway. He didn't say a word as he walked in but he didn't have to. Those desire filled eyes did all the talking for him. She was unable to peel her gaze from that handsome face, those finely sculpted muscles of his chest and those powerful, long legs. He was barefoot too and Thyri was greatly turned on by the sight.

He had a wine bottle tucked in the crook of his tatted arm. In his left palm he held a wine glass and in his right he held what looked like a white notepad with a flower design on its borders...

Wait a minute... that looks like my...

On closer inspection, Thyri was able to realize that the book was her notepad that she'd dropped earlier and forgotten about.

"Thanks for grabbing my notepad," she said, watching him arrive in front of the small dining table.

He gave her a simple nod as he sat the wine glass to the cream oak table then the bottle of the red wine, followed by her notepad.

Thyri observed as he lifted the bottle with one hand and unscrewed its lid before pouring the red liquid into the thin rimmed glass. He still hadn't spoken up and his lack of communication did nothing to ease the nerves rushing through every fiber of her being. Just moments ago when they'd been in the main beach house, Killian told Thyri to head to the second villa's master suite and that he would meet her there. He didn't give his reasons for wanting them to split up but now that they'd been reunited, Thyri understood the reason behind his departure. He'd gone to get some liquor and of course picked up her notepad along the way.

He finished filling the glass and Thyri watched as he reached for it while still holding the bottle. He took his time as he sauntered over to her, refusing to take his eyes off her. Once he'd arrived in front of her, Killian brought the glass to her lips and like a good girl, Thyri placed her lips to the glass, allowing him to pour the liquid into her mouth. The red wine spilled eagerly down her throat and Killian let her have a small sip before pulling away. But Thyri quickly reached for his hand, making him place the glass back to her lips and she opened her mouth wider as she drank the entire drink.

Killian was already hard as concrete as he watched Thyri drink but the fact that she'd just finished the damn glass, that he'd filled to the rim, had him ten times harder and he felt a wetness leak out the tip of his shaft.

"Damn," he commented, removing the glass from her lips once she'd finished it.

Thyri released the breath she'd been holding while drinking the dry tasting wine and remained looking up at Killian as he stood over her.

"And here I thought you'd only need a small sip to help calm those nerves," he said before raising the wine bottle and slugging back the remainder of the alcohol.

He knew she was nervous and that both surprised and pleased Thyri. He was starting to know the littlest things about her without her even having to tell him and going out of his way to put her at ease. Thyri loved that shit. She'd also noticed the slowing down of her heartbeat, letting her know that Killian had successfully eased her apprehension.

She studied him closely, her skin tingling at his Adam's apple moving up and down and the way his full, pink lips accommodated the bottle. She reached for his abdomen, rubbing her hands along his smooth muscles while hungrily looking up at him.

Killian stopped drinking and lowered his head to look at

163

Thyri. Her touch had electrified him and he could feel his attraction for this beauty reaching the point of no return.

"Open up that pretty mouth for me," he demanded and she did, allowing him to empty the remaining red wine down her throat.

Thyri drank every last drop and Killian happily watched. Once she was done, he pulled the bottle away from her lips and walked to the dining table to drop the empty glass and bottle. He then turned to face Thyri, giving her one last lustful stare. He took bold steps back towards her and reached for her neck when he towered over her.

"No holding out on me tonight, Bubba."

He tightened his hold around her throat, causing her breathing to restrict and a frenzy instantly raced through her at his firm hold. She didn't realize how much she liked being choked until now. Only he had the power to choke her and make her wet at the same damn time.

"And you take every inch."

She confidently nodded, trying to convince him of her understanding and obedience to his instruction. He slowly leaned closer to her, crashing his lips to hers and giving her a nasty tongue kiss that had Thyri releasing a moan between their lips. The deep sweeping strokes of his tongue combined with the red wine she could taste on his tongue had her gushing down below. He continued to feed her strong doses of him with his lips and dominated her mouth like a true king would.

Killian soon let go of her neck only to reach for her waist and lift her up from the bed's edge. His lips branded to hers once more and while they tongued each other down, Killian dropped Thyri to the center of the bed. He let their tongues dance together for a few moments before he broke away from her and started sliding down between her toned legs.

Thyri sighed and lifted her lower body up when she felt her shorts being tugged down. By the time they were to her ankles, Thyri angled a glance down at him and seeing the way he was looking at the spot between her thighs was enough to make a fluttery sensation form in her stomach.

"You're not wearing any panties, Thyri," Killian announced in an aroused tone.

He slid her shorts off her ankles, chucking them to the floor while keeping his eyes locked on her exposed treasure.

"I'm not," Thyri replied, loving the sight of Killian's white teeth sinking into his bottom lip. "I haven't been able to wear them properly on this trip."

Killian reached for her calves, slowly sliding her down the bed until her freshly waxed pussy was just inches away from his lips.

"Why?" he asked, unable to stop marveling at her womanly center.

He could see her piercing - two silver balls on each side of her clitoral hood - and he was turned all the way on by how pretty it looked on her pussy.

"Because they've just been getting wet every time I..."

Hearing her mention the very thing that he could see dripping out from her tightness made his dick throb. His eyes met hers and that was the connection she'd needed in order to keep talking.

"Every time I see or think about you, Killian."

Fuck.

Killian could no longer take it. He leaned forward, darting his tongue out and delivered a slow, sensual lick along Thyri's wetness, earning a gentle moan from her. He gripped her warm thighs, raising each one to his shoulders and gave her yoni another slow lick.

"Were you thinking about me tonight?" he queried after his lick, pressing a finger to her clit. "On the beach?"

Warmth spread through her at his touch.

"Yes," she whispered. "I... I was writing about you."

Killian's cheeks hiked and his finger kept nudging her sweet spot.

"Tell me what you wrote about me," he demanded before pressing his lips back to her folds and devouring her in the way he'd wanted to from the second he'd first laid eyes on her in his shop.

"I... I wro... I wr... Killian, shit..."

Thyri was now finding it extremely hard to concentrate. His soft lips were sealed to her pussy and he sucked, licked, and lapped on her moist folds, keeping an even tighter grip on her thighs that were pressed to the side of his head. He would let his tongue lick up to her piercing, flicking against the silver balls before running his tongue back to her entrance and diving into her tight core.

Thyri threw her head back, her eyes struggling to stay fully open and her body rocking to the steady beat that Killian had created with his talented tongue moving in and out of her. They were only seconds in and already Thyri was getting addicted to his mouth. He was a pro with it, knowing exactly what to do to have her going crazy for him.

He suddenly lifted his mouth off her pussy and she deeply sighed, dropping her head down and staring deep into his brown orbs.

"Tell me," he demanded, dragging his tongue along her right inner thigh. His soft beard tickled her skin.

"I wrote about how you make me feel," she responded in a breathless tone.

Killian's tongue moved to her left inner thigh and her heart skittered as he made a slow trail towards her pussy. She needed to feel his lips on her once again and she knew that in order for that to happen, she needed to tell him her truth.

"...How I haven't been able to stop thinking about you and how I wished you were on top of me... fucking me."

Killian smiled, bringing his tongue to the top of her thigh, and sucking on her warm, espresso brown skin. He sucked for a few seconds before releasing her flesh and looking up at her.

"Fucking you fast or slow?"

Thyri's gaze lingered over him, taking in everything that he had to offer and loving the sight of it all. Killian was a gorgeous man. There were no denying it. He had a gorgeous face, gorgeous eyes, and gorgeous lips. And from those lips he'd just asked her a question that had her feeling very nasty.

"Both," she answered. "Fast and slow."

"Fuck, Thyri... don't say that shit," he replied in a low tone. "Don't say that shit unless you mean it."

"I mean it." She shot him a confident gaze. "I want you to fuck me, Killian. Fast and slow... and hard. Teach me a lesson for taking so long to realize that I belong to you."

Killian lifted his head, leaning away from her thigh and pinning her with a dangerous look. It was a dangerous look because it told Thyri that he planned to give her everything she wanted and more. *Much more.*

"Remember what you just said to me, Ri," he told her carefully. "Because I promise you I ain't gonna forget."

The sudden entry of two fingers inside her tightness made Thyri jolt up and release a loud whimper.

"And I have no problems—" He slid them both out then pushed them right back in, earning another passionate cry from Thyri. "Reminding you of what you said."

He didn't bother waiting for her response and he buried his head between her legs, pushing his fingers back inside her cave and latching his mouth onto her clit.

Thyri began to lose all sense of control when Killian's tongue and fingers worked her middle in perfect sync. While his fingers rocked back and forth, his tongue would flick up and down on her clit, taking her to the greatest of highs.

"Killian... Oh my... aghhh!"

This man was dangerous. This was their first ever night together, the first time he'd been granted access to the treasure between her thighs and here he was, doing all the right things to make her moan for him and he hadn't even slid the ammo he was carrying under his shorts into her yet.

"Kill... please, oh, fuck!"

Thyri's head fell back and she reached for her breasts, squeezing them tight as Killian's fingers dived deeper inside her. *In. Out. In. Out.* He didn't miss a beat and his mouth was still sealed to her clit, teasing the soft bud to the point of no return and once an intense wave came rushing through her, Thyri couldn't stop shaking and squirming in her spot. Her reaching an orgasm didn't stop Killian from continuing to consume her moist center.

He changed tactics, by slipping his fingers out of her and lifting his lips off her clit. Thyri heard the sound of him spitting and she looked back down to see his now wet fingers. He then spat on her clit before rubbing his slippery fingers onto it and sinking his tongue into her warm slit. He used his freehand to grip her left thigh, pushing it all the way back while his tongue and fingers continued to send her over the edge.

"Kill!"

He was a beast with it and Thyri was finally starting to understand why his nickname was 'Kill' because that's exactly what he was doing to her pussy with his mouth and fingers.

Killing her.

His groans and hums of pleasure filled the room alongside her moans and hearing how much he was enjoying tasting her only sent Thyri over the edge more. Before Thyri knew it, another uncontrollable wave washed through her but before she could get fully lost in it, her body was flipped over and Killian started eating her pussy from the back, sending her to complete nirvana.

Thyri moaned when her head was pushed down to the mattress and she arched her back. Her thighs were wedged further apart, giving Killian perfect access to suck and lick her passage. He stuck his tongue out, using it to quickly thrust in and out, making Thyri feel like she could no longer take all that he was giving her right now. She shifted forward, trying to run but it was a big fat mistake the second she thought of doing it because Killian gripped her thighs tighter, keeping her locked in place as he used his tongue to fuck her from behind.

"Killian!"

"Where... the... fuck... you... going?" he asked her between each thrust of his tongue. "Who... the... fuck... told... you... that... you... can... run?"

Thyri's moans and cries heightened and every part of her body was on fire. The faster Killian's tongue dove within her wet walls, the hotter her body burned. His tongue slipped out her pussy, sliding up her soft inner lips until he reached her ass and pushed deep into her tight opening.

If Thyri thought she could handle Killian's tongue game before, she'd been greatly mistaken because now that he was eating her ass and fingering her pussy at the same time, she was sure that she was a goner.

She gripped the cream linen sheets under her, trying to find some sort of way to release the pressure she could feel constantly building within her. However, it was no use. There was no escaping the spasms that were rolling through her core. She was cumming back to back and there was no running from it.

169

Thyri felt her backdrop, no longer having the strength to keep her arch.

"Uh-uh." Killian stopped feasting on her briefly and lifted a hand to smack her ass twice. "Arch that mothafucking back."

Thyri quickly obeyed, grabbing the little strength she had left and arching for him.

"That's my girl," he praised her. "Now twerk that pretty ass in my face, baby. I'm not done eating you yet."

Thyri obeyed once again, throwing her ass back on Killian's bearded face as he devoured her. The faster her ass cheeks pushed against his face, the faster he fucked her with his tongue and the louder her moans got. Thyri was afraid that she would wake up the entire island with how loud she was getting but she knew Killian didn't care. He wanted her to get as loud as possible and didn't care who heard them.

After multiple climaxes, Thyri was made to lie on her back and Killian lifted her cami top over her head, chucking it to the side and smiling down at her exposed boobs. The sight of her pierced nipples made Killian's erection lengthen and he reached for both her breasts, squeezing them tight as he stretched over her. He dropped his mouth to her right breast, latching onto her nipple and sucking on it hard. He bit into it a couple times, causing Thyri to whimper. He soothed the pain with gentle flicks before moving onto the opposite one. He kept hold of the one he'd just tended to and gently massaged it.

Thyri's hands went to the back of his head, stroking his low cut waves as his tongue did wonders to her body. Once he was done teasing her nipples, he let his lips drop to the tattoo he'd completed just over a week ago and planted soft kisses to her inked skin.

The fact that he now had his lips on the artwork that he'd

created just for her made Thyri become even more of a feen for him than she already was.

While his lips peppered her tattoo with kisses, his hands caressed her waist, slowly sliding down to the apex of her thighs. He rubbed on the spot where she was moist and desperate for him to slide inside her. Their eyes met and he planted one last kiss to her skin before announcing, "No running, Ri."

She nodded, sighing deeply as her breathing returned to its normal state. She let her hands fall from his scalp, stroking down the strong muscles of his back and reaching for the band of his shorts. She slid the purple fabric down his legs but stopped when her wrists were grabbed.

"Hold on, Bubba... I gotta strap up."

She'd become so lost in the desire she felt for this man that she'd forgotten about the most important component of their night.

Protection.

"I get tested regularly," he informed her. "But still safety comes first."

Thyri nodded.

"I get tested regularly too."

Now it was Killian's turn to nod and he reached into the left pocket of his shorts, pulling out a gold square packet. Thyri watched as he slipped the plastic between his lips and seeing him tear it open with his white teeth was one of the sexiest sights ever to her.

He raised his body over hers, letting his shorts slip down his long legs and kicking them off his ankles before shielding his shaft with the latex.

Killian lowered his chest onto hers, reaching for her thighs and bending them back and placing them on his waist. The same moment that she felt him press his lips to hers was the same moment that she felt him push past her entrance and make himself right at home.

Thyri tensed up as slices of pain ran through her lower body. She hadn't had the chance to look at his dick but she didn't need to. She could feel how big he was as he pushed through her walls. Prior to this night, she'd had her suspicions about him carrying a large weapon because of the way he walked with a slight limp, as if he had something heavy holding him down. Tonight she was experiencing what that heavy weight was.

"Easy... baby," he whispered between their kisses, noticing the light gasp she'd released while he entered her. "You got this."

She released a shaky breath and butterflies took flight in her stomach as Killian stroked her lifted thighs.

"This is your dick," he said, gently easing out of her only to slip right back in. "Take it."

The pain started to fade seconds later and all that followed was the deeply satisfying pleasure that his slow strokes were now providing.

The ride began.

Every thrust felt incredible, every touch he gave her felt amazing and every kiss he provided was breathtaking. This was ten times better than Thyri could have ever imagined. One hundred times better! How could she be such a fool and deprive herself of this connection? She should have never tried to convince herself that she didn't want him... she should have never tried to convince herself that they weren't meant to be. What a huge error that had been.

"Shit... Ri, you feel so damn good," Killian groaned, entering her deeper and deeper.

Thyri opened her mouth to reply but no words came out. All that followed were her sweet moans and cries. The sweet ride continued.

In. Out. In. Out.

Killian kept a steady, smooth rhythm and Thyri was unable to think straight. All she could think about and see was Killian and she'd never been happier to have a man inside her than right now. Every hair on her scalp stood to attention, every skin cell tingled and every nerve fired up.

"Your pussy is so fucking wet... I can feel her through the condom."

Thyri's arousal heightened at his words and her wetness only dripped out faster, causing the squishy sounds of him diving in and out of her to be heard.

"Shit... I like how that sounds," he voiced.

His pumps began to increase in speed and momentum. Each time he pushed inside her, Thyri could feel herself getting closer to her climax. Getting a vaginal orgasm during sexual intercourse was a rarity for her so the fact that she could feel one approaching, she knew that this man right here was one extremely blessed man.

Moments later and things took a completely different turn as Killian stood onto his feet but remained crouched over Thyri. He pushed her legs further back so they were bent over her head and kept a firm grip on her thighs as he began to enter her at a downward angle.

"Killian!"

Thyri was in pure shock as he fucked her in the piledriver position and her moans were endless at this point. Her heartbeat wouldn't stop pounding at the same speed as Killian's pounds to her pussy and she could feel her juices running down her thighs. He quickly reached for her throat, gripping tight as he kept a firm look at her below him.

"You kept my pussy away from me... for this long..." The sound of his skin slapping against hers loudened and Thyri cried out, loving every bit of how he was fucking her right now. "Too fucking long, Thyri. How could you?"

"I'm... I'm sorry, Kill... I'm sorryyyyyy!" she apologized without him even having to ask. That was the power he now held over her. At the drop of a hat, he had her wherever he wanted her to be. She was convinced that she could do anything he wanted and if she somehow couldn't fulfil his wishes then she would find someone who could. Anything to please him she would do. "Forgive me!"

He paused his pounds only to slowly rotate his hips while his dick was buried inside her.

"Tell me that shit again."

"Forgive me, baby," she begged softly, her eyes suddenly moist with tears. "Please."

Killian flashed her a toothy smile, loving the way she was begging for him while he had her completely weak for him. He continued rotating his hips, hitting every part of her walls before pulling out, getting back onto his knees, and slamming back inside her pussy. He reached for her thighs and brought them to his sides.

"You ain't getting forgiven just yet, Thyri."

He brought his mouth to her left ear, biting down hard on it and curling his lips around the soft lobe. He gently sucked on it and let his tongue make a slow trail down her ear. Then he lifted his lips from her ear to say, "Not until I teach you a lesson for keeping my pussy away from me."

Thyri gasped when he suddenly pulled out of her. He tightened his hold around her neck and brought their lips within the same breathing space. His dark eyes were locked on hers and he remained silent, shooting a salacious stare her way.

"Now turn the fuck around," he said. "You're getting this dick from the back too tonight."

It wasn't a request, it was an order and Thyri wasn't about to disobey him. How could she? Killian had her under his spell and she'd be a fool to deny it. He was the only man she wanted – no, the only man she *needed* exploring between her thighs every night. The spell he'd casted was one that Thyri didn't see ever breaking. They were in this deep now.

Way too deep.

Chapter Thirteen

"Kill... Killian!"

A hand was suddenly placed over her mouth, muffling her moans.

"Don't make a sound," he whispered into her left ear. "I told your ass you were taking every inch tonight."

His deep strokes quickened with each passing second and goose-bumps raised across her skin as his lips brushed her ear.

"Every... fucking... inch," Killian said between each pump.

He had her lying on her stomach as he eased in and out of her from the back. His hand was still covering her mouth and she felt lightheaded by all the lust rushing through her.

"All that shit you was talking... ain't this what you wanted?"

"Thyri."

"You wanted to be taught a lesson remember? For taking so long to realize that you belong to me."

The faster and harder he went, the better it felt.

"You... belong... to... me," he groaned between each pump.

Even with her mouth covered, her moans made an appearance

and refused to let up because of his strokes. His stroke game that was out of this world ama—

"Thyri."

Thyri rapidly blinked and her head shifted to the right, allowing her to gaze into familiar brown eyes.

"Girl, you don't hear me calling you?"

Thyri drew in a long breath and rubbed her hands on her bare thighs.

"Sorry, sis... I got lost in my thoughts."

"What were you thinking about?" Truth queried, studying her sister closely.

"...Umm..." Thyri's head slowly turned and when she found those irresistible eyes that she'd looked into all night and the early hours of this morning, her body flooded with heat.

He lifted his champagne flute to his lips and sipped from the glass without breaking eye contact from her. The sight of him drinking his mimosa reminded her of the way he'd drank her juices last night and she quickly looked back over at Truth.

"Nothing," Thyri finished her sentence, ignoring the wetness she could now feel dripping out of her. "What were you saying?"

"Nigel offered to give Alana a few swimming lessons and I told him I'd think about it. You know how I'm a bit nervous for her to start early... but I think I'm gonna go ahead and take him up on his offer. Will you and Nai get in the pool with us while he's teaching?"

"Of course," Thyri agreed, her cheeks hiking as she watched Alana place a small mango slice into her mouth. "I could never miss my princess' first swimming lesson."

"Neither could I," Tanai chimed in. "No way am I going to miss seeing my baby in action."

Truth smiled at her sisters, glad that they were both on board to support their niece. She loved how much they loved her daughter and treated her as their own. She knew that if anything ever happened to her, Alana was in safe hands.

It was twelve-thirty p.m. right now and the gang were currently enjoying breakfast in an outdoor dining hut on the beach. Everyone was gathered around a large white clothed table and had been served breakfast by two stunning Caribbean women. It was great to be able to sit down and eat together as a group. That was one of the many things that Thyri loved about this vacation, the fact that they would all sit down together to eat a meal.

When Thyri first got settled at the table, she focused on eating her breakfast and not engaging in conversation with anyone. Not even her sisters. But of course Truth was too much of a talkative person to not have a conversation with her sisters. Thyri initially didn't want to talk because all she could think about was last night and how the man sitting across from her, had rocked her world in ways she didn't think were possible. While she ate and drank, flashbacks of their night came flying into her head and she didn't bother trying to push them out. She wanted to remember their phenomenal night and she didn't want to ever stop remembering them.

While Truth tended to Alana, making sure she'd eaten up all her breakfast, Thyri let her thoughts slip back to early this morning, when she'd been in his arms.

"How the hell do you look even more beautiful in the morning?"

Thyri felt the heat of a blush on her cheeks. She let her hands rub over the smooth panes of his chest and studied him with bright, pleased eyes.

"You don't look so bad yourself, handsome," she replied, her voice slightly raspy. "And considering all the work you put in a few hours ago I'm surprised you look this good."

Her hand found his face and she brushed her palm on the side of his beard.

"Work that I definitely intend to put in again this morning." Killian slid a hand under the sheets, landing on Thyri's soft folds. She sighed softly at his touch.

"Kill... we need to get back before everyone wakes..." She drew in a sharp breath when he pushed two fingers inside her. "Wakes up."

"You know I don't give a fuck about who sees us, Ri," he said, slowly moving his fingers in and out of her. "And you shouldn't either. You're mine, I'm yours. End of story."

"But Kill..." She released a quiet whimper as his fingers moved. "Soraya."

"Fuck her."

"Yeah that's what... that's what your ass already did to her."

His eyes widened at her reminder of his past and he quickened his finger movements, resulting in Thyri's moans to sound.

"That was way before you, Thyri, and I told you that it ain't gonna happen again. Ever."

Her mouth curved into a smile.

"Good... but I don't want her knowing about us yet, Kill. Not while we're still on this trip with her... please, Kill... not yet."

"Fine," he reluctantly agreed. "But as soon as we get back to Atlanta, everyone's knowing about us. And that lil' break that you and that other nigga are on is now permanent."

Thyri nodded, agreeing with him wholeheartedly. While they'd been taking a break during their mind blowing sessions last night, Thyri had revealed to Killian about the status of her relationship with Chosen and how he'd ended things between them. Killian was glad to know that Thyri had come on this trip single but in his mind it changed nothing. Whether she'd been on a break with Chosen or not, it didn't change how Killian felt about her and it didn't change the reality of their situation. They were together now and nothing was going to change that.

"Killian, we still need to go... Killiannnnn!"

His fingers worked in and out her tightness faster and her eyes began rolling back.

"We go when I say we go," he instructed. "I wanna taste you right now then I'm gonna fuck you ten times better than I did yesterday. Then we can go."

Before she could even think about protesting, Killian's lips meshed with hers.

Luckily for Thyri, they'd managed to get back to the main villa just in time without anyone being awake yet. They'd parted this morning and reunited at breakfast with everyone else.

It pissed Killian off at not being able to hug and kiss on Thyri as soon as he laid eyes on her at breakfast but he relaxed himself as best as he could. He wanted to respect Thyri's wishes and not make her uncomfortable on their vacation. This was her first vacation ever and he wanted to make it an enjoyable experience for her. Trying to force her to be public with him as an official couple when her sisters were still under the notion that she was in a relationship with someone else wouldn't be an enjoyable experience. He understood that she wanted to be able to tell her sisters privately about their situation and of course there was the issue of Soraya.

Thyri had told Killian last night about how Soraya had started acting funny after he'd asked Thyri to ride with him on his jet ski. It was clear that she was jealous and Killian didn't care – in fact, he was willing to check Soraya about her attitude towards Thyri – but he was starting to understand how much of an empath Thyri was. She didn't want to worsen Soraya's existing jealousy. He had no choice but to respect and honor his girlfriend's wishes.

My girlfriend.

Killian let his eyes wander back to Thyri and he smiled as he watched her talking to her sisters.

Damn, I really can't believe she's mine... I mean I can believe it

181

because I manifested that shit but damn... she's really mine. All min—

"Yo, Kill?"

Killian's eyes met the cognac eyes of his younger brother.

"Kay and I need to holla at you later on."

Killian's eyes narrowed at Kadiri.

"About what?"

"You know what," he replied in a low tone.

Killian looked over at Kason who sat next to Kadiri and from the serious look on Kason's face, Killian knew exactly what was coming from his brothers.

A lecture.

Killian observed as Kadiri licked the edge of his freshly rolled blunt. He then carefully sealed the marijuana filled cone and brought out his lighter from his right pocket. Killian's eyes darted toward his other brother who currently leaned against the balcony of the room they were situated in. Killian's room. It was the place that Kadiri suggested they all go to get the privacy that they desired. Now that privacy was here, Killian expected his brothers to reveal whatever it was that they had to say but their silence was deafening right now and he hated it.

"Are you niggas gonna say what you need to say or what?"

"Whoa." Kadiri held up his palms while his lit blunt sat between his right index finger and middle finger. "Easy there, tiger. No need for the cold tone."

Killian's expression hardened and he leaned back, allowing his back to meet the velvet armchair he sat upon.

"We know you slept with Thyri last night, Kill," Kason announced.

Killian's heart skipped several beats.

How the hell did they find that shit out without me telling them first?

"Kadiri was already up by the time you got back from the other villa. He saw you two walking in together and he—"

"He told you," Killian calmly interrupted Kason.

"Yeah." Kason sighed. "He did."

Killian decided to remain silent as he kept a fixed gaze on Kason.

"So what do you have to say for yourself?" Kadiri piped up after taking a pull from his blunt. Smoke curled from his lips as he spoke.

"Nothing, kid," Killian replied, watching as Kadiri passed over the blunt to Kason.

Kadiri's eyes bulged.

"Nothing? Nigga she's in a whole ass relationship."

"Yeah with me," Killian confirmed.

"What?" Kason frowned and started shaking his head from side to side. "Nah, I'm pretty sure Nai told me she's with some nigga called Chosen... runs a cigar bar in one of our buildings."

"Oh yeah that nigga," Kadiri chimed in. "One of my men runs it with him and he's been telling me about the new building they want for their future expansion."

Killian hadn't even known that Thyri's ex had a cigar bar in one of their buildings. He didn't care about Chosen so he'd never bothered to look him up and even now his stance hadn't changed. He didn't care about Chosen at all.

Kason leaned forward and held out the blunt for Killian to reach for. Killian grabbed it, lifted it to his lips and took a long pull from it before releasing a thick cloud of smoke.

"Nope she's not with that nigga anymore. She's with me."

"You're not making any sense... how can she be with you when she's been with him and was with him back in Atlanta?"

Killian felt a tightness settle into his face after Kadiri's question. He hadn't expected his brothers to find out about him and Thyri so soon. Thyri wanted time to tell her sisters privately after this trip about them and Killian thought that it was best to do the same. Only now that Kadiri had spotted them this morning, the cat was certainly out of the bag. Now Killian was left with no choice but to explain the situation with him and Thyri. And he knew that explaining was what he had to do because he could tell by his brothers' statements, questions, and the suspicion creeping in their eyes, that they were definitely feeling some type of way about their older brother involving himself with a taken woman.

"Before she came to Grenada, him and her got into an argument. He decided to break things off between them. She arrived on this trip single but she's leaving as mine."

Killian was fully aware of what had happened between Thyri and Chosen in Atlanta. She'd told him about Chosen's desire for her to be a stay at home wife and mom and her disapproval towards his wish. She'd also told Killian about her putting hands on Chosen, something that she'd deeply regretted. Killian understood her reasons for slapping Chosen but he made it clear last night that she could never do that to him. He didn't care how angry she got, putting hands on him could never be an option and Killian would never do the same to her. He'd never put his hands on a woman in his life so far and he had no plans to ever do it. Killian also made it clear that he would never force Thyri to give up her dreams in order to be his wife and the mother of his children. She could do it all and he would be by her side to support her through it all.

"Well damn," Kadiri remarked after taking a pull from the joint that he'd just received from Killian. "I knew your ass liked her but for you to have cuffed her this damn quickly... especially after she just got out of a situation."

"That don't mean shit," Killian replied. "She's mine and has been mine from the second I laid eyes on her."

Killian spotted Kason's lips curving into a smile and he wanted to ask him what was so funny but Kason spoke up before Killian could talk first.

"And that's exactly how I felt when I laid eyes on Tanai... and y'all thought I was going crazy for marrying her that quick."

"And I still think your ass was crazy for marrying her that fast but that's a story for another day," Kadiri commented as he threw Kason a side eye. "But back to you—" Kadiri's eyes landed on Killian's dark browns. "You barely know the girl and you've already decided to cuff her. Are you sure that's a good idea?"

"It's not a good idea," Killian stated. "It's the best idea I've thought of all year."

"But what about Chosen?" Kason asked. "He's still in the picture, Kill. He might have broken things off but we all know how niggas can be with their exes. That possessive shit can be a mothafucka."

"Unless he's tryna lose his life, he better stay away from her." Killian's angry gaze sliced Kason's face. An angry gaze that Kadiri immediately spotted.

"You really need to fucking relax." Kadiri let out a light chuckle. "This nigga's really willing to go to jail over a girl he just met."

"Time ain't nothing but a number, baby," Kason said, lightly shrugging. "I told you that he's had a crush on her ever since he tatted her."

"Yeah you did, you did."

"I just didn't think that he would make his move on her this fast."

Killian's eyes shifted from both his brothers. It was at that moment that Killian came to the realization that his brothers had been having private conversations about him and Thyri this whole time.

"So y'all have been gossiping about me the whole damn time, huh?" he queried, a smirk quickly forming on his lips.

"I mean with the way you were staring at her at Kay's reception and now this vacation, it's been kinda hard not to," Kadiri stated. "And let's not forget the shit you said to her in front of everyone..." A loud laugh slipped out of Kadiri's mouth at the memory in his head.

"Look at me when I'm talking to you, Thyri." Kadiri mocked Killian by putting on his best impression of his brother's deep voice. "This nigga was really out here talking to her like he was her daddy or something."

After last night and this morning, I most certainly am her daddy now.

"You must really like her ass."

"I told you he does," Kason chimed in.

Killian went silent again, a wide grin plastered on his face as he watched his brothers.

"And I'm happy for you, bro. I really am... but aren't you forgetting someone?"

Killian's left brow hiked up at Kason's query.

"Soraya," he continued. "You were the one that brought her on this trip, Kill. You really finna handle two women at the same time?"

"Hell fucking no," Killian snapped. "Soraya and I were messing around in the past but that's over with. I belong to nobody else but Thyri."

Now it was Kason and Kadiri's turn to remain silent. They both stared deeply at their brother, recognizing how serious he was about his new relationship. Although it was a shock to hear that their brother – who they'd always assumed was a covert player – was now a taken man, Kason and Kadiri were happy for him and would support his new relationship. They each congratulated Killian on his new commitment, giving him a solid dap and Killian thanked them both for the love.

"Thyri hasn't told her sisters yet, so I'd appreciate it if you both act like you don't know, especially you, Kay. I know how much you love telling the wifey everything but Thyri wants to tell Nai and Truth *after* Grenada, in private."

"A'ight." Kason nodded as he accepted the blunt from Kadiri. "My lips are sealed."

The brothers spent a few more minutes smoking and sharing their feelings about their vacation. This was their last day in Grenada and quite frankly, none of The Miller men wanted to leave the island. It had become their sanctuary and they really didn't want to leave it so soon. But sadly all good things had to come to an end at some point, right?

After chopping it up with his brothers, Killian departed from them to head to the one person he'd been dying to be close to since they'd parted this morning. While him and his brothers had been smoking and conversing on the balcony of his ocean front room, Killian had seen her leave the breakfast table to head inside the villa. So he knew exactly where she was right now.

Killian took quick, bold strides across the walkway leading to the other side of the beach house. Within seconds he was outside a white door and he reached for the door's handle, eagerly turning it to enter the room. He stepped into the suite only to frown when he realized that it was empty.

"Tru?" Footsteps were heard moving through the bathroom. "I'll be down in a sec..."

Thyri's words trailed off once she noticed who stood in the

center of her room. Her cheeks flushed at the sight of him in cream shorts and a matching vest.

His swept his eyes up and down her body and seeing her in a tan bikini set had his hands suddenly aching with the need to touch and explore her stunning physique.

"Kill? What are you doing here?"

Killian was quiet while reaching for the bottom of his top, slowly pulling the cotton fabric up his body and over his head. Laying eyes on the sculpted muscles of his chest sent shivers down her spine.

"What do you think I'm doing here, Bubba?" he asked, chucking his top to the side, and inching forward to where she stood in the middle of the bathroom's doorway.

"Kill... I can't... Alana's swimming lesson..."

Thyri paused, biting her lip as Killian stopped walking and pushed his shorts down his long legs. His thickness sprang forth and the thought of him being inside her made her pussy pulsate and tingle with pleasure.

"Alana's swimming lesson?" he repeated her last words. "Finish what you were gonna say, Thyri."

His shorts had dropped to his ankles and he'd kicked them out the way. Now he was pressing closer towards her once again and this time he was completely naked.

"I... I can be late."

Killian grinned before slowly moving his head up and down, agreeing with her new decision.

"Oh, you're definitely about to be late." He arrived in front of her, reaching for her waist and pulling her into him.

"Not too late, Kill," Thyri whispered, leaning in to press her lips against his and giving him gentle pecks. She began talking between each one. "I still... gotta... go."

"Uh-huh... I know, baby." Heat flooded his insides when her

hands went to the back of his neck and stroked his skin. He let her peck him a few more times before he leaned back and pinned her with a lustful gaze. "But you're not going anywhere just yet."

With his hands still holding her waist, he pushed her backwards, leading them both into the bathroom. Neither of them could take their eyes off each other's face and the desire radiating between them was electrifying.

"Not until I'm done with your sexy ass."

He joined their lips together for a more passionate kiss, sliding his hands to the sides of her bikini thong and pushing the thin fabric down her body.

Thyri knew that she wasn't about to be on time for Alana's lesson but she just prayed that Truth didn't get too angry with her about her lateness. She would make it up to her sister and niece but right now the only thing she wanted to make was great sex with Killian Miller. Nothing else mattered but being with him.

Chapter Fourteen

Thyri rushed down the villa's white steps while fixing the folded strap of her bikini top. Once reaching the last step, she leaped off it and ran through the villa's open front door.

"Kick those legs, Alana... nice, big kicks... there you go!"

"That's my baby girl! Keep kicking, baby."

Thyri approached the main pool and spotted her sisters, her niece and Nigel, their sailor, inside the pool. She'd heard Nigel and Truth's voices before she'd seen their faces and a smile formed on her lips at how encouraging they were being to Alana. It wasn't until Thyri got closer to the pool that she noticed Kadiri in the pool too.

"Thyri, there you are!" Truth turned around and noticed Thyri's presence.

"Sorry I'm late, guys." Thyri's apologetic look settled into her face. "I lost track of time."

"Oh I bet you did," Kadiri commented, the corners of his mouth quirking up as he studied Thyri carefully.

It was at that moment Thyri's shoulders went tight and a weight seemed to press on her chest, robbing her of breath.

Shit. He knows.

"No worries. Come on in, Nigel's just started coaching Alana on leg kicks and arm strokes," Truth explained, smiling from ear to ear as she looked at Alana floating in the pool.

"And she's a pro already," Kadiri said. "Ain't that right, Lani? You're a beast at this shit already."

"A beawst! A beawst! A beawst!" Alana yelled, causing Kadiri and everyone else to laugh except Truth who currently donned a frown.

"Not you cursing around my baby, Skinny Boy."

"Not you still calling me that shit when I told your ass to stop."

"Can both of you relax," Tanai intervened, noticing the glares that they both shared. "Nigel, please continue."

Nigel nodded and began teaching Alana once again. Thyri now stood by the pool and came to sit at the edge of it so she could dip her feet into the water and move across the pool. Once she'd entered the cool water, she swam over to where everyone surrounded Alana and smiled at the sight of her niece in her pink Minnie Mouse swimsuit. It was a one piece and had a tutu that looked adorable on her.

For her lesson, Alana had been given a long, pink noodle to float with rather than individual armbands because Nigel didn't want her becoming dependent on fixed floatation. He had the armbands on standby by the edge of the pool in case Alana got uncomfortable using the foam noodle. So far she was doing well using the noodle alone and Nigel was glad at how fast she was learning to be dependent on floating on her own weight accompanied by the noodle.

Thyri observed as Nigel continued teaching Alana's swimming

lesson and what surprised her the most was how paternal Kadiri was acting towards Alana. He refused to leave her side and would physically help guide her whenever he felt necessary. Of course he'd let Nigel do his thing and didn't interrupt his teaching but whenever he found an opening to talk to Alana he would take it.

It was very sweet to see their interaction. Whenever Alana got nervous performing a swimming technique, she would look over at Kadiri and he would give her an affectionate gaze followed by a few encouraging words and her nervousness would dissipate.

At first Truth didn't know what to make of their newfound closeness. She wasn't expecting Kadiri to be in the pool for Alana's first lesson and when he arrived, all she did was shoot him a dazed look that seemed to ask, *Why are you here, nigga?*

Kadiri didn't bother explaining himself though. He simply got in the pool and stayed at a close enough position to Alana. He had told himself when he'd first laid eyes on Alana that he was tripping about his urge in wanting to know her. But it'd been a lie from the jump. He wasn't tripping and when he'd overheard Truth telling her sisters at breakfast about Alana's swimming lesson, he knew he wasn't missing it. There was something about the three year old that he just couldn't shake. He felt the need to protect her and provide for her in any way he could.

"Breathe, Lani, you've got this, girl. Just make those kicks stronger and you'll be good. A'ight?"

Alana nodded at Kadiri and followed his instruction by kicking her feet stronger than before.

Their closeness was cute to watch and Truth knew she'd be a hater trying to deny it. Despite all the tattoos that were inked into Kadiri's golden honey skin, they did nothing to deter Alana from warming up to him. The more she studied the pair of them, the more Truth realized that they were forming a bond that she wouldn't be able to come between. Not that she actually wanted to become between them... she just hadn't expected Kadiri of all people to become a father figure to her daughter. And quite frankly, she was afraid.

While Nigel demonstrated back floating to Alana, Truth let her eyes wander over to Kadiri whose gaze was still fixed on Alana. Her gaze lingered over him as she analyzed each feature he possessed. From those hooded cognac eyes, those plump lips, those bushy brows to the detailed tattoo pieces that covered his upper chest, arm and back, Truth knew she would be a deluded woman if the words *'He's not sexy'* ever slipped out of her lips. And how could she gloss over the fact that he had an athletic build that looked extremely attractive on him. Yeah she teased him about being skinny but that's exactly what it was - *teasing*. He was in great shape and those abdominal muscles she could see on his torso whenever he dipped in and out of the water, had Truth's heart rate picking up slightly.

When Kadiri felt the stare of someone on him, his eyes shifted to Truth's direction and she quickly looked away, not wanting him to get gassed by her staring. But it was too late. He'd caught her eye just before she'd looked away and he grinned at the realization of what she was doing.

Nigel helped Alana get on her back to perform a back float and it wasn't long till Alana was floating on her back without the pool noodle. Everyone started clapping and cheering at her, making her grin.

"You're doing amazing, Lani. Look at you being a better swimmer than all our asses. High five!"

"High fiwve!" Alana yelled out as she lifted her tiny hand to hit Kadiri's.

Damn it, this nigga really is being so sweet to my baby, Truth mused as she fought against the smile trying to curve her lips. *He's*

even given her a personal nickname. Lani. It's cute... I can't even lie.
But my God, they're getting really close on this trip.

About thirty minutes later and Alana's swimming lesson was done. Nigel said his goodbyes to Alana and everyone else before making his way towards the pool's steps. Truth followed him and thanked Nigel for all his help before turning around to head back towards the center of the pool where everyone still was. She noticed that Alana was now sitting on Kadiri's shoulders while they played together in the pool. Thyri and Tanai watched from a short distance away. Truth swam over to her sisters and they both turned to face her while they floated in the water.

"I believe Lana's got a new best friend, sis."

Tanai's statement accompanied a pleased smile that made Truth roll her eyes.

"I'm the only best friend she'll ever need," Truth replied. "I still can't believe how close they've gotten today."

"I mean all the guys have pretty much taken a liking to her... she is the baby of the group and the cutest," Thyri explained. She too wore a smile as she observed Kadiri and Alana playing together.

Thyri wasn't lying when she mentioned how the Miller brothers had taken a liking towards Alana. So far on this trip, she'd fallen asleep on Kason's chest after their time on the boat and jet skis yesterday, shared sweet potato pone - a Grenadian desert - with Killian during dinner last night and now she was playing in the pool with Kadiri. Clearly the little girl was having a hold on the brothers and it was really great to see, especially for Tanai who was glad that her husband and his brothers were getting close with her niece.

"I know you and Kadiri haven't gotten along in the past but surely you can put your differences to the side for Lana's sake, sis?"

Tanai's question made Truth pout and instead of replying, she let her body ease back into the water and she floated on her back, looking up into the clear blue sky. Her thoughts raced through her mind at the same time that worry raced through her core.

It's not like Truth had a real issue with Kadiri. Was he rude? Extremely. But she could easily take his brashness. What she couldn't take was the number one person, she would lay her life down for in a heartbeat, becoming attached to a man that wasn't going to stick around for the long run. Truth had already experienced one man coming in and out of Alana's life whenever he saw fit and she didn't need another one being added to that equation. She was afraid about Alana becoming close with and fond of Kadiri, only for him to suddenly pull away like her father constantly did.

Truth raised her body out the cool water and came to stand on the soles of her feet again so she could stare at her sisters.

"I don't want her getting attached to anyone she doesn't need to get attached to," Truth revealed. "I already get enough stress from the fact that Jodell refuses to be consistent in her life and when he does choose to be consistent it's at a time that suits him best."

"But Kadiri's family now, Tru. He's not going anywhere."

"You can't be certain of that, Nai. Men change like the weather and I have no idea if your relationship with Kason will stand the test of time."

An empty look formed on Tanai's face whereas on Thyri's formed annoyance.

"Truth, don't say shit like that."

"What?" Truth shrugged and the water around her rippled at her shoulder movement. "I'm just being honest."

"Tanai's right and you know it. Kadiri isn't going anywhere so I don't see the problem with him being close with Alana. You know deep down there isn't a problem with him being close with her either. You and he had a pointless beef at the reception but that's been over with. There's no real issue here unless you make one and I really don't see the harm in him being close to Alana."

"There really isn't no harm," Tanai added, causing Truth's frustrations to mount at the way her sisters had tagged team on the topic of Kadiri being close to her daughter.

"At the end of the day, I'm Alana's mother and I have the final say on who she can be close with," Truth concluded before turning to where Alana was situated with Kadiri.

She swam over to them and once close enough she said, "Lana, baby. Let's go."

Both Alana and Kadiri looked her way and said nothing. Alana sat on Kadiri's back while he swam around in the shallow end of the pool and he slowly turned to look at the three year old, only to see the disappointment easing into her adorable face.

A sudden coldness hit Truth's chest when Alana shyly shook her head from side to side.

"I don't wuanna go."

"Lana, you've been swimming for a while now, baby. I'm sure you're tired. Come on, it's nap-nap time."

Once again Alana shook her head from side to side and this time Truth's heartbeat wouldn't slow down.

"She's good right here with me," Kadiri announced, shooting Truth a confident gaze. "Ain't that right, Lani?"

"Yesssss!" Alana screamed, only pissing Truth off further.

"I'll make sure she's down for a nap after we're done here," Kadiri promised before turning away from Truth to resume him and Alana's swimming game.

I don't believe this. Truth's expression hardened as she watched the happy pair play like she wasn't even there, like she didn't even matter, like she didn't even exist. She wasn't even an afterthought at this point. It was just the two of them, off in their own little world.

Truth decided that if her daughter wasn't about to leave the pool then neither was she. She would wait until Alana had tired her little self out and make sure she was by her side when it was time for her nap. She turned to face her sisters once again and the grins that danced on both their lips had her rolling her eyes and dipping her body into the water so she could go down below. She didn't want to see their joy of what was happening between Kadiri and Alana because quite frankly, Truth wasn't sure she approved.

Call it jealousy, call it dislike... all Truth knew was that she didn't like the idea of another man being added to Alana's life so soon. Alana had already received enough broken promises and heartbreak from her father. There was no need for anymore to be added to her young life. She was only three and Truth didn't want any problems in her baby's life. As her mother it was her responsibility and priority to make sure that Alana stayed a happy girl and she would always make that a priority until the day she took her last breath on this planet. No one came first but Alana Capri Wright.

Hours later and nighttime finally arrived. Since it was the gang's last night in Grenada, the plan was for them to all head to a local nightclub not too far from Calivigny island. Everyone was down for the plan except Kadiri. He knew that Alana was way too young to be following them to the club and he understood that she would be supervised by the island's nanny, Anita, who Kason had paid good money to ensure Alana's safety but being away from her just didn't sit right with Kadiri. So he came up with the lie that he was too tired to go the club and decided that he would stay back at the island.

Kiana wanted to stay behind with him but he managed to convince her to go have fun with the girls and turn up without him. When she warmed up to the idea of being without him, Kadiri sighed a breath of relief, glad that she wasn't about to be bound by his side all night wanting some dick. Sure, she could get some when she came back *if* he was awake but that wasn't something he really craved tonight. Peace away from Kiana was what he needed because of how she'd been following him around like a lost puppy. The only time he managed to get a break from her was when he'd been spending time with Alana today in the pool because she hated kids. Something she'd openly told him and shown him in the past because whenever they were out in public and there were noisy kids around, she would always complain.

Truth appreciated Kason hiring a nanny to take care of Alana but she'd already known from the moment that she'd come on this trip that she had no plans to use the nanny. She didn't feel like going out to the club tonight and decided that staying behind with her baby would be best.

"Are you sure you don't want to come out tonight? It'll be fun, Tru!"

"I'm sure it will be," Truth agreed, nodding at Tanai. "But you two have fun without me. I'm trying to get an early night tonight for our flight."

"Our flight that's in the late afternoon you mean?" Thyri's left brow arched.

"I still want to get an early night, pooh. Now stop worrying about little old me and get ready for your night, my darling sisters."

That left Kason, Tanai, Thyri, Kiana, Killian and Soraya heading to the night club off the island. The five minute boat ride off the island was quiet. Way too quiet for Killian's liking. Kason and Tanai sat in their own little corner on the right hand side of the yacht's love sofa. Having their own private conversation while they hugged and kissed on one another like the true love birds they were. Thyri and Kiana sat in the middle with Soraya sitting to the left of Kiana and Killian sitting on the end of the sofa next to Soraya. He'd left a reasonable sized gap between them because he didn't want Thyri feeling any type of way about his interactions with Soraya. It's not like he wanted to sit next to Soraya in the first place, he would much rather be sitting next to Thyri right now. In fact he was tempted to make Soraya and Kiana scooch over so that he could sit next to his Bubba. But it was a temptation that he couldn't indulge in. Not when they'd agreed to keep their new union a secret for the remainder of this vacation.

But God was it killing him. The more he caught her eye during their boat ride, the more he wished he could be next to her, holding her and kissing her. She looked fucking amazing tonight. The white floral print maxi dress she wore was a bold statement on her womanly figure. It had a deep v neckline, allowing an ample amount of her cleavage to be seen. Killian had no problems with Thyri showing off her girls, they were beautiful and how could he be mad when he'd clearly cuffed a bad bitch? He wasn't about to stop her from being the baddie that she truly was. He just wished he could kiss and hold on his girl. Call him clingy or call him needy all you liked – Killian didn't care. All he cared about was being able to have Thyri in his arms whenever and wherever he wanted. And when they got back to Atlanta, he had no plans to be shy about it.

Five minutes later, their boat ride was finished and the gang were escorted into a Range Rover SUV that had been waiting for them in the main town. Thanks to the connections that Kason had in Grenada, they were being properly taken care of and had security taking them and following them to their destination. It took thirteen minutes for their driver to arrive outside Bananas, the night club that the group were partying at tonight.

As soon as they pulled up, upbeat music grabbed their attention and lured them to the lively location.

I see her
She came with her nigga
Mm, but she gon' slide right to my side, I know

Bananas was packed full with bodies tonight. As the gang were led in by their main security guard, they each caught eyes with various strangers looking their way. With the way they'd stepped into the function, it was kind of hard not to look at them. Everyone was drawn in by the pretty girls walking ahead and the even more handsome men walking behind them. The ladies couldn't take their eyes off the men and despite the fact that Kason was holding on to Tanai's hand while she walked in front of him, that didn't stop the endless stares coming his way. Tanai knew she had a fine ass husband and she had no insecurities about the looks he got from other women. In her eyes, all they could do was look but they most certainly couldn't touch what was hers. She had nothing to be worried about because she was the one that had his heart.

"Welcome, friends! It's a pleasure to have you all here tonight! Kay, my main man!"

They'd been led upstairs to a private section and a short, bronze skinned man with dreads pulled up into a bun stood in the center of the room. He'd just greeted them and had his arms stretched out as he looked over at Kason.

Kason gently broke away from Tanai's hand, moved forward and stretched his long arms out to embrace the man.

"Gray, my man."

The two men embraced and patted each other on the back.

201

They then broke away from each other and turned to face everyone else with wide grins.

"Guys, I'd like you to meet Gray, he's the owner of the club that I was telling you about in the car." The memory of Kason talking about the club owner that was taking care of them tonight flew into Thyri's head. "Anything you need, he's got it handled."

"I do indeed," Gray promised. "It really is a pleasure to meet you all."

Everyone took turns greeting Gray and once greetings were said and done, Gray told the gang to get comfortable in their VIP area.

There was a c-shaped sofa for them all to sit on, glass coffee tables with white LED lighting and star lights on the ceiling above them. From their section they were able to look over a glass balcony to the main club below and see the cascade of souls turning up on the dancefloor. The girls each took their seats while Killian and Kason remained standing as they conversed with Gray about the drinks that the gang would be consuming tonight.

"Whatever y'all need, I promise I got you. You're like family to me, Kay, so your family is my family."

"Appreciate you always, man," Kason told Gray before rattling the first order of drinks he wanted for their table.

"This is our last night in this beautiful country, sis," Tanai announced to Thyri, reaching for her hand, and squeezing tight. "There's no way we're not getting drunk tonight."

"Amen to that," Kiana chimed in.

Thyri nodded and a smile took ownership of her lips at the same second that her eyes landed on Killian.

Alongside the starlight that were above their heads, the night club had purple and blue strobe lighting that would occasionally flicker on the side of where their VIP section was. The purple and blue lights were now in their section and now that Thyri was staring at Killian, she could see the lights radiating off his golden tone, emphasizing those sexy features he owned.

He was looking extremely good tonight. The beige button down shirt and matching shorts that he donned brought the nastiest thoughts to Thyri's mind. His legs were out on display too and those long, powerful legs never looked better. His shirt was unbuttoned too, exposing his broad and powerful chest, that chest that Thyri wished she could place her lips on. Right here. Right now. She hadn't even had any liquor inside her yet and she was already feeling nasty. That's just the way Killian made her feel. A silver Cuban link chain hung around his neck and the color silver against his light skin was a sight that made Thyri's panties get wetter than they already were.

Their tense eye contact continued for a few more moments before Killian was distracted by Kason talking to him about something. Thyri soon found herself distracted by the catchy and melodic songs being played by the DJ.

Oh, wait, you a fan of the magic?
Poof, pussy like an Alakazam
I heard from a friend of a friend
That that dick was a ten out of ten

The night went on in full effect. Bottles of Don Julio and Clase Azul were sent to their table in ice buckets and alongside those buckets came bottle girls, holding sprinklers and shot glasses. Shots were poured out and everyone grabbed one. Kason said a few words about how great of night tonight was going to be while everyone was huddled in the middle of the section with their glasses raised in the air. They toasted before gulping down their first shot of the night. The first of many.

"We go again!" Tanai yelled over the loud music and no one

disagreed with her.

After her fifth shot of the night, Thyri was starting to feel the effects of the tequila as it raced through her system. Her heart was racing and she couldn't stop smiling all of a sudden. The two tells of her intoxicated state making an appearance.

Yeah, yeah
Sexy love, what she need from a bad boy like me
Yeah, yeah
Sexy kisses, the thing that she end for my lips

As the sweet sounds of Rema filled the club, Thyri peered over the balcony at the dancefloor below to see multiple couples grinding on each other. Once she heard kissy sounds being made, her eyes lifted and found Tanai dancing on her husband in the right hand corner of their section. Kiana was the one making kissy noises and giggling at the married couple. The alcohol had clearly gotten to her head and Soraya's too, who was now twerking on top of her seat.

Kiana's attention went over to Soraya who was doing her damn thing on top of the sofa right now. The black mini dress Soraya had chosen to wear tonight left little imagination for the naked eye and allowed her ass cheeks to pop as she thrusted her hips back and forth. It was a sequin mini dress, had one shoulder and cut outs across her cleavage area, her abdomen and on her left hip. Kiana began to cheer Soraya on, moving closer to her and spanking her ass. They'd grown close on this trip and it was good to see them having fun together.

Shorty say she feeling sore
She grab my neck and she whisper, 'Please'
Shorty give me dirty splash on my chest to my knees

The liquor coupled with the sultry vocals of Rema, made Thyri's eyes wander to find the one man she couldn't stop thinking about. He was leaning against the balcony, cup in hand and raising it to his lips at the exact same time that their eyes connected. His eyes stayed locked on hers and Thyri's body flooded with heat as she watched him sip on his cup.

Yeah, yeah
Shorty got a lot in her bucket list
I give her number one, she need a bucket quick
And when we done, she feel me like a majesty

Thyri wanted to feel his hands on her body while she danced on him. Fuck the whole keeping their relationship a secret. She could no longer take not being able to be close to her man. She could no longer take not being able to have his lips against hers tonight. The liquor racing through her veins had her forgetting all about her plan to make their relationship public once they were back in Atlanta. All she knew was that she wanted Killian next to her for the rest of this night. The same second that Thyri slowly got up from her seat was the same second that Soraya jumped off the sofa and sauntered her way over to where Killian was posted by the balcony.

By the time Thyri stood up straight, Soraya was standing in front of Killian. She turned around so that her back was facing him. A wide, devilish grin clung to her lips as she bent over and started grinding her butt on him. Thyri could hear the blood rushing through her head as she watched Soraya dance on him and a pain quickly formed in her jaw. But as quick as that pain had formed, it also disappeared just as quick when she observed Killian stepping to the side so that Soraya was no longer dancing on him. She was basically dancing with air. Soraya looked over her shoulder to see that Killian had moved out of the way and a frown settled on her face.

"What the hell, Kill?" She stood upright and walked over to the spot that Killian was now in. "Why the hell are you acting like that?"

The nightclub's music was loud but because of how loud Soraya was talking, everyone could hear her over it. And Thyri was glad she could hear because she wasn't trying to miss a single word of what was now going down.

Killian remained silent with a nonchalant look. He had his red cup lowered while he stayed leaning against the glass balcony.

"Like you ain't had this ass all up in your face while fucking me!"

She lifted her finger and wagged it in his face.

"You ain't fucked me once on this trip, Killian! Why the fuck is that?"

Soraya's yelling had attracted everyone's attention and Tanai had stopped dancing on Kason, much to his dismay, and was now walking over to where Soraya and Killian were standing by the balcony.

"Soraya, what's going o—"

"Ask this nigga!" Soraya mean mugged Killian and made a move to nudge his forehead with her finger. Well it was more of an attempt because even with her heels on, Killian still remained taller and the moment he sensed her trying to touch him, he grabbed her wrist, stopping her from doing something that he would make her regret.

"You need to chill, Soraya."

Before I make your ass chill.

He could tell by her glossy eyes and aggressive tone that she was drunk. He'd never been around her in this state before but he'd heard stories from his employees about how wild his manager got in her inebriated state on nights out with her girls. Tonight he was finally getting to see her wild side with his own eyes and he most definitely wasn't a fan.

"Get the hell off me!" Soraya snatched her wrist out his firm grip. "Oh I know why you won't fuck me!" She let out a callous chuckle, throwing her head back like she'd just heard the funniest joke in the world. "Because you're too busy fucking your new bitch, Thyri!"

The mention of her name made a chill crawl down Thyri's spine and her sight set on Tanai whose eyes had widened.

"Let that be the first and last time you ever call her out of her name," Killian warned, stepping closer to Soraya, and looking at her dead in the eyes.

"So you admit it then! You are fucking her, aren't you? You invited me on this trip but she's the one you've been paying attention to, not me! Admit that shit, nigga!"

"I don't need to admit anything about my personal life to you, Soraya."

"Fuck you, Killian! Fuck—" Soraya yanked his red cup out of his left hand. "—You!"

She lifted it and chucked the remaining liquor in the cup, onto his face. Then she threw the empty cup to the floor and stormed out of their VIP section with teary eyes. Killian simply lifted the bottom of his shirt, using it to dab his face dry.

Feeling inclined to go after her friend, Kiana rushed out of the VIP section to attend to Soraya whereas Tanai remained standing a short distance away from Killian. The bewilderment spreading across her face was unmissable.

"What the hell just happened?" she asked, placing her hands on her hips, and looking from Killian to Thyri.

Kason came to stand next to her, trying to wrap his arm around her waist but failing when she shrugged him off.

"I know I'm not talking to myself right now." Her face hardened as her eyes darted between Killian and Thyri. "What is Soraya talking about?"

Thyri swallowed the lump that came into her throat as she avoided looking into her sister's eyes.

This isn't how I wanted her to find out. Fuck!

"Do you wanna tell her or should I?"

"Tell me what?" Tanai answered Killian's question that was directed at Thyri.

You need to tell her. Now, Ri.

Thyri sighed deeply, finally finding the courage to stop pussy footing around and stare at Tanai.

"Killian and I... we're together now."

Tanai's hands dropped from her hips and her lips parted at the same time her brows raised.

"What?" Her voice was laced with disbelief. "Together how? Aren't you with Chosen?"

"She's no longer with that nigga, Nai, she's with me," Killian intervened.

Tanai went quiet as she stared at Killian, taking in the words he'd just revealed. Her gaze went to Thyri who wore a guilt-ridden look.

"Nai, I swear I was gonna tell you at the right time after our vacation."

A million thoughts rushed through Tanai's mind but she couldn't snatch and hold on to a single one. She suspected Thyri's attraction to Killian and his to her at the wedding reception last week but what she never could've suspected was the two of them entering a relationship.

"...Oh wow... this is all just so sudden," Tanai commented.

"Exactly how you and I got together, baby," Kason chimed in, securing an arm around Tanai's waist and this time she didn't

REAL LOVE FROM A REAL ONE

shrug him off. "When I found out about them all I could think about was how similar their situation is to ours." Tanai went stiff but Kason failed to pay attention to her change in body language. "Killian knew he wanted her from the jump, the same way I knew I wanted you."

"When you found out?" Tanai looked over her shoulder to inspect him. "You knew about them before tonight?"

"Yes, Nugget... I found out this morning from Kadiri. I wanted to tell you ASAP but Killian told me not to."

"Only 'cause Thyri wanted to tell you in private back in the A," Killian explained, leaving the balcony and walking over to where Thyri sat on the sofa. "Bubba, are you okay?"

She'd gone silent and it wasn't sitting right with Killian at all. The blank look she wore wasn't allowing him to read her emotions. He took the empty seat next to her and reached for her hand, bringing it to his lips and pressing a soft kiss to her knuckles. Her heart warmed at the sweet gesture but the truth was, she was far from okay.

What was supposed to be a night of fun had turned into a complete mess. Watching the scene that played out between Soraya and Killian just minutes ago made Thyri feel like she was in her own personal episode of Love and Hip Hop. Drama was the one thing she couldn't stand and it'd been thrusted her way.

"Thyri." Her chin was raised, forcing her to look up into his enchanting dark browns. "Talk to me... please."

What could she say? There was nothing that could be said to repair the damage of this night. There was nothing that could fix this shit. All Thyri wanted to do at this current moment was go home. Not home to their villa on Calivigny island but her home back in Atlanta. That's all she needed right now.

Her real home.

Chapter Fifteen

"Mommy, look! A swing!"

"Yes, baby. A swing. You wanna go on it?"

"Yesssssss!" Alana shrieked, causing Truth to laugh at her excitement.

One of the hidden gems of this island was a treehouse that the island's designers had built for guests with children. Truth hadn't found the time to take Alana to the treehouse because of all the activities they'd been doing that had kept them preoccupied and by the end of the day, Alana would be worn out and Truth's priority would be getting her to bed.

It was only now on their last night that Truth had found some time to take Alana up to the treehouse and boy was she glad that they'd found the time now.

This was no typical treehouse. Instead of having a rope ladder for people to climb up, this treehouse had polished wooden stairs that led into the house. The treehouse had three main rooms. The first room was a playroom with an outdoor swing, an indoor swing, a slide that led into a ball pit, a blanket fort, a painting and drawing area and various toys. The second room was a bedroom that looked as good as the rooms in the main beach villa and the third was a living room that housed faux sheepskin sofas that looked extremely comfortable. Truth tested that theory and found that the sofas were just as comfortable as they looked. The tree-house also came with an outdoor pool, a rope hammock and a balcony that overlooked the gorgeous view of Calivigny island.

While Truth pushed Alana on the outdoor swing, she was left in awe at how captivating this island was. She was grateful to Kason and Tanai that she'd gotten to experience such an island for the weekend. It had been amazing but what wasn't amazing was the fact that they were leaving tomorrow afternoon.

Zing! Zing! Zing!

Vibrations sounded off from Truth's back pocket. She reached into her pocket for her phone with her left hand while keeping the other hand alert to push Alana's swing whenever it came towards her. Her eyes lowered on the screen and her body locked up with rage at the caller ID. Just as she made a move to press decline, the sounds of footsteps coming upstairs were heard and Truth looked to the right to see Kadiri walking onto the balcony of the treehouse.

Alana had turned to the right too and seeing that face she'd grown fond of made her jump off her swing and race towards him.

"Kad Kad!"

A smile flickered on Truth's lips at Alana's nickname for Kadiri. One thing she always found cute was how Alana's nick-names for family were usually a part of their name but duplicated. For Thyri, it was RiRi, for Tanai, it was Nai Nai and now for Kadiri it was Kad Kad.

"There's my favorite girl," Kadiri said as he crouched down and opened his arms for Alana to run into. "You've been having fun up here without me, huh, Lani?"

Truth turned around to face the pair and observed their hug. Alana started rattling off all the things she'd done in the treehouse so far and it wasn't long till she was pulling Kadiri into the playroom so she could show him exactly what she'd been doing.

"Truth," Kadiri greeted her with a simple nod as he walked past her.

"Peanut Head," Truth responded, returning his nod.

He frowned instantly and Thyri simpered.

"What? You said I can't call you Skinny Boy, right? So I don't see nothing wrong with calling you Peanut Head." She cackled to herself. "After all that is the shape of your head."

Before Kadiri could verbally make his disapproval known of Truth's new nickname for him, the sound of vibrations filled the space and Truth sighed as she lifted the phone to her central line of vision.

"I need to take this." Her eyes fell on Alana holding Kadiri's hand and looking like tiny ant next to his six two frame. "Lana, baby, I'm gonna leave you to show Kadiri around your new playroom while mommy takes a quick call. Okay?"

"Okay!" Alana exclaimed, pulling Kadiri along. "Come on, Kad Kad!"

Kadiri happily allowed Alana to lead the way into the playroom while Truth pressed the green answer button and walked across the balcony to enter the living room on the other side of the thousand square foot treehouse.

"Hel—"

"Have you actually lost your raggedy ass mind, Truth?"

Truth released a harsh breath once his deep baritone came on the line. She entered the living room and the motion sensor lights came on, allowing her to lay eyes on the center seating area.

"Hello to you too, Jodell."

"So now you've suddenly remembered to answer the mothafucking phone when I've been calling your ass for the past two days."

"I've been busy, Jodell," she calmly replied, sitting on the nearest couch, and tucking her legs underneath her body before sitting on top of them. "The same way you said you were too busy to spend time with Alana this weekend."

"Oh I know just how busy you've been." He scoffed, choosing to ignore her reminder of his choice of not spending time with Alana this weekend. "Grenada, really, Tru?"

"My baby and I needed a vacation so we took one. End of story."

"Are you fucking crazy? You took my daughter out the country without my mothafucking permission, Truth. And I bet you have her around another nigga too, don't you? I swear to God if you were in front of me right now I would choke your stupid ass the fuck out."

"And I'd love to see you try that shit, nigga, once I've shot you twice in the dome for playing with a bitch like me."

"Bring my seed home. *Right. The. Fuck. Now.*"

Truth lifted her phone off her ear and glared at it like it was an infectious disease that she wanted no parts of.

"Your seed? Who the fuck do you think you're talking to, negro?"

"Your stupid as—"

"*My daughter* and I will be home tomorrow like I told your ass via text. It's funny because I really could've taken my daughter out the country without your ass finding out a damn thing. But I told you out of the kindness of my heart but we both know you don't really give a damn about Alana's wellbeing. Please refrain from calling my line and yelling at me like you don't have any got damn sense. Have a good night, Jodell."

"Bitch, I swear to Go—"

Truth cut the line before he could finish the vicious sentence dying to leave his lips. She pressed the power button and lowered the volume to switch off her device. Once it was off, she flung her phone to the other end of the cream couch and reached for a white pillow only to squash her face into it as she let out a scream. The scream was muffled nonetheless but she was just glad to get it out. She kept the pillow over her face as she felt tears prick her eyes.

Don't you dare, Tru. Don't you fucking dare.

Her situation with Jodell aka *Helldell* was what one would call... *complicated.* Like all relationships in the beginning, theirs started off sweet. Once upon a time, Truth was convinced that Jodell was the love of her life. What a big fat lie that turned out to be. He was far from it. He was more like the devil reincarnated. He'd been emotionally abusive, physically abusive too but Truth wasn't a pusillanimous woman. She'd thrown around a few fists with him and wasn't shy when it came to hurting him which is why he quickly learned his lesson after the first time he'd tried to beat her ass. Her late father hadn't approved of their relationship at all. In fact, he'd hated Jodell the first time he met him and from that moment on Truth knew she could never bring Jodell around her father again. She'd just wished she'd listened to her father when he told her to stay away from him but the stubborn mule in her made her disobey his wishes and do her own thing. Why she ever thought she was wiser than her father, she would never know. The only good thing that had come out of her relationship with Jodell was Alana. Alana was a blessing that Truth would never be able to stop thanking God for.

She took a deep breath, letting the pillow fall from her face and the second she could see her surroundings again, she noticed Kadiri standing in the doorway of the living room.

"You good?"

She was anything but good but she had no plans to share any personal details of her life with him.

"Fine," she retorted, blinking back tears, and getting up from her seat.

She made her way towards the living room's exit, determined not to stare at Kadiri as she was fearful he would read the pain in her eyes. As she got closer to the exit, she realized she had a problem on her hands. She was blocked by Kadiri's frame still standing in the center of the doorway and there was no way out unless he moved. Eventually she was standing in front of him and silence filled the space around them.

Feeling like she had no choice, Truth gazed up into his cognac eyes without saying a word. She didn't have to say a damn thing though because Kadiri could see the sadness within her. He wanted to say something... anything at all to ease her suffering but he didn't know what to say. Instead he lifted a hand to her face and stroked her cheek, loving how soft her skin felt.

From the second he laid eyes on Truth at his brother's reception, he was aware of how attractive she was. Who could ever deny it? She had chocolate brown skin with not a single spot or blemish in sight. Her oval face housed small eyes, thick brows with a slit in her left brow that looked sexy on her, full lips, and a well sculpted nose. She was petite and her head only made it to the lower region of his chest but despite her small shape, her body was filled out in all the right places. Her jet black hair was pulled up into a ponytail, allowing that alluring face of hers to shine more. The more he stared at her, the more he found himself getting lost in her dark brown eyes. They were magnetic, pulling him in more and more to the point of no return. And at this point, Kadiri wasn't sure he wanted to return.

Truth would be lying if she said his touch didn't provide her with a comfort she needed but she'd be a big fool to accept his kindness. He was a man and in her eyes they were all one in the same.

Cruel human beings.

She pushed his hand off her face and pushed past him to go be with the one person she was sure could never disappoint her in this life.

Her daughter.

Chapter Sixteen

"Thyri."

Thyri pushed the silver handle of her bedroom door and rushed in without bothering to turn around and face the voice desperate for her attention. The room's motion sensor lights spilled in, splashing everything with its warm, cool light.

She suddenly dropped her Bottegas to the floor and made a beeline for the open door of her en-suite. She could hear his footsteps trotting along behind her but she paid them no mind.

Once inside the bathroom, Thyri hit a switch and approached the sink. Standing in front of the vanity mirror allowed her to see just how over this night she was. Those dull eyes were unmissable and the downturned facial features she currently housed were another sign of her reaction to just how shit this night had been.

That little bitch!

Thyri gripped the edge of the sink, tilting her head down and closing her eyes as she tried to slow down her racing heart.

All Thyri had wanted was the chance to have a private conversation with her sisters about her new relationship *after* their vacation but Soraya had ruined that. Now Tanai knew the truth and Thyri knew that it was only a matter of time before Truth found out too.

Though her eyes remained shut, Thyri heard his footsteps come to a halt behind her. She could sense he was standing close without having to open her eyes and actually look at him. Though she was angry, she knew that she owed him a response after he'd called her name.

Thyri lifted her head and opened her eyes only to see his reflection standing behind her. The minute her eyes locked on his, she felt the discomfort clouding her heart begin to fade away.

"Do you need some space?"

Thyri immediately shook her head 'no'.

He slowly stepped forward, circling an arm around her waist, and pulling her into him so that her back pressed against his chest.

Space from Killian was the last thing she wanted. Yes, she was angry... angry at the entire situation that had gone down tonight but she wasn't about to take that anger out on the one person she needed in her orbit.

As they both faced the mirror, their gazes were fixed on one another and Thyri couldn't get over how handsome he looked standing behind her. She was convinced she could stare into those almond shaped eyes forever and those lips? Baby, those lips were the only lips Thyri wanted to kiss on, suck on, bite on and feel on her second set of lips that lived between her thighs. His hold on her waist got tighter and Thyri lightly sighed once his lips settled on the side of her neck. He peppered her flesh with soft kisses for a few moments before planting one last peck to her cheek.

"I get that you're angry, Bubba... and trust me you have every right to be. I'm sorry that I put you in this fucked up position. If I could change this entire set up I would. But I can't. These are the cards we've been dealt so we need to handle it, baby. And we will. The right way."

Thyri continued to watch his reflection in awe at how one man could be this good at communication. The last time she'd experienced a man being this skilled at communicating was with her father.

"Tomorrow morning I need to apologize to Soraya. She didn't deserve to be placed in the position that she's in right now and though I didn't plan for shit to end up like this, she still deserves one. But the same way I owe her an apology is the same way she owes you one, Ri."

Thyri's chest tightened at the thought of having to talk to Soraya. They hadn't talked after Soraya had stormed out of their VIP section. When she came back, she sat in one corner and refused to grace anyone with words. Not even Tanai could get through to her. The only person that eventually got any communication from Soraya was Kiana and even then it still wasn't much. Soraya sat the whole night huddled in a corner with her nose buried in her phone.

Seeing the lack of communication his sister-in-law received from Soraya made Killian decide on not talking to Soraya for the rest of the night. He wasn't impressed with the fact that she'd thrown a drink in his face and now she was ignoring Tanai who was the only person who cared enough to want to hear her side of things. Quite frankly, he didn't care for her emotions. All he cared about was Thyri and since the cat was out of the bag about their relationship, he had no interest in keeping up the charade of them pretending like they weren't together. He spent the rest of the night holding and touching Thyri whenever he felt the need to which Thyri didn't object to because that's all she'd wanted to be able to do all night.

But she was still too pissed off to enjoy herself and even when

Tanai tried to get her to loosen up and dance, Thyri couldn't get into it. She just wanted to go home and be far away from Soraya. Home time came eventually and now here the two of them were. In Thyri's bathroom.

"She never should've called you out your name. I don't care how angry or jealous she is, you're my woman and she will respect you."

My woman.

The corners of her eyes crinkled as her mouth lifted into a smile.

"Your woman, huh?"

"Yes." Killian's mouth now mirrored hers as a smile took control of his lips. "*My* woman."

"I love..." Thyri slowly turned in her stance, causing Killian's arm to fall from her frame. "The sound of that."

She now stood facing him and lifted her hands to his nape, stroking his warm skin.

Killian's arms found her waist once again and this time once he had a secure hold around her body, he pushed her up against the sink and kept his chest pressed against hers.

"I'm proud of you."

Thyri's brows furrowed.

"Proud of me? Why, baby?"

"Because you listened," he explained. "I told you at the reception that I never wanted to see you get out of character and tonight you remained calm...ish." He chuckled at the memory of Thyri shooting daggers at Soraya as she sat in her corner, paying no one any mind but her smartphone. "I know how bad you wanted to put your hands on her, especially after she called you out your name, but you didn't."

"I didn't," Thyri repeated after him. "I guess someone's having a hold on me after all."

A pleased expression formed on her visage as he studied her.

"For real though... I really am sorry, Bubba."

"You don't need to keep apologizing, Kill. You didn't know I was going to be on this trip, the same way I had no idea that you were going to be here. I know if you'd known, you wouldn't have invited her."

"Hell no," he whispered, lifting his right hand, and stroking her cheek.

Thyri smiled at his touch and kept her eyes connected to his. His hand slid down her cheek and landed on her throat, causing her breaths to quicken. Her hands that had been on his neck, she dropped and let fall to his lower torso. He circled his hand around her neck and Thyri's smile turned into a grin.

"You forgive me?" he asked, leaning in to press a kiss to her forehead.

"Yes, Killian." She nodded. "I do."

He released her forehead and bent his head low so he could whisper into her ear, "That ain't enough for me, Ri."

Her brow lifted but the second she felt his lips brush her ear, her brow dropped and goosebumps lifted across her skin.

"I need to know just how much you forgive me, Thyri."

"Hmm... you do?"

His head went up and down as a teasing smirk crossed her lips. I need you to show me just how much you forgive me."

Just as she parted her lips to respond, Killian's mouth curled around her ear lobe, sucking gently on her skin.

"Kill," she moaned, rubbing her hands against his sculpted middle.

His lips continued to work their magic as they sucked, licked, and bit her ear, making all sorts of nasty thoughts fly into Thyri's mind. At the same time his lips worked, he still had a hand wrapped around her throat and his other hand slid around her waist, falling down the small of her back until he was able to grip her booty through her dress. He started squeezing her soft cheeks and that was enough to heighten her moans.

"Kill... I will," she breathlessly promised. "I'll show you."

He lifted his lips from her ear to ask, "You will?"

"Yesss," she hissed as his hand hugged her pussy from behind. "I will, baby."

After her confirmation, Killian decided to release his hold on all parts of her body and stepped away from her.

Thyri caught her bottom lip between her teeth as she let her gaze cruise down Killian's body. All night she'd been wishing to have her lips on that fine ass body of his and the time had finally come.

She inched forward, closing the small gap between them, and reaching for his right hand. She then led the way out of the bathroom, into her bedroom and brought them both by the edge of her bed. Once she had him where she needed him, she pushed him down causing the mattress to shake as his mighty body fell on it.

Adrenaline rushed through Killian's veins at the sight of Thyri standing over him. His fingers twitched, reminding him of his urge to want to touch and hold her. But from the way she was looking at him like she wanted to eat him up, Killian suppressed his urge and remained still.

Thyri crouched over Killian's body, leaning down, and pressing her lips to his warm chest. Tonight of all nights, she was glad that he'd decided to wear nothing but a shirt to the club which he'd left unbuttoned, giving her easy access. She kissed on his abdominal muscles, sucking, and licking on them before making her way further up his chest.

Killian's head fell back and his eyes shut as he felt tingles flood his body at her lips moving on his skin. Her lips arrived on his left pec and she darted out her tongue, licking across his flesh until she was able to wrap her mouth around his nipple.

"Shit... Thyri."

His nipples were one of his most sensitive spots on his body so for Thyri to now have her lips on one with that damn tongue piercing of hers... Killian knew he was in trouble.

Big trouble.

Her sucks were delicate and her tongue joined in on the action, flicking against his hard bud and teasing Killian to the point of no return.

"Fuck... Ri."

Hearing his groans brought a smile to Thyri's mouth and she bit into his nipple, causing him to release a soft whimper.

Yeah that's right, baby. Moan for me.

She released his left nipple and made a trail of wet kisses to his right nipple. She worked her charm once again, pleasing his nipple in the best way, making his moans fill the room louder and louder.

After sucking his nipples, Thyri kissed down his stomach, over his belly button and stopped at the waistband of his shorts. She reached for the woven fabric and pulled them down his thighs. Killian lifted his hips, allowing Thyri to tug his shorts down to his ankles and remove them from his body.

Thyri's eyes sparkled as she looked at the thickness standing at attention between Killian's thighs. He had such a beautiful dick. It was thick and long with a slight curve that had Thyri's mind blown every time she felt it inside her.

She lifted her right hand to her mouth, spitting on it a few times before wrapping it around the base of his shaft while keeping her eyes on him. She had this teasing glint in her eyes that made Killian both intrigued and nervous. The second emotion was foreign to him during sex. Getting nervous because of woman's ability to pleasure him? That never happened. But with

Thyri, shit was just different. Too damn different. She was in a league of her own. She had him feeling things he hadn't felt in what felt like forever and doing things that he didn't even need to ask her to do. She just did it.

Her hand that was wrapped around his dick slowly moved up and down his length, causing him to bite his lip. She held him prisoner with her stare and her hand movements quickened.

Killian not only felt weak in the knees each time she stroked him, but he could also feel that weakness spreading across every fiber of his being. He wanted more from her – no, scratch that – he *needed* more.

"T-Thyri... Please."

Thyri shot him an innocent look as her hand continued to move up and down his hard flesh.

"Please what?" she asked, dropping her head down and darting her tongue out to tap against his tip a couple times, while still moving her hand up and down his base. She then paused her tapping only to start slapping her face with his dick, making it hit both her cheeks before resuming her tapping motion with her tongue.

Her actions almost had Killian squealing like a little bitch but when she stopped tapping her tongue against him and acted like she hadn't just teased him in the worst way, Killian sighed deeply.

"You really gon' make me beg you, baby?"

Thyri grinned, her teeth flashing white against her espresso brown skin.

"Do you want me to suck your dick?" she shyly asked, lifting her hand in a slow motion until it reached his smooth head.

"Yes, Bubba... you know I do."

"Ask me nicely..." She removed her hand from his dick and her open mouth came down on him. Her lips tightly encircled his hardness and sucked him in all the way to the back of her throat.

Then she quickly moved upwards and released him. "And you might just get what you want."

She didn't have to tell him twice.

"Please, Thyri," he begged. "I want you to suck my dick."

His wish was her command and she wasn't about to waste any time now that Killian had told her what she needed to hear. She got on her knees, extending her body forward so that she was positioned between his thighs that hung over the bed's edge and got right to work.

"Thyriiiiii... fuck!"

Times like these, Thyri was grateful that short hair suited her because it provided a great incentive for her to regularly get her hair cut. Because of the short cut she'd rocked on this vacation she had nothing in her way as she pleasured her man in the best way.

Up and down her lips moved and Killian was left in awe at her ability to multi-task. While her mouth did the main work on the upper half of his dick – sucking, licking, and spitting on him in ways that had Killian's eyes misting – her two hands stayed rooted at his base, twisting, and stroking his source of arousal.

"Shit... you... you bad... bad, bad girl."

When her lips dropped to his ball sac and she took the first one in her mouth, Killian was certain that if she asked him to clear out all of his bank accounts and put the large sums of money in her account, he would do it.

"You are so... mothafucking bad."

If she asked him to sell all the shares he had in the stock market just so she could reap the benefits of his long term investments, he knew he'd do it in a heartbeat. Anything she wanted from him in this life, she could get. She had his nose wide open and he wasn't ashamed to admit it.

Her lips moved to the second ball, tending to it just like she'd done to the first. All while doing this, she stayed moving her hands up top, not wanting to neglect his most sensitive spot.

Unable to stop himself, Killian yanked her hair, lifting her head and placing her back in position by his dick. Her mouth came down on him again and she found her heart racing as Killian pushed her head up and down his length. Quicker and quicker he moved her and Thyri felt her wetness flow out of her faster at how rough he was being.

"Just like that," he coached in a low tone, watching her move. "That's a good girl... eat your dick up... just like that."

The sounds of her choking filled the room and she'd be lying if she said she didn't like it. Eventually Killian released his grip on her hair, letting her head go and just as Thyri started doing her thing again, Killian sat up.

Thyri popped her lips off him and looked over at him, reading the hunger burning in his dark pools.

"Take your dress off," he ordered. "Now."

He didn't have to tell her twice.

Thyri got up from her knees, stepping away from Killian and reaching for the thin straps of her dress. The same second her straps lifted over her shoulders was the same second that he lifted his shirt over his. Their eyes refused to break away from one another as they stripped each article of clothing from their bodies.

Once Thyri stood in nothing but her thong, Killian made a move to rise on his feet but seeing Thyri back away and shake her head 'no' made him freeze.

"I'm not done showing you I forgive you, Killian."

Her statement made him realize that she was right. She wasn't done and he'd be a fool to not let her finish doing her thing.

Killian nodded before lying back and allowing his back to meet the bed. His head was lifted slightly, allowing him to see her as she slid the white lace fabric down her thighs. His mouth became moist the more he watched her in all her glory.

Her thong dropped to the floor and she stepped out of it, sauntering over to where Killian lay with an extremely wet mouth and an even harder dick. Thyri climbed on top of him, rubbing her hands across the hard planes of his muscles and smiling down at him.

"You know how sexy you are, right?" Killian asked as he looked up at her.

His eyes landed on her pierced nipples, her tatted arm, her belly button piercing and the sternum tattoo that she owned because of him. He could never get tired of knowing that a part of him was on her body forever.

Thyri's smiled turned into a shy one at Killian's query.

"And you looked way too sexy in that dress tonight, Ri. I should've just made you stay in and wear that dress for me. No one elsssssshit."

Killian groaned at the tightness of her walls molding around his dick. She'd raised her hips, held his dick upright and placed her opening above his tip before sliding herself down him.

"No one else?" Thyri chuckled as she slowly raised herself up and down Killian's rod.

"No one fucking else," he groaned through gritted teeth as Thyri rode him at a steady beat.

He reached up to grab her waist but it was a big, fat fail because she grabbed his hands before he could latch them onto her waist and pressed them down to the space above his head.

"Uh-uh." She shook her head from side to side, flashing him a mischievous grin. "No touching."

She continued to rock up and down, soft moans slipping out her mouth each time Killian's dick filled her up.

"Only I'm allowed to... uhh... allowed to touch," she said, keeping his hands pressed to the bed.

Killian had no choice but to surrender and sit back, letting her do her thing. Not that he was complaining. Having Thyri ride him was something he could get used to. *Very* used to. But he'd be lying if he said he didn't want to be in control right now. He wanted to be able to latch his lips onto her breasts as they bounced up and down and he badly wanted to be able to grip her waist while he pounded into her with his hips thrusted in the air. But for now he'd be patient and let his Bubba take the ropes.

She was doing an amazing job. Each time she slid her pussy down his dick, Killian was left with wide eyes and an even wider mouth. She knew exactly how to ride him. Not too fast. Not too slow. Just right. And she had the stamina to keep moving up and down. Those stallion knees of hers were no joke and Killian was gassed at how strong her knees were.

"Killian... you feel... so good inside me."

He bit down on his bottom lip, both eyes sealed on her as her love faces washed across her pretty face.

"Ahhhh, fuck!"

Feeling the lust overwhelm her, Thyri let go of Killian's hands and grabbed her breasts, stroking and massaging the soft flesh as she kept riding him.

His hands being free allowed him access to her waist and he quickly latched on at the same time his hips lifted. Thyri's moans and cries only heightened as Killian pumped into her from below.

"Killiannnn!"

"Yes, baby?" His pearly whites flashed in smile. "You feeling that dick?"

"Kill... fuck... yes." Her breaths were tiny pants and quickening with each passing second.

Beads of sweat had broken out on both their skin and their racing heartbeats showed no signs of slowing down.

Thyri suddenly reached for Killian's throat, squeezing tight as their eyes remained locked.

"Shit," Killian cursed, heat flooding his core at her action. "Tighter, Thyri. Squeeze that shit tighter."

She obeyed, applying more pressure to his neck. Her choking him tight coupled with the tightness of her pussy choking his dick had Killian on cloud nine right now. It was more like cloud one hundred because this feeling right here was too fantastic. He never wanted it to end.

"This is it, Thyri."

Thyri's lust filled face mixed with confusion so he knew he needed to keep talking.

"This... you and I," he explained. "I don't want to be in anyone else but you, Bubba. I only want you."

Thyri felt her heart melt at his words and she loosened her grip on his neck. She could hear the sincerity in his tone and it only melted her heart more and more. He was being real about his feelings and she felt the need to be real too.

"I only want you too."

And that was the honest truth. Thyri bent low to bring her face close to his and pressed her lips to his. He was all she wanted from here on out.

Chapter Seventeen

"About damn time you grew some balls and told me the truth that I already knew about five hundred and fifty years ago."

Five hundred and fifty years ago? Thyri couldn't stop the corners of her lips from lifting. *This girl is so damn dramatic.*

Tuesday morning had arrived and the girls had arrived back in Atlanta yesterday evening. You would think that the seven hour flight would have been enough to keep the girls knocked out and glued to their beds for the next twenty four hours. But no. Tuesday morning was here and the girls were eager to get back to their regular scheduled programming. Working at their company didn't actually feel like work for them so it wasn't a hassle for them to get back to their company's headquarters and get right back to work.

Now that they were back in the city and had all the privacy they needed, Thyri took this moment to reveal to Truth the truth about her and Killian. A truth that Truth already knew from her own suspicions and observations. She had a feeling that Thyri and

Killian had already messed around in Grenada, especially after seeing their interactions together. They'd been fooling themselves thinking that they could hide their connection.

Thyri finally filled her sisters in about how Killian and her made things official and how things with her and Chosen were over. She also chose to take her revelations all the way back to the day she'd first laid eyes on Killian at his shop. She revealed the truth about her attraction towards him and how despite thinking she was never going to see him again, he remained stuck in the back of her mind. Now fate had brought them together through the union of Kason and Tanai.

"You were over here playing games when you knew damn well that Killian was who you wanted from the jump. Took you long enough but you finally came to your senses and made the right decision to leave that other bum ass nigga alone."

"Truth," Thyri pouted as she watched her sister who sat in the seat opposite her.

The sisters were seated around a round conference table. They were in their meeting room with their cups of Starbucks coffee, MacBooks, iPads, notepads, and pens all sitting in front of them. Tanai was into all things digital which is why she had her MacBook, iPad, and Apple Pencil to jot down notes but Thyri was an old schoolgirl which is why she had a physical notepad alongside her Mac. Truth hated writing things down which is why she had her MacBook alone to type and her iPad for google searches.

"What?" Truth shrugged. "You thought I didn't notice the way you were looking at him the entire time in Grenada? Girl, please." Truth waved her off. "I know you better than you know yourself and I was lowkey rooting for the two of you from the beginning. Why do you think I was pushing you to get on that jet ski with him? You needed your back blown by a real nigga and guess what, you finally got it. So congratulations, sis, no more small pee pee for you."

Tanai let out a soft giggle as she jotted down the remainder of her iPad notes. The sisters were having a meeting about all the work they had to get done this coming month. They still needed to make their final decisions about their products for their cleaning line, had new businesses that were trying to sign their company on to clean their buildings and Tanai wanted to go through her PowerPoint presentation that showcased all the ideas that she had thought of while on her hiatus away from her sisters and the city. Though her time away had placed a dark cloud over her relationship with her sisters, she was hoping that the new ideas she had to share would eradicate that dark cloud, replacing it with a rainbow and allow her sisters to see that during her time away, their company had always been on her mind.

"Chosen's dick wasn't small, Tru," Thyri commented, frowning at Truth's assumption.

A very fake assumption. He wasn't packing as much as Killian and didn't have the skills that Killian had but he wasn't small by any means.

"Whatever helps you sleep at night, sis." Truth smirked. "But ew, I can't believe the both of you heifers are cuffed to the Miller brothers. Y'all really are keeping it in the family, huh?"

Tanai looked up from her notes and tapped her Apple Pencil against her iPad's screen. Her lips mirrored the smirk that currently sat on Truth's mouth.

"I mean what can I say... the Miller brothers are just built different." Tanai's tongue darted out her lips and she slowly wet them, keeping her eyes on Truth as she said, "*Very* different."

"Your nasty ass," Truth commented. "At the rate I know you and Kay Billy are going, I won't be surprised if your ass ends up pregnant before the end of the year."

Tanai smiled, lifting the white pencil, and tapping it against her cheek. Tanai's sudden quietness had Truth's mind spinning and she gasped at her realization.

"Don't tell me your ass is already pregnant, Nai!"

"No, no, no." Tanai repeatedly shook her head from side to side, dropping her Apple Pencil to the top of her iPad.

"So why you smiling so hard like you are?" Truth queried.

"Because you just reminded me of Sonny's proposition on the night before we got married."

"His proposition?" Thyri's raised a brow.

"Yeah..." Tanai shyly nodded. "He said if it was up to him, I'd be pregnant right now and he asked me if I wanted that to happen because he was more than willing to spend the entire night making sure it did."

"Well damn, he sure as hell ain't tryna waste no time." Truth tittered.

"He really isn't." Tanai released a soft sigh, her eyes sparkling with joy as the mental images of her husband popped into her brain. "But he's still cool on my decision for us to wait a little while longer. We're just trying to enjoy marriage right now especially since we didn't really take the time to be boyfriend and girlfriend first. So for now the focus is just on us... but I'd be lying if I said I don't get baby fever every time I'm with Alana or see another baby. I lowkey want to give him a baby right now."

"And like I said before I wouldn't be surprised if you get pregnant before the end of this year," Truth repeated.

"I mean we don't use protection so I wouldn't be surprised either. He really just be nutting in m—"

"Ewwww, girl! TMI, TMI!" Truth yelled, covering her eyes to block her view of Tanai.

Tanai laughed, remembering how much Truth hated talking about sex. She could only talk about it on a surface level but hearing about bodily fluids and specific positions made her cringe which was funny because she was the one with a child out of the trio.

"Sorry *Ms. Frigid.* I forgot how much sex isn't something you like diving too deeply into even though you've already had plenty of it diving in you." Tanai laughed once again and even Thyri sported a grin at Tanai's use of rhyme.

"You are so corny, you know that, right?" Truth flipped her the bird. "I don't mind doing it, I just don't like hearing about the specifics, y'all know that."

"Yeah we know," Thyri replied. "Moving on though... I'm sorry for not telling you both in Grenada about Killian and I. I just wanted to tell you guys once we were back home and away from everyone else."

"It's cool, I'm not sweating over that. It's not like you were going to keep it away from us forever," Truth said. "I'm just glad I wasn't in that club when Soraya called you out of your name."

"You and me both," Thyri agreed, knowing how much hell Truth would have raised that night.

When it came to fights, Truth was definitely the biggest hot head out of the sisters, followed by Thyri whereas Tanai was more of a pacifist. Truth fought with hands, Thyri fought with words and Tanai was always the one trying to end all the fighting or stop it before it could get too far. It had only been at her wedding reception that she couldn't find the strength to intervene with the arguing happening between her sisters and Kason's family because she was too emotional about all the insults that Kason's mother had thrown her way.

"I was even wondering why she took an earlier flight without saying goodbye... now it makes total sense."

"Yup," Tanai confirmed Truth's words, rolling her eyes at the memory of Kason telling her that Soraya had left the island early.

"She wasn't trying to stay any longer than necessary and she didn't even thank Sonny for the free accommodation. But whatever. Karma will definitely deal with her ass."

Yesterday morning in Grenada, everyone had woken up and arrived downstairs for breakfast only to be told by Kason that Soraya had taken the earliest boat off the island so she could get on her flight. It was a surprise to Truth that Soraya had dipped off so early but after finding out what had happened at the club with her, Killian and Thyri, she was no longer surprised. In fact she was glad that Soraya had taken the initiative to run. Truth didn't want that woman anywhere near her or her sisters from here on out. She didn't care about how jealous Soraya was about Killian's situation with Thyri, that gave her no right to call Thyri out of her name. Soraya's issue was with Killian and should have stayed between her and Killian. In Truth's book, It had nothing to do with Thyri and Truth didn't want to have to hear anything in the future about Soraya stepping out of line again.

"Thyri."

Thyri looked over at Tanai and nodded in response.

"Are you sure things between you and Chosen are done done?"

"Yeah." She nodded once more. "We're no longer together."

"But you mentioned that he put you two on a break..." The wheels in Truth's head started turning as she spoke up. "That doesn't actually sound like your relationship is totally over."

A frown graced Thyri's lips.

"But it is. We haven't spoken and I have no intentions of speaking to him again."

"And if he suddenly pops up today, what will you tell him?"

"That we don't have anything to talk about." She shrugged, giving Truth a blank stare as she answered her. "He ended things and I'm keeping things like that."

"Let's just say for arguments sake, he never put a break on your relationship... would Killian and you even be a thing right now?" Truth queried with a curious gaze. "Because at the end of the day you would still be with small pee pee and Killian would still want your ass. So how exactly would that have worked?"

"I mean... if Chosen and I were still together before Grenada I definitely wouldn't have had sex with Killian, if that's what you're asking."

"But how can you be so sure, sis?" Tanai intervened. "You said it yourself, you've been attracted to this man since you first met him at his shop. There's no telling what you wouldn't have or would've done with Chosen still in the picture."

Damn.

Now that Thyri really thought about it - her sisters had a valid point. Her attraction to Killian had no bounds and as much as she tried fighting it off, their time alone in Grenada had sealed their fate. Even if she had arrived to Grenada as a taken woman, how could she be sure that she wouldn't have jumped on the chance to be with Killian? Everything about that man oozed alpha male and though she'd always been an independent, don't need a man for shit woman, Killian brought that submissive side out of her without even trying. Him just breathing in the same space as her made her want to submit to him and do anything to please him.

"You need to talk to Chosen... you don't need to see him but at least call him or maybe text would be better. But make it clear to him that you've moved on. For good. Yes he put a break on your situation but he was under the assumption that you were coming back to him. But you're not and he deserves to know that."

Thyri pondered over Tanai's words, realizing how right she was.

"I'm also gonna keep it real with you, sis... as much as I'm happy for you and Killian and as much as I never liked Chosen for you, I'm still wary about how fast you've moved into this new situation with Killian. You've been with Chosen for two years... on and off yes but still two years. That's a long ass time to be in a relationship."

"It is," Tanai agreed. "But time ain't nothing but a number. The time she's shared with Killian is clearly more than anything she's shared with Chosen."

"And I'm not doubting that but I just wish you'd given yourself some time to be free, Thyri. To be single and live a hot girl summer before thrusting yourself back into a new relationship. But you're grown and you're gonna do whatever the hell you're gonna do. So as your sister I'm gonna support you through it all regardless of my personal opinions about the situation."

Thyri's eyes darted from sister to sister, seeing the way they both watched her with care and affection.

"Just be careful, Ri. I don't want you getting hurt again."

"She'll be fine," Tanai insisted, reaching for her Starbucks cup, and taking a quick sip of her iced chai latte. "Killian ain't Chosen. That's a grown ass man right there who doesn't play about anything. Y'all saw the way he handled his mom, his brother and your asses at the reception."

"Oh we definitely saw it all." Truth grimaced, thinking back to how Killian had her wrapped around his finger that evening. "How could we ever forget it?"

Neither of them had forgotten Killian's kingly nature that day. His ability to get everyone to listen to him was unmatched. Thyri knew it all too well now because his kingly nature always made an appearance in the bedroom.

"Yeah he seems like a real one but Ri, just be careful. I only want what's best for you..." Truth glanced over at Tanai as she said, "What's best for both of you. I know how tough I can be on you both but know it comes from a place of love. I don't want my sisters being placed in a fucked up situation. That ain't cool."

"I hear you, Mom," Thyri teased, making Truth shoot her a side eye which quickly softened into a loving smile. "I'll be careful. I promise."

"Good... now about those anti-microbial candles, Nai. You were saying they kill germs in the air?"

The Wright sisters continued their meeting, getting back to their conversation about their upcoming cleaning line and Tanai's new product ideas. One thing that Thyri would always love was the fact that she got to work Monday to Friday with her sisters and although business was always a priority, they could also talk about their personal lives, creating a healthy balance between their business and personal lives.

Ding!

About fifteen minutes later, Thyri's phone went off and she apologized to her sisters before reaching for the device to put it on do not disturb. She'd forgotten to put it on do not disturb prior to their meeting, something she rarely did because when she was with her sisters she liked to be able to concentrate on them alone.

She lifted her phone, her eyes glossing over her newest text.

Dayana: *Can't wait to see you for lunch!*

She typed back: *Can't wait to see you more,* pressed send and put her phone on DND. Her focus went back on Tanai as she shared her PowerPoint that she had open on her MacBook.

Three hours later and lunch time finally arrived. Typically lunch was something the sisters had together but from time to time they would go off course and decide to have lunch with their friends outside work. Today was Thyri's turn to go off track.

"Someone's missing me already, huh?"

"Maybe."

"Oh a'ight." He released a hearty chuckle that brought a hot spot in the center of her stomach. "I'ma remember you said that when I next see you."

Thyri smiled to herself, finding herself getting lost in the sweet memories of them together on vacation. Oh how she missed him. It hadn't even been a week since they'd been away from each other and still she missed him.

"How about you remember that tonight?"

Her Louboutins clicked against the concrete floors as she drew nearer to the restaurant with the white sign 'Toast On Lenox'.

"Tonight?"

She could hear the smile in his voice and that was enough to strengthen her own.

"Yes, tonight." She reached for the silver handle of the front entrance and pulled it open. "I'm cooking salmon tonight, my favorite – I'm sure there'll be a plate for you... if you make it on time."

"Hmm... I'll have to check my schedule and get back to you."

Thyri now stood inside Toast and greeted the caramel skinned hostess with a smile.

"Hello ma'am. Welcome to Toast. Do you have a reservation?"

Thyri nodded.

"Kill, hold on, babe," she spoke into her AirPods, before addressing the hostess.

Killian waited patiently, listening in on Thyri speaking to the hostess about her reservation. She gave her name and the booking time.

"You can call me back later, Bubba, when you're done with lunch," he said once the hostess told Thyri to follow her through the restaurant, giving him the opening he needed to talk to Thyri.

"It hasn't started yet, silly." He heard her footsteps as she moved through the restaurant. "Dayana isn't here yet and besides you're on your lunch break too, right?"

Killian's eyes dropped to his desk that his Cajun chicken Caesar salad sat upon.

"Yup."

"That's what I thought. Besides, I haven't heard you tell me all about how you'll be clearing your schedule tonight for me only."

Killian laughed, reaching for the lid of his salad box, and opening it.

"I haven't heard you tell me that you miss me, Thyri."

"Ooooo, real smooth, mister." She giggled. "Of course I miss you, Kill."

"I can't wait to hear you tell me that tonight when I'm deep inside yo—"

"TT!"

A familiar female voice now calling Thyri's name told Killian all he needed to know about the status of their call.

"I'll see you tonight, Bubba. Have fun on your lil' lunch date. Oh and I hope you know that salmon isn't the only thing I'm eating tonight."

Thyri felt the heat of a blush on her cheeks. Before she could respond, Dayana had made it over to her and rushed to hug her, leaving Killian to say a final goodbye to Thyri and ending their call.

"You left me all alone in the A without even saying goodbye! What if I'd died or something!"

Thyri snorted as they hugged. She was sitting in her seat but that hadn't stopped Dayana from running into her arms.

"I missed you too, drama queen."

"Drama queen?" Dayana released her, pulling her head back as a shadow of dismay crossed her face. "When was the last time you laid eyes on me?"

Thyri paused, trying to scan her mind for the memory of the

time she'd seen Dayana last. One wasn't coming to mind right away though, making her face grow warm with shame.

"Exactly," Dayana confirmed what they both already knew without either of them having to say it. It had been too damn long since they'd seen each other.

"I'm sorry, girl." Thyri took out her AirPods, observing as Dayana took the emerald seat in front of her. She placed her AirPods in their case. "Life has been a real rollercoaster these past few weeks."

The women had been a given two person table in the middle of the restaurant.

"But I've missed you so much," Thyri said, reaching across the white marble stone table for Dayana's hand.

Dayana shot her a look of fake disgust which made Thyri cackle. The look faded into a grin and just like that Dayana was done pretending like she didn't miss Thyri.

"I missed you more, *Ms. I'm Looking Way Too Sexy With My Tan.* You need to tell me everything! How was Grenada?"

Ding! Ding!

The sound of her phone going off made Thyri take a quick glance to the lower right, reading the texts that had appeared on her home screen.

Killian: *Make sure you shoot me a payment request on Apple Pay for your lunch bill when you're done eating.*

Killian: *Lunch is on me.*

Killian: *And it's not up for debate either.*

Thyri's heart skipped several beats and she felt a smile form on her lips but it vanished when she felt her hands shake. Her eyes lifted to her hands and she realized that Dayana was shaking her hands, trying to get her attention.

"Earth to TT. Girl, this is my time. Leave your phone aloneeeee and tell me all about Grenada."

"Alright, alright, I got you," Thyri replied.

Their hands remained joined as Dayana asked Thyri a million and one questions. She wanted to know exactly how Grenada had went, how it was meeting Tanai's new husband and all the juicy tea that Thyri had to spill about their vacation. As much as Thyri loved and appreciated her bestie, she wasn't about to tell her every single detail about the vacation. Especially not the bits about her and Killian hooking up.

Dayana was still under the notion that Thyri was in a relationship with Chosen and had no idea about their breakup or the events that had led up to their breakup. They were in a public setting and although the restaurant wasn't packed full with bodies, Thyri didn't feel comfortable spilling out her life story to Dayana right now. She was still dealing with the truth behind Truth's words in their meeting this morning.

Things between her and Chosen weren't fully over until she made them so. And that was a whole other issue she would need to deal with another time. For now, Thyri wanted to keep things light and enjoy brunch with Dayana. Toast was one of their favorite breakfast spots in the city because of their fluffy French toast and mouthwatering honey fried chicken.

Thyri told Dayana about her vacation, how much she'd enjoyed it and all the things she'd done on the island. Between Thyri filling Dayana in on Grenada, their waiter came and took their orders. They hadn't needed to look at the menus because they knew what they wanted. Her relationship with Killian and the drama that had happened with Soraya would have to be a conversation for another day.

Once Thyri was done talking, the girls' meal had arrived and they thanked their waiter for the fast service before tucking into their meals.

Now it was Dayana's turn to tell Thyri on all that she'd missed in her life and surprisingly it wasn't much. Things with Ethan were on the mend since their last hiccup because of his jealousy towards her tattooing male clients. Dayana told Thyri how she'd followed her advice and actually had a conversation with Ethan. Thankfully, he understood that he was just overreacting and that he had nothing to worry about with his girl dealing with male clients.

Thyri was glad to know that they'd addressed Ethan's insecurities and were moving forward from it. Dayana also filled Thyri in on her time at House of Hayes and it was clear not only by her words but the way her face lit up as she spoke that she loved working at the shop.

"Killian's such a great boss... I mean in the first week he was a little tough on me but I understood why. He wasn't happy about how I kept coming in late for appointments and when I missed your appointment, he wasn't happy at all. However he recognizes my talent and is motivating me more and more to do more complex designs. Sometimes I shy out and feel like I can't do it but he believes in me."

Thyri couldn't stop the smile currently dominating her face even if she tried to. Hearing her best friend tell her all about her boyfriend being a great boss was an instant mood lifter and Thyri couldn't wait to see him tonight.

"And his manager Soraya? She's great vibes. I think you'd like her if you met her."

Thyri's heart tightened at Dayana's mention of Soraya.

Oh best believe, I've already met her and I'll never like her ass.

Dayana wasn't aware that Soraya had been in Grenada with Thyri and Thyri had no desire to tell her about it. Thyri chose to change the subject, asking Dayana about how her mother was doing since her car accident. Thankfully, Dayana's mother was doing fine and still on bed rest at the order of her husband, Dayana's no-nonsense father.

Thyri was glad to hear that Dayana's mom was doing good and the friends continued to eat, sip on their mimosas, enjoy each other's company and catch up on lost time. Dayana also offered Thyri the chance to get a free tattoo, her way of apologizing for missing Thyri's appointment.

Thyri reluctantly agreed – her reluctance had stemmed from the fact that she didn't feel comfortable not paying her girl for her hard work. But she would let Dayana think she was giving her a free tattoo and slide a couple bands in her account once she'd completed the piece that Thyri already knew was going to be amazing.

An hour later, Thyri covered their lunch on behalf of Killian but since Dayana was still unaware of their relationship, Thyri chose not to bring up the fact that Killian had covered their lunch. She also texted Killian before leaving to not only tell him about their bill but tell him that she hadn't told Dayana about them yet. She didn't want him feeling some type of way when Dayana returned to House of Hayes and didn't thank him for covering her lunch. Thyri had a feeling he wasn't about to be happy about her still trying to keep them a secret but she just wanted to tell her girl in a more private setting. Her home for example. She would tell Dayana soon enough, she just hoped that Killian could be a little more patient with her.

The girls exited the restaurant and once outside in the parking lot, they kissed each other goodbye. Thyri then drove back to the office in her Lamborghini Urus.

Ding!

It's cool, baby. I understand you want to tell her in a private place. Just don't keep her in the dark too long. She's your best friend and deserves to know the truth about us.

Killian.

During her drive, Thyri's mounted phone had sounded off, alerting her of a new text. Reading Killian's words had her ten times more smitten than she already was for him. Why was he such a sweetheart? He understood her wishes and respected them while also giving her advice. He really was wifey material and though wifey material was something associated with women, Killian had those qualities that made him an ideal partner.

He better watch out before I end up putting a ring on his finger, Thyri mused, chuckling to herself at the thought of her proposing to Killian. The alpha in him would never let her do it and she knew it. But still it was fun to toy with the idea.

She arrived at the office ten minutes later, pleased to be reunited with her sisters and dived into all the tasks she'd needed to do. Home time arrived at five-thirty p.m. and even though Thyri liked to stay longer some evenings, she was more eager to get home so she could prepare dinner for Killian. She'd texted him her address earlier while working and told him to come any time after six p.m. Although dinner wouldn't be ready at that time, she wanted him watching her cook because she had a treat in store for him. She'd never cooked in lingerie before and tonight she planned to do exactly that.

It took her less than fifteen minutes to arrive at her apartment building located in midtown Atlanta. Ariana Grande's vocals melted into her eardrums, telling Thyri all about how she'd been waiting for that special someone who was now in her life.

She inserted her silver key into her door's lock and pushed the door, stepping into her vacant home. Her attention went to her living room that she quickly walked into, placing her Givenchy handbag to her teal couch followed by her encased MacBook and pink water bottle. She kicked off her heels once she'd placed her items down and made a beeline for the corridor leading to her bedroom.

Tems had made an appearance on her Apple Music shuffle, pouring her heart out about all the *Crazy Tings* happening in her life at the hands of a man.

"Crazy tings are happening," Thyri sang along.

She gently bobbed her head to the upbeat tune, pushing her door's silver handle.

"Crazy tings are ha—"

Thyri gasped and her posture went limp, as if all her bones had dissolved away leaving only her skin to make do with standing. She ripped out her right airpod, bringing her music to a stop.

"Ri."

On the edge of her bed sat the last person she expected to see tonight.

"You're back," he said, standing to his feet and a smile broke through his pink lips. "I missed you."

It was at this moment that Thyri realized that Tems singing in her ear all about crazy things happening had been nothing but facts.

Crazy things were happening.

Chapter Eighteen

"Chosen... what are you doing here?"

Every fiber of Thyri's being was on fire. It didn't matter how hard she tried to calm herself down, every part of her refused to cool down. Anger swelled in her guts, in her heart, in her head – *everywhere*. And she knew that the only way for her to get that anger to vanish was if the current elephant in her room left.

"Thyri, aren't you happy to see me?" he asked, his brows squishing together at the harsh tone that had poured from her lips. This wasn't the reaction he was hoping to receive from his girlfriend. "We haven't seen each other in over a week... I thought my girlfriend would be happier to see me."

She cringed internally at his use of the word 'girlfriend' and shook her head from side to side as she said, "Chosen, you lost the right to call me your girlfriend when you decided to break up with me via text."

Chosen folded his arms across his chest and raised his brows.

"I didn't break up with you, Thyri," he insisted. "I simply said that we need to take a brea—"

"That's the same damn thing, Chosen, and you know it," she cut him off. "I'm not your girlfriend anymore and you aren't allowed to be coming into my apartment without my permission. You need to leave."

"What?"

"You heard what I just said. You need to leave and please leave your copy of my key on the counter before you go."

A blank stare washed over his face and he remained silent, trying to figure out if this was a joke or something. But not a vestige of humor showed on her face, causing worry to flow through his veins.

The more Chosen stared at the girl who he believed to be his girlfriend, the more he realized that there was something different about her. She seemed... distant... yet assertive and dare he say, *rejuvenated*. Prior to her walking into her bedroom, he'd heard her singing along to one of her favorite R&B singers. She sounded happy. *Happier*. Much happier than he remembered seeing her last. Even the glow she donned on her face made him privy to that happiness.

What the hell has gotten into her?

He'd expected her to be cut up over him putting a sudden end to their situation and he'd felt joy over the weekend believing that she was emotionally scarred by what he'd done. He'd felt joy knowing that he would be paying her a random visit during the week to find her still heartbroken over him putting a pause on their relationship. He wanted her to feel pain, the same way he'd felt pain when she said that they weren't going to get married. The same way he'd felt pain when she'd made him feel like less of a man by refusing to agree to be a stay at home wife and mom.

But Thyri being cut up was far from the truth and the more

he looked at her glowing skin, the more he realized that she housed a tan.

A tan?

Chosen uncrossed his arms, stepping forward to get closer to Thyri. She remained unmoved, glaring at him as he made his way over to her.

There was only one way that she could've gotten that tan and you know damn well that it ain't from Atlanta's weak ass sun, nigga. The weather was shit this weekend. No sun whatso-fucking-ever.

Chosen arrived in front of her. His eyes narrowed as he scanned her face and it wasn't long 'til his own face hardened. It took him less than five seconds to connect the dots and the moment he did, he could hear the blood rushing through his head.

"Who is he?"

Thyri sucked her teeth, turning to leave her bedroom but failing miserably when her arm was pulled.

"Unless you want a reminder of what happens when you grab me without my permission, I suggest you let go of me and give me fifty feet."

Without having to be told twice, Chosen released her but chose to ignore her request of giving her space.

"Who the fuck is he?" he spat, glaring down at her.

"Move away from me, Chosen. *Now.*" She turned to reach for the door's handle but the second the door slightly opened, it was pushed shut, forcing Thyri to remain trapped in her bedroom. She faced him, raising her eyes to his face, and seeing the annoyance growing within him. "Chos—"

"Answer me," he ordered, pressing his body against hers which ultimately pressed her against the wooden door.

"Get the fuck off me!" she yelled, shoving his chest in the hopes of getting him off her.

Another huge fail because Chosen's frame was pure muscle, giving him the ultimate advantage over her. She was no match for him. He reached for her wrist, keeping it locked in his palm as his eyes bored into her soul.

"Tell me who the fuck has been dicking you down in another country, Thyri. Right. Now."

Chosen wasn't dumb. He was far from it. He knew this girl like the back of his hand and he knew how she acted whenever she had the best sex of her life. Sex that he used to give her on a regular. She would be singing nonstop with her head held high and her energy on high. You couldn't tell her shit and that's the vibe he got from her right now.

This glow is from new dick. It has to be. I ain't seen her glow like this since the start of our relationship... but what if you're tripping, man? What if she's just happy because she's happy. Nothing else. Why it gotta be about another nigga?

Chosen's jealousy would forever be his Achilles' heel because it had him spiraling in his thoughts. One part of him was certain that she had someone new in her life, blowing her back out in ways he didn't want to think about. Then the other part of him was kicking himself for being so dumb to think that his girl would choose another over him. She loved him. She would never let anyone else in after him. They were locked in for life, right?

"Ri." He let out a breath he hadn't even realized he was holding. "Just tell me the truth... please, baby. Is there someone else?"

What Thyri really wanted to say was, *'None of your business'*. However what she chose to say instead, because of the deadly look she'd seen flicker in his eyes just seconds ago, was, "No one."

"No one?"

"No one," she affirmed. "Yes, I went on a short vacation this weekend with my sisters but that was it. A girls only vacation."

It was a bold faced lie but Thyri didn't feel like she owed

Chosen the truth right now. She didn't want to bring Killian into the mess she was in with Chosen. Killian was currently the greatest thing in her life and she wasn't trying to mess that up by bringing him up because she knew that Chosen's jealous streak would have him cursing Killian the hell out. Her and Chosen weren't together and despite the time they'd shared together in their relationship, it changed nothing about her feelings towards him. She wasn't in love with Chosen and quite frankly, she wasn't sure she ever was.

Are you in love with him?

Killian's question from over a week ago floated in her mental, reminding her of the day she'd realized that she'd never actually been in love with Chosen. She had love for him, yes. But was she ever crazy in love with him? *No.*

"Tanai wanted us to take a quick trip out the city to Grenada so that's what we did."

Chosen released a sigh of relief, realizing that his suspicions had been incorrect. Her glow wasn't from new dick but from being abroad, away from the A. He freed her wrist and Thyri snatched her hand away from his reach.

"Thyri, I'm sor—"

"You still need to leave," she voiced, finding the strength to push him back as far as she could and turning to reach for her door, tearing it open as she spoke. "What I do with my life from here on out is none of your concern. I'm not your girl anymore."

And who I have dicking me down, is none of your concern either.

She stepped through the open doorway and walked into her corridor.

"Yes you are," she heard from behind her, making her roll her eyes.

*I don't care what he chooses to believe right now. I need him out. Killian's going to be here soon. I **can't** and **won't** have them meeting in my home.* She winced at the idea of the two men encountering one another in her apartment. *Hell no! Not happening.*

She rushed down the corridor, trying to get as quickly as possible to her front door. She could hear his footsteps hurrying along behind her and as much as she was glad that she had him moving out of her bedroom, she was irritated at the current predicament she was in.

"Just because we took a break, that don't mean shit, Thyri. That don't mean you don't belong to me because you do."

Oh my God!

Thyri groaned, freezing in her stance, and throwing her arms in the air.

"Chosen, I'm only going to tell you this one more time," she snapped once she'd turned to face him again.

Her eyes briefly fell to his feet and she cringed internally at the fact that he'd been wearing his sneakers in her bedroom. Her biggest pet peeve.

He was a short distance away from her in the corridor and her groan had caused him to stop walking towards her.

"We are no longer together. I didn't want to have to do this shit today but since you've decided to enter my home without my permission I guess I have no damn choice." She paused, huffing out a breath before continuing to talk. "Do you remember the bullshit you said to me in your text message?"

She arched a brow at him and before he could part his lips to talk, she was quick to answer her own query.

"No? Because I do. You said we should take a pause on us so that I can think about what you really want from me and figure out if I'm willing to be all I need to be for you. Not if you're willing to be all you need to be for me but only for me to think about how to please *you*. And that's the damn problem. That's always been the fucking problem with you! You don't think about anyone else but yourself. You only thought about how things were going to ever affect you in this relationship."

"I thought about you all the time, Thyri."

"Oh really?" She placed her hands on her hips and lifted her head up high. "When you took your business trips out of town every few weeks and only hit me up when you felt like it, were you thinking about me then?"

A guilt ridden look marred his face.

"Thyri..."

"When you opened your cigar bar and made me stay by your side the entire night, refusing to let me dance with my sisters and my friends, were you thinking about me then?"

"I... I just wanted you to myself that night."

"You mean you wanted me by your side so you could flaunt our relationship to your ex. The same ex you promised me wasn't coming?"

Chosen went silent.

"Yeah, that's what I thought." Thyri smiled, not finding a damn thing funny but still smiling out of the crazy she could feel twitching inside her. What she really wanted to do was go off on Chosen but she realized that it would all be a waste of time. What was going on between them right now, was a huge waste of time. He wasn't her man and she wasn't his woman. This was done. They were done.

"I'm glad you decided to break up with me, Chosen, bec—"

"I didn't break up with you, Thyri! Are you not listening to what the hell I'—"

"Because I definitely would've broken up with you by the time I came back from Grenada," she continued talking over him and once she'd said her final sentence, Chosen's jaw twitched, telling Thyri that she had definitely hit the mark.

"What the hell did you just say?"

"You heard me."

"Nah..." He released a cold chuckle, shaking his head from left to right. "I don't think I did because what I heard sounded pretty fucking stupid."

"It's not stupid at all, Chosen. It's the truth."

"You mean to tell me you were just going to throw away all the time we've spent together and the great memories, like I meant nothing to you?"

"No, I appreciate the good memories we have together but they're nothing compared to the bad ones. You and I both know that this relationship hasn't been the same for a while now. I was just holding on for the sake of holding on. You and I have been done for a hot minute."

"That's a lie and you know it, Thyri." His eyes squeezed into thin slits as he stepped forward. "I don't know what kind of crack you've been smoking these days but you need to stop acting like you and I are done, when we're not do—"

Ding Dong!

Thyri's heart thudded in her chest and she lifted her wrist, reading the gold face of her Gucci watch to see the time was six-fifteen p.m.

Fuck! Fuck! Fuck!

She needed to run, to scream, but her body had become petrified stone.

You've been standing here arguing with this man for so long that you've failed to get him out in time. You stupid, stupid, stupid girl!

Chosen immediately noticed the panicked expression that flittered across her pretty features. Even with them arguing, he couldn't help but notice her beauty. Those chocolate brown eyes still knew how to pull him in and those full lips he still longed to kiss despite all the crap that had come out of them about their relationship. Their relationship that still existed in his eyes.

"Who's at the door?" he asked, concern heavy in his tone.

Yeah they were having issues right now but that didn't change the care he would always have for her. Clearly something was wrong and he wanted to know what was wrong so he could somehow fix it. If he could just prove to her that he was the one for her then maybe she would drop this stupid rhetoric of their relationship being done.

Thyri was left speechless and her breath stalled.

Get yourself together, girl. You can handle this. You're a grown ass woman. Woman up.

"I'll be right back," she announced in a hushed tone.

She turned away from him, trotting along the corridor to get to her living room.

"Okay," he replied, choosing not to follow her. He needed to get back in her good graces and in order for that to happen he knew he needed to stay on her good side. "I'll be in your bedroom waiting for you, Ri."

Thyri released a breath after he said that but didn't turn around to respond. She just kept her focus on getting to her front door. When she arrived in front of the door, she took a deep breath, exhaled, and reached for the handle.

One look into those heavenly eyes of his and her mind turned into a buzzing mess of static. All the negative emotions that had built inside her, vanished and all that remained was the sweet feelings she had for him.

"Bubba."

A grin appeared on his lips, splitting his face in two. She returned that grin and allowed her eyes to cruise down his tall frame, taking in his outfit. He was clad in a cream sweater, black jeans, and black Balenciaga speed runners on his feet. A gold chain hung around his neck and locked in both ears was a diamond stud. He was looking like a snack that she wanted a big taste of.

"Killian... you're here."

He nodded, his eyes sweeping down her figure and seeing that she had on a beige belted jumpsuit. She looked formal yet sophisticated and sexy. From the look of things and the lack of smells coming from her home, he had a feeling that he had arrived too soon.

"I'm too early."

"No, no, no." She shook her head from side to side, stepping out her apartment to reach for his left tatted hand. "You're fine. I've been wanting to see you all day."

"So have I," he said, pulling her into him and circling his arms around her waist while her hands went to his sides. "You've been on my mind since I woke up."

Her heart swooned at his words and she stared up at him, letting her eyes fall on those soft lips of his. Those lips she'd missed. He leaned in to kiss her at the exact time she did and their lips meshed together in perfect harmony. His tongue met hers and the dance began. He kissed her with a passion that took her breath away and her memory too because she began to forget about the fact that her ex was waiting for her in her bedroom.

When she felt Killian gently push her back into her apartment, red flags started shooting in her mind and she broke their kiss, freezing in his arms.

"Kill... there's something I have to tell yo—"

"You little fucking liar."

An unknown voice made Killian's head lift and meet the dark eyes of a stranger. The stranger's hands were tightened into fists by his side and he skewered Killian with an unflinching look. Accepting the glaring anger that poured from the stranger's eyes, Killian kept Thyri tight against him.

"I was right the whole damn time!" he yelled, watching as

Thyri glared at him over her shoulder. "You've been fucking someone else behind my back like a little whore."

"Chos—"

"You better take back what you just called her."

"And who the hell are you mothafucking talking to, nigga?" Chosen barked.

"You," Killian calmly replied. "This is the final time I'm going to tell you. Take it back."

"Man, shut the fuck up! You over here kissing a woman that doesn't belong to you and now you think you can tal..." Chosen's words drifted off once he saw Killian release Thyri from his hold and rush past her to enter her apartment.

"Kill, no!" Thyri begged, clutching the back of his sweater, and keeping him from getting over to Chosen. "Please, don't."

Killian's head snapped in her direction and he reached for her soft hands, trying to peel them off him. Thyri refused to let go though. She could see the fire in his eyes. He meant business and he wasn't about to let Chosen get away with calling her a whore.

"Thyri. Get. Off. Me. Now."

"No."

Chosen stared at their interaction with vexation and shock. He was vexed that his suspicions had been correct and that Thyri had indeed been fucking with someone else. But he was shocked by their connection. They seemed... *close*. Like they knew each other much more than Chosen had known Thyri.

"Kill, please," she said, holding him as tight as she could. She knew that if he really wanted to, he could push her to the side with ease and reach Chosen as desired but she was praying for Chosen's sake that he didn't.

Chosen tittered at Killian's struggle to get to him and crossed his arms against his chest.

"Please, baby... he's not worth it." Her words had Chosen's

261

amusement disappearing from his body and all that remained was more rage than he'd felt when he'd first laid eyes on them kissing by her door.

"I'm not worth it? Bitch, you really got me fucked u..."

The minute Thyri felt her grip on Killian release, dread rushed through her. It all happened so fast. One minute Killian was next to her, then he was in front of Chosen. Thyri's eyes widened once Chosen lifted a fist in the air but that fist never landed because Chosen's collar was tugged and he was raised into the air.

"Killian!"

She rushed over to the men, seeing Chosen's body crashing against her kitchen counter and Killian's fist lifting in the air above Chosen's face.

It was at this exact moment that Chosen had registered who the hell this man was. He'd heard Thyri call him by the name 'Kill' but he hadn't connected the dots in his head as to who *Kill* actually was. But now that she'd called him by his actual name, Killian, it was enough to ring bells in Chosen's head.

Killian Miller's fucking my bitch?

"Don't do this! I'm begging you!"

Chosen's eyes bulged with fright as he stared up at Killian. The collar of his shirt was lifted, forcing his head up and making him have no choice but to look into the cold eyes above him.

Killian had his fist raised but he hadn't dropped it onto the one spot he desperately wanted to. All he could think about was Thyri pleading with him to not go through with hurting her ex. He couldn't take hearing him call her a whore but he'd tried his best to let it slide. The key word here was *tried*. Then he heard the word 'bitch' and that was all the confirmation he needed to do damage on Chosen's face.

Killian deeply inhaled, lowering his fist, and using his hand to grip Chosen's collar tighter. Now he had both hands on Chosen's shirt as he glared down at him.

"Listen closely to the shit I'm about to tell you because I promise you, if we have to have this conversation again, I won't be doing any talking," Killian announced. "This is the last time you will ever step foot in this house, the last time you'll call her out of her name and the last time you'll get to breathe the same air as her. She's not your concern anymore and who she's fucking, which is me, is definitely not your concern. Do not make you being in her presence and mine a habit because I put this on everything I love that it'll be the last habit you ever make."

Killian dragged him across the counter and pushed him in the direction closest to the door.

"Drop your copy of her key on the floor before you leave."

Chosen wasted no time in doing what Killian had ordered. Now that he knew who this man was, he knew that trying to fight him back wasn't a smart idea. Not only was Killian physically powerful by his physique but he was also powerful because of the weight and influence of his last name.

Miller.

Chosen reached into his jeans, pulling out the silver metal and dropping it to the floor. He turned to the door, shooting Thyri a venomous look and walking towards her front door. Thyri stepped out the way, making sure to be in the direction that Chosen wasn't coming in and watched him leave.

Once he'd stepped out her apartment, she rushed to her door and pulled it shut just as Chosen turned to face her. She met his unrelenting stare.

"This ain't over," he quickly mouthed and the door shut, blocking him out.

She sighed, turning around, and resting her back against the door. Her eyes drifted to Killian who stood near her kitchen counter. He held her gaze for a moment before looking away without a word.

"Killian, I'm so sorry. I had no idea he was..."

Killian heard her talk but he quickly tuned her out. It wasn't something he could help because whenever he got angry and someone tried to talk to him, it was pointless. He was boiling with so much fury and clenching his jaw so tight that it hurt. It all fucking hurt.

It hurt that he didn't beat Chosen to a pulp as he'd wanted to and it hurt that he'd heard his girl get disrespected twice.

I should've killed him. He should be dead right now.

Speaking on death wasn't something that phased Killian at all. He'd handed quite a few souls in this life their death sentences earlier than planned and he'd felt no ways about it. Anyone who disrespected or tried to harm his loved ones had felt his wrath. That was nothing new to him and those who truly knew him. But Thyri had no clue about his dark side and he didn't want her seeing that side. *Ever.*

His anger continued to burn through him and while he watched Thyri's lips move, he could no longer hear anything she was saying. All he could hear were his inner thoughts telling him that he needed to leave Thyri's apartment, find Chosen and kill him.

"That shouldn't have happ—"

"Take your clothes off."

Thyri blinked and a fluttery feeling formed in her stomach. "Huh?"

"Clothes off, Thyri," he ordered, lifting his sweater, and hiking it up his frame. Those hard muscles of his revealed themselves to her and her breath caught in her throat at the sight of his exposed upper body. "Now."

Like a good girl, she obeyed and started unfastening the belt of her jumpsuit. Then she pushed her jumpsuit down her body and it pooled at her feet. Leaving her in a purple bra and matching lace panties. She unhooked her bra, releasing her breasts and chucked the garment to the floor before pushing her panties down her thighs till they dropped to her ankles.

"Sofa."

His gaze on her was a mixture of desire and frustration. She sauntered over to her seating area and took a seat in the middle of the teal sofa. She looked over at Killian to see him walking over to her and removing his gold Hermes belt from his jeans. He dropped his belt to the floor, stopped walking to push his jeans down and removed them from his body, followed by his boxers.

Then he made his way over to her and got on one knee in front of her. His right leg remained bent, allowing his right foot to stand on the floor while he stayed kneeling on his left leg. She could see the frustration still heavy in his eyes and she knew that the only way for all that aggression and anger to leave him was if she gave him what he needed.

Her.

Killian grabbed her calves, sliding her down the couch and twisting her body so that she was lying on her side, facing the left side of the couch.

"Put your right knee on the floor and keep it against the sofa."

She obeyed, placing her right knee on the floor, and keeping it against the sofa. Killian then lifted her left knee, bent it, and kept it lifted as he shifted himself more closely to her middle.

Her upper body remained on the seat and her arms were bent, keeping her upright and stable. He lifted his hand up to his mouth, spitting on it a couple times before placing it down to his dick and rubbing on it. He placed her bent knee over his right hip and tightened his grasp on her calf at the same exact moment he pushed himself into her tight opening.

"Shit, Killian."

She gasped at his entry. Even with how much sex they'd had on vacation, she still wasn't used to his big size. He pushed as deep as possible, sliding out in a smooth motion before pumping right back in. Not missing a single beat.

In. Out. In. Out.

He didn't stop and his pace got quicker and harder with each passing second. And the position he had her in – the jack sex position – made her feel everything more intensely.

"Ahhhhh, Kill! Too... too deep," she moaned, throwing her head back as his thrusts got harder. "I... I feel you in my stomachhh, baby, uhhh—"

"Shut the fuck up."

His freehand reached for her neck, gripping tight as his eyes held her prisoner. His right hand remained on her right calf, keeping her thigh bent over his hip.

"You ain't let me beat that nigga up so guess what? I'm beating that pussy up," he retorted, working his dick deeper, faster and harder inside her. "I'm beating *my* pussy..." He pulled out only to slam back into her, causing her to whimper. He retreated only to do it again.

"All... the... way... up," he affirmed between each thrust.

Thyri could not only feel how wet she was, but she could also hear it because of the squishy sounds that filled the space.

This is crazy, Thyri mused, biting her lip hard, an attempt to release the pressure she felt building within her. *He's really fucking the shit out of me right now.*

She badly wanted to moan and could feel one forming at the base of her throat but he'd already told her to shut the fuck up and she wasn't trying to disobey him. Until he told her it was okay to make noise, then she would do so.

When she felt like she could no longer take the pressure, she lifted her hand, pressing it to his chest in an attempt to get him to slow down.

"Move your fucking hand."

"Killian!" she cried out, no longer able to keep her moans at bay. "Uhhhhh!"

"I ain't gon' tell you again, Thyri."

She moved her hand, her eyes shutting tight at the pleasure overwhelming her soul. She couldn't think properly, speak properly, or see properly. Inky black dots gathered along the edges of her sight, threatening to put out her vision.

He freed her neck, sliding his hand in the gap where her butt was and slipping his thumb into her hole. His finger moved in and out of her ass at the same speed his thickness moved in and out of her tightness.

"Mine," he growled, turning Thyri on in the worst way. "Mine... mine... mine."

This was not how Thyri expected her evening to go and she knew that another conversation about Chosen was enroute but for now, she would let Killian do his thing and let out all his frustrations.

As toxic as it was, using sex as a release for anger, Thyri needed this just as bad as he did. She needed him to beat her pussy up and she had no complaints about him using her as therapy. He could use her any day, any time, any place. She'd be ready and his for the taking.

～

"Take it off."

"Kason!" She laughed. "I need to go downst—"

"Take it offffff," he drawled in a needy tone.

"Sonny, no," she affirmed, gently pushing on his chest. Her

fake way of getting him to leave her alone. "I need to go down-stairs. Your mom will be here any second."

"She can wait."

Kason's hands went to Tanai's waist, tugging at the band of her velour joggers. But Tanai gripped his hands, stopping him from pulling her pants down. His head shot up and he gave her an unimpressed look.

"Tanai."

"Kason."

She giggled, leaning in to peck his lips before lifting his hands from her body. Once she was free, she let go of his hands and moved towards their bathroom's exit.

The second she tried to leave him, Kason's hands latched onto her waist, pulling her back in place in front of him.

"Kasonnnnn! Honey, please! I gotta go."

"Where you going, huh?" He smirked, pressing his lips to the side of her neck. "You and I have unfinished business, Mrs. Miller."

Tanai giggled, loving his use of her marital name.

"Is that right?" she asked, no longer able to act like she didn't want him.

"We... definitely... do," he whispered between his kisses, working his way up her throat, onto her face and sealing his lips to hers.

He gave her an affectionate smooch before pulling away to set his eyes on her.

"So you're just gonna have to be late to meet my moth—"

"Sonny, no." Tanai shook her head from side to side. "This is the first time we're spending time with one another. I don't wanna make a bad impression."

"And you won't," he replied with a smirk. "She'll understand once you tell her that you and your hubby had a very important meeting that couldn't wait."

"A meeting?" Her right brow shot up. "Where, Sonny?"

"In our bedroom," he explained, letting a hand slide down her backside, and spanking her right cheek.

"Kason!"

He chuckled, rubbing on the spot he'd just hit.

"You are so silly." She playfully nudged him, throwing him a side eye.

"Ain't that why you love me, baby?"

The corners of her mouth turned up at his familiar question. The question they regularly asked whenever they were teasing each other. She slowly nodded, watching him lift her hand and place it to his lips.

How did I get so lucky? Tanai asked herself as he kissed her hand. She was unable to peel her gaze from her husband and she stared deep into his mahogany eyes, finding herself getting lost in his essence.

He's everything I've ever wanted and more. Caring, funny... nasty and all mine. I just love him so damn much. I love his voice, his face, his personality, his mind... everything. I finally understand the shit India Arie was talking about in her song, he is 'The Truth'. My truth and I am a reflection of him. I love hi—

"Nai."

Tanai blinked a couple times, focusing in on Kason's lips, realizing that he'd been talking.

"Sorry, babe... I zoned out."

Kason didn't say anything and simply looked at her, slightly tilting his head to the side as he inspected her.

"What?"

Tanai noticed a little cocky smirk appear on his face.

"Look at you... thinking about me and shit. Oh you definitely want some dick."

He reached for her waist, spinning her around and making her face the LED mirror hanging on the cream wall in front of them.

"You want some dick don't you, Tanai Kristen Miller?"

Tanai sighed, staring at their reflections in the mirror and biting her bottom lip when his hand squeezed her right boob.

"I do," she admitted in an aroused tone. "But later, Sonny. I promise I'm all yours."

"You ain't gotta promise me shit that's already true," he told her, pinching her nipple. "You're already all mine."

"You right." She nodded, grinning at him.

Kason let his other hand join in on the fun and was now stroking her breasts with each palm.

"What were you saying, baby... when I zoned out?"

"I asked you how work was with your sisters," he replied, pressing a kiss to her nape while his hands massaged her ample cleavage.

"It was good... I told them all my ideas including the one about your company becoming one of our clients."

Ever since Kason had found out about Tanai owning a cleaning company with her sisters, the wheels had been turning in his head. He loved the fact that his wife was making paper but he wanted her making a hell of a lot more and any way he could assist in that process he was here for. He'd given Tanai the idea of her and her sisters' company, The Wright Way, being the new cleaner of the headquarters for Kason's tech company, Shield. Not only did he want her company being the only one taking care of his building, but he also wanted their new hand sanitizer product made available as dispensers throughout his building.

Furthermore, the homes and offices across the country and the world that Shield protected, Kason wanted The Wright Way's cleaning products given to them alongside the Shield security system that they owned. It would be a great way of marketing The Wright Way's new products and getting their name across the shores. He also planned to have The Wright Way take care of the gym he owned with his brothers, KMG and have them contracted to take on the clients of the various buildings Miller Industries owned across the city so that they would be the ones in charge of the buildings' hygiene. It was a multi-million dollar contract that Kason was flying their way and he was more than happy to fit the bill to ensure that his wife's company became bigger and better than it already was.

"Good. They like it?"

"They loved it," she said, making Kason smile at her through the mirror.

"Just like I knew they would. Y'all are amazing at what y'all do – it's only right my company works with yours. This is only the beginning, bae and I can't wait for the three of y'all to be at the gala this year. You'll be able to meet Shield's board mem—"

Ding Dong!

Both Kason and Tanai's eyes widened at the sound of the doorbell. Tanai rushed towards the door, thinking she was free to go until her arm was pulled.

"Kason, your mother's here! No more playing."

"Uh-uh, where's my kiss before you go?" he asked, pulling her back in front of him.

This time she faced him. She gave him a quick closed mouth kiss then made a dash for the door.

"That wasn't a real kiss, Tanai!" His yell made her chuckle as she ran through their bedroom. "But don't worry, I'ma hold you to that. Just wait 'til I have you all to myself tonight."

Tanai slipped her feet into her LV fur mules before running

out her bedroom's door, sprinting across the hallway leading to the stairs.

When she heard familiar voices greeting one another, she went to the balcony that overlooked the front foyer and looked over it to see Kason's mother being assisted with taking off her coat by Camila, Kason and Tanai's head maid. Tanai made a beeline for the steps and once at the top of them, she took a deep breath before walking downstairs.

"Tanai, there you are, my dear."

Temilola had noticed Tanai coming downstairs and a warm smile graced her lips as she watched her daughter-in-law. The tension that was starting to form in Tanai's chest instantly dissipated.

"Hello, Mom."

Tanai arrived on the final step and her heart warmed at the sight of Kason's mother opening her arms. She sauntered into her arms and sighed happily once they embraced. A sweet vanilla scent filled Tanai's nostrils as they hugged, making her feel right at home.

Damn, she smells so good, Tanai mused.

"Thank you," Tanai mouthed to Camila who had just finished hanging up Temiola's coat on the nearby rack.

Camila smiled and nodded before leaving the pair alone.

"How are you?" Temilola asked while they remained hugging. "I hope that son of mine hasn't been bothering you too much."

"I heard that, Momma."

Tanai smiled at the sound of her husband's voice. Their hug ended, allowing Tanai to turn around and see Kason standing on the balcony overlooking the foyer.

"You were supposed to, son," Temilola commented. "Is that any way to greet your mother?"

"Coming, Mom," Kason obediently answered, moving away from the balcony to head downstairs.

He arrived within seconds, greeting his mom with a loving hug and kiss.

This evening, Temilola had come over to Kason and Tanai's home to spend time with her daughter-in-law. She not only wanted to make up for her behavior at their reception but she wanted to get to know Tanai better and teach her one of Kason's favorite meals.

Pounded yam and egusi soup.

Temilola Miler was half Nigerian thanks to her mother and half African American thanks to her father. And it was because of Temilola that Kason was a quarter Nigerian and had grown up embracing the Yoruba culture that had his mother was from. Tonight, Tanai was getting a taste of that culture and she was excited to learn more about her husband's heritage.

After greeting his mother, Kason decided to leave his two favorite girls alone. They needed some privacy and time to talk without him being all up in their business. And Kason wasn't one to stay in women's business. He knew his wifey could handle her own and was rest assured that his mom would be on her best behavior tonight.

Once he'd left, Temilola linked arms with Tanai and the ladies headed through the house to the kitchen.

"Camila tells me that you personally went out to buy all the ingredients for Kason's meal."

"Yes." Tanai nodded. "I just wanted everything to be perfect."

"Well that's sweet of you to be so attentive, dear."

They arrived in the kitchen and just as Tanai had requested, not a single one of her kitchen staff were in sight. She'd told them to take the evening off because she didn't want anyone interrupting her time with Temilola.

"Let me just start off by apologizing once ag—"

"Oh no, you don't need to," Tanai insisted.

"I do," Temilola confirmed with a firm head nod. "I had no right treating you the way I did at your reception and I'm sorry. I was just hurt that Kason eloped. I wanted him to have a traditional wedding and a normal white wedding of course. And since I was robbed of that I took it out on you."

"I'm so sorry for us eloping. If I'd known th—"

"If you'd known it wouldn't have changed anything. I know my son and I know stubborn he is."

Tanai cracked a small smile and nodded.

"He sure is."

"What's done is done. At least I'll have Killian and Kadiri's weddings to plan. Let's just move on and focus on the future including when you're going to make an old lady like me a grandma."

"Ummm..." Tanai nervously chuckled. "Not anytime soon."

"Oh come on." Temilola gasped, shifting closer to Tanai, and reaching for her stomach to caress it. "Young, pretty girl like you. This is the perfect age to carry one."

"I mean sure we'll have children but right now we're just enjoying marriage."

"Enjoying marriage indeed." Temilola smirked, releasing Tanai's stomach. "I see that glow, young lady. I'm surprised you have so much energy today and are walking straight."

Tanai's cheeks burned hot scarlet and embarrassment settled on her face.

"Mom," she shyly called Temilola.

"What? I know all about sex, my dear. How do you think I had three sons?" She laughed, squeezing Tanai's cheeks before deciding to change the subject. "Alright, alright, let's get started on cooking."

Tanai enthusiastically nodded.

"I wanna hear all about your vacation, my darling. How was it? Memphis and I have been meaning to take a trip to Calivigny but just haven't found the time yet. Tell me everything."

Tanai was very glad that things between her and Kason's mother had changed for the better. It was great to be able to talk to her without feeling like there was bad blood between them. For the next two hours, Temilola taught Tanai how to make pounded yam and egusi. Like a good student Tanai paid close attention, listened carefully and asked questions whenever appropriate.

During the process, Tanai felt the urge to get on insta stories and document the process of learning how to cook one of her husband's favorite dishes. She hadn't been on Instagram in a few days because honestly... the app was becoming a bit stressful for her.

Ever since Instagram blogs had posted intimate photos from her wedding reception, a cascade of random accounts had come over to her page, leaving all types of hate comments under her posts. She had to limit her comments to only those she followed and lock her page because of how chaotic it got.

The worst part wasn't even the comments, it was the DM requests she received telling her to:

- *Go somewhere and die, whore*
- *Stay away from Kason's fine ass*
- *Stop pretending to love him when everyone knows you're only with him for his money*
- *Choke in your grave, you gold digging bitch*

Yeah... it was bad. And the funny thing was, Tanai hadn't told a soul about it. Not her sisters or her husband. She didn't want to burden them about something she was sure she could handle herself. They hadn't noticed the hate comments under her Instagram posts because she'd had Camila delete them all and limit her comments to people she followed, the day after her wedding reception, the same day that photos of their intimate reception had leaked to the blogs.

Though it was a shock to receive the hate comments, they didn't mean anything to her because Tanai knew that they were only jealous of what she had. They were only jealous of the fact that she'd become Kason's wife and there was nothing they could do to change that. She was his wife and they were going to spend the rest of their lives together.

Forever.

Chapter Nineteen

"Y̲ou okay, Nugget? He's not hurting you too much is he?"

"Sonny..." she simpered. "I'm fine, honey. This ain't my first rodeo you know."

"I know, I know but I just don't want you in too much pain."

"I'm fine. My brother-in-law is doing a great job."

A smile flickered on Killian's lips at her words.

"Besides he's not the one hurting me... the needle is. He's simply doing his job."

"Good because he knows I'll fuck him up if he fucks this up."

Killian's brows furrowed and he tore his eyes away from Tanai's wrist to look over at his younger brother who sat on the stool next to her seat.

Killian shot an amused look his way as if to say, *You know damn well you can't do shit to me*, before turning his focus back on Tanai.

"We're almost done, Nai. Hang in there just a little longer."

She nodded at him and her existing smile strengthened. Killian applied pressure on her skin with the needle he held and continued tattooing her.

Today Kason and Tanai had come to House of Hayes to get matching tattoos. When Kason had first told Killian about their plans to get tattoos together, Killian was all for it and already knew that Kason wanted him being the only person doing them.

Despite being the owner of one of the best tattoo shops in the city, Killian didn't do tattoos as much as he used to. He'd been in this game for over thirteen years and when he first started, he'd been hungry as ever, doing anyone who wanted a tattoo from him. Then as the years passed, Killian became more focused on creating a squad that he could trust and nurture to be as good as him - even better than him if they were willing to work hard. Mentoring his artists was inevitable and he wasn't complaining about becoming one because he enjoyed taking artists under his wing to show them the ropes.

He'd become selective with who he tattooed because he honestly didn't have as much time on his hands as CEO of House of Hayes. Those he tattooed nowadays were either celebrities, close friends, or family. And if you weren't any of those and you still wanted a tattoo by him, you were put on a waiting list and would have to be patient until he could fit you in. Atlanta's A-list celebrities automatically wanted his hands on them because of his reputation and talent. That was nothing new and even his waiting list currently had over one hundred names, patiently waiting for his availability to free up. The city recognized Killian as one of the best tattoo artists and passing up a chance to have him ink you up was a no go.

About twenty minutes later, Killian applied the final coat of Vaseline across Tanai's skin before wiping it away.

"Oh my God... Killian, this is amazing."

Amazing it was.

The matching tattoos that Kason and Tanai had decided to get were matching puzzle pieces. She had one piece of a puzzle and he had another - each piece fit one another. On Kason's puzzle piece there was a heart lock whereas Tanai's piece contained a heart key that had an end the same shape as Kason's lock. The tattoos were on their right wrists and Kason brought his right wrist next to hers, allowing the puzzle pieces to be next to one another. Despite being separate puzzles on each of their skin, their pieces aligned, appearing connected because of the way Killian had designed them.

It was such a romantic tattoo and Tanai was in awe at how realistic her and Kason's puzzles looked. Killian's talent was undeniable and Tanai was grateful that her skin had been graced with his undeniable skills.

"Thank you so much," she said, lifting her wrist and inspecting her tattoo closely.

"Appreciate you, bro," Kason informed Killian. "You killed this shit as you always do."

Killian grinned, giving them a nod of thanks and observing as Kason reached for Tanai's chin, pulling her into him so he could kiss her. Just the sight of them being affectionate made Killian think about one person and one person only.

I miss her.

A week had passed since he'd seen her last. A week had passed since the day her stupid ex had shown up at her apartment. Killian's thoughts went to that night, when he'd had her in a karma sutra position and fucked her senseless on her couch. After that, she'd been too tired and despite her trying to convince him that she could still cook them dinner, Killian told her not to bother. He ordered them some Thai takeout which they ate over a Netflix show. They barely spoke and when they were done with dinner, Killian led Thyri into her bedroom so she could get some sleep. He'd noticed her yawning and her lids slightly closing while eating which is why he knew putting her to bed would be the best thing. She made sure that Killian got in bed with her and he wrapped his arms around her as she lay her head on his chest. Seconds after her head hit his chest, she was out like a light and he began to watch her sleep, admiring everything about her but hating what had happened earlier.

During the week they'd texted from time to time, checking in on one another but that was really it. No one had brought up what had happened last week so the air was still awkward between them.

After taking pictures of Kason and Tanai's tattoos then wrapping them, the lovebirds thanked him again, collected their tattoo aftercare kits, and said their goodbyes to Killian before leaving his shop.

Killian sanitized his studio by wiping down his worktable, the chairs, cleaning his tattoo machine and all the equipment he'd used. Once he was done, he made his way to his office upstairs, not surprised to see that the main shop hallway was vacant and the doors of the various studios were all shut. All his artists were fully booked today and hard at work which were the two of the many things he loved.

He arrived on the second floor and stepped towards his office door with purpose. When he stood in front of it, his hand reached for the door's handle and he pushed the door open, looking into the space. A tightness formed in his gut at the woman sitting opposite his desk. She had her back to him but upon hearing the door open, her head turned and her eyes shifted nervously to his face.

"Hey, boss."

He remained silent, stepping deeper into his office, and letting the door shut behind him as he made his way towards his desk. He approached his seat, pulling the leather chair out from under his desk and sitting down. He turned to face her, resting his right hand on his thigh while allowing the other hand to rest on top of his desk.

Soraya's empty feeling in the pit of her stomach worsened at his tense stare. The silence between them was deafening but neither party spoke up to end it. Killian continued to just shoot daggers her way as memories of what she'd done in Grenada came into his mental.

"Killian, I'm so sorry about what I did in Grenada. I never should have..."

No longer having the bravado to remain quiet, Soraya decided to speak up and although Killian could see her lips moving and hear words coming out her mouth, he wasn't actually listening to a single word she was telling him.

Now that he was finally laying eyes on her, Killian was reminded of all the negative feelings he'd felt towards her in Grenada. She'd been jealous, rightfully so but the calling his girl out her name was something that he couldn't let slide. He didn't know what it was but every time he'd heard someone disrespect Thyri, he got a twitchy feeling in his jaw and his hands, telling him that he needed to take action. Luckily for Soraya, she was a woman and Killian would never lay a finger on her.

"I'm willing to do whateve—"

"You finally remembered that you have a job, huh?"

Soraya rapidly blinked, suddenly thrown off track by Killian cutting her off.

"I never forgot," she replied in a timid tone. "I had Cleo tell you that I needed a few days off. She said she told you."

"Oh she told me," he confirmed, lightly tapping his fingers against his glass desk.

"Okay." She shifted in her seat. "Well like I was saying

before, I'm willing to do whatever it takes to make things right between us. At the end of the day we still need to work together and I don't want my drunk mistake ending our business relationship."

"You should have thought about that before you called my girlfriend a bitch," he retorted.

"And I'm really sorry that I did," she apologized once again, eyeing him closely and reading the darkness crossing his eyes. "Please, Killian... you can't seriously be considering firing me over one mistake?"

"I most definitely am." His nods were stiff as his fingers continued to drum the table.

"So you're going to fire me because I rightfully reacted to a situation that you placed me in?" She crossed her arms against her full chest. "I never asked to go to Grenada, you invited me."

She made a very good point. Her coming to Grenada had all been part of Killian's plan, not hers.

"I know I put you in an awkward position but believe me, I never knew Thyri was gonna be on that trip. If I'd known, you and I wouldn't have gotten on the damn plane together."

She shot him a hurt look and Killian quickly realized that he'd been unnecessarily rude. He couldn't help it though. Soraya had angered him with the way she'd behaved towards Thyri. Could you blame him for not wanting to be friendly to her?

Silence formed between them once again and as their eyes remained stuck on another one, Killian was left lost with his thoughts.

She's a good manager but let me not act like she's not replaceable because she is... but ain't no one gonna be able to run my shit as good as her. Shit, man, I really don't know what to do. On one hand I want to get rid of her ass because of that disrespectful, sick shit she pulled in Grenada but on the other hand she's good as fuck at her job

REAL LOVE FROM A REAL ONE

and I don't really wanna lose her as a manager... what the hell should I do?

Killian was torn and he hated it. The more he stared at Soraya, the more his conflicted state grew.

Ding!

Killian's eyes went to the sound that had come from his phone and he gazed down at the newest text.

Bubba: *I hate the fact that I haven't seen you in so long, Kill.*

Ding!

Bubba: *Please come over tonight so we can talk?*

Warmth radiated throughout Killian's body and he leaned forward, reaching for his phone, and unlocking it to enter his device.

Soraya watched as he tapped on his screen for a few seconds before placing his phone to his ear and allowing their eyes to meet once again. There was a glow in his brown pools as he waited for the line to pick up and Soraya was curious to know who he was calling. When he spoke the word, "Bubba" into the phone, her curiosity vanished and all that remained was envy.

"I'm good... yeah, I saw your text... of course, I'll be with you tonight... I've got a quick favor to ask, baby... I'm with Soraya and she's got something to tell you. That okay?"

Soraya's heart raced and she uncrossed her arms, sitting up straight in her seat.

"Alright, I'ma put you on speaker," he told her before lifting the phone from his ear to do exactly what he'd said.

After tapping on his screen and placing it down to the desk, his joy filled eyes went to Soraya's and the joy faded from his eyes as he nodded at her to speak. Soraya let out a breath and leaned forward to do what he wanted.

"Hey, Thyri..."

"Hi."

Her voice was as soft as a feather yet her nonchalant tone was unmissable.

"I want to apologize for what I called you in Grenada. It was wrong and I never should've called you out of your name. I hope you can find it in your heart to forgive me."

The line went quiet and Soraya's eyes aimlessly darted around the room as she avoided Killian's frosty gaze.

"Thank you for your apology," Thyri spoke up seconds later in a more pleasant tone. "Apology accepted. I apologize on behalf of Killian for putting you in that situation... We didn't plan for things to pan out the way they did and I'm sorry that you were placed in the middle of our situation."

Both Soraya and Killian were surprised at Thyri's apology. He hadn't expected her to ever say sorry to Soraya, especially not after how annoyed she'd gotten with Soraya that night in Grenada. But it was evident that Thyri had gotten past the situation and Killian greatly respected her growth.

"No worries," Soraya replied.

"Thyri, are you good with Soraya remaining my manager?"

"Definitely," Thyri agreed.

Soraya released a sigh of relief, resting against her seat and looking at Killian to see the smile flickering on his lips as he took his phone off speaker. He raised his phone back to his ear and turned in his seat to face the white wall behind him.

"Look at you... apologizing on my behalf. Why you gotta be so cute for, huh?" He chuckled. "Yes, baby. I'll be there. It's been a busy couple days since we've seen each other but I promise I haven't forgotten about your pretty ass... I miss you more. You sure you don't wanna come over to mine tonight?"

Hearing him get comfortable on the phone gave Soraya the incentive to get up from her seat and leave his office. She turned around and made her way towards the exit but the call of her name stopped her in her tracks.

"Hold on, Bubba... Soraya?"

She looked over her shoulder and met his gaze.

"Appreciate you apologizing to my girl," he stated. "And I apologize for putting you in the middle of me and her. We cool?"

"We're cool," she said with a smile that didn't quite reach her eyes but since Killian was a distance away from her, he couldn't properly notice her artificial smile.

"Cool," he concluded before turning in his seat and continuing his call with Thyri.

Soraya gave the back of his head one last look, her throat tightening at the sound of his exhilarated tone as he spoke on the phone to another woman that wasn't her. She left his office and didn't look back.

"So what do you fancy for dinner tonight, baby girl?" Truth's eyes drifted to the front view mirror, allowing her to stare into those adorable peepers belonging to her heart in the physical form.

"Umm... Mackie Dees!"

"Lana, baby, you had McDonald's last Friday..." Truth eyes went on the road ahead and she indicated left before taking the turn. "What about your favorite... Spaghetti Bolognese?"

"Mackie Dees! Mackie Dees! Mackie Dees!" Alana yelled, throwing her hands in air, and waving them like she just didn't care.

"Lana, no, you need to eat something better than that junk. Having McDonald's is okay once in a while but not all the time."

"Mackie Dees! Mackie Dees! Mackie Dees!"

"You can shout as loud as you like, my love, but you're not getting McDonald's tonight. Choose something else."

"But mommy, I want Mackie Dees," she said. "Plwease."

"And I want a million dollars in my account," Truth countered. "But we don't always get the things we want right away."

"Plwease."

Truth's eyes met Alana's small, brown ones in the front view mirror and her heart began to melt at the sight of her three year old staring innocently at her.

"Uh-uh, that puppy dog look ain't gon' work on me tonight, baby girl. No *Mackie Dees*," Truth told her with a firm 'no' head shake. "Sorry."

Alana huffed and shifted in her car seat so that her body was facing out the window rather than towards her mother. Truth noticed her change in position and couldn't help but smirk at the sight of Alana sulking. It was something that Alana rarely did so when she did do it, it was funny to see.

About fifteen minutes later, Truth drove her G-Wagon into the parking lot of her apartment building. She parked her car in the first available spot she noticed, reached for her handbag, hoisting it over her shoulder before getting out the car. She opened up the back passenger door to be greeted to Alana's cute face that still donned a sulky look.

"There's my baby pooh," Truth lifted her hands to her soft cheeks, stroking them gently. *"My baby pooh, my baby pooh, my baby pooh."*

The second her singing mother started tickling her face and armpits, Alana started wiggling in her seat and laughter burst out from her.

"You still mad at Momma, Baby Pooh?" she continued to sing and tickle Alana, making her giggles increase. *"Baby Pooh, Baby Pooh, Baby Pooooh."*

Alana's pleasant laughter filled the parking lot and once satisfied that Alana's mood was no longer in a funk, she unclipped the straps of Alana's car seat and released her.

"Okay, come to Momma." Alana's hands lifted and Truth cupped her armpits, pulling her up into her arms. Alana rested her head on her mother's shoulder and sighed softly, feeling at ease in her mother's arms.

Truth locked the car and led the way to the parking lot's exit so she could get the both of them inside their apartment building. Within minutes, they were on the elevator, waiting for it to arrive on their floor. The elevator dinged and the silver doors slid out their way, allowing Truth to step onto her floor and walk towards their door. Her eyes fell to Alana to see her sucking on her thumb.

"Have you decided what you want to eat, Lana?"

She shook her head 'no' and Truth smirked, knowing fully well that Alana knew what she wanted. She just couldn't have that particular thing tonight.

"Okay." Truth looked ahead down the corridor to see that they were getting closer to their door. "Do you want mommy to choose fo..."

Truth found her words trailing off when she noticed a tall figure standing slightly further down the corridor, by their door. Her steps became slower and she held onto Alana's small frame tighter.

Wait... there's no way that's—

"Kad!" Alana screamed, excitement evident in her tone as she turned to face the figure that stood a short distance away.

"What's up, Lani?" His deep voice echoed across the walkway. "You miss me as much as I've missed you?"

Truth remained frozen with a dazed expression plastered on her face as she watched Kadiri saunter over to them.

What the hell is he doing here?

287

She was in too much shock to take real notice of Alana wriggling in her arms, trying to get free. But the moment she felt Alana poke her chest with her elbow, tightness formed in her face and her heart.

"Alana, calm yourself," she ordered, reluctantly bending low to let Alana jump free from her arms.

She observed as Alana ran into Kadiri's arms that were outstretched for her. He'd crouched down low so the cutie could hug him.

"There's my favorite girl," he announced, pressing a kiss to her forehead, and rubbing on her back as they hugged. "You okay? How was school today?"

Truth continued to watch their interaction and it was only now that she was noticing what Kadiri held under his arm.

A brown paper bag that donned a yellow 'M' logo.

No he didn't.

A frown quickly formed on Truth's mouth.

"What's up, Baby Mama?" Kadiri finally addressed her while Alana still had her arms wrapped around his tatted neck. Truth was too pissed about the McDonald's bag he held to notice the name he'd called her. "I came to say hello to Lani and surprise her with her favorite food of course."

Alana leaned back and looked under his arm to see what he was holding. He pulled it out for her to grab hold of and she opened the paper bag, her eyes lighting up once she caught a glimpse of the happy meal box.

"Mackie Dees! Mackie Dees! Mackie Dees!"

How the hell did he even find out where we live? Truth mused, unmoved by the way Alana was going crazy about Kadiri bringing her favorite meal.

"Shware with me?" Alana asked him and his heart melted at her question.

"Course I'll share with you, Lani. Thanks for thinking of a nigg—"

Truth cleared her throat, gaining both their attention as they turned to look at her.

"Thanks for the unwarranted visit but she's not allowed McDonald's tonight," Truth voiced in a strict tone.

Alana's eyes bulged.

"But Momma! He bought for me," she said in her cute, tiny voice that almost made Truth crack but she remained strong on her stance.

"No, Alana. You had it last Friday." Truth shook her head from side to side, causing Alana's heart to break. "You're not having it again. We've already discussed this, Alana, so just forget about having... Alana." But she stopped shaking her head and a sigh escaped out of her once she noticed the watering of Alana's eyes. "Alana, don't."

The first tear dropped out her lid and Truth's heart broke at the sight of her daughter tearing up.

"Uh-uh, Lani," Kadiri called out to her, reaching for her shoulder. "Since when do you do that cry baby shit? You're a big girl, Lani. You don't need to cry."

She fell into Kadiri's arms once again and her head fell on his chest. Her chest started heaving up and down as her sobs came out louder and faster.

"Lani, baby, stop," he cooed to her gently and rubbed on her back.

Truth's sorrow shredded her insides as Alana cried.

Oh my God, this little girl really has me wrapped around her little finger!

"Alright, alright!" Truth rushed over to Alana. "You can have McDonald's tonight, Baby Pooh."

Alana turned to face her mother and her watery eyes looked up to see her mother's guilty face.

"But no more for the rest of this month, Alana. I mean it."

Alana's mouth curved into a small smile and she nodded in agreement with her mother's words.

Truth carefully looked down at Alana and was left in awe as Kadiri lifted a hand to her little face, wiping away her tears that had formed and telling her not to cry because she was too pretty to cry. The more Truth watched the way he was treating Alana, like she was his own, the more Truth came to the realization that Kadiri was now a permanent fixture in Alana's life and that there was nothing she could do to tear them apart. He was now a part of their lives for good.

Chapter Twenty

Her eyes locked on his and her body came to attention at the way he was studying her. Like she was the only subject he needed to be educated on. Like she was the only view he needed to lay eyes on for the rest of his days on this earth. His piercing eyes were liquid pools of desire, swearing to memorize every part of her.

My God... that dress on her... perfection.

She wore a red off the shoulder gown that stuck to her curvaceous figure like a second layer of skin. It had a floral lace design on the dress' top half that trickled into the skirt and her mermaid train graced the limo's floor. She had on a silver diamond necklace with the initial 'K' in the center of it, a necklace he'd gifted her with last week, matching diamond earrings locked in each ear and an iced out silver Audemars Piguet strapped to her left wrist that matched the one he currently wore on his wrist. She was looking too good for her own kind and the more her husband watched her, the more the part of him that made him male expanded.

A smile danced on her lips as she reached over to her left for the champagne flute waiting for her. Just as she placed the chilled glass to her lips, she felt his large hand grip her thigh and she turned to face him, taking a quick sip from her champagne.

"God was truly showing off when he made you."

Her heart swooned at his statement.

"You're making me wanna tell Saber to turn this damn car around..." His eyes sparkled with lust and he looked over at the partition that separated them from their driver. "Fuck it, we're going home, Nugget. I need yo—"

"Sonny, no." Tanai laughed, quickly placing her glass back into its holder before she reached for Kason's hand that had pressed on the intercom above his armrest.

When her hand came crashing on top of his, he grabbed it, keeping it at bay from turning the intercom off.

"Kason, don't you dare!"

"Saber."

"Yes, boss?"

"Turn the car around."

"...Umm... sir, are you sure? We're almost there."

"Saber, ignore him," Tanai told their driver, unable to contain her giggles.

"Turn the car around, Saber."

"Saber don't listen to him! He's crazy, trust me."

"Umm... ma'am, are you su—"

"Saber, you know damn well I'm not crazy but I'll definitely show you crazy if you don't turn this car around right now."

"Okay, sir. I wil—"

"Saber, please, ignore him!" Tanai's laughter continued. "Please keep driving."

"Saber, I need to get my wife home right this second. She's looking too sexy tonight and I need her back home with me so I can have my way with her. Fuck the gala. I need my puss—"

Kason's words became muffled and an amused expression formed on his face as he realized what Tanai had done.

"Saber, thank you for the great driving. Keep it up," Tanai said.

"Yes ma'am." Saber's amusement was laced in his baritone. "I'll let you know when we've arrived."

"Thank you," she concluded before pressing the intercom's button to turn off their microphone.

Her eyes went to her husband who had his mouth covered by her hand.

"You ready to stop playing?" she asked him with a soft giggle.

He nodded, shooting her an innocent look. She then decided to release his mouth only to suddenly giggle when he launched himself at her, circling his arms around her body and burying his face into her neck to bite her.

"Kason," she cried out.

"You must really want your husband to go to jail tonight, huh?" he whispered between his bites and sucks on her flesh.

"Jail, Sonny? For what?"

"For murdering any nigga who tries to take you away for me."

Loud laughter erupted out of her again.

"Oh, Sonny... everyone in Georgia knows I belong to you."

"They better."

He lifted himself from her neck to gaze into her deep set eyes. His hand landed on her cheek, caressing her soft skin, and loving everything about what he had in front of him. The woman he had by his side was the best partner, confidant, and soulmate he could've ever asked for. She was everything. *His everything.* And he knew that as long as God kept his heart beating and his lungs filled with air, he would forever be by her side. He would forever be hers.

"Tanai?"

"Yes, honey?"

"I love you."

Tanai's knees weakened and her white teeth flashed in a smile.

"I love you more, Kason."

"Impossible," he disagreed, shaking his head from left to right.

She shot him a silly grin.

"I'm nothing without you, Nai. Nothing. You are my world... my everything. I just want to make you happy twenty-four-seven."

"Awww, Kason, baby." She lifted a hand to the side of his face, stroking his beard.

"I'm serious," he said, placing his hand on top of hers to rub on her skin. "Be real with me, Nai... am I making you happy? Is there anything you want or need from me that I'm not already doing? How can I make this marriage even better for you?"

He leaned forward to place a sweet peck to her lips.

"Tell me, baby. Whatever you need, it's yours. Even if I have to go steal the damn moon for you, consider it done."

"Sonny, stop being so sweet... you're gonna make me ruin my makeup."

"Fuck your make u—"

"Mr. and Mrs. Miller," Saber's voice sounded through the limo's speakers just as the car came to a halt. "We've arrived."

Kason sighed, disappointment crossing his features at their arrival.

Tanai smiled even harder at him before whispering, "You are the best husband I could've ever asked for. I've lost count of the amount of times you've made me happy because you constantly make me happy, Kason. But you know what would make me even happier right now?"

His left brow arched.

"If we're not late than we already are for your gala, Mr. Miller."

Kason sighed once again and Tanai chuckled before leaning closer to him. Thinking she was about to kiss him, Kason shut his eyes, expecting to feel her lips crash against his.

"Saber, we're ready to go."

But when he heard the press of their intercom button and her talking rather than kissing he realized he'd been played. His eyes popped open to see her reaching forward for her red Jacquemus purse.

"You know I'm not letting you leave this car without kissing your husband, Tanai."

"Oh is that right?" she asked in a teasing tone.

"Bring your sexy ass over her—"

The cool night air rushed into the car, lashing against their cheeks and the couple turned to see their car door open.

Tanai made a dash for the door but was halted when her hand was grabbed. She turned to look at Kason, reading the seriousness in his eyes.

"You know I'm just playing with you, honey."

"That's what I thought. Now come over here and give your man some love."

She grinned and nodded obediently, falling into his arms, and providing him with a hot tongue thrusting kiss.

After their kiss, Kason let Tanai go first and she was escorted out the car by Saber. Kason quickly followed and once they were both standing outside the car, flashes of white light suddenly stung their eyes.

"Mr. and Mrs. Miller over here!"

"Kason! Tanai! This way!"

Kason and Tanai were ambushed by a cascade of paparazzi and already knowing how his wife got nervous around large crowds of strangers made Kason place an arm around her to lead her into the venue.

"Sorry y'all, I gotta get my beautiful wife inside where it's warm. You can catch us on the red carpet in a few minutes," he told the paparazzi as him and Tanai walked into the prestigious venue.

Tonight was the night of Shield's yearly gala – a night where Kason rounded up all the employees, investors, and high value supporters of his company to celebrate the company's success.

Shield had become a billion dollar company just over a year ago and was now on its way to become a multi-billion-dollar company and tonight Kason wanted to turn up with his company as they celebrated Shield's growing success.

Once they entered the building, the coat check greeted them and asked to take their coats. When her coat was removed by Kason, Tanai's dress was on full display, allowing all to feast their eyes on the gorgeous gown she was clothed in.

Kason reached for her hand, kissing it before leading the way into the venue's main hall.

"Oh my God, Tanai! You look amazing!"

The first person that complimented Tanai was a woman that she didn't know but nonetheless she thanked her for her kind words. Then the compliments kept pouring in as the married couple walked into the banquet hall. The sounds of Dua Lupa's *Levitating* boomed through the large room.

Tanai felt all eyes on her and her heart raced each time she caught eyes with someone new. The hostess of the night, one of Shield's senior leaders and the woman that had planned majority of the night, Danita, approached the couple to say hello and lead them to their table.

"There your asses are!" Kadiri exclaimed as he got up from his seat. "Took you long enough!"

A lightness formed in Tanai's chest when she laid eyes on her sisters, brothers-in-law, father-in-law, and mother-in-law. Everyone was here and had been waiting for them.

"You know we had to make an entrance, bro," Kason told his brother.

Kason led Tanai over to his parents and they all hugged as they greeted one another.

"My darling, I definitely need to steal that dress from you," Temilola announced, making Tanai giggle. "You look absolutely beautiful."

"Thank you, Mom. So do you!"

Then the rest of the family greeted the couple. Tanai squealed with delight when her sisters rushed over to her and the trio huddled in a group hug.

"Bitchhhh, that fucking dress is everything on you," Truth voiced. "You're givinggg real rich bitch energy tonight!"

"No but I'm so jealous. Red really is your color, Nai," Thyri commented.

Tanai thanked them for their compliments before gassing them up too. They both looked breathtaking tonight. Truth had on a navy fitted gown with a pretty lace pattern and Thyri had on a black sultry looking gown that had sequins covering the dress' bodice.

Kason dapped and hugged his brothers, gassing them up due to their expensive designer tuxedos.

"You sure do clean up well, bro. Almost had me thinking you were homeless with the way you dress on a regular," Kason teased Kadiri which made Kadiri flip him the middle finger before he chuckled.

"Just tryna look better than you as always," Kadiri replied.

"Both of y'all cleaned up well. You learned from the best so there's no surprise there," Killian voiced. "I taught you both well, kids."

"Your old ass must have been doing all that teaching in your dreams," Kadiri said and the brothers chuckled at his teasing remark.

Once greetings were all said and done, Tanai and Kason took their seats and the evening finally got started.

Danita got on the mic and greeted all the guests, cracking a few jokes about Kason being the worst boss in the world which made everyone laugh before introducing the first performers of the evening – two professional salsa dancers who were world champions from Chile and Argentina. Everyone watched in awe as the dancers did their thing and showed off their award winning dance moves.

The night went on in full effect and Tanai remained in high spirits as she ate, drank, took photographs on the red carpet, and danced on the dancefloor alongside her sisters, husband, and his brothers.

She like the way that I dance
She like the way that I move
She like the way that I rock
She like the way that I woo
And she let it clap for a nigga

Tanai and her sisters laughed as they watched The Miller Brothers huddle together on the dancefloor, doing a popular dance known as 'The Woo'. When Drake's *Way 2 Sexy* came on, the brothers only danced with more and more excitement.

"That's their bad bitch anthem," Truth said into Tanai's ears, causing more laughter to pour out of her.

A few minutes later, Kason led Tanai off the dancefloor and back towards the main seating area.

"Baby. I wanna introduce you to some more people. That cool?"

Tanai nodded, understanding that even though tonight was a night of fun, it was also a night of business. All of Kason's investors, shareholders and board members were present today and they all wanted to meet her. She'd already met a few and was prepared to meet some more.

Table by table, they went and greeted the various important members of Kason's billion dollar tech company. Eventually, they arrived at the table of a warm beige skinned man that donned a smirk the second Kason lifted his fist out for them to dap.

"Kason, my man."

"Sebastian, what's up?"

"I see you finally decided to stop being shy and bring your beautiful wife out with you tonight."

Kason chuckled, patting the back of Sebastian as they hugged. Sebastian made eye contact with Tanai over Kason's shoulder and the way his eyes were rapt on her face had Tanai slightly uncomfortable but she shook it off.

"Sebastian, my amazing wife, Tanai," Kason announced as their hug ended. "Nai, this is Sebastian, one of the shareholders at Shield."

"It's a pleasure to finally meet you, Tanai," Sebastian greeted her, extending a handout for Tanai to place her hand into which she did. "Your pictures do you no justice... you truly are a beauty."

Tanai observed as he lifted her hand to his mouth, pressing a soft kiss to her knuckles.

"It's a pleasure to meet you too, Sebastian."

He let her hand go but kept his piercing gaze on her.

"Kason, you are definitely one lucky man."

"Oh believe me, I know." Kason grinned, reaching for Tanai's hand and holding it tight. "Thank you for coming out tonight, man. I hope you're enjoying yourself."

"Without a doubt. I don't know how you managed to do it but you definitely topped last year's gala."

The men continued to talk while Tanai listened, joining in whenever Kason felt the need to involve her. Once their conversation was over, Tanai felt the urge to pee and told Kason that she would be right back. He kissed her goodbye before letting her go. Tanai made her way to the restrooms, greeting all those who greeted her and thanking all those who complimented her outfit.

She arrived inside the restroom, finding it empty and choosing the first cubicle she laid eyes on. After peeing, she flushed and made her way to the sinks, placing her purse to the white marble vanity top.

The tone of a chord was heard and Tanai's eyes fell to her Jacquemus bag. After washing and drying her hands, she reached for the bag, opened it, and brought out her phone. She tapped its screen, allowing her to view her notifications and the alert of an email labelled 'No Subject' had her intrigued. She unlocked her device to head to the email and once it opened, her heart skipped a beat at the first line of the email.

He's still mine.

Attached to the email was a movie file and she clicked on it, only to suddenly wish she hadn't.

"Ahhhh!"

"Don't you dare stop taking that dick."

The video wasted no time in loading and Tanai's eyes widened at the sight of a female's ass going up and down a thick, large, and wet penis.

"Kaaaaaason!"

"Take that dick... yeah." His pleased chuckles sounded. *"Fuck... your pussy feels so fucking good."*

"Daddyyyy!"

"Who's pussy is this?"

"Yours, Kayyyy! Forever yours."

Tanai instantly locked her phone, cutting off the moans and groans coming from the video.

Her eyes shot up to her reflection and she saw that the color had drained from her face. She knew that laugh, she knew that voice and she most certainly knew that dick.

He's... He's cheating on me?

Tanai squeezed her eyes shut, trying to fight back the tears that had pricked her eyes. The restroom's door suddenly opened, making her eyes pop open and she noticed an attractive Caucasian woman enter the bathroom. The woman smiled at her just before she rushed into the nearest cubicle.

Tanai picked up her purse and made a beeline for the door, taking deep breaths as she headed back to the main hall.

She'd made it just in time for the next performance which was a violin performance by one of Atlanta's top violinists. Tanai took her seat next to Kason and he pecked her lips when she was seated.

"You okay, Nugget?"

She nodded without gracing him any eye contact or emotion.

Thinking nothing of her silence, Kason looked towards the main floor, watching the African American violinist take her center stage seat. After the magnificent performance, it was time for Kason to make his speech and everyone cheered him on as he took the mic from hostess, Danita. Everyone except Tanai.

"Thank you... thank you." He smiled at the entire hall. "Thank you all for coming out tonight. One of the best things about owning Shield is knowing that I have all of you amazing people on my team. Without all of you, Shield would not be where it is today and I am truly thankful for you all."

More cheers and whoops filled the room.

"But before I continue this speech any further, I can't not thank the one woman who has made me a better man... the one woman who I'm blessed to be able to wake up to every day."

Awwwwws then filled the room and Tanai's heart raced as she felt all eyes shift to her. Even her sisters, brothers-in-law, mother-in-law, and father-in-law were all looking her way.

"Tanai, baby... my Lil' Nugget... I love you so much. Thank you for being the best wife I could've ever asked for, thank you for supporting me through everything. I love you, sweetheart. Forever."

Tanai's mouth curved into a small smile and she let her eyes wander around the room, gazing upon all the smiles coming her way. Smiles from total strangers who didn't even know the battle going on in her mind and heart right now. Strangers who didn't know the betrayal she felt by the one person she loved more than anything in the world. She didn't even have time to process what had just happened to her in the bathroom. She didn't even have time to be alone with her thoughts and contemplate the fucked up shit that was going on.

Someone had gone out of their way, to get her email and send her a copy of her husband's sex tape. She didn't know who had sent it and hadn't checked the sender's email address. She didn't want to check the sender's email address because that would mean she would need to head back to the email and Tanai wasn't sure she could handle that right now.

Was this recent? No... can't be. He wouldn't do that to me. He wouldn't do that to us... right? He wouldn't cheat on me. He loves me... right? Tanai's panic worsened inside her as her thoughts continued to spiral out of control. *When you're away from him, you have no idea what he could be doing. You have no idea who he could be fuckin—*

"Sis."

A hand reached for hers under the table and she looked over at Thyri, who was staring at her with concern.

"You okay?"

Tanai quickly nodded, shooting her a weak smile before turning to look back at Kason. Her smile instantly faded at the sight of him and the tears that pricked her eyes made her blink rapidly to keep them at bay.

Tanai wasn't okay. She wasn't okay at all.

Chapter Twenty-One

Kiana: *You need to let me take you out for dinner or something.*
    Kiana: *All this texting back and forth is only making me miss your ass.*

Truth sent two laughing emojis before replying: *Miss you too.*

Truth: *We definitely need to link up soon.*

After Grenada, Kiana and Truth had kept in touch. They'd gotten to know each other on the private island and exchanged social medias. Now two weeks had passed since their vacation and they were still in contact.

Truth enjoyed texting Kiana because not only was she friendly, but she was also very funny and Truth loved women that could make her laugh. They'd been texting back and forth on iMessage for the past two weeks but now that Kiana had put up the offer of taking her out, Truth was all for it.

Kiana: *Okay cool, let me know when you're free and we'll go out.*

Kiana: *And you don't need to worry about finding a babysitter* *cause you know Kadiri will jump at the chance of taking care of Alana.*

Truth: *Oh believe me, I know, girl.*

Truth: *I might as well hire his ass as my new babysitter while you and I paint the town!*

Kiana sent two laughing emojis into their chat.

Kiana: *I know that's right!*

Kiana: *He really loves her and it's quite sweet, don't you think?*

Truth: *Yeah, I can't even lie... it is.*

Kiana was well aware of Kadiri's fondness for Alana because Truth had told her. She didn't want Kiana to feel some type of way about not knowing that Kadiri was getting close with Alana because she wasn't trying to get in the middle of what they had going on. She just wanted to keep things honest with Kiana especially since they were becoming friends.

Surprisingly, Kiana wasn't jealous about Kadiri spending time with Alana. She was cool with it and actually admired her man being so fond of the little girl. She knew that if she ever had his babies - which was unlikely since she hated kids - then he would be a great father.

Kiana: *How was Kason's gala?*

Truth: *Really good!*

Truth: *I had so much fun.*

Kiana: *That's good.*

Kiana: *You made it home yet?*

Truth: *Almost.*

Truth: *My Uber's five minutes away from my block.*

Kiana: *Alrightie.*

Kiana: *Let me know when you're home.*

Truth: *Will do.*

Five minutes later, Truth's Uber arrived outside her apartment building and she thanked her driver before leaving the car. She entered the building and made it up to her apartment floor, bringing out her key as the elevator doors slid out her way. Within minutes she was in her home and staring into youthful hazel eyes belonging to her babysitter.

"She was an angel as always. We had milk and cookies before I put her to sleep. She was trying to fight her sleep thinking she could wait up for you but she eventually gave in."

Truth smiled at Yasmine, the young biracial woman who took care of Alana whenever Truth needed her to.

"Thank you so much, Yas, and thank you for coming to my rescue on such short notice."

"No problem! You know I'll always drop everything to come take care of my special girl."

They continued talking for a few moments. Yasmine filled Truth in on everything Alana had eaten, drank, watched, and gave her the usual feedback on how their time together had been. Truth was glad to hear that things between Alana and her babysitter went well which wasn't a surprise because Truth knew how much Alana adored Yasmine. Truth paid Yasmine her fee for the night plus an extra *just because you're so great* fee that had Yasmine smiling so hard that her face started aching.

Yasmine then packed her things, said her goodbyes before leaving Truth's home. Truth sighed happily as she made her way to Alana's bedroom, being extra careful as she quietly pushed open her bedroom door.

The sight of Alana laying in her crib had Truth's heart melting and she approached the baby pink, butterfly toddler bed and looked down at her sleeping three year old. She bent low to kiss her cheek, whispering to her how much she loved her before backing away and leaving her bedroom.

Just as she shut Alana's door behind her, the sound of the

doorbell went off and Truth's brow arched as she looked at the other end of her living room where the front door stood.

She made her way through her home and arrived at the front door. Without checking the door's peep hole, Truth pulled the door open only for her to scowl at who had been standing on the other side of her door.

"Hello to you too, nigga," he announced, giving her a lopsided grin.

"You know you're picking her up tomorrow morning, right?" She had a hand on the side of the door and a hand on the side of her hip as she sized him up.

"Yeah I know." He stepped forward. "It's you I came to see."

"Uh-uh." She stepped back when he started coming too close. "Relax, bro. You don't need to come any closer than you already are."

Jodell's grin faded and his sienna brown eyes stared deeply at her face.

"Quit acting so cold, Tru. You know how many times I've said sorry?"

Nowhere near enough for me, nigga, she mused, examining his face, and reading the remorseful look he housed.

These past two weeks, Jodell had been doing a whole lot of groveling through texts and even the times he'd come to collect Alana, he'd constantly apologize to Truth, trying to get her to forgive him. He'd become regretful about the way he'd lashed out at her on the phone when she'd been on vacation and though it was a surprise to hear him admit that he was wrong to act like that towards her, Truth was glad to hear it. But his apologies still didn't change the fact that he'd disrespected her.

"Whatever you want me to do to fix things, I'll do it."

Truth said nothing but her eyes did plenty talking as they scanned his face. She knew her ebony skinned baby daddy was fine. She'd be a fool to act blind to his handsomeness. He had bright sienna brown eyes, bushy brows, dimples, and a small chin beard to match the thin moustache that bordered his thick, moist looking lips. And how could she forget about that sexy height? As he towered over her now, she was reminded of just how tall he was. He had a low Caesar haircut that was faded at the sides and lined perfectly at the front to form a crisp hairline.

"I never should have reacted like that... you have every right to take our daughter on vacation whenever you want to," he said.

Truth let her eyes wander down his tall frame, seeing the black fitted North Face tracksuit he had on and thinking about all the times she used to see him naked.

"And I'm sorry for calling you a bitch. That was outta pocket."

It was outta pocket... but I really do wanna see him outta those damn clothes.

Blame it on the liquor swimming in her bloodstream right now, because that's exactly what she was blaming for her sudden want of the one man that had brought her nothing but misery in this life.

"Can I come in?"

She looked at his lips, licking her lips at the thought of feeling them on hers and slowly nodded before she opened the door wider for him to come in. Seeing her grace him entry made Jodell's lips lift into a smile and he walked closer, stepping into her apartment but stopping when he'd made it right in front of her.

"You look beautiful tonight by the way," he said in a low tone.

Her gown was the first thing he'd laid eyes on once she'd opened the door and as beautiful as it was, he'd be lying if he said that the reason why he'd come here tonight was to see her fully clothed.

"Thank you," Truth replied.

Silence formed between them as they continued to ogle one another. Truth could feel her body heat rising by the second and before she knew it, his lips came crashing on top of hers and her hands went to his neck.

It all happened so quickly. One minute his hands were on the back of her dress, zipping it down and then her hands were at the bottom of his hoodie, pulling it up and over his head. The door slammed shut and Truth was pushed against it as her dress was pulled from her frame and his sweats fell to his ankles.

Once she was naked, she turned around, pressing her right cheek to the door, and sighing deeply as her thong was yanked down her thighs. The second he pushed into her tight opening, Truth was in nirvana.

Ultimate nirvana.

"Oh my... God."

"Fuck... I've missed your ass."

It had been so long. So *fucking* long since she'd had the chance to feel this feeling. Too long since she'd had the chance to feel this bomb ass dick.

"You missed this dick, huh?"

"Yesssss," she moaned, arching her back as he fucked her from the back. "I did."

Helldell was toxic as hell for her, that she knew for sure. Tonight she was choosing to ignore the depths of his toxicity because one thing she could never forget about was how good that toxic dick felt and tonight she needed it bad.

There was no one else that wanted her but him, no one else that desired her and no one else to make her feel good so sadly he would have to do for tonight.

Chapter Twenty-Two

"Tanai, tell me what's wrong. Right now."

He'd noticed. Of course he'd noticed. It would have been criminal if he hadn't. There was no way he couldn't feel and see the shift in his wife's energy. He'd first felt a hint of it when she'd returned to their table from the restrooms but he'd dismissed it because he thought he was stressing over nothing. He'd thanked her during his speech and noticed how miniscule her smile was. However, he let his mind convince him that everything was fine. She was good. They were having a great night together and nothing was going to ruin it.

But how very wrong he'd been.

Upon returning to their table after his speech, Kason reached for her hand which she reluctantly gave him and that was more than enough confirmation to him about something being wrong with his wife. She was cold, distant, and irritated and before this night was over, Kason planned to get to the bottom of it.

He inspected her as she looked out the tinted window next to her and his jaw clenched at her lack of communication. She knew how much he hated being ignored.

"Tanai, I know you hear me talking to you."

I do and I really wish you'd stop, she mused, sighing deeply as she continued to look out the window, allowing her to stare at the brightly lit streets they drove past. But her staring was short lived because she felt a hand grab her chin and twist it to the right, forcing her to stare into his dark brown orbs that were burning with annoyance.

"Do you want me to die? Because that's exactly what's gonna happen if you keep ignoring me."

His dramatic ass, she mused, lowkey wanting to laugh at what he'd said but she wasn't in a laughing mood.

"You and I are a team, Nai. A team. There's no I in team which is why *we* need you to stop ignoring your husband and tell him what's wrong."

His eyes softened and the hand that sat on her chin, gently caressed her skin. However, his caressing stopped and his hand fell off her face when she pushed it away. Kason frowned, feeling his frustrations mount at Tanai's behavior.

"Tanai, what the hell has gotten into you tonight?"

Tanai felt tears prick her eyes and she quickly turned away from Kason, but once again Kason didn't let her avoidance last long. This time he got on his knees, on the limo's floor and came to kneel right in front of Tanai.

She tried to push him away but her lifting her hands made him hold onto them and pull her in his direction.

"K-Kason, please," she said in almost a whisper, squeezing her lids shut in the hopes of keeping her tears at bay. "Leave me alone."

Her voice had started breaking, her number one tell of when she was about to cry.

"Never," he replied, holding her hands tightly in his as he looked up at her.

Despite her sealing shut her eyes, it did nothing to stop the first tear from falling and Kason's heart broke at the sight.

"Nugget, please tell me what's wrong. What have I done, baby?" he asked, letting go of one of her hands so he could wipe away her falling tears. "Please, Tanai, talk to me. Tell me what it is so I can fix it."

Tanai's tears fell faster and faster with each passing second and times like these she was reminded of how much she hated her emotional side. It was hindering her from having the strength to confront Kason.

But could you really blame her?

The thought of Kason being with another woman wasn't something she ever wanted to have to think about. He'd assured her that she wouldn't have to worry about any other woman but herself.

Tanai started shaking her head, finally opening her eyes which only made her tears worsen. No longer standing the sight of his woman crying, Kason lifted a hand to the armrest that sat between their seats and pressed the silver button.

"Saber, stop the car."

Tanai's eyes grew large at Kason's order.

"Boss... are you su—"

"I didn't ask for questions, Saber. Stop the damn car."

"Yes, boss."

Saber could tell by his boss' harsh tone that something was wrong because Mr. Miller never got rude to him. *Ever.*

The car came to a stop moments later.

"Saber, give us a moment."

"You got it, boss."

The sound of the car door opening was heard then it shut.

"We are not going home until you tell me what's wrong, Tanai Miller," Kason announced in a strict tone. "I don't care how long this takes. It can take all night, I really don't care but what I do know is that you are going to communicate with me."

By now, Tanai's crying had stopped and as she stared down at Kason on his knees in front of her, she was reminded of how much she usually loved him in this position but tonight she hated it.

Enough of this crybaby shit, Nai. Time to find out the truth.

She took a deep breath, released it, and looked him dead in the eyes as she asked, "Are you cheating on me?"

Kason's brows knitted and a sudden coldness hit his core.

"What kind of fucked up question is that, Tanai?"

"Answer it," she snapped, shooting daggers his way.

"Hell fucking no I'm not cheating on you," he fired back. "Why would you even ask me that bullshit?"

"Because one of your bitches' sent me a video of you fucking her from the back!" She yelled, snatching her hand out of his grasp, and pushing him away from her.

"What?"

A dazed look formed on his face as he remained rooted in his spot in front of her. She was attempting to push him away and doing a terrible job at it because Tanai's strength was nothing compared to his.

"You were fucking her and clearly enjoying it while recording the two of you!" Tanai's yelling worsened.

Kason didn't even have to think too long to put the pieces together and realize who had sent his sex tape over to his wife. A sex tape that he'd been under the impression only had one copy. *His copy.* A copy that had been deleted the very first day he'd laid eyes on Tanai.

"Just admit it, you're cheating on me, aren't you?"

"Tanai, I'm not! I swear to you I'm not."

"So who the hell is sending me an email of your sex tape with the caption, he's still mine! Who the hell is feeling comfortable enough to step to me! Your wife!"

A bitch that's definitely going to see me soon, Kason thought to himself but remained silent as he gazed into Tanai's glossy eyes.

"Someone who isn't important," he finally said.

"Not important?" Her face contorted. "But clearly she was important enough for you to record the both of you fucking!"

"Nai..."

"You don't even know what it's been like having to deal with women from your past and women who think you belong to them... I've had to deal with so much bullshit..." Tanai sighed, feeling her eyes well up. "So much fucking bullshit."

Her tears started falling again and sadness tore at Kason's heart.

"Nai... what are you talking about? You've had to deal with what?"

Tanai had done a pretty good job at keeping Kason in the dark about all the hate messages and comments she'd received on Instagram. However, now that tonight had turned into the night of confrontations, Tanai knew that confessions were getting added to this night too.

So she revealed it all.

Kason listened and watched as his wife poured her heart out to him, telling him all about the hate she'd faced at the hands of total strangers and although she'd done a pretty good job at handling it, tonight's email had been the final blow to her ego and most importantly, her heart.

When Kason asked to see the email, Tanai pulled out her iPhone from her purse and handed it to him. Kason typed in her passcode – their wedding date – and headed to her emails. He clicked on the first email with no subject and spotted the caption that Tanai had mentioned earlier.

He's still mine.

Then he clicked on the movie file and his jaw tightened once female moans filled the car.

Tanai's eyes remained stuck on him as he remained silent. His golden honey face reddened the more he stared down at her bright screen.

"Fuck... your pussy feels so fuck—"

Kason exited the video and clicked on the sender's email. The email was a fake address as it had a bunch of random numbers and letters that didn't make any sense. But Kason didn't have to know the email address because he already knew who had sent the email. He sent the email to the trashcan before locking Tanai's phone and putting it on the empty seat next to her.

"Nai," he called out to her, lifting his hands to her thighs, and holding onto her. "I swear to you on my life and yours that I'm not cheating on you. I would never cheat on you. I made a vow to never cheat on you and I intend to stick to that vow, baby. This video..." Kason released a deep sigh as he realized someone from his past was messing with him. "This video was taken over a year ago with a woman that I haven't seen or ever intended to see once I met you. But now that she's decided to play these bullshit ass games, I'm gonna see to it that she never even thinks of stepping to you again. I promise you that no one from my past will ever step to you about me again. I'll make sure of that. And the Instagram DMs I'll take care of too. Anyone and everyone who tries to disrespect you is getting their account shut down. I don't give a fuc—"

"Kason, no." Tanai shook her head from left to right, knowing how much power her husband had in the tech industry. "There's no need for all that."

"Yes, there is," he affirmed, leaning forward to peck her lips. "Yes, there is. You are my wife and no one disrespects you. *No one.*"

He kissed her lips once more.

"I'm sorry about everything, Nugget. Please forgive me. I know this is all my fault and I promise you that I'm gonna handle everything. Just say you forgive me... please, baby."

The more Tanai gazed into those irresistible eyes belonging to her husband, the more she found her heart opening back up to him like it always did. The more she found herself forgiving him.

"I forgive you."

Those were the three magic words Kason needed to hear and as soon as she'd said them, he pressed his lips to hers, trying to prove to her just how sorry he was.

Tanai's back met the leather seat and she released a light breath as Kason's kiss intensified. His tongue pushed past her lips to collide with hers. The deeper their kiss got, the more her libido increased.

"Son... Sonny..." She broke away from him, pushing against his left pec. "We still need to head home."

Kason ignored her, reaching for the back of her dress, and letting his hands slide up her back until he found her zipper.

"Sonny, Saber's outsi—"

"I don't mind calling him in but that's not changing the fact that you're about to ride my face."

Her inner thighs heated up at his words and instead of protesting, she decided to give in, allowing her husband to pull her dress off her frame. Once it was down to her ankles, Kason pulled it off her body and chucked it to the limo seats behind him.

He marveled at the sight of Tanai in nothing but a red lace thong. Her breasts were sitting pretty and perky which wasn't a surprise since she had work done a few years ago. He leaned forward, squeezing her soft boobs as his lips captured hers.

"Mmmh, Kason," Tanai moaned between their hot kiss.

His mouth tore away from hers only to kiss down her face, onto her throat and neck.

"I... promise... you... I'm... yours," he told her as his lips peppered her neck with kisses. "Only yours."

A sharp bite on her neck caused Tanai to whimper and she squeezed on Kason's shoulder.

"You got that?"

"Yes." She nodded, reaching for the side of his face so she could lift his head up.

His desire filled eyes focused on her and she let her hand slide down his face to his jaw which she took in hand. She held it tight, pulled him closer to her face and gave him strong eye contact as she squeezed his jaw.

"Don't you ever allow another bitch to send me a video of you and her fucking. You got that?"

He nodded, completely turned on by how Tanai had grabbed his jaw, forcing him to look at her.

"You belong to me and this dick—" She grabbed his crotch with her free hand, causing Kason to groan. "Is mine. No one else's."

He nodded again but that wasn't enough for Tanai and her face hardened as she ordered him to, "Say it."

"This dick is yours, baby. No one else's."

"Open your mouth."

He instantly obeyed and opened wide for her. Tanai moved closer to him to spit into his mouth before opening her mouth across his and devouring his mouth with deep sweeping strokes of her tongue. Kason groaned as she used her tongue to swirl her saliva around his mouth, making their kiss extra sloppy.

Moments later, she pulled away from him and noticed the smile on Kason's lips. She knew how much he liked her doing that to him and because she'd done it, she'd now released his wild side that had no intentions of being hidden.

He reached for her long legs, lifting each one to his shoulders as he crouched down between her open thighs. Kason knew he had a lot of making up to do tonight because of the embarrassment Tanai had faced at the hands of another woman. Their time together in the car right now was only a sample of all the ways he intended to make it up to her. One thing was certain, neither of them were getting any sleep tonight.

~

It's all over
I lost my composure
I got love to show you
Would you let me love you, me love you, baby?

Warmth spread through Killian's system at Thyri's rubs on his nape. She had the softest hands and whenever they were on his body, they always seemed to bring him a remedy that he could never get sick of having. He turned his head to the right, taking a quick glance at her sitting in the passenger seat next to him.

That gown on her tonight had been the best dress he'd seen in a very long time. The color black had never looked better and if it wasn't for the fact that he needed to drive home, Killian was convinced he could admire her for all eternity. He let his eyes face the roads as he focused on driving them both to his home.

"You hungry, Bubba?"

Though they'd just come back from a gala filled with endless food and drinks, he knew how much she loved her food and despite her slim figure, she wasn't a slim eater.

"No..."

A smirk graced his lips, causing an identical one to form on hers.

"I mean not right now."

He chuckled and nodded as he approached a stop light. He smoothly brought his Bentley to a stop.

"And I know exactly what to feed you when we get to mine," he announced, lifting a hand to her thigh, and squeezing tight.

"Yours?"

The surprise in her voice made him turn to her.

"Yeah, mine."

"I thought you were taking me home, Killian?"

Huh?

His brows drew together as he watched her like she was suddenly speaking gibberish because in his mind, she was.

"I am taking you home," he confirmed. "With me."

"That's not my home though, Kill... that's your home."

The stop light turned to amber then green, causing Killian to mash the gas pedal and place one hand on the steering wheel while the other that had been on Thyri's thigh went to his lap.

The attitude in her voice had caught him off guard and he wasn't understanding why him taking her home with him was an issue.

"So what are you telling me right now, Thyri? You wanna go home?"

She caught the sudden note of hardness in his voice and it made a tightness form in her chest.

Way to go, Thyri. You've made an issue out of nothing when you and your boyfriend have had a great night so far. Way to fucking go!

A great night they'd had indeed. Kason's gala had been their first public appearance as a couple and although Thyri was nervous to encounter Killian's mother after their last encounter at the reception, Temilola greeted her with open arms, easing her discomfort completely. The night had been amazing. Her and Killian danced together with the rest of the family, enjoyed the gala's food together and since Killian was driving her home, he hadn't drank any alcohol tonight but he enjoyed watching Thyri sipping on her liquor while she looked right back at him. He was consumed with nasty thoughts of being able to sip on the juices that slipped out of her when they were alone later on tonight in his home. Later on had finally come and Killian now felt the tension in the air rise because of Thyri's opposition to his decision to take her home with him. Though they hadn't discussed where Thyri was ending up at the end of the night, he thought it was an assumed undisclosed agreement that she was coming home with him.

"No," she voiced. "I'm fine with going home with you."

"You know I'm never one to play games, Thyri, so I ain't about to start playing any games with you. If you wanna go home, I'll take you home."

"No," she repeated, reaching for his tatted hand that had been sitting on his lap. "I want to go home with you."

Killian said nothing and kept his concentration on driving them home, allowing the vocals of Drake to fill his mental. Hearing him rap all about how he'd been losing friends and finding peace was enough to keep Killian distracted and quiet.

Thyri didn't even have to hear Killian talk anymore to know he wasn't happy with her. She could not only feel it but she could see the way his lips had pressed together and the way his expression had dulled. She'd grabbed his hand and was holding onto it but he wasn't holding onto her.

Thyri decided to stop holding him and just give him some space. Clearly what she'd said had thrown him off guard and she didn't want to add any more salt to his wound by touching him when he didn't want to be touched by her right now. But the second she lifted her hand away from his was the same second Killian reached for it and slowly raised it to his lips.

Thyri's skin tingled and her lips lifted into a smile as he kissed her hand repeatedly before setting it down to the middle of his thighs. Where she could feel... *him.*

The rest of the car journey they sat in a peaceful yet desire filled silence and it only took five minutes for Killian to pull up into the private parking lot under his apartment's building.

"Oh wow... I see someone has taste after all," she said as she walked into his home and he chuckled at her teasing.

When Thyri stepped through Killian's front door, she couldn't stop smiling. Not only did his apartment smell nice but it was clean, modern and had a masculine vibe that suited his persona well. The colors black, white, gray, and silver coated his space and despite those colors largely being considered as boring for a home, in Killian's home they were far from it. They brought a debonair vibe to his space and reminded Thyri all about how this man had class. A class that couldn't be bought, earned, or stolen. It was something you had to be born with and baby, Killian had been born with a whole lot of it. Too much of it in fact but she wasn't complaining at all. Her man had class and she loved it. Even the black Tom Ford tux he'd donned tonight was an example of that.

His house was a three bedroom penthouse with hardwood floors, expensive looking artwork on various walls and floor to ceiling windows that only made his home look ten times more expensive than it already was.

"I wanna show you something, Thyri."

She nodded as she kicked off her heels and allowed him to grab her hand. He led her through the three thousand square foot space to his studio which had her mouth falling wide open.

"Oh my God... Kill... this is amazing."

Amazing it was. He had all his artwork framed on the four white walls enclosing them. From his sketches to his drawings to his paintings - they were all here. And Thyri couldn't stop beaming as she caught sight of each one. This man - no, scratch that - *Her* man was so damn talented!

She suddenly gasped when her eyes met a white framed sketch in the center of the wall across from them. How the hell she'd missed it, she didn't know but now that she'd seen it, she quickly walked over to it and her pulse raced the more she gazed at it.

"I drew that the first day I met you," he announced, his steps echoing on the hardwood flooring as he sauntered over to her. "Couldn't get that face out of my head so I knew the only solution was to draw you."

Tears filled her eyes and she couldn't believe that she'd been brought to tears by a sketch but she was.

What happened to you being a tough bitch, Thyri? Not you crying over a sketch.

She couldn't help it though. The sketch was magnificent. There weren't enough words in the dictionary for her to describe how great it was. He'd captured every feature of her face, not missing a single part of her.

Thyri felt his large hands on her arms and he slowly stroked her skin through her dress.

"Killian... this is... this is..." She quickly turned to face him, grabbing his face, and giving him a long overdue kiss.

Killian wrapped his arms around her waist, pulling her in closer to him as their kiss got deeper. She took full control of the kiss, trying to show him her gratefulness and love for what he'd done. He'd managed to make her whole night and even though she'd experienced a great night at Kason's gala, Killian had made it one hundred times greater.

"Thank you," she whispered to him moments after kissing him.

She'd ended the kiss and he groaned as she pulled away but Thyri just had to thank him.

"Thank you for being so talented... you're amazing."

"Not as amazing as you," he replied. "You're the one making your father proud alongside your sisters. He would be so proud of you, Bubba."

Why is he so sweet?

Yeah he sure is... but you definitely weren't acting sweet when you gave him that attitude earlier.

A weight settled on Thyri's heart as she remembered her behavior during their car ride.

"Killian, I'm sorry about the way I acted earlier."

"Don't be." He shook his head 'no'. "I should've asked you if you wanted to come home with me... I guess I'd just been feening to have you in my crib that I forgot to ask what you wanted."

"No but I'm really sorry... I let old shit get in my head and I lashed out on you because in the past I wasn't given a choice on whether or not I wanted to go home after nights out with..."

Her words trailed off as she realized she was about to bring up the name of a man Killian hated.

"With me you're always going to have a choice, Thyri. We've talked about this," he explained, caressing the small of her back.

"I know," she replied, remembering all the conversations they'd been having these past two weeks.

The day that Soraya had apologized to Thyri, Killian had come over to her apartment and they'd had a long heart to heart about what had happened with Chosen. Thyri made it clear that Chosen coming in the middle of them wasn't going to be a thing and that she was completely done with him. Killian also made it clear about his intentions for Thyri. He was in this with her for the long run and was serious about making her his wife one day soon. Though it may have seemed too soon for the couple to be talking about marriage after only being together for just over a month, Killian wanted to make sure that Thyri understood how serious he was about her.

"I will never force you to give up your independence. Don't forget that."

She nodded, feeling her lips curve into a loving smile. Killian smiled back at her and she stepped on her tippy toes to crash her lips to his. Their heated, sensual kiss continued and Killian slowly stepped back as their lips remained locked, leading the both of them through his home to his bedroom. Once he had her by the edge of his bed, he gently broke away from her and helped her get out of her gown before she helped him strip from his tuxedo.

When the lovers were naked, Killian carefully set Thyri down to the center of his bed, sliding down to her thighs, but Thyri stopped him with the following words, "Kill... I need you... I need you inside me."

He let his hand drop to the apex of her thighs, feeling into her warmth and realizing how wet she was.

Shit... she's wet as fuck right now.

She wasn't lying about needing him and he wasn't about to deprive her from the one thing they both desperately wanted.

"Killian... shit."

The first thrust inside her brought a frenzy to her mind and Thyri held onto him tighter, sighing deeply as he pulled out. Then he slid right back in place, exactly where he belonged and the ecstasy rushing through her didn't stop.

His pumps were gentle, slow and everything she been craving all night. He brought his mouth to hers, entwining their lips in the best way.

They always had great sex but this session right here... Thyri could feel her soul tying to his. This session right here was confirmation that they were in this for the long run. This wasn't a joke. Their feelings for each other were only getting stronger and stronger each day. Nothing could pull their magnetic force apart.

But there was one person keen on trying to keep them apart.

Chapter Twenty-Three

"Thyri, stop blocking my number. I need to see you. You know shit ain't done between us. Don't make come find you. You know I don't care about that wack ass nigga."

It was a lie as soon as it had dropped from his lips.

Of course he cared about Killian. How could he not? He cared that Killian Miller was messing with Thyri and he was still in so much shock by what had happened in her apartment two weeks ago. Because of Killian's new presence in Thyri's life, Chosen was too scared to go over to Thyri's apartment. He didn't want to run into Killian, especially not after the warning he'd given him the last time they'd encountered one another.

"Just call me, Thyri. Please," he concluded before hanging up the line.

Her phone had gone straight to voicemail but that didn't stop him from leaving a voicemail with the new number he'd gotten to get in touch with her. This was the third new number he'd gotten in the space of a week and quite frankly, Chosen had no plans to stop changing his number until he got through to Thyri. He knew there was a strong chance she could just change her number so that he wouldn't have a way to call her but he was betting on her not changing it. He knew how important her current number was because all the important people in her life currently had that number and changing it would be tedious.

After pocketing his phone, Chosen turned around to pull open the glass door behind him and step into the establishment that usually never failed to put a smile on his face.

"Man, what the fuck has gotten into you tonight, nigga?"

"Nothing," Chosen retorted, walking towards the bar that already had one seat occupied.

"You sure?"

Chosen shook his head 'yes' and took the empty seat next to his boy.

"A'ight," Jodell replied, deciding to drop the issue. He knew how private his boy was and he wasn't about to press him to share some shit that he clearly didn't want to share.

They were close but they weren't that close so it wasn't that deep to Jodell that Chosen wasn't willing to share the troubles of his life. He was a pretty private person too and wasn't going to start blabbing his mouth about his life drama either. They had a few things in common, after all the women they were each connected to were sisters and it was on the day of Jodell's birthday party two years ago that Chosen and Thyri had met.

"So our second building," Chosen announced, reaching for the bottle of scotch that sat in front of them. "You've secured it?"

"By tomorrow I will," Jodell confirmed, watching as Chosen poured equal amounts of liquor into both of the crystal tumbler glasses opposite them. "You know things like that take patience. I needed to prove my worth and now that I have, he owes me big time. That building will be ours and we can finally get shit moving quicker."

"That's what I like to hear." Chosen closed the bottle and set it down to the countertop before reaching for his glass. "This is only the beginning."

"The beginning," Jodell said, also reaching for his glass and lifting it so they could clink glasses.

Chapter Twenty-Four

"Profits have been up over sixty five percent with each of your companies, sons. To say that I'm happy would be a fucking understatement right now."

"Yup, I'm definitely telling Momma about you cussing, Dad." Memphis laughed and shook his head at his youngest son.

"That's cold, Kadi, and you know it," Memphis responded as he dipped a spoon into his bowl of caviar. "Snitch on me and I'll simply let your mother know about the night you decided to smoke your best friend, Mary Jane, in our theater last month."

Killian let out a loud chuckle just before he took a bite into his lobster. Today he was enjoying a meal with his brothers and father at one of Atlanta's finest restaurants – Bacchanalia.

Kadiri's eyes narrowed at his father's words.

"You wouldn't."

Memphis smirked as he lifted his filled spoon to his mouth.

"Oh she's definitely gonna kill your ass. You know how much she hates weed in the house," Kason intervened with light chuckles leaving him at the memory of their no nonsense mother catching them in the past smoking.

"Man, whatever." Kadiri waved his brother off. "Your ass is still overdue for an ass whooping after you and Tanai eloped."

"Pretty sure she's over that now," Kason smugly stated. "Her and Nai have been getting on a like a house on fire. I'm definitely convinced she loves Nai more than she loves me."

"I'm not surprised either. Tanai's way prettier and nicer than your ugly ass," Kadiri teased, causing Kason to smirk.

"I've been meaning to show you something," Kason announced to Kadiri as he slowly cradled the side of his face with his left hand.

"Oh yeah what's tha..."

Kadiri's words trailed off and a frown formed on his lips at Kason turning his head to the right so that Kadiri could clearly see the middle finger he'd extended with the hand he'd used to hold his face.

"Your dumb ass," Kadiri muttered before laughing at his brother's goofiness.

"Alright, boys, back to what I was saying before... I'm really proud of y'all. You're all killing it with your ventures and I know it's only up from here."

The Miller brothers had come from wealth thanks to their father's construction company – *Miller Industries* – that he was currently the CEO of, but rather than remaining in the shadow of their father for the rest of their lives, the brothers had each created their own empires that complimented the empire that their father had first created.

Killian owned House of Hayes, the biggest tattoo shop in Georgia, Kason owned Shield, a billion dollar tech security company and Kadiri owned Kadiri's Kustoms, the best custom car shop in Georgia. And as a collective, they owned KMG, their luxury gym.

Each of their companies' headquarters had been constructed by Miller Industries, putting their father's company on payroll and each of their buildings were protected by Kason's tech company, putting him on payroll too. The Miller Brothers were all next in line to inherit Miller Industries once their father retired, making them all the rightful owners of their father's empire.

It was a win-win system for the entire family and Memphis was grateful that his sons had made a name for themselves outside of the name he'd created for them. He was also glad that they were working together as a unit because family always came first. No matter what.

The construction industry had been and still was cutthroat. Memphis had dealt with a lot during his time including naysayers and enemies. Enemies who had tried to get in his way and get a taste of the power that The Miller name had.

Memphis had been strong enough to deal with everything with his brother, but his oldest son, Killian had provided much more assistance once he was old enough to understand just how deep the Miller family's power went. Anything his father ever needed from him, Killian got done. It wasn't something he questioned or challenged, he just did it. That was the same for Kason and Kadiri too. Their father's wishes reigned supreme in their household and that's just the way shit went.

There were secrets amongst The Millers that they planned to take to the grave, which they were fine with because nothing came first but family.

"Dad, I've been meaning to share this with you for a minute now but just haven't had the chance to... basically Tanai and her sisters will soon be in business with Shield. You remember their cleaning company I told you about?"

Memphis nodded but remained silent.

"I want them to be Shield's chief cleaning company and I not only want them cleaning our building, but I also plan to make their products available alongside Shield's. You know to create some type of hygiene and technology synergy."

Once again Memphis nodded as he took a sip from his wine glass.

"Killian and Kadiri are down for it too. They're considering signing the girls on to be in charge of their buildings in the near future – obviously, we don't want to overwhelm them with too much work because they're still a small company."

"This all sounds great, son, but are you sure you want to mix business with pleasure?"

Kason's face went blank.

"Pleasure?" he asked his father.

"Yes, son. *Pleasure*. I understand the goal here is to make your wife richer but she's still your wife at the end of the day. Do you really think it's a good idea involving your wife in business affairs?"

"I think it's a great idea," Kason confirmed. "When people see my wife I want them to know that not only does her husband have money but she does too."

"I hear you, Kay. I really do. But just be careful about mixing your money in the place you lay your head at night... most importantly the place you slide yourself into at night."

This time it was Kadiri's turn to nod without saying a word. He understood what his father was saying but he wasn't about to listen to him because he'd already had it set in his mind that he was doing this. He was going to make his wife a very rich woman with her sisters. She was the love of his life and he definitely wasn't about to leave her hanging. Anything to make her happy he would do and that included hunting down the devil that had sent her that sex tape last weekend.

Trinity Carter.

Kason had every intention of ruining Trinity's life once he set eyes on her. The only problem was Trinity wasn't in the city. She wasn't even in the state and at this point, Kason's personal hackers weren't even sure she was in the country anymore. They were searching high and low for her online and so far they had nothing.

Absolutely nothing!

It angered Kason to know that the woman who was suddenly hell bent on putting a wedge between him and his wife was nowhere to be found. How she had suddenly fallen off the face of the earth was confusing. All her social medias had been deactivated, her bank accounts inactive and her apartment she no longer lived at. All Kason knew was that he needed her found. She'd suddenly come up with this crazy plot to destroy his marriage so he felt no remorse about destroying her. He needed her found sooner than later so he could deal with her for trying to ruin what he'd built with Tanai.

He hadn't even seen Trinity in over a year so for her to have popped out of nowhere with a copy of their sex tape that he had no idea she had in the first place, Kason was livid. Most importantly, he wanted answers. Now.

After enjoying a meal with their father, the brothers each went their separate ways back to work. Killian made his way to House of Hayes and arrived ten minutes later in the parking lot of his shop.

"Boss," Cleo greeted him with a warm smile as he stepped through the front door. "You have a good lunch?"

His head went up and down as he said, "I did. You?"

"It was decent," she replied, shrugging lightly. "Thyri's here by the way."

His body sizzled at the mention of Thyri.

"Cool."

He took a quick glance at the waiting area on his left, spotting a cinnamon skinned man sitting with one leg crossed over the other as he gazed down at his phone. When Killian looked over at him, the man's head lifted and he greeted Killian and Killian greeted him back before walking through the walkway leading to Dayana's studio.

Knock! Knock!

"Come in."

Killian pushed the door's handle, stepping into the room and feeling his heart skitter at the smile that now danced on his Bubba's lips.

"Hey, boss," Dayana addressed him, sending a friendly smile his way before focusing back on Thyri.

"Hey you," Thyri greeted him, her smile growing bigger and bigger by the second.

He returned her smile, walking deeper into the space to get a closer look at what was being done to his woman.

Thyri was lying flat on her side on the tattoo chair while Dayana sat on a stool that was next to Thyri's head, allowing Dayana to lean low as she tattooed behind Thyri's ear.

Once he was close enough, Killian was able to see Dayana's process. A cute, detailed butterfly sat on the skin behind Thyri's ear.

"I hope I'm doing a good enough job tattooing your woman, boss."

Laughter erupted out of Thyri.

"Hey. Keep still, girl. You wanna end up with a long black line behind your ear?"

"I'm sorry," Thyri apologized, laughing some more but

keeping as still as possible. Her eyes flashed up to meet Killian's and she could see the smile in his eyes.

From Dayana's statement, Killian was reminded about what Thyri had done two weeks ago. She'd finally made it known to Dayana their relationship. And he knew by how extra nice Dayana had been towards him these past two weeks, that she approved of the two of them together.

"You're doing a great job," Killian complimented her, bending low to kiss Thyri's cheek which made her blush. "I'll be in my office waiting on you, Bubba."

"Okay. See you in a few."

He nodded and gave her one last look before saying goodbye to Dayana and leaving her studio.

About ten minutes into him sitting in his office, working on a new tattoo design, the door slowly opened and in popped Thyri's pretty face.

"I'm all doneeeee."

She walked into the large space and made her way to the other side of his desk where he sat. Killian dropped his pen, grinning as she came closer to him and admiring her fit. She had on a beige off the shoulder bodysuit, a denim mini skirt and clear stiletto heels on her feet. He spun his chair in her direction and reached for her thighs once they were in his reach. He brought her down to his lap and joined his lips to hers.

"You like my new tatt?" she asked him moments after their kiss, turning her head so he could get a good look at her new ink.

"I love it," he answered, admiring the adorable design. "Look at you cheating on me with Dayana."

Thyri giggled as she wrapped her arm around his neck.

"I mean technically I cheated on her with you. She's always been the one tatting me."

"Yeah but that was before I changed your life."

"You mean before *I* changed your life," she teased, making him chuckle.

He started peppering her face with kisses and she sighed happily as he loved all up on her.

"You ready for our date?"

Killian had set up a private pottery class for the two of them to learn how to mold clay. Ever since he'd discovered that Thyri was a creative just like him, he knew she'd appreciate creating things which is why he knew a pottery class was the perfect date night idea for the both of them.

"Oh absolutely," she voiced. "I can't wait to see how bad you are at molding clay."

He scoffed.

"That's a lie and you know it. You know how great I am with my hands."

"I mean you're a'ight."

"I'm a'ight?" His left brow arched. "Oh a'ight, clearly you've forgotten how good I am with these hands." Killian's hand that had been holding her waist, he brought forward and slowly moved up her stomach. "But I have no problem reminding you."

She shook her head 'no' in a teasing manner and felt her body heat rise when his hand stroked her left boob. Lust blindsided her and she stared at him, seeing the desire sparkling in his magnetic eyes.

"Uh-uh." She reached for his hand but the second she did, he squeezed her breast causing a flood to rush out of her. "Kill... no, you can't." She sighed. "You're making me wet."

"That's my job." He squeezed tighter. "You knew what you were doing when you decided to wear that short ass skirt. Go lock the door, Thyri."

"We have a date," she reminded him, her weakness for him evident in her tone. "That I've been looking forward to all week."

I know we do," he nonchalantly said. "Go lock the door."

"Killyyyyy."

Her calling him by the new name she'd coined for him a few days ago brought a smirk to his face.

"The door, Ri."

She shot him a puppy dog look and he continued to stare at her with a smirk. The more he gazed into her deep set eyes, the more he felt his heart weakening for her like it always did.

"Alright, alright." He finally gave into her protesting. "Fine. Date first."

"Date first," she agreed, carefully removing his large palm from her chest.

"But after that date..."

"You can finally remind me just how great you are at using your hands," she told him, causing a large grin to split his face into two.

The lovers kissed one last time before making their way out of Killian's office. They walked through his shop to head outside. Along the way, Soraya had just stepped out of an artist's studio and spotted Thyri and Killian walking out together, hand in hand. They hadn't seen her because she was behind them on the other side of the shop but she'd definitely seen them.

Her stomach hardened as she watched Killian open the door for his lady and allow her to step out first. He smacked her butt, causing her to giggle before he followed her out the door. They were perfect for one another and although Soraya didn't want to admit it, it was the truth. They were the perfect couple.

"They're so cute together, right?"

Soraya turned around to see Dayana walking towards her.

"They're okay," Soraya replied with a shrug.

Dayana came to a stop next to her, eyeing her with an intrigued look.

"You don't approve, huh?"

Soraya remained silent but gave her a look that said, *You know I don't.*

Soraya knew that Dayana and Thyri were close friends so she knew that Dayana was well aware of what had went down in Grenada.

"I'm sorry about the shit that went down in Grenada," Dayana apologized. "I had no idea myself that they liked each other."

"Don't be sorry," Soraya told her. "You're not the one who got in my way."

Soraya then walked off, leaving Dayana in the hallway of the shop.

Chapter Twenty-Five

Once Thyri sat in the passenger seat of Killian's Bentley, she smiled and giggled as Killian made sure she was strapped in safely by doing her seatbelt for her before shutting the door to head to his driver's seat.

He's so damn swee—

The ringing of her iPhone disrupted Thyri's private thoughts. Her gaze dropped to her Prada shoulder bag and she unzipped it, bringing out her phone to see an unknown number. Her muscles tensed because she knew exactly who this unknown caller was.

He just doesn't know when to fucking quit!

She quickly hit decline and went to her call log just as Killian's car door had opened.

Killian noticed from his peripheral the way her fingers were tapping hard on her screen. Like she was pissed off and he could feel her shift in energy.

"Bubba."

She turned to look at him.

"You good?"

"Yes, handsome," she replied. "Just fine."

He had a feeling she was lying but he wasn't about to press the issue further. Clearly whatever it was she wasn't willing to share right now and usually Killian would be determined to get to the bottom of her problems but he didn't want to pry. When she was ready to tell him, he would be here waiting. Right now they had a date to get to and all Killian wanted to do was enjoy the rest of the day with his girl. Anything else just didn't matter.

Kadiri headed to his car shop and pulled up to his bustling establishment fifteen minutes later. He'd always loved cars from the second he'd realized what one was. He remembered stealing his father's various sports cars between the ages of fifteen and seventeen, always getting into trouble with the law for driving without a license but thanks to his father's deep pockets, he was always let off easy.

Kadiri walked through his business, being greeted by all his employees, and heading straight to his office at the back of the shop's garage, only to be halted by the call of his name.

"Boss, wait up."

Kadiri turned around to see one of his best employees, Jodell, walking up to him with a pleased expression.

"Jo, you good?'

They dapped once Jodell stood a short distance in front of him.

"Yeah, man, I just wanted to holla at you about what we discussed a few weeks ago. The new building I was telling you that me and Chosen are thinking of getting... we need that now, boss."

Kadiri nodded, remembering all about how Jodell had explained to him his plans with Chosen for their cigar bar. Jodell was one of his best workers at Kadiri's Kustoms and he hadn't even been working at the shop for that long. He'd started working for Kadiri just under four months ago, claiming that he needed a change of scenery from his old office job. Alongside working at the car shop, he'd recently joined his friend Chosen in running his cigar bar in downtown Atlanta. A cigar bar that the boys were looking to expand.

Jodell was one of Kadiri's best mechanics but just because he was one of Kadiri's best men that didn't mean that Kadiri was going to stifle his growth and stop him from seeking out other interests. That went for all his employees too. He was all for them pursuing their dreams and he would be here to support them in whatever way he could because that's just the type of boss he was. Kadiri was all for making sure Jodell secured his next building at a slightly cheaper rate because of how good of an employee he was.

Now despite Chosen being Jodell's business partner and Thyri's ex, that didn't have anything to do with Kadiri in his mind. He was mainly supporting Jodell and his ventures. Chosen was simply tagging along for the ride and Kadiri had never spoken to Chosen a day in his life. It was only Jodell he talked to about business.

"And I got you. I'll get the paperwork set up, get my people to call you and you'll be all set."

Jodell's eyes lit up with joy at his words.

"Thank you so much, boss. You're the best, man."

"No worries, Jo. You stay being good to me and I stay being good to you."

The men continued to talk for a few minutes. Jodell filled Kadiri in about one of the new Bentleys coming into the shop today for a custom job. Then when their conversation was over, Jodell got back to work and Kadiri headed to his office to look over some emails about new car parts he had coming in next week.

Ding!

Minutes into him checking his first couple emails, his phone went off and he picked up the device to see a name that had him sighing deeply.

Kiana: *So are you taking me out tonight or what?*

As much as he had love for that girl, she sure knew how to get on his nerves with her demanding ways.

Nah, I've got work to do all night, he sent back then locked his phone and dropped it down to his black ceramic desk.

Ding!

He reluctantly lifted his phone once again, realizing that he wasn't about to focus unless he got her off his back.

And what about tomorrow? Her response was.

He quickly typed, *'I'll let you know'* and stared at the screen as her read receipt came in.

Instead of replying, she liked the message and Kadiri decided to place his phone on DND so he could focus on going through his emails.

Things with Kiana had always been... *complicated.* He knew that he had love for her, being in love with her was the part he knew he could never be though. They'd been on and off for the past year and every time Kadiri told himself to just put her out her misery and end things between them, he found himself staying put.

She'd complained to him about not being invited to Kason's reception and he understood her frustrations but honestly, he didn't care. Yes, he'd met her mom, aunt, and a few cousins but that didn't change the fact that she wasn't about to meet his mother. *Ever.*

The only woman who Kadiri ever planned to introduce to his mother was the woman he planned to get married to and that wasn't her. It was selfish of him to stay in a relationship with

344

Kiana when he knew it wasn't going anywhere but he didn't have the time or effort to find someone else right now. Being with Kiana was convenient... for the most part. She had good pussy, could cook, and did his laundry whenever she was over at his crib. He was only with her for the moment and he knew that sooner or later that moment would pass but for now, he would let it run its course.

Once Kadiri was done with work, the time was seven-thirty p.m. All his workers had gone home which wasn't a surprise because the shop closed at six p.m. but he liked to stay behind to get extra stuff done. Now that he was done, he had one place in mind and it wasn't the place that he rested his head every night.

"Kad Kad!"

"There she is." He smiled as he felt her tiny hands wrap around his long leg and he crouched down to pick her up into his arms. "Thought your lil' ass would be getting ready for bed by now."

She was already in her Hello Kitty pajamas but when the door was opened for him, he'd spotted her sitting on the living room couch watching Cocomelon without a care in the world.

"I'm big girl," she affirmed with a stern look. "I go bed when I want."

"Nice try, young lady," the voice of her mother sounded, making Alana's stern look vanish. "You're going to bed now and you know it."

Alana pouted before burying her face into Kadiri's tatted neck.

"Want me to read you a bedtime story, Lani?"

"Yes plwease," she whispered to him, gently nodding.

"I got you, sweetheart." He began leading the way to her bedroom, feeling Truth's stare on him from the kitchen.

"Uh-uh, not with those shoes you don't," Truth ordered, making Kadiri stop walking and sigh deeply.

"Relax." He kicked off his J's, leaving him in his white socks. "I got it, Baby Mama."

Truth watched as he walked to Alana's bedroom. She was low-key glad that Kadiri was here to put Alana to sleep because she'd been having a tough time trying to get her to go. All she wanted to do was watch another episode of Cocomelon despite knowing that she had to be up early for school tomorrow.

I might as well pour me a glass of wine and curl up with a good book, Truth mused to herself before deciding to do exactly that. She'd had a long day and needed to relax.

No, what you need is some dick, girl.

Truth immediately shook her head at the thought.

Hell no. I'm not calling Jodell. That night we shared last weekend was a mistake. And it's not happening again. Hell no.

Truth meant it. She didn't want to go down the toxic path of fucking her baby daddy because it wouldn't end well. And the last thing she needed was to get pregnant by him again. Her and Jodell were strictly co-parents. That was it.

Chapter Twenty-Six

Truth's eyes cracked open and she squinted as a few stray rays of sunlight filtered through her curtains, lighting her surroundings. An instant pain in her neck caused her to raise her head but she suddenly froze when she realized that she felt the hardness of a chest against her back.

What the...

She looked over her shoulder and her eyes bulged when she realized what was behind her... *who* was behind her. Truth's panic rushed through her as she examined his face.

He was still asleep and lost in his own private world which she was glad about because she didn't want him to wake up and realize the position they'd fallen asleep in. A very unexpected position that Truth never would have thought she'd be in. She'd woken up with her body draped across the body of the last person she'd ever expected to be this close to.

Her eyes darted over to the center coffee table and seeing the two empty wine glasses that stood in place including the empty bottle of her favorite Merlot, made the memories of last night flood into her mental.

"*She's finally out for the count.*"

"*Thank you for doing that, Kadiri.*"

"*No need to thank me.*"

"*Still, thank you. You don't need to be doing that but you want to anyway.*"

"*Anything for my Lani. That's my baby.*"

"*At first I was skeptical about you wanting to be close to her but I get it now, you love her.*"

"*Yeah... I do.*"

"*You treat her like she's your own and I know how much she loves and appreciates you.*"

"*Look at you, being nice for a change. That red juice got you feeling sappy, huh?*"

"*No. I'm always nice and FYI it's not juice.*"

"*So what is it then?*"

"*Merlot.*"

"*Oh I shoulda known you were the type to drink that bougie shit. I see you.*"

"*It's not... I mean shit... it was kinda expensive.*"

"*There's nothing wrong with liking the expensive shit, Baby Mama.*"

"*You ain't ever gonna quit calling me that, huh?*"

"*Nope.*"

"*Even though I've stopped calling you Skinny Boy?*"

"*Don't matter. It has a ring to it and we both know you love it.*"

"*No I don't.*"

"*Keep lying to yourself if that's what helps you sleep at night, love.*"

"*You ever try Merlot, Skinny Boy?*"

"*Oh so now we're back to Skinny Boy.*"

"Yes we are."

"Look at you smiling and shit, you've loved calling me that from the jump even though you know there ain't nothing skinny about me."

"Whatever you say, Skinny Boy... so answer my question. Have you tried it?"

"I don't think I have."

"Wanna try it now?"

"I don't see why not."

She poured him a glass and he took his place next to her on the couch. He began to ask her how her day went and she told him before asking him about his. Their natural conversation flowed and it wasn't long till Truth was pouring Kadiri another glass of Merlot. Then another and another and another.

He became an open book, expressing his love for Alana and how he couldn't wait to be a father one day. When Truth asked if him and Kiana were ready to have a child together, she was shocked to hear him say, *"Hell no."*

He kept it real with Truth and told her how he didn't see a future with Kiana. He had love for her and always would but she wasn't the love of his life.

"So why not break up with her if you don't see a future with her?"

"Every time we break up we just end up getting back together. I can't be bothered to break up just to fuck and make up again."

"Wow."

"What? I'm just being honest. Besides, I don't really wanna see her ass with anyone else right now."

"So you're selfish and toxic. Got it."

"Like I said I'm just being honest, man. She's mine for the time being and when she's not she'll be free to bounce to the next dick that she wants."

"And what if she decides to bounce early because you're not taking her seriously?"

"Then I guess I gotta say hasta la vista to her ass and get a piece of that pussy one last time."

"Oh my God. Your toxic ass! I can't stand you."

Truth lifted her body off Kadiri's and planted her feet on her gray rug before standing on her feet. She turned around to read the time of the black analog clock mounted on her wall and released a sigh of relief at the time – *7:05 a.m.*

She still had plenty of time to not only get Alana ready for school but she had time to get herself ready for work. Truth's eyes lowered to the sleeping being on her couch. As peaceful as he looked, Truth needed to get her day started and she didn't want Alana to wake up to find Kadiri still here. Truth knew her baby like the back of her hand and knew that seeing Kadiri would not only excite but have her getting the wrong impression thinking that Kadiri could always stay the night at their house. For a three year old, Alana was pretty smart and she understood relationship dynamics between women and men. That was one of the many reasons why Truth didn't want to mess with Jodell anymore. She didn't want Alana getting confused by thinking that Mommy and Daddy were back together when they were not.

"Kadiri."

Truth gently called out to him, hoping it would be enough to pull him out of his slumber. It wasn't though because he didn't move a muscle. His chest continued to rise and fall as he peacefully slept.

"Kadiri, get up." She dropped a hand to his shoulder, tapping it repeatedly.

He snapped awake, his cognac eyes revealing themselves to her.

"I gotta get Alana ready for school and I got work, nigga. You gotta go."

Kadiri rubbed the sleep from his eyes with one hand and covered a yawn with the other.

"What time is it?" he asked, his morning voice extra deep and raspy.

"Time for you to go." She walked in the direction of Alana's bedroom with her phone in hand.

"Lemme take a quick shower, Tru."

Truth froze in her stance, frowning at the thought of him using her amenity. A small smile creeped up on Kadiri's face as he watched her turn to face him with a frown.

"C'mon. Just a quick shower won't hurt," he voiced as he sat upright. "Besides, I thought you were being nice to me for a change, Baby Mama?"

Truth's face softened.

"Or is that only when you have that red juice in your system?"

"The same red juice that had you telling me all your life secrets you mean?"

He chuckled as he stood up from the couch.

"You mean the red juice that had you falling asleep on a nigga's chest?"

Truth's cheeks burned.

"Yeah that juice," he confirmed with a never ending smirk still in place on his handsome face. "You gonna let me shower or what?"

She deeply sighed.

"Towels are inside the bathroom, in the cupboard on your left."

He smiled, shooting a wink her way before making his way to her bedroom. While he went to shower, Truth made her way to Alana's room to check on her. Finding her still in a deep slumber wasn't a surprise because Alana wasn't a morning person at all. Getting her up for school in the mornings was always a struggle which is why Truth always made sure that she left plenty of time in the mornings for Alana to complain, roll around in bed and groan about wanting more sleep.

Truth decided to give Alana a couple more minutes of shut eye, kissing her forehead before quietly exiting her bedroom. Since Kadiri was using her shower, Truth decided to head back to her living room and browse her phone while she waited on him to finish.

As she took her seat on her couch, her eyes met their empty glasses from last night.

Still can't believe we fell asleep. That Merlot really knocked us the hell out.

Truth lightly shook her head, unlocking her phone and heading to the Gmail app. She opened a few emails, responded to about five before deciding to scroll through Instagram and see what was new with the people she followed.

Ding!

A new text had come in from Kiana.

Dinner Saturday night? My treat x

Truth clicked on the message so she could respond.

"Yo, Tru."

The call of her name made her look over her shoulder only to suddenly wish she hadn't. She'd been so engrossed in her phone that she'd failed to notice the shower turning off and the sound of her bathroom door opening.

"Where's your lotion at? I need that."

Truth blinked slowly and it felt like every muscle in her body had frozen.

"Truth."

She focused in on his face, realizing that he'd been talking to her and she hadn't responded.

"My dresser. Top left drawer."

"Appreciate you," he thanked her and headed back into her bedroom.

Truth was left alone again and she returned to her phone, trying to distract her mind from what she'd just encountered. However, it was too late. Her mind wasn't interested in anything or anyone on her phone. Her mind was far more interested in dissecting what she'd just seen.

Kadiri Miller had just come out her bathroom with nothing but her lilac towel wrapped around his lower frame. And Truth couldn't deny how good he looked with those washboard abs of his. Water had been dripping down his sculpted middle and those tattoos inked into his light beige complexion never looked better.

Yeah he's fine but that's a problem I don't want or need. He's a father figure to Alana and a friend to me. That's all he'll ever be to me. A friend.

Truth entered the chat she had with Kiana and responded to her dinner proposal.

Saturday night is perfect for me.

Truth pressed send and left their chat so she could head back to Instagram. While on Instagram she promised herself that she would never take things any further than friendship with Kadiri. It could never and would never happen. And she would never disrespect Kiana like that.

Ever.

Chapter Twenty-Seven

"**N**o but this deal... My God, girls... this deal is about to change your lives."

"*Our* lives, Mama Tee. There's no way we're doing this without you," Thyri said which brought an instant smile to Theresa's face.

"How could we pull this off without our best momager in the world?" Tanai's rhetorical question only made Theresa's smile strengthen.

"You're the only person who we trust to handle this alongside us. The only person we trust to help us hire new employees and the only person we trust to encourage us when we feel overwhelmed with it all," Truth added, causing Theresa's eyes to mist.

"Girls... you're gonna make me cry." She laughed, lifting a hand to each eye to press underneath them in the hopes of keeping her waterworks at bay.

"We love you," Thyri cooed, getting up out of her seat to hug Theresa.

"We really do," Tanai agreed.

"Always will," Truth echoed her sisters' sentiments.

The sisters had all gotten out of their seats and huddled around Theresa, hugging her tight and stroking on her back as she cried tears of joy.

"Your father would be so proud of the three of you. So, so, so proud."

The girls nodded, knowing that Theresa was absolutely right. Their father would be proud to know how far his company had come and how far it was going because of his three daughters who had inherited his legacy. They'd inherited his legacy and turned it into a powerful household name that would last for many generations after them. Their father had left them the greatest gift of all - *generational wealth* - and they would forever be grateful for his ambition and great mind.

"Okay, okay, enough with my crying... let's finish eating."

The Wright sisters nodded in agreement before getting back into their seats and resuming their meal. It was seven-thirty p.m. and they were currently at Theresa's townhouse on the outskirts of Atlanta, enjoying a meal with their favorite woman in the whole wide world. Theresa was already aware of their new upcoming deal with Shield but now that they had gotten more details from Kason's team, they were eager to share with Theresa the rest of the information involving their collaboration.

Theresa was surprised and proud to know that Kason was involving their company alongside his. This was about to be a whole new ball game for The Wright Way because not only would their company be on a lot more radars, but they would also need a lot more employees to handle the huge workload coming their way. However, the girls weren't complaining at all. They were excited and ready for the big opportunity coming into their lives.

For dinner, Theresa had prepared various southern dishes just for them. She'd made all their favorites. Fried chicken, collard greens, cornbread, shrimp, mac and cheese, red beans with rice, chicken pot pie, corn pudding and fried okra. There was so much food still laid out in front of them despite how much they'd already packed on their plates and taken into their stomachs. Theresa never hesitated in over feeding her girls and tonight was no different. She kept encouraging them to keep taking more food from the various bowls laid out in front of them, not caring about how much food they'd already eaten.

"So Thyri, Truth... are wedding bells soon in the midst for you?"

"Hell no," Truth countered, grimacing at the thought of her walking down the aisle. "That's definitely not for me."

"Don't say that, Tru. You could meet that special someone any day now."

"That's what I keep telling her Mama Tee but she's not listening to me," Tanai intervened. "He could just walk into your life one day and boom! *First comes love. Then comes marriage. Then comes baby in the baby carriage.*"

Thyri and Theresa laughed at Tanai singing along to an old childhood rhyme. The only person not laughing at her singing was Truth, who wasn't finding anything amusing about what Tanai had prophesied for her life.

"Uh-uh." Truth shook her head 'no'. "Ain't no baby in no damn carriage. Marriage ain't for me. At all."

Theresa pouted at Truth's certainty towards marriage not being for her. She prayed that Truth didn't have this negative mindset towards marriage for the rest of her life because she would love to see her settle down with someone one day. She wanted all her girls to find that special someone and she was glad that Tanai had already found hers.

"And what about you, Thyri?"

"Oh you ain't know?" Truth's brow arched. "She's practically already married."

"To whom?" Theresa asked with shock while a shy look crossed Thyri's face.

"Killian," Truth revealed.

"Kason's older brother?"

"The one and only," Tanai confirmed. "They've been attracted to each other ever since he did her tattoo over a month ago. Once they got to Grenada, that pretty much sealed the deal for them."

The sound of a chord filled the room and Tanai's eyes landed on her phone that had lit up. One glance at the bright screen and she felt numbness infuse her body as she spotted her new email's title.

'No Subject.'

The last time Tanai had received an email with that label, she'd felt like her entire world had turned upside down.

God no. Not this shit again.

Instead of giving into her thoughts that were telling her to open the email, Tanai decided to clear the email's notification from her lock screen and focus back on dinner with her family. Whatever that email contained wasn't important right now and she wouldn't allow a complete stranger to ruin her evening.

But Tanai would be lying if she said she didn't want to know what the email contained this time. Was it another part of Kason's sex tape with the unknown woman? Was it a different sex tape? What if Kason had been lying to her all this time? What if he was still seeing this woma—

Please snap out of it, Tanai. You're at dinner with your family. This isn't the time to start worrying about shit that just doesn't matter right now. You'll deal with it later.

Tanai decided to listen to herself and kept her focus on the conversation that her family were having about Thyri and Killian.

Theresa was glad to know that Thyri had found someone who treated her with respect and brought her happiness. She'd known about Thyri's previous relationship with Chosen but hadn't really approved of him. There was something off about that boy that she could never seem to put her finger on. Now that Thyri had moved on from him, she was happy for her and praying that her relationship with Killian stood the test of time.

Nine p.m. came around and the girls decided to say their goodbyes to Mama Tee. They'd had a wonderful dinner, a delicious pecan pie dessert and had shared great conversation. Now it was time for them to go their separate ways and head home.

"Text me as soon as you both get through the door," Truth instructed, making Thyri and Tanai both nod as they each kissed and hugged one another goodbye.

Tanai walked towards the parked Mercedes S-Class limo waiting for her a short distance away from Theresa's front yard. The driver's door opened and a suited, ivory skinned man appeared, walking to open the right rear door.

"Good evening, Mrs. Miller." He smiled at her.

"Hey, Saber." She smiled back as she approached the open door.

"You enjoy your evening?"

"I did," she replied, gently nodding. "Thanks for picking me up."

"It's my job, ma'am."

"I know... but still, thank you."

He nodded respectfully at her before helping her get in the car. Once she was seated, he shut her car door and made his way to the driver's seat.

Along their journey home, Tanai was as silent as a ghost. Not even hearing her favorite band, *The Internet*, via the car's speakers was enough to get a sound out of her. Saber was privy to her music taste because she'd connected her phone to the limo's speakers along many of their journeys together. It had gotten to the point that she didn't even have to connect her phone because he had her music choices queued up for her. But tonight, music couldn't do anything for Tanai. She was too anxious for music tonight.

You can't ignore it forever, Nai. Open it.

She looked down at her phone that was sitting face down in her lap. Her nerves were rushing through her and only getting worse by the minute. She knew she needed to see what she'd been sent but she couldn't bring herself to unlock her phone. Her nerves weren't allowing her to.

Just do it, Nai. Get it over with.

She took a deep breath, peeking out the tinted window next to her and then exhaled. She lifted her device, bringing it to her face so her Face ID would grant her access. Once it unlocked and took her to the home screen, she pointed a finger towards the mail app. Seeing her finger shake made her take a deep breath and she tapped on her screen to enter the app.

The *'No Subject'* email was first on her inbox list and she braced herself before opening the message.

I'm sending this to the blogs in twenty four hours but I figured you deserve to see this first. He belongs to me and always will belong to me. I had him doing things and feeling things that you won't ever be able to do so good luck trying, Mrs. Tanai Miller.

Attached to the bottom of the email was a movie file, just like the first email she'd sent had. Tanai clicked on the file and the video began playing.

This time the video had an angle of both Kason and... *her.*

She was on her knees with her back arched but her face was positioned towards the camera as Kason thrusted into her from behind. Tanai examined her face, seeing that she was light skinned, had curly hair and a curvaceous body.

"Kay, baby... aghhhh!"

He pulled out of her and Tanai observed as he reached for something on the bed. She couldn't see exactly what it was because it was too small to see on camera. His fingers did a twisting motion and he lifted the object to the woman's butt hole. Tanai realized that the object was a small container and her eyes bulged when she realized what it contained.

He started tapping the container, sprinkling out the white powder that it held into her butt hole and reached on the bed for a green piece of paper that had Tanai's heart racing.

"Mmmh... you doing that sexy shit you love doing on my ass, huh, Daddy?"

"Damn straight," he replied before whispering, "Such a pretty ass."

He started rolling the dollar bill into a thin cylinder and lowered the cylinder to the woman's asshole. Once it was in place, he lowered his left nostril while keeping the right one closed with his finger and Tanai suddenly exited the video just as he started snorting.

She let go of her phone and lifted her hands to cover her face as the tears rushed down her cheeks.

Seeing her husband snort cocaine out of another woman's ass was triggering. Extremely triggering as Tanai had lost one of her closest friends at the age of twenty to a cocaine overdose. She'd been suffering with a cocaine addiction for three months. An addiction that she'd hid well from her family and friends. Not a single soul had known about her weakness for the white powder except her dealer. The last cocaine she'd been supplied with had been laced with a high dose of fentanyl and it had taken her life with no remorse or hesitation. Locking her body away in a coffin forever.

So for Tanai to see her beloved husband doing the one act that had taken the life of her friend – a death she'd confided in him about – fucking hurt!

Tanai wasn't even mad about the unknown woman's plan to expose the video. She was pissed and heartbroken about Kason doing coke and although it had been way before they'd gotten married, it had still happened. He'd taken the substance without delay, like it was second nature to him.

The remaining journey home, Tanai's cries continued and her mind swirled with dangerous thoughts. Thoughts of a word starting with D.

You promised to have and to hold your husband, Tanai. For better, for worse, remember that? This is worse and instead of sticking beside him you're trying to flee?

He's doing cocaine! How am I supposed to just erase that from my mind? How am I supposed to just act like everything's fine?

To love and to cherish, 'til death do you part, Tanai. Kason told you he doesn't know the meaning of divorce and won't ever sign any papers to release you from being his wife. He won't let you g—

"Mrs. Miller," Saber's baritone filled the car. "We're home."

Tanai sighed, wiping her wet cheeks dry before pressing the intercom in the armrest beside her.

"Thank you," she said in a low tone.

Moments later, the car door was opened for her and she stepped out into the cool night, holding onto Saber's arm as he led her to the front door. Tanai looked ahead to see a figure standing in the open doorway and when she spotted the grin on his face as they came closer, a weight settled on her heart. Her hold on Saber's well-built arm tightened.

"Is everything okay, Mrs. Miller?" Saber questioned her in a hushed tone.

"Yes," she whispered as they inched nearer to the front door.

"Thank you for bringing my wife home safe as always, Saber," Kason announced as he stepped out the doorway, extending his arms out for Tanai to walk into.

"You welcome, sir."

Saber turned to Tanai to say goodnight and she loosened her hold on his arm as she said goodnight. He then left the couple alone.

"Nugget, I missed you."

His arms were still stretched out and feeling like she had no choice but to, Tanai walked into his arms and allowed him to hug her.

"How was dinner with Theresa and your sisters?" he asked as he held her tight, stroking her back through her Burberry trench coat. "You eaten enough or you still want something to eat?"

"I'm good," she replied and Kason broke their hug, nodding at her with understanding.

"Okay lemme rephrase that." He smirked. "Do you want something to eat or do you want to be eaten?"

He tried to pull her closer to him but she shrugged him off and avoided his gaze. It was at this moment that Kason noticed how red her eyes were. A worried expression marred his face as he closely scanned her face. Realizing that he was starting to notice her mood, Tanai walked past him to enter their home. The pull of her arm stopped her from reaching the stairs.

"Tell me what's wrong."

Tanai lowered her head and felt a tightness form in her throat.

"N-Nothing," she croaked out.

"Don't lie to me, Tanai."

She heard the front door shut behind her and his pull on her arm tightened. He started pulling her backwards, trying to get her to face him once again but she remained rooted in her stance, not wanting to face him.

"Tanai."

"I-I can't... I don't wanna go through this shit."

"What?" Kason's brows squished together. "What shit?"

"Just let me go," she ordered, tugging her arm out his reach and succeeding in being let go from his hold.

"What are you talking about, Tanai?"

She ignored him, racing towards the stairs, and running up them. Before climbing the first step, she kicked off her heels and dropped her Chanel bag to the floor.

"Tanai!"

She heard his footsteps chasing after her but she pressed ahead, determined to get upstairs to her room and get to her bathroom. Along the way, she unbuttoned her trench coat, pulling it off her shoulders and dropped it to the floor behind her without a care about the risk of someone tripping over it.

"Tanai, I'm talking to you!"

She continued to ignore him, reaching the top of the stairs, and rushing across the hallway leading to the master bedroom. Once she was inside the room, she sprinted across the large space and ran into the en-suite. The second she turned to shut the door behind her, a large hand came pounding hard on the door, keeping it wedged open.

"Kason, leave me al—"

"I'm never doing that shit so dead it out of your mind right fucking now, Tanai," he snapped, glaring at her without blinking.

Tanai stepped away from the door, not wanting to be close to him but having no choice as he barged his way into the bathroom.

"You need to tell me what's going on," he bossed. "That isn't a request either, it's an order."

"I'm not your child so don't talk to me like I'm one!" she yelled, pointing a finger at him. "And stay the fuck away from me! I don't want you anywhere near me tonight!"

Kason's heart almost stopped at her words and he froze, feeling like he'd just been shot. His lips parted but no words came out. He didn't have anything to say to what she'd just said because it had shocked him to the core. The whole world seemed to be moving in slow motion. He felt like he was walking in a dream world; a horrific, nightmarish dream world.

Tanai's eyes misted with tears as she stared into his eyes. His eyes that were filled with anguish because of the harsh words that had fallen from her lips. Harsh words that were only the small preview of the many harsher things she intended to say to him tonight.

"I had no idea that I married a cokehead."

He blinked rapidly, feeling heat flood his insides.

"I had no idea that I married a *cokehead* who likes doing lines out of bitches' asses!"

The mention of coke, doing lines and asses was more than enough information for Kason to register what was going on. More than enough information for Kason to realize why his wife had been crying before she'd arrived home to him tonight.

"She sent another video."

"Yeah she sent another fucking video!" Tanai yelled. "Another video of you doing coke, Kason. Cocaine!"

"Nai..."

"You know what that drug's done to my life! You know who I've lost because of it!" The tears that had formed in her eyes dropped and before she knew it, she was crying.

Kason could feel his heart breaking as he watched her cry and he couldn't stand it. He walked up to where she stood in the center of the room, ignoring her head shakes and her attempt to keep him at bay by lifting her hands.

"No, l-leave me al—"

"Baby, I'm sorry. I'm so sorry."

Tanai's chest caved in as he pulled her into him, wrapping his arms around her and refusing to let go. Even as she hit against his hard chest, trying to get him to leave her alone, he only held on tighter.

"Just tell me what to do to fix this and I'll do it, Nugget. I promise."

Tanai's loud sobs filled the room, breaking his heart more and more.

He promised you that you wouldn't be disrespected again and look what's happened tonight, Tanai. You've been disrespected and humiliated. And the humiliation is only going to get worse once she leaks that video to the blogs.

Tanai eventually got herself together and stopped crying. She looked up to see Kason's pained filled eyes locked on hers. Knowing that she wasn't about to be released from his arms without showing some sort of compliance, Tanai extended her neck to plant a closed mouth kiss to his mouth.

The kiss was unexpected but Kason quickly welcomed it, loosening his arms from around her body to lift his hands to her face so he could deepen the kiss. The second Tanai felt his arms leave her body, she yanked herself away from him and shot him a cruel look. Kason's heart dropped as he realized that he'd been played. The kiss was nothing but a tactic to get him to drop his guard and it'd worked because now he no longer had a hold on her.

He stepped forward to try and grab her again but she stepped far away, edging towards their bathtub at the far end of the room. He decided to stop following her and his shoulders dropped with a sigh.

"She's leaking that video to the blogs in twenty four hours and I don't want to be here when it's out."

"She's not leaking shit. I'll make sure of that."

Tanai scoffed.

"The same way you made sure that she wouldn't contact me again? Sure."

A few days after Tanai had received the first email from the woman, she realized how the woman had found her email in the first place. On The Wright Way's website, all the sisters had put their business emails up for clients to be able to contact them individually if need be. The woman had found out Tanai's company website and seen her email on there.

"My guys have been searching for her, Nai, but she's disappeared without a trace. She's been planning this for a minute because every record of her from the internet has been wiped. Even her bank accounts in her name were closed down the same date our elopement made headlines."

"I don't care about her," Tanai retorted. "I can't do this."

Kason's face hardened.

"I can't be here in this house with you, Kason. I just can't."

How tonight had turned into a complete shit show, Kason wasn't sure but what he did know was that this was the last thing he needed to happen tonight. His wife was supposed to be his peace and their house, their sanctuary but tonight everything between them had turned to chaos in a matter of minutes.

Trinity's tricks had showcased again tonight and she'd sent over another video that Kason had no idea existed.

That bitch must have been secretly recording me. Fuck!

The more Kason thought about what Trinity had done and was doing to his marriage, the more heated he got. But what was really pissing him off was Tanai's inability to just listen to him. She was more focused on trying to leave him tonight which would only cause further problems between them rather than solutions. He understood that seeing him do coke had been a triggering experience for her but it's not like he was doing the shit today. Why she was blowing this out of proportion, Kason didn't understand. She was acting like she'd been present in the room with him and Trinity when he'd done it when she hadn't. It had happened long ago and it wasn't happening again. Why wasn't she getting that?

"I'm packing a bag and goin—"

"Nowhere, Tanai. You're not leaving me," he cut her off and she looked at him without blinking. "Are you really trying to leave me over some bullshit from my past? My past that had nothing to do with you." He paused, contemplating about the situation at hand. It was fucked up yes but Tanai was blowing things out of proportion. "I'm sorry you lost your friend and I know how much it hurt to see me do the one thing that cost her life but I'm not a cokehead, Tanai. I'm your husband and I'm not letting you use this situation as an excuse to walk away from us. There is no walking away from us. Me and you?" He pointed from him to her. "This is it. Till both our hearts stop beating. You know that so stop tryna act brand new. My past is in the past and right now I'm only focused on my present and future which is you."

Tanai was silent for a few seconds, bringing a slight discomfort to Kason's heart.

"I need some space."

When she finally spoke up, that discomfort only worsened.

"And you can have all the space you need in the comfort of our bed," he replied, sternness ingrained into his visage. "You're not leaving your husband."

"I said I need space. What aren't you understanding?"

"And I said you can have plenty of space in our bed. Don't make me have to repeat myself."

"You can't make me sleep in the bed with you."

His left brow arched in a manner that seemed to ask her, *Wanna bet?*

She decided to stay quiet and looked at him as he looked right back at her.

Tanai took the silence that formed between them as an opportunity to think. It was evident that he wasn't about to let her leave their house tonight even though that's what she really wanted and it was clear that he wanted her sleeping in their king sized bed even though that's the last thing she wanted to do. So there was only one other option and Tanai knew she had to be smart in order to make sure it happened.

"Fine," she reluctantly announced. "I'm not leaving."

Relief coursed through his veins at her words and he nodded in agreement.

"You're not leaving."

Tanai slowly inched forward, shortening the gap that had formed between them. He could see the mixture of anger and hurt flashing in her eyes as she came closer to him. She then stepped around him, heading towards the door but before she could completely walk away, he gently grabbed her hand.

"Nai, I'm gonna make things right. I swear to you."

She said nothing but the anger and hurt disappeared from her eyes after he'd spoken. A weak smile graced her lips before she said, "Can you let me go so I can get ready for bed?"

He nodded and let her hand go, allowing her to walk past him and leave the bathroom. Kason sighed and turned around to head out the bathroom too. The second he turned around, he spotted Tanai running through their bedroom and that's when his heart started racing.

"Tanai!"

He immediately ran after her, worry snaking through him at

the thought of her leaving him when they'd both just agreed she wasn't going anywhere.

Tanai didn't stop or say anything in return to him as she dashed out their bedroom. She knew how fast he was but she wasn't about to give him the advantage of catching up to her. She went through the hallway and straight into the guest bedroom on the other end.

"Tana—"

Bam!

The sound of the door locking was heard just as Kason had made it to the door. He lifted a fist and let out an exasperated breath.

Knock! Knock! Knock!

"Tanai, open the door."

"I told you I need space, Kason. So leave me the hell alone!"

Knock! Knock! Knock! Knock! Knock! Knock!

She flinched as his knocks on the door became louder and quicker.

"Tanai, open the door. Now."

"No."

"I haven't gone a single night without you being by my side as I sleep, Tanai, and I don't intend to start doing that shit now. Open the door. Right now."

"Just leave me alone!" She yelled. "I don't want to be around you, I can't stand the sight of you and I'm disgusted that you think just because the video is from your past, I'm not allowed to be upset. I'm allowed to be upset, Kason! I'm allowed to be fucking upset! I'm sleeping in this room alone whether you like it or not. You can't and won't control me. I'm not the bitch you smoked coke out of. You make me fucking sick and I regret marrying you."

Silence.

370

Nothing but silence followed her monologue. Silence so loud that you could hear a pin drop if it fell on the ground right now.

Tanai stared at the door, expecting to hear something come from the other side. But nothing came. Not his knocking or his yelling came bursting through.

It was just silent.

Pure silence.

Then moments later, she heard his footsteps departing from the door and then shortly after a door slammed. Tanai felt her heart crumble and tears swam in her eyes. She buried her face in her hands as her tears fell, realizing that things between her and Kason would never be the same again.

Chapter Twenty-Eight

S leep was good for the soul and needed for the brain to relax and recharge. It was supposed to be a refuge from the craziness of life but for Tanai, sleep had been exhausting. And I know that probably didn't make any sense because how could sleep be exhausting when it's entire purpose was to replenish the mind, body, and soul? But for Tanai it had been nothing but exhausting.

All night she'd been consumed by dreams about her husband. She'd seen him with the unknown woman in the sex tapes and seen him with women that her mind had completely made up. His promiscuous nature prior to their marriage had dominated her mind nonstop. She'd not woken up out of her sleep once during her dreaming. Something about the dreams - no the nightmares - just sucked her in and kept her asleep. Forced to be subjected to the fears and insecurities of her mind about her husband being with women that weren't her.

Tanai's eyelids gave flutter like brand new butterfly wings hoping for flight. She suddenly fixed on a figure through a lazy squint and confusion snaked through her at her mind deciding to play tricks on her.

I know damn well I slept in this room alone so why am I seeing someone here?

Her eureka moment suddenly happened as she realized who the figure was.

God no!

Her eyes grew large at the sight of him sitting on a chair beside her bedside. His arms were crossed over his shirted chest and his eyes puffy with dark circles underneath them.

No! No! No!

She jolted up out the bed, trying to turn away from him but was stopped by her left hand refusing to cooperate.

She looked over at it and her heart skipped several beats as she noticed the silver metal cuffed around her wrist. Her eyes followed the chain attached to it that led to the oak bedside table next to the bed. The other end of the handcuff was secured to one of the bedside table's wooden legs, keeping her locked in place.

"Release me," she ordered. "Now, Kason."

Her eyes met his and she glared at him before looking over at the bedroom door that was open.

She'd been so deep in her nightmares that she'd failed to hear him picking the lock of the guest bedroom and she'd failed to defend herself before he could handcuff her to the side table.

"Release me now!" She screamed, frantically jerking her arm, causing the table to shift slightly at her movement.

He didn't respond and chose to keep surveying her with a blank stare. Tanai groaned at her trapped state, continuing to fuss and move until she could no longer be bothered. She eventually remained still, huffing, and sighing as frustration bubbled up inside her.

"You done?" he asked moments later but Tanai was quiet, no longer having the strength to say a word to him.

"You had plenty of time to talk all your shit last night but now it's my turn and you're going to listen, Tanai, the same way I listened to you."

Tanai sighed deeply, feeling like she wanted to scream their entire house down but she knew there was no point. He wasn't going to let her go.

Kason first began with the video.

"I am not that man anymore, Tanai. I'm your man, your husband and I'm not allowing the past to come between us. I'm sorry that you had to see that shit and I'm sorry that I didn't admit to you my past use of cocaine but like I said before it's in the past and it's not something I ever intend to do again."

Then he went on to explain how he was handling the situation.

"While you slept all night in here, I've been up with Harris."

Harris was Kason's attorney, a man that Tanai knew quite well because the day she became Mrs. Miller was the day Harris also became her attorney.

"We've sent out warnings to all major blog pages about their future decisions to post any inflammatory and defaming information about you or me. My hackers are at the ready too in case any of them choose to defy my warning then that's their precious blog careers gone."

He also went on to explain how Trinity was being taken care of.

"We've tracked her down in Idaho. She used a fake identity to cross state lines and a new number to communicate with her younger brother. She'll be found in the next hour and be brought back to Atlanta by the end of the day."

Lastly, he brought up the harsh words that Tanai had spoken last night.

"You said you regret marrying me." His eyes darkened with pain. "You really mean that shit, Nai?"

She said nothing, allowing her head to fall as she thought back to last night.

Of course I didn't mean it. I was just so damn angry.

"No," she replied in a low tone.

"Nai, look at me."

Her head slowly lifted and she met his pleading eyes.

"You regret marrying me?"

"No," she repeated and his heart skipped with joy. "But I'm not going to lay here and act like everything's good between us because it's not. And you know it's not, Kason."

"I'm trying to make things right, Tanai. I've been up all night trying to find that bitch and ruin her plans of leaking that ta—"

"I don't give a fuck about her!" she yelled. "I give a fuck about my sanity and if you truly gave a fuck about making things right between us you would've given me the space I needed last night."

Kason immediately started shaking his head 'no'.

"You had your space when you slept in our guest bedroom."

"The same guest bedroom you've broken into and chained my hand to the fucking side table, Kason!" she screamed and angrily yanked her arm, causing the oak table to slightly shift.

"If you're about to tell me the same bullshit about you packing a bag and leaving me—"

"That's what I wan—"

"The answer still remains the same as yesterday, beloved." His eyes were suddenly cold as ice as he said, "No."

"Kason!"

He ignored her and rose to his feet.

"Kason, let me g—"

"I said no," he spat the words out through gritted teeth. Frustration and disdain were wrapped in his instruction. "You are not leaving me and that's final. As much as I hated you sleeping in this room rather than ours, I'm gonna respect the fact that you'd rather sleep alone for a few more nights. I'll take one of the guest rooms and you can take our bedroom. But all this talk of packing a bag ends now, Nai. This is your home, *our* home and I'm not letting you walk away from it. Now I can't and won't ever stop you from going out to work, to your personal appointments and doing whatever else makes you happy, but after that's all said and done, you will be returning to one place – this house. Disobey me and I promise you I'll not only come and get your ass, but I'll be also handcuffing every part of you to our bed, Tanai."

"You monst—"

"Camila!"

A tanned skinned woman came rushing into the bedroom and Tanai's eyes widened at the arrival of her head maid.

She's been here the whole time?

"Uncuff her," he ordered before taking bold strides to the exit to leave the women alone.

"Have a great day today, Nugget," he said over his shoulder. "I'll see you later on tonight."

Tanai watched as Camila lifted a silver key out of her white half apron and came closer to uncuff Tanai.

"Camila, do you see what he's done to me?"

Camila gently nodded, sporting a sympathetic look as she released Tanai.

"He won't let me go despite knowing how much he's hurt me."

"He loves you, Señora."

"Well he has a pretty messed up way of showing it."

Tanai rubbed on her wrist and huffed out a breath. Her gaze went to the handcuffs that Camila now held.

"How the hell did he even find handcuffs..." Tanai's words trailed off as she came to the realization of how Kason had gotten his hands on handcuffs.

They'd been in his closet where Tanai had left them after the amazing night they'd enjoyed together. A very freaky night indeed.

"You can't keep teasing your husband like this, Tanai... baby, you need to uncuff me."

"Be a good boy tonight and I just might."

"Baby, you see how hard my dick is right now?"

"Oh I definitely see how hard he is... and I promise you if you keep being a good boy for me then you'll be able to put him anywhere inside me that you want."

She shook her head at the sexual memory, slipped out of bed and thanked Camila for letting her go. She made her way to the master bedroom, suddenly stopping when she assumed Kason was in there. The sound of their front door opening and closing reminded her of his goodbye:

I'll see you later on tonight.

She was suddenly reminded by his attire. He was already dressed in a white button down shirt and black slacks. One of his work outfits that Tanai always found sexy and sophisticated on him.

I need to get out of this house. Now. Tanai raced towards her bedroom. The only thing on her mind right now was leaving this house. Nothing else mattered.

Chapter Twenty-Nine

Tanai: *I promise I'm fine, I just have a few things I need to take care of.*

      Tanai: *I'll be in next week bright and early.*

Tanai: *Love you both so much.*

Thyri stared down at the latest texts from Tanai and felt her scalp prickle.

Something was off.

Tanai had claimed that she was fine in their group chat but the restlessness that Thyri could feel creeping up inside her told her different. Her sisterly instinct was shooting out red flags at Tanai's lack of attendance at work today.

She couldn't put her finger on what it was but something was definitely off with Tanai and Thyri knew that she would need to get to the bottom of it when she next laid eyes on her sister.

Thyri grabbed her lavender Telfar bag at the edge of her bed, dropped her phone into the bag and made her way out her bedroom. Once she was in the living room, she went to her shoe rack to grab her Nike sneakers and placed them on.

She took one last look at herself in the mirror hanging in her front foyer before opening her door and leaving her apartment.

Minutes later, she was inside the parking lot of her building, walking towards her Lambo. When she arrived at the driver's door, the sound of a car door opening was heard but she paid it no mind as she pulled open her car's door.

"Thyri."

That was until she heard the call of her name and a baritone that she recognized very well. Her body tensed and she stood facing her car as she heard footsteps approach her from behind.

"You really thought ignoring me was going to work forever, huh?"

Thyri refused to turn around and face him but she didn't have to because Chosen arrived at the trunk of her car.

"Thyri, how could you do this shit to me? To us?"

Thyri almost wanted to laugh at his questions but instead she chose to remain quiet. Keeping her body facing her car and her line of gaze looking at the row of cars parked along hers.

"Answer me, Thyri!" he yelled, slamming on the trunk of her car. An action that immediately made her spear him with a glare.

"Don't slam on my car," she snapped. "I don't know if you've gotten amnesia or something but my boyfriend made it very clear that you aren't allowed to make being in my presence a habit and here you are disobeying him. He doesn't play about me so if you knew better you'd do better by staying the fuck away from me."

"Wow." Chosen lifted his hands and repeatedly clapped them together. "You really have been brainwashed by the biggest player in the city."

"I haven't been brainwashed." She paused, wanting to ask him what he meant by *biggest player* but decided not to. "Just stay away from me, Chosen."

"He won't ever love you the way I do, Thyri, and you know

that. But let me tell you what you don't know. You don't know his reputation with women in the city and how he treats them like they're just another number on his hit list. He hurts people, Thyri and pretty soon he'll hurt you."

He's lying, Thyri. He's just mad that you chose Killian over him.

"Don't end our relationship because of a man you barely know... all the time and history we've shared together, you're really going to throw that away, Thyri? I know I haven't always been the best man but I promise to do better... I'll be better for you, for us. I'll stop trying to pin my dreams on you and actually listen to you, Ri. I promise."

It's a little too late for that, nigga. I've moved on and I'm happy. Much happier than you ever made me.

"Move away from my car unless you're tryna get ran the fuck over, Chosen," she spat out, opening her car door wider and getting inside her car.

She quickly shut the car door before Chosen could get another word in. Following her warning, Chosen stepped out the way so that he wouldn't be hit by Thyri's car reversing out the parking bay. He knew Thyri wasn't playing about running him over. She really would do it.

Chosen's shoulders slumped as he watched Thyri drive out the parking lot and once her car was out the lot, he began to boil with so much fury that he had to grit his teeth for control.

How the fuck have I lost her to that nigga, man? Fuck! I can't allow this. She's mine and mine only.

As much as he tried convincing himself that Thyri was his – the fact remained she was with Killian and not him.

Chosen let out a breath, reaching into his back pocket for his phone and heading to his contacts. When he found the name he was looking for, he clicked on it and initiated a call. The call was picked up on the first ring.

"Yeah?"

"I need that thing we discussed done ASAP. Are you still in?"

"Yeah I'm in. You ready to cough up that bread?"

"Money is no object. Just as long as you get the job done."

"It'll be done don't you worry."

"Cool." He started walking towards his Range Rover. "You home?"

"Yeah." She giggled. "You missing this pussy already, huh?"

Choosing to ignore her query, he stated, "Leave the door open. I'll be over in a few minutes."

"Alright. See you soon."

She wasn't Thyri but she'd do for tonight. Chosen needed to release some stress and he needed to release it fast. He was done trying to get through to Thyri with words because in his mind his words alone weren't working.

Unbeknownst to Chosen, his words had definitely struck a chord with Thyri. As she drove to her destination she was left reeling at what he'd said.

He hurts people, Thyri and pretty soon he'll hurt you.

Killian would never hurt her... right? He'd put too much confidence in her when it came to their relationship so why she was even entertaining Chosen's foolish lies she didn't know. What she did know was that she needed to stop entertaining the stupid thoughts of her ex. Her and Killian were solid.

Less than twenty minutes later, Thyri was in the arms of the only person she wanted.

"You... smell... so... fucking... good," he whispered as he kissed into her neck.

"Thank you, baby... mmh, Kill... didn't you say you wanted to do something important with me tonight?"

Friday night had finally come and what better way to bring in the weekend than being with her favorite man in the whole wide world? Killian was all for Thyri spending her Friday night with him and he'd told her how he had planned something important that he needed her for.

"Yeah... but this is important too," he replied, reaching for the straps of her mini dress. "I know for a fact that you taste as good as you smell so I'ma need a taste of that right no—"

"Killian," she giggled, pulling out his arms and lifting a finger, shaking it left to right as she shook her head 'no'. "I wanna know what was so important."

Killian let his eyes sweep up and down the tight fitting, black mini dress she had on and sunk his teeth into his bottom lip. When he'd helped her take off her coat earlier and seen what she was wearing underneath he couldn't stop admiring her which is why he knew he had to get his hands on her and his lips all up on her. But sadly she'd stopped him and the stern look she wore told him that she had no intentions on giving him some *special quality time* until he revealed to her what was so important.

"Okay, fine," he said, giving into her like he always did. "Take your clothes off."

"Killian!"

"What?" He laughed. "I'm being serious. Take your clothes off. This is important."

Her right brow hiked and he laughed some more at her.

"I want to paint you," he revealed, causing surprise to flood Thyri's core. "Will you let me paint you, Bubba?" He stepped closer to her and kept his desire filled eyes stuck on her. "Will you give me the honor of painting that heavenly body of yours?"

Her head slowly went up and down at the same moment his hands held onto her waist, pulling her in close to him.

"Yes?" he asked before bending low to brush his soft lips against hers.

"Yes," she confirmed. "Yes, yes, yes!"

Kilian beamed at the excitement evident in her voice. Even the way her brown eyes were glowing with joy told him about her exhilaration for what he had in store for her tonight.

"Alright, let's get you ready."

Killian led her to his bedroom where he had his Versace robe and slides waiting for her. He told her to get undressed, put on the robe and meet him in his studio. Then he gave her some privacy and headed to his studio.

As he waited for her to undress and come join him, Killian felt a fluttery feeling form in his stomach and he tittered at his current emotion.

Nervous to paint your own girlfriend? Come on, nigga.

He couldn't help it though. He was honored to be painting her for the first time and he really didn't want to mess this up. He wanted this artwork to be one of his best artworks – possibly the best – and he wanted it to be perfect.

Moments later, his studio's door slowly opened and his beauty stepped into the room. Even with just his robe on, she still looked like the best piece of art he'd ever laid eyes on.

"So... where do you want me?" Her shy tone filled the room as she walked deeper into his space.

Killian grinned, walking towards her at the same time she walked towards him. He held out his hand for her to latch onto when they were close and led her towards the blue velvet sofa in the center of the room.

"Right here."

Thyri noticed the sofa and the new set up of his studio. He had a blank canvas sitting on an easel stand in the right hand corner of the room and a table next to it that carried his acrylic paints, brushes, and palette knives.

He held her hand as she took her center seat and pressed a kiss to her hand once she was seated.

"What position do you want me in, Kill?"

"Any position you like," he replied. "Whatever position you feel comfortable in, is the position I want you in. Tonight's all about you, Bubba. Nobody else but you."

Then he stepped away from her and took his position behind the canvas. Thyri untied the robe's belt before pushing the cotton robe over her shoulders and letting it fall off her frame. She chucked it to the floor then got on the sofa to lay on her side, making sure Killian had an entire view of her body.

"Damn, I really have the best view right now."

Heat burned her cheeks and she simpered at his comment.

Killian's eyes travelled down her womanly frame, admiring her naked body and when he caught a glimpse of a gold chain secured around her left ankle, he focused his gaze on it and noticed the letter 'K' hanging off the chain. Killian got a warm, fuzzy feeling at the realization of what she'd done. She'd gotten an anklet with his initial on it.

"You know damn well I'm the only one allowed to buy you jewelry, Thyri."

She giggled.

"I wanted to surprise you."

Surprised he was and he got the sudden urge to ditch their painting session just so he have her on her back and her legs in the air so he could see, and hear that anklet jiggle while he gave her the deepest strokes.

Later, nigga. You've got a job to do, he told himself, shaking away his filthy fantasies.

He decided to put his glasses on and got started on setting the mood of his studio for his girl to be extra comfortable. Thyri was surprised when Killian said he'd created a playlist just for her and he played it in the background while putting his brushes to the canvas.

He had all her favorite artists in rotation. Summer Walker to make her feel empowered and remind Thyri all about how *Girls Need Love* too. Miguel to soothe her soul and *Adorn* her. Beyoncé to remind her how *1 + 1* equals two and confirm to her what she already knew about her having Killian's heart. Doja Cat to remind her how much of a *Freak* she was for Killian and how she was a good girl who did bad things to him. The Internet to make her never forget how she was Killian's *Girl* and how anything she wanted was hers. Thyri was left in awe at his attention to detail. He knew all the artists she liked listening to and had placed them into a playlist made specially for her. She continued to listen while Killian painted away.

There was nothing greater than seeing her man create. He was a chasm between his mind and soul, juggling the two as he placed his vision to the white canvas. He was a storm that couldn't be tamed. Each emotion that crossed his face was charming and yet terrifying. But terrifying in a good way. Terrifying because he looked so damn godly as he poured his heart out onto the canvas. Like a king that could never be shaken off his throne. The way he would stop and concentrate on his work, staring at it hard like it needed to obey his every wish and command, was a turn on. The way he would let his eyes land on her, devouring her face and figure with his gaze, was another huge turn on. Every part of him was a turn on in fact and Thyri was convinced she could never get bored feeling that heat build inside her as she watched him.

It took him just under two hours to finish his art and when she thought it was time for the big reveal, he shook his head 'no', much to her dismay. He came to stand in front of her as she sat upright on the sofa with her feet planted on the floor.

"But Killy..." she pouted and stared up at him. "I wanna see it."

"And you will, Bubba. When it's one hundred percent done

and ready. I promise."

She continued to pout and he grinned as he cupped her chin in his palm.

"Thank you for being my muse tonight, Thyri. That shit really means a lot to me."

"You mean a lot to me," she responded, lifting his hand that had been cupping her chin.

"You mean everything to me, Ri…"

He watched as she brought his tatted hand to her lips, wrapping her lips around his index finger and sucking on it slow. She moved her mouth around his finger as if she was sucking on a piece of candy. He felt a drop of precum leak out his tip and wet his boxers. Then she popped his finger out her mouth, shooting him an innocent smile.

This tease, he mused, sinking his teeth into his bottom lip as he watched her.

"You know what I think you should do right now, Killian?"

He had a strong feeling that he knew but he decided to act oblivious, taking a page out of her book by being a tease. He shook his head 'no', causing Thyri to let go of his hand. She let her back meet the sofa and widened her legs, allowing Killian to get a greater view of her moist center.

"I think you should get on this couch and show your muse just how much she means to you."

The fire that was building up inside him increased and his eyes continued to hold her hostage.

"If I get on this couch, Thyri, we're not leaving it all night. You're getting put in all the positions we're yet to try and I don't care how many times you tell me you're cumming, we're not stopping."

Her mouth became moist at his words and she felt the heat of a blush on her cheeks.

"So position me, Killian." Her innocent smile strengthened. "You know I'm all yours."

She didn't have to tell him twice. Within seconds, Killian got naked and told Thyri to stand up so he could sit down. He leaned back against the couch with his legs spread slightly apart.

"Sit on top of me with your knees bent and your feet flat against the sofa," he ordered and she quickly obeyed.

He caught sight of her gold anklet, the anklet with his initial and he couldn't help but smile at the piece of jewelry she'd decided to wear tonight. He then adjusted her seating position so that she was sitting on his hips before reaching for her arms and telling her to lean back.

Within seconds they were in the 'tug of war' sex position. Killian held her by her arms and Thyri held onto his too. They began swaying back and forth with Killian's dick pushing into her every time they both went forward.

"You feel amazing, Ri... fuck... every single fucking time you know how to make me weak."

He told no lies. Every time they had sex, it was like they'd unlocked a whole new level in the ways they could make each other feel good. And each level was better than the last.

"Kill... uhhhhh!"

"Would you look at that... look at that pretty pussy..."

Her eyes followed his, dropping to the gap between them.

"Look at you taking that dick... your dick."

His emphasis on his dick belonging to her was a reminder to her about how solid their bond had become. It was reminder to her that he belonged to her and no one else. Any doubts she'd had prior to coming over to his house had all washed away. There wasn't a single doubt in her mind about him being the only man for her. They were locked in for good and she was looking forward to strengthening their blossoming relationship.

Chapter Thirty

"Have you packed everything?"

Her little head went up and down.

"Are you sure?"

"Ywes, Mommy."

"What about your toothbrush?"

Alana was quiet and her chin dipped to her chest as her posture slumped.

"Lana, that's one of the most important things you need," her mother told her, a slow smile growing on her lips as she watched her daughter. "Lucky for you I already packed it into your Elsa backpack."

Alana's eyes lit up and she raced towards her mother, clutching onto her legs as she hugged her.

"Thank you, Mommy."

"You welcome, Baby Pooh." Truth reached down to pick her up into her arms and turned to face the door once she held her.

"You ready to spend some time with Daddy, Alana?"

Alana nodded at her smiling father, watching as he stepped away from the door with his arms reaching out.

Truth kissed Alana's forehead, whispering to her how much she loved her before handing her over to her father. Once he had Alana in his arms and she rested her head against his shoulder, he gave Truth a look she knew all too well. The same look he'd given her on the night of Kason's gala, the night they'd joined their bodies as one. They hadn't had sex since then and Truth had no intentions of having sex with *Helldell* again.

When he'd arrived to pick up Alana, he'd come in with the assumption that they were about to do what they'd done last Friday. But he was very much mistaken because Truth pushed him away the second he tried to kiss her.

"Uh-uh. Don't touch me, boy."

"Come on, Tru... why you acting like I wasn't dicking you down last week?"

"That was last week when I was drunk and horny."

"So you used me?"

"The same way you used me you mean? Yup."

It was clear to him by her dismissive nature towards him that she didn't want or need him dicking her down anymore and he couldn't lie, it made him salty as hell. She was the mother of his child yes, but in his eyes, she was also his home pussy – the one place he felt safe in and could always come back to whenever he felt like it. From here on out, he had no intentions of just co-parenting with Truth without sex being involved but for tonight he'd let it slide.

Alana and Truth said their final goodbyes and before Truth knew it she was home alone. She let her eyes wander around her abode and released a heavy sigh.

It hadn't even been five minutes since Alana had left and Truth was badly missing her three year old already. She brought life into their home with her lively, humorous, and sweet spirit and Truth loved her more than life itself. Missing Alana whenever she went to spend time with her father was nothing new for Truth. That was her kid and she could never stop missing her. Sometimes she really hated the fact that Alana constantly went back and forth between two households but it was what it was.

After getting over her wave of sadness and loneliness due to her daughter's absence, Truth headed to her en-suite to make a new batch of the products she used on Alana's hair. Alana had kinky, thick, and healthy hair. At only three years old, she had shoulder-length hair that she loved wearing in various braiding styles.

Truth wasn't a fan of a lot of the hair products out there in the market because of all the chemicals they contained so she started making natural hair products for Alana once her hair started growing super long at the age of one and she hadn't stopped since then.

Truth brought out her essential oils and herbs then got to work.

Ding Dong!

An hour later, Truth was interrupted by the ringing of her doorbell and she took off her white latex gloves before leaving her bathroom to head to her front door.

"Baby Mama."

A dazed look crossed her face, making him frown.

"You gonna let me in or am I gonna have to invite myself in?"

Truth's dazed look remained and Kadiri could feel his patience wearing thin at her lack of words.

"Yo, Lani!" he yelled, looking over Truth's shoulder, into her apartment. "Your momma's acting strange as hell tonight. Where you at, pretty lady?" He stepped forward to enter her home. "I hope you ain't been watching Cocomelon without me."

He felt a hand to his chest and felt a flutter in his stomach at her touch. His eyes dropped to meet her brown ones.

"Alana's not here, Kadiri. She's with her father this weekend."

His heart dropped.

"Oh shit... my bad."

"Why didn't you text..." Truth paused as she came to the sudden realization that there was no way Kadiri could have texted or called her because he didn't have her number. They'd never exchanged numbers and 'til this day, Truth wasn't privy to how he'd found her address.

"I guess this would've been a good time to have your number, huh?"

She nodded and watched as he took a step back, causing her hand to fall from his chest.

"A'ight, no worries. I'll see her some other time then."

He reluctantly started to turn away until the sound of her voice made him freeze.

"Not you only showing up for her," Truth remarked in a teasing tone. "You don't care about your baby mama after all."

He met her eyes again and a laugh broke through his lips.

"Shoes off. You know the drill," she instructed as she opened her door wider for him and walked away from it.

Kadiri entered her home with a smile. He caught a whiff of rose and vanilla and spotted her reed diffuser in the center of her kitchen island. He could always count on her to have some good smelling shit in her crib.

He kicked off his Alexander McQueen sneakers and placed them nearby the door before turning to face her living room, only for his brows to squish together at her disappearance.

"Tru? Where the hell did you go?"

He started walking to her bedroom.

"You ain't even offer a nigga something to drink or something to nibble on. Where's your southern hospitality, girl?"

He arrived in the doorway of her en-suite, watching her standing by her sink with a bunch of tools, bottles, and bowls on the vanity countertop below her.

"Kinda in the middle of something," she muttered, lifting her mixing spoon to her bowl.

"What the fuck are you doing?" he asked, leaving the doorway to get closer to her. "You mixing up weird potions and shit?"

"No." She shot his reflection a rude look once he came to stand next to her. "I'm making Alana's hair products."

"Her hair products?"

"Yeah. I make all the stuff she needs for her hair, to help it grow and keep it healthy. You see how long her hair is, that didn't just happen overnight. Took a whole lotta love and care from yours truly."

"Oh wow... so these are the oil you us... *Ow!*" Kadiri yelled at her slapping his hand just as he reached for one of the filled mini bottles.

"Hands off, Skinny Boy." She chuckled at his dramatic yell. She hadn't hit him hard at all but he'd shouted out in pain like she had. "No touching the merchandise."

"You're a hater." He quickly grabbed a bottle before she could stop him and lifted it into the air.

Truth observed him closely eyeing the mini bottle and shaking it.

"So these are the oils you put in my Lani's hair to make it grow long and shit. This is pretty amazing," he complimented her, taking her by surprise. "I can tell this takes a lot of hard work but you love doing it. I respect that shit a lot."

"Thank you, Kadiri."

393

"No worries." He lightly shrugged. "But back to your inhospitable ass. Where's my drink?"

Laughter came into her eyes as she read his stern expression.

"You know where the refrigerator is. Go get it."

He kissed his teeth and playfully pushed her shoulder. Truth laughed and before she could push him back, he was racing out her bathroom to head back to her living room.

About ten minutes later, Truth was done making Alana's products, washed her hands and went to her living room to find Kadiri laying on her couch as he watched TV. She spotted a carton of apple juice on the center coffee table and she scowled at the sight.

"Kadi, I have cups in this house for a reason."

He grinned but didn't turn to look at her. He could already feel the daggers she was shooting his way.

"Couldn't find them."

"That's why you ask." She sighed, arriving at the foot of her couch.

She expected him to move his feet for her to sit down but he didn't so she sat on top of them, making him groan at her squashing his feet. She laughed at his annoyance.

"That's what your ass gets for not moving your smelly feet."

"You know damn well they don't stink, girl."

He slid them out from under her and positioned himself upright on the couch so he could sit next to her.

"So what we eating tonight, Baby Mama?"

"I didn't know you speak French." His confusion marred his face so she kept talking. "You said we. You meant *oui*, right?"

"Haha, very funny. No what are *we* eating tonight."

"You mean what am *I* eating tonight?" She pointed to herself.

"Tru." He gave her a serious look. "*We.*"

394

She playfully rolled her eyes before telling him, "I've got left-over beans and rice that I made last night."

"Yeah that's what's up. Fix me a plate."

"Nigga, you know damn well I ain't your maid."

He chuckled.

"I mean shit you can be. I'll get you the whole outfit, don't even worry about that, baby, just tell me - how much do you charge per hour?"

"Your annoying ass." She got up from her seat.

"Cause I'ma need your ass all day at my beck and call," he tittered. "You need health insurance too or can I work your ass to the bone without any hassle?"

He got up and followed her to the kitchen, laughing nonstop as he teased her about becoming his maid.

For the next few hours, Truth and Kadiri ate together, drank together, and talked about everything under the sun. Well almost everything. After three glasses of Merlot, Truth found herself opening up to Kadiri about her father's death, telling him about how much her father meant to her, his great personality and how honored she felt to be carrying his last name. Talking about her father almost bought tears to her eyes but she held it together as best as she could.

Eventually midnight came and Truth and Kadiri hadn't even realized how carried away they'd gotten talking.

"Shit, is that really the time?" Kadiri gazed down at the silver face of his iced out Rolex. "I should get going..."

"Didn't you drive here?"

He nodded.

"You've been drinking, Kadi, remember?"

They'd finished a whole bottle of wine together and although Kadiri was convinced that he was fine, he could definitely feel tiredness worming its way through him. Driving tonight was a huge no and he knew it too.

"Stay the night," she offered. "You can crash on the sofa like last time."

"A'ight," he agreed. "I'll stay."

Truth got up to get him some extra pillows and a duvet cover but he told her that he was fine.

"Are you sure? It gets pretty cold out here, Kadi."

"I'll be fine."

She then left him in the living room and made her way to her bedroom to get ready for bed. She stopped when she was halfway to her door and turned to see Kadiri taking off his jewelry.

"Good night," she told him.

"Night, Baby Mama," he replied with a smile that reminded her of just how sexy he was.

She continued walking towards her bedroom, entered her room and closed the door behind her. It took her fifteen minutes to get ready for bed. She flossed and brushed her teeth, did her nighttime skincare routine, and dressed into her lace nightgown dress. She pulled back her silk sheets and got under them, ready to let sleep take her soul for the night.

The second she closed her eyes, two quiet knocks sounded on her door and she stared at the white door without saying anything.

Knock! Knock!

Again two knocks sounded and she remained silent as a shadow.

The door's silver handed started moving down and the door was pushed open. Her room was void of light but she could still make out his golden face and that shirtless frame of his thanks to the light filtering through from her living room. Her heart raced as she stared at him half naked.

"Tru?"

396

"What's wrong?" She sat upright as he came into her room.

"Your couch is uncomfortable as fuck," he explained as he came to stand by the edge of her bed. "And it's cold out there."

I told his ass, she mused as a small smile grew on her lips.

"A nigga can't sleep."

Truth remained silent and so did he. Since he was standing at the edge of her bed, he could clearly see her tangled in her purple sheets. She had a black bonnet on her head but she still looked attractive to him.

She didn't respond to his dilemma but she didn't have to. The pulling back of her sheets told him all he needed to know. He climbed in her bed and took the empty spot next to her and slipped his body under the sheets.

"Thank you," he whispered once he lay next to her.

She continued to remain silent and laid back on her side, facing her back towards him as she shut her eyes.

Kadiri got comfortable, rolling onto his side but keeping his chest facing her. Though she had her back to him, he still wanted to face her.

Truth shut her eyes, trying to fall victim to her slumber but it was a huge fail. The heat of his body radiated through the sheets and heated her up. She could feel her skin tingling too and despite her telling her mind to just go to sleep, her mind refused to listen. The presence of a man in her bed had her feeling things she couldn't fight off.

Go to sleep, Tru. Go. To. Sleep.

Truth felt him move and when his chest brushed against her back, she felt the wetness of her excitement leak out of her.

"Shit... sorry, Tru," he apologized in a low tone, moving slightly away from her.

"It's cool." She leaned back and her back hit his chest again.

This time Kadiri didn't move and he felt the hardness of his arousal increase. He'd already become hard as a brick as he lay next to her, inhaling her sweet rose perfume but now it had gotten one hundred times worse.

He slowly raised a hand to her waist and pulled her in closer to him. She willingly followed his direction, sinking her body into his. His right arm went across her chest and his left arm he pinned beneath her.

They were now spooning and Truth felt his erection poking her butt. Neither of them brought it up though and Truth kept her eyes shut as she tried to fall asleep.

"Sweet dreams, Truth."

A kiss landed on her neck and her heart warmed at his action. Within seconds they were both out like a light.

Chapter Thirty-One

"**Y**ou have got to be fucking kidding me!"

No one could look him in the eye. They were all struck with guilt and shame for what had gone down.

"You mean to tell me none of y'all can do your jobs, that's what the fuck you're telling me right now? I told you both to return back to Atlanta with her, not without her!"

"Boss, she knew we were coming for her. Her hacker wanna be brother put her onto us finding out her new identity. She's fled Idaho under a new identity neither we nor her brother know. Sh—"

"I don't mothafucking care!" Kason bellowed. "Don't call my line again until you find her!"

He ended the facetime call before throwing his phone to the wall opposite his desk.

Today had shaped up to be one of the worst days of Kason's life. Trinity had disappeared again. How she'd managed to go off the grid in the first place was thanks to her eighteen-year-old brother, a tech kid genius who had skills that not even Kason's hackers had mastered yet. He'd been the one to remove all digital traces of Trinity's online presence. When Kason sent his men to Idaho with the task of bringing Trinity back to Atlanta, he thought it would be a piece of cake, but clearly it hadn't been.

How the hell an eighteen year old and his crazy sister had outsmarted Kason's men was something Kason was failing to comprehend. He didn't want to hear about where Trinity had fled to. He just needed her back in his city now.

Was he going to kill her?

No.

But he was definitely going to make her wish that she was already dead.

It was currently nine-thirty p.m. and after being at Shield's headquarters all day, trying to distract himself from the war going on in his mind and his marriage, he decided to go to the one house he could always seek refuge.

"Omo mi, *(My child)*, are you okay? Have you eaten? I have some left over jollof in the refrigerator."

"Yes, Momma. I've eaten."

"Okay well there's nothing wrong with you eating some more. You're looking a little skinny these days anyway. Is Tanai not feeding you?"

"Temi, leave the boy alone. He clearly came here with something to tell us. Kason, what's going on?"

"Oluwasegun, what's wrong?" his mother asked, calling him by his Nigerian name. A name she only called him when she was being serious with him.

Sometimes Kason hated how much his parents knew him like the back of their hands. His Georgia born and raised father knew to relate to his son in ways only a man could and his Nigerian mother sure knew how to soften her son's tough exterior up every single time. The two of them combined were a powerful force and they could always tell when their son had something heavy on his mind.

"It's Tanai... I think she might leave me."

His parents' eyes bulged and his mother started howling like she'd suddenly lost a loved one. After Memphis got his dramatic wife to calm down, he raised a hand to Kason's shoulder and told him to explain what was going on in his marriage.

Kason confided in his parents about everything. From the sex tapes to Trinity's games, he told them it all. Now though it may have seemed weird for Kason to admit having a sex tape to his parents, it wasn't weird to him. Memphis and Temilola had raised their sons to always be upfront and honest with them about any and everything knowing that they wouldn't be judged. They were here to protect and nurture their sons, not kick them down for being their true authentic selves. Though Kason loved and appreciate his parents dearly, he knew they would lose their shit if they found out he'd done cocaine in the past so he conveniently left that part out.

"Mom... Dad... What do I do? I can't lose her. I *won't* lose her."

"And you won't," Temilola told him, caressing his cheek. "Yes, you're going through a rough patch right now but this too shall pass, ololufemi *(my darling)*. Tough times don't last forever and I know Tanai loves you. She's just hurt right now, rightfully so, but she'll come around. She has to come around."

"Marriage is full of ups and downs, son," Memphis added. "Tanai made a vow when she took your last name and I know she doesn't want to break that vow. She loves you. Just give her some space, son, as much as you don't want to – it's for the best."

Kason listened to his parents' advice and thanked them for their wisdom. He could always count on them to provide him with words of hope and empowerment. He spent a few more minutes with them before deciding it was time to head home to his wife.

It was ten-thirty p.m. when he arrived home and after parking his Rolls Royce in their garage, he rushed upstairs, desperate to be in the arms of one person tonight.

When he arrived outside their bedroom, he took a deep breath and released it before pushing open their door. His heart and face fell at the sight of their empty bed. But he suddenly heard flushing and his eyes wandered to the closed door of their en-suite. He'd been so focused on their bed that he'd failed to notice the light that shone under the bathroom door. The door was pulled opened and as her pretty face appeared, a smile warmed his lips.

A smile she didn't return.

Tanai approached their bed, pulling back the Egyptian cotton sheets and got acquainted with the bed. She didn't grace him with a hi, a smile or even a good night. She simply acted like he wasn't there and it felt like he'd been stung by a deadly bee.

He wanted to walk up to her, pull the sheets off her body to admire that sexy nightgown gracing her body and make her talk to him. He didn't care if she cursed him out for what he'd done this morning, handcuffing her to the bed like she was his prisoner, he just wanted to hear something from her. Anything at all would do.

But he fought against his desire to get his wife to talk to him and walked out the door he'd just come through to head to their guest bedroom.

Just give her some space, son, his father's words echoed in his mental as he gently shut their bedroom door behind him.

He prayed that his father was right. He didn't want to lose Tanai. At all.

Chapter Thirty-Two

"About time you finally let me take your ass out to dinner."

Truth simpered as she lifted her chopsticks and shoved a spicy tuna roll into her mouth.

"All this texting just hasn't been the same."

Truth nodded as she gently chewed and swallowed her sushi.

Truth had finally taken up Kiana on her offer for them to go out for dinner and tonight they were enjoying sushi at MF Sushi.

"I know, girl. I know. My bad for taking so long but I've just been busy with work and Alana of course."

"I know and I totally get it," Kiana replied. "How is the little cutie anyways?"

"She's good."

"Good." Kiana lifted her glass to her lips and sucked the paper straw.

"How have you been though?" Truth inquired. "What's new?"

"Well, nothing much, girl. I've..."

Kiana began to fill Truth on the activities of her life. From the texts and calls they'd exchanged in the past few weeks, Truth had found out that Kiana was a bottle girl working in one of the city's hottest clubs, *Euphoria*. Bottle girls in Atlanta were bringing in a lot of money ranging between five hundred dollars to three thousand dollars a night. It all depended on your personality, your clients, and the popularity of the club you worked at. And of course being pretty definitely helped and Kiana had no problems in that department because she was a very beautiful girl. Like Truth, she had espresso brown skin, owned big, brown eyes and her jet black hair was currently braided into knotless braids that fell past her waist.

Truth had no clue that bottle girls were making that much paper until Kiana told her and if you were really good at it, you could easily make six figures in less than six months.

"As much as I love being a bottle girl, I want more for myself, you know? I have a lot of money saved up in the bank and I'm thinking of starting my own nightclub."

"Oh my God, Kiana, that sounds amazing!"

"Thank you, girl." The corners of Kiana's mouth curled upwards into a smile. "So yeah, that's what I'm working towards now. I know it's not going to be easy but I've been a bottle girl for almost three years now, I'm ready for a change."

"Change is good. Yeah starting a business ain't easy but if you say committed to it, I'm sure it'll stay committed to you," Truth replied.

Kiana's head went up and down as she said, "Yeah, definitely."

"Have you thought of a name for it?"

"I'm thinking of naming it after myself. So Kiana's. Is that too vain?"

"No not at all. Your name is pretty and Kiana's nightclub sounds hot. That's a spot I'd definitely have to visit."

Kiana giggled with happiness and continued sharing her plans for her future club.

The girls ate, talked, and drank for the next two hours. The more time that Truth was spending with Kiana and getting to know her better, the more she realized that she really did like Kiana. She was funny, pretty, and good vibes. Truth really enjoyed her company and talking to her. And because of how much she was enjoying Kiana's time, she knew that what happened last night with Kiana's boyfriend could never happen again.

Nothing happened though... all we did was cuddle.

Yeah all they'd done was cuddle but that still didn't change the facts. She'd cuddled with a man that belonged to the girl that she was becoming closer to.

What happened last night between you and him can't happen again, Truth. End of story.

"I don't wanna leave you yet," Kiana announced after they'd paid the bill for their sushi and drinks.

"Neither do I," Truth admitted. "I'm having so much fun with you."

"Okay so let's have some more fun."

Truth's brows lifted as she watched a sneaky look appear on Kiana's face.

"Let's go turn up."

"Girl, I'm not dressed for the club."

Tonight Truth had put on a chocolate bandeau top, denim jeans and clear heeled sandals. A dainty gold chain was secured around her neck with matching studs in each ear and a gold Burberry watch was strapped to her left wrist. Her natural hair was slicked back into a long braided ponytail and she had a natural beat of makeup on. In her eyes, she looked too casual for the club.

"Girl, are you crazy? You look gorgeous!" Kiana exclaimed, reaching across the table for Truth's hand and squeezing it tight.

"Niggas ain't gonna be able to take their eyes off you tonight."

Truth remained silent and frowned at Kiana's words, not really convinced that she looked good enough for the club tonight.

"We're going, girl. You deserve a night of fun because of how hard you've been grinding and taking care of Alana."

"Hmm... I mean you're right about that."

Kiana's eyes lit up.

"Exactly! So let's go turn up."

Truth thought about her words some more before deciding to just give in. It was clear by Kiana's tone and expression that she'd already had her mind set on them going to the club. Truth knew that if she said no, she wouldn't hear the end of it so it was best she just gave into Kiana's wishes and followed her to the club.

"Alright, alright. Let's go."

"Yayyyyyyyyyyyy!" Kiana screamed and Truth giggled before shushing her because of the attention that her loudness had drawn to their table. It was a Saturday night which meant that restaurants were packed full with bodies and the restaurant they'd dined at tonight was definitely filled up.

"Okay let me just tell Kadiri that I'm on my way with you now."

"Kadiri?" Truth's heart skittered.

"Yeah, girl. He's at the club now celebrating his boy's birthday. So we're gonna go turn up with them."

"Okay," Truth simply said, watching as Kiana brought out her phone to text Kadiri.

She was surprised to hear that they would be with Kadiri tonight but she chose not to think too much about it.

The girls then gathered their things, went outside to hop in Kiana's car and headed to their destination. Kiana had been kind enough to pick Truth up at her home before their date at MF Sushi which is why Truth was car-free tonight.

Fifteen minutes later, they pulled up in front of a club with a bright white neon sign that read 'Euphoria'. Truth quickly realized that Kiana had brought them to the club she worked at and she felt butterflies take flight in her stomach at the amount of people lined up outside the club. But thanks to Kiana's employee status at the club, once she'd parked and they walked up to the front entrance, the big, stocky bouncer let them in.

"Thanks, Enzo!"

"No problem, K. You and your girl have a good time tonight."

"We will. Thank you." Kiana then grabbed Truth's hand and led the way into Euphoria.

The dark club was packed with souls. Some on the dance floor, letting the DJ's tunes take over their bodies and some in their VIP sections, turning up with their bottles and lifting their cameras in the air as they tried to document how much fun they were having to social media.

Always askin' "What you doin'?", tell 'em take you shoppin'
If he don't do it for you, baby, get a different option
Got you comin' out the crib and he ain't comin' out of pocket

Don Toliver's rapping echoed through the club and Truth held on tighter to Kiana's hand as they moved through the large space. All of the bottle girls they encountered along their walk greeted and hugged Kiana, making Truth realize just how popular her friend was at Euphoria.

Seconds later, they arrived on the other end of the club where a muscular Caucasian man stood in front of a red rope. When he spotted Kiana and her friend coming closer, he gave her a respectful nod and moved out of the way as he unhooked the red rope.

"Thanks, Cade."

He let them pass through and Truth's eyes focused in on the large section they'd walked into.

There was a large red booth that seemed to seat an endless amount of men.

Truth locked eyes on the man in the center of the booth and her heart almost went into cardiac arrest at those familiar cognac eyes. She didn't understand why she was acting shocked when she knew he would be here tonight. He'd spotted her too and got up from his seat.

A smug grin sat on Kiana's lips and it only got stronger as Kadiri approached them.

"Hey you," she greeted him, releasing Truth's hand so she could walk into his arms.

He opened an arm out to pull her in. She landed a kiss on his lips before embracing him and Truth felt her heart drop at the sight.

"What's up? Y'all good?" he asked as they hugged, looking over Kiana's head at Truth who was watching him with a blank look.

"Yeah," Kiana replied. "Where's Q?"

"Sitting down," he replied as he let her go.

"Okay let me say happy birthday to him. Kiana turned to Truth. "Truth, you coming?"

She nodded and stepped closer to her. Kiana then led the way towards the VIP booth. Just as Truth walked past Kadiri, she heard him say in a tone loud enough for only her to hear, "So you can't say hi now, Baby Mama?"

She stopped walking and turned to look at him.

"Hi."

"That's more like it." A sexy smile graced his lips, causing butterflies to take flight in her stomach. "You good?"

She nodded.

"Good," he replied, letting his eyes run down her frame and loving the fit she had on.

Seeing and feeling his heated gaze on her, she quickly turned to follow Kiana and arrived in the VIP booth. She felt multiple eyes on her as she stood next to Kiana.

Truth soon realized that tonight was a big night at Euphoria because of a man named Quinton. It was his birthday and he'd invited all his friends to come turn up with him tonight. Quinton was a very popular man in the city of Atlanta since he owned the biggest radio station in the city. Almost the whole city had shown up for him tonight and a few Atlanta celebrities had shown their faces too.

"Happy birthday, Q. I trust the girls are treating you well tonight," Kiana told him after pecking his cheek.

"They definitely are. Why ain't you working with them tonight, K?"

"I needed a break," she explained.

"I feel you..." His eyes drifted to the brown skinned beauty standing next to her. "Who's your friend?"

"This..." Kiana reached for Truth's hand, pulling her in front of her. "Beautiful lady is my girl, Truth."

"Hello, Truth," Quinton greeted her. His desire filled eyes sweeping down her body, loving what he was seeing.

"Happy birthday," Truth told him in a friendly tone.

"Thank you, beautiful. You want something to drink?"

Feeling like she had no choice but to say yes, Truth nodded and Quinton's eyes lit up like diamonds at her response. He shifted to the right, making room for Truth to come sit next to him and Kiana gently nudged her in his direction.

Once Truth was seated next to him, Quinton reached into one of the many ice buckets sitting on the center table opposite him and pulled out the tall bottle of Don Julio.

"You cool with taking shots with the birthday boy?" He flashed her a smile as he unscrewed the tequila bottle.

"Yeah, I'm cool with that."

Truth looked over at Kiana to see that she'd walked over to Kadiri and wrapped her arms around him, leaning closer to steal a kiss from his lips.

The more she thought about this night, the more she realized that Kiana had only come down to Euphoria to be booed up with Kadiri. She wasn't really here to turn up with the birthday boy, she was here to love up on her man and she'd only brought Truth along to be her wing woman.

I knew I should've said no to the club. Kehlani was dead right in her song cause I really do hate the club!

Truth knew there was no way she'd be able to go home now that the birthday boy had her next to him. However, she wasn't complaining about being stuck by Quinton's side all night because he wasn't bad to look at all. He had dreamy brown eyes, clear bronze skin and a bushy beard that looked as soft as cotton.

Might as well enjoy myself and enjoy these free drinks, she told herself before deciding to get comfier with Quinton.

She took a couple tequila shots with him and after her third one, she could feel her buzz getting stronger. Before she knew it she was laughing at all of Quinton's lame ass jokes and letting him place an arm around her waist, keeping her close to him.

Kiana and Kadiri were sitting in the booth, drinking and vibing to the songs being played. The booth had been given hookah to smoke and smoke surrounded the atmosphere as everyone inhaled their hookah pipes.

Seeing the way Kiana sat on Kadiri's lap and grinded on him to the beat of the song currently playing, was enough to make Truth down two more shots.

"You gonna dance with me, beautiful?"

"Of course, birthday boy," Truth replied and allowed Quinton to lead her out the VIP section to the main dancefloor.

Just as they made it to the center of the dancefloor, the DJ decided to play a dancehall song and the club started going crazy as Vybz Kartel's vocals filled the room. Couples rushed to the dance floor to whine to Vybz Kartel's *Bicycle*.

Quinton grabbed Truth's waist and she immediately got into position in front of him.

"Damn, girl," Quinton commented as Truth started to do her thing.

Truth grinded her butt on his crotch area, feeling his erection grow with each hip movement she made.

"I think I might need to take you home with me tonight," he whispered into her ear.

"I think you just might," she agreed, working her hips faster and faster to the rhythm of the music.

"You go, girl!" Truth heard a familiar voice shout and she turned to the left to see Kiana cheering her on at the same time she whined on Kadiri.

Truth hadn't even realized that they were on the dancefloor and she suddenly felt exposed as she caught Kadiri's hard stare on her. He was looking at her like she was doing something that she wasn't supposed to be doing. Truth sent a smile Kiana's way and continued to do her thing, dancing on the birthday boy while he held her tight.

The night went on in full effect and once the clock hit eleven p.m. Truth was ready to call it a night. But the birthday boy was most certainly not.

Eleven p.m. was the time for the club to get more popping because all the latecomers had finally shown their faces, but Truth had been here since nine p.m. and she could feel a wave of tiredness constantly rushing through her with each passing minute.

When more people started coming into the VIP section to greet the birthday boy, Truth became an afterthought. Quinton was too preoccupied with greeting all who greeted him and when more women started flooding to his side, he forgot all about Truth.

Truth took this as her cue to go home. She looked over at Kiana, seeing her downing shots with Kadiri and his boys and knew that there was no way that Kiana was about to drop her home. And she didn't want to spoil her girl's fun by telling her that she was done with the club for the night.

So she requested an Uber and got up from her seat to head outside the club. She thought no one noticed her departure but someone definitely had. Truth's Uber arrived ten minutes later and she hopped in, glad to be heading home.

Ding! Ding!

Five minutes into her journey, her phone went off and she stared down at the bright screen to read her new notifications.

GIRL!!!!!!!!!!!!!!!!!!!!

WHERE THE HELL DID YOU GO?????

Truth unlocked her phone to respond to Kiana's texts.

Truth: *Sorry, girl. I tapped out early. I'm too damn tired.*

Kiana: *You didn't even say goodbye!!!*

Five angry faced emojis popped into their chat.

Truth: *I'm sorry.*

Truth: *I wasn't trying to interrupt you and your boo.*

Truth: *But I had fun tonight. Thanks for bringing me out.*

Kiana: *You welcome girl.*

Kiana: *Get home safe.*

Truth locked her phone and stared out the car window for the rest of her ride home.

Tonight had been fun... ish. She'd enjoyed flirting with Quinton and owning his attention for a while. And even though she'd had no real intentions of going home with him tonight, she'd entertained the thought of having a one night stand.

"We've arrived, ma'am," her Uber driver announced twenty minutes later.

Truth thanked him and reached for her YSL purse on the seat next to her before leaving the Audi.

Home sweet home.

Truth entered her dark home, flicked on a light switch, and shut the door behind her. She kicked her heels off and made a beeline for her bedroom, ready to lay her head down on her pillow and forget all about the events of tonight. Especially the way her chest tightened every time she caught sight of Kiana kissing Kadiri. She wasn't jealous. There was no way in hell that she was jealous! Truth Wright didn't get jealous and there was no way she was about to start getting jealous now.

After washing off her make up, doing her skincare routine, flossing, and brushing her teeth, Truth changed into her silk night dress, wrapped her ponytail into a bun, put her bonnet on her head and got into bed. She got comfortable before shutting her eyes and allowing sleep's comforting embrace to consume her. A comforting embrace that didn't last for very long.

Knock! Knock! Knock!

Truth jolted awake to the loud sound of knocking on her front door twenty minutes later.

What the hell!

She reluctantly swung her warm feet out of bed and into her LV fur mules. She stumbled towards the door, still feeling the effects of REM sleep in her system. She arrived in front of her door seconds later and pulled it open, ready to curse out who was on the other side.

"What the fu..."

That was until she locked eyes on... *him.*

The minute she'd noticed him in the club tonight, she was reminded all over again of how fine he was. He had on black jeans, a gray crew neck tee, white Air Forces on his feet, three silver chains hanging from his neck, a silver stud in each ear and a silver watch around his wrist. Simple yet effective. Effective at making her wet at the sight of him.

"Kadiri?"

"You never said goodnight, Baby Mama," he announced, stepping forward and reaching for her waist.

"Umm... I-I..." Truth's words fumbled as he held onto her and pushed her back into her apartment. "Kadiri, what are yo—"

"But it's cool," he cut her off before she could finish her sentence. "You can say good night now."

He let go of her waist and turned around to shut her door.

Truth stepped away from him when he started making his way closer to her again.

"Kadiri, what are you doing here?"

"You never said good night, Tru."

Each step she took back only made him take another step forward.

"Good night," she quickly said, still stepping back. "You should get going. It's late."

"Nah..." His eyes swept up and down her body, causing a shiver to run through her. "I wanna stay."

"Kadiri. You can't stay." She continued to step back towards her bedroom and he continued to follow her.

"Why not?" He stopped briefly to kick his Air Forces off.

"You know why," she replied, making it to the doorway of her bedroom and lifting her hands to the door's frame, creating a barrier to stop him from coming through.

His brows pulled together in a frown as he kept sauntering over to her.

414

"Kadiri..."

He stopped once he towered over her and placed his hands to her sides, pulling her into him. Her eyes fell from his and heat flooded her insides at his touch on her body. She could smell his cologne and she didn't realize how much she loved the scent of bergamot until now.

"Kadiri, go home."

She kept her eyes to the floor, avoiding his gaze as his hands tightened on her waist. Her chin was suddenly lifted and her breath caught in her throat once her eyes met his.

"No."

"Kadiri, go ho—"

"Enough with all that damn talking. A nigga tired as fuck right now and I need my arms around you while I sleep."

Truth felt her feet lift and her eyes bulged as he picked her up only to move out his way.

"Kadiri!" She yelled as her feet met the floor and he walked past her to enter her room.

"Shut up and let's go to sleep."

She was in pure disbelief as she watched him walk up to her dresser. He took his jewelry off and placed it onto her dresser, straightening his silver chain as if it rightfully belonged there in the first place.

I don't believe this. He's really not listening to...

Truth's thoughts got distracted when Kadiri's shirt lifted off his upper body, revealing his tatted chest. The light from her living room had spilled into her bedroom, providing more than enough light for her to see him. All of him. She became breathless at the sight of him half naked and felt her nipples harden under her dress.

He placed his shirt to her table stool and reached for his

Hermes belt. Truth quickly turned away from him, not trying to appear like a creep watching him undress.

"Kadiri, you really need to go home," she said, rushing over to her bedside and taking a seat on her bed's edge. Her back now faced him which she was glad about because she wasn't sure she could take looking at his face anymore. He was driving her crazy.

"You still talking after I told you not to?" he asked with a smirk, pulling down his jeans as he watched the back of her head.

She pouted, crossing her arms against her chest as she heard him drop his jeans to her stool.

"You have five seconds to lay your head down on that bed before I lay you down myself."

He's not the boss of you, Tru, she mused. *Don't you dare lay down.*

"One."

Her heart skipped a beat as his count down began.

"Two."

Her body began to sizzle.

"Three."

Her knees felt weak.

"Four."

She released the breath she hadn't even realized she'd been holding and lay on her side.

Kadiri glowed inside as he watched her lay down and get under her sheets. Then he strolled over to the bed.

Truth soon felt the bed dip and his body drew nearer to hers under the sheets. Once his tatted arm went across her chest and the other pinned itself under her body, Truth gave in and rested her back against his chest.

His intoxicating cologne surrounded her, making her feel like putty in his palms. He placed his head on the side of her neck, inhaling her rose scent and holding her tighter. He felt the hardness of her nipples poke his arm and the bulge in his boxers expanded.

No one said a single word but nothing needed to be said. She could feel how bad he wanted her and he could feel it too. But he wanted to feel more. *Much more.*

A light gasp broke from Truth's lips when she felt his arm press tighter into her, pushing against her breasts and hard nipples. When his arm started moving and rubbing against her chest, Truth shifted backwards, pressing her ass cheeks into his bulge, and slowly grinding into him.

"Kadiri."

The moan of his name was all the confirmation he needed to drop his arm from her chest and replace it with his palm which he used to cup her right breast. Truth gasped once again as he palmed her breast and squeezed her flesh tight, making her grind her butt faster against his erection. He started rubbing his finger against her nipple at the same time he squeezed her boob, driving her insane.

"Kadi..."

The next moan of his name made him drop his hand from her breast and slide it down her stomach. He hiked up her silk dress, letting his hands fall between her warm thighs and groaned when he felt the soft folds of her pussy.

"God damn it, Tru... you ain't got no panties on."

She opened her legs wider, giving him better access and he stroked on her pussy's lips, feeling how warm and wet she was. He almost wanted to cum right there and then when her juices drowned his fingers.

"Kadiri, we... we can't."

"We can't what?"

"We canmmmmh!"

His finger slipped in and she couldn't help the sounds of pleasure that escaped her. He gently pushed into her tightness and she couldn't stop the lust from overwhelming her. The damage had been done. Every part of her now ached for him.

"Kadi..."

"You are so mothafucking wet, Tru," he whispered, dipping his finger in and out of her at a slow, steady pace. "I make you this wet?"

Her moans and cries heightened as he worked his finger back and forth.

"Yesssss," she hissed, grinding her butt at the same speed that his finger moved in and out of her cave.

He suddenly pulled out, making her feel empty for just a second until he dove right back inside her with two fingers this time.

"Kadiriiiiii."

"You better ride those fucking fingers," he spoke directly into her ear, his cool breath fanning her skin. "Ride that shit, baby."

She quickly obeyed, thrusting her hips up and down as she matched his energy and rode his fingers. Moments later, she reached behind her with her right hand, tugging at the band of his boxers.

Kadiri shifted back slightly, sliding out his arm that had been pinned below her and using it to help her pull his Versace boxers down to his thighs.

His dick sprang forth and Truth grabbed it, feeling her eyes grow large at how big he felt. She still had her back to him so she couldn't see it but she didn't have to see it to know he was huge. Huge and wet with pre-cum.

"Fuuuuck, Tru..."

She stroked him with one slow motion and Kadiri's groan was unmissable. He continued to move his fingers in and out her tightness while she remained focus on sliding up and down his swollen flesh. Her moans filled the room and so did his as they each pleasured each other with their hands.

"You made me jealous tonight... you know that, right?"

A smile danced on her lips at his revelation.

"I wanted to snatch you away from him so bad."

"Kadi!"

His fingers pushed deep into her and remained deep, resulting in her screaming. Kadiri pushed her hand off his dick with his free hand and lifted his head from her neck, looking down at her as he worked his fingers in and out faster with each passing second.

"You like making me jealous?" he asked while fucking her with his fingers alone.

"Kadiriiiiii." Her eyes rolled to the back of her head and her legs began to shake.

"You like making me jealous by letting another nigga touch you? Huh?"

She could no longer form coherent sentences or words. All that came out of her were sounds of ecstasy. She felt her orgasm overwhelm her and she couldn't keep still or think straight. Even as he watched her climax, he refused to stop and kept fucking her with his fingers.

"That's right... nut on my fingers."

Her juices rushed out of her, doing exactly as he commanded. Once she'd rode her first orgasm of the night, Kadiri pulled his fingers out of her and rose up on the bed, making a move to position himself in the middle of her legs.

The second his lips came crashing down to her lips was the exact moment Truth heard vibrations fill the room. They both froze, caught off guard by the interruption.

Truth tore her lips away from his, looking over at her bedside table to see her vibrating phone and its bright screen that read:

TANAI

Without thinking twice about it, Truth slid out from under Kadiri towards the edge of her bed and reached for her phone.

"Nai?" She let out a deep breath. "You okay?... Slow down, I can't understand yo... Oh my God!" Truth pushed Kadiri off her and jumped out of bed. "What the fuck!"

Kadiri's worry snaked through him at Truth's panicked tone and the look that accompanied it.

"Where is she now? Okay, okay, okay, I'm on my way!"

She ended the call and ran to her walk in closet. Kadiri got out of her bed and followed her.

"Tru, what's going on?"

"I'm going to jail tonight," she said to herself as she grabbed the first pair of jeans she could find.

"Truth!"

There was too much anger spiraling from the pit of her stomach for her to respond but the second Kadiri's hands grabbed her body and turned her around, she had no choice but to talk to him.

"Kadiri, let me the fuck go!"

"Not until you tell me what's going on."

"You need to let me go." She pushed against his chest, trying to get him away from her but of course her petite size was no match for his athletic one.

"Talk to me, Tru. What's going on?"

"It's Thyri!" she yelled, feeling the tears she'd been fighting away, pricking her eyes. "She's been attacked!"

"Attacked?" His eyes popped wide. "By who?"

"That bitch, Soraya. I'm gonna fucking kill her ass!"

Chapter Thirty-Three

"Y ou and Killian are cute together I can't even lie."

A smile broke through Thyri's face and she watched Dayana lift her hose to her lips.

"Just don't break his heart, cause I have a feeling he'll take it out on me since I'm your girl and I don't wanna lose my job," she concluded before sliding the hookah's hose between her lips and deeply inhaling. A bubbling noise was heard as Dayana inhaled.

"Lose your job? You wouldn't lose your job, Day."

"Yes I would." Dayana chuckled as smoke drifted from her lips. "I'd definitely lose my job for fucking him up after he decides to disrespect me."

Now it was Thyri's turn to laugh and she took a quick pull from her hose before deciding to respond.

"Girl, you know damn well you can't fuck my man up. You seen how big he is, right?"

"I mean I sure can try..." Dayana paused, thinking to herself about her chances of beating Killian. The more she thought about those muscles he owned the more she came to her senses and realized she was definitely no match for him. "Actually you're right. My tiny ass couldn't do shit to him." Dayana laughed and Thyri smirked, lifting her hose back to her mouth once again.

"So things between you and Chosen are really done?"

Thyri nodded.

"We're done."

Dayana slowly arched a brow.

"What's that look for?" Thyri frowned. "We are."

"Are you sure? Because I remember saying that same exact thing when I first ended things with Ethan."

"Yeah but your situation with Ethan is different. You're actually in love with Ethan."

"And you're not in love with Chosen?"

Thyri's head went from side to side.

"I'm not."

"And what about Killian?" Thyri felt her skin tingle. "Are you in love with him?"

"Yes."

Dayana's bottom lip dropped, exposing her mouth and Thyri's laughter rang out at Dayana's reaction.

"Thyriiiiiii!" Dayana shrieked, dropping her hose, and reaching for Thyri's shoulders. "You know what you just said, right?"

"I doooo." Thyri's laughter continued as Dayana shook her.

"And you know there's no taking it back, right?"

"I know." Thyri stopped laughing and her eyes bulged as she realized what she'd just admitted to her bestie. "God, did I really just say that?"

"Yes you did," Dayana confirmed with a grin. "Wow, girl. I don't know what he's done but he has you wide open. You haven't even been together that long."

"I know."

"But I guess when you know, you know," Dayana replied, nodding at her with assurance. "It's clear he's making you very happy."

"He is, I can't even lie."

"And I still can't believe he painted you? That's so romantic."

A scarlet heat warmed Thyri's cheeks as she remembered the memory of Killian painting her in his studio.

"I just hope it all works out for you both. All I want is you happy and if he's doing a good job at doing that then I guess he's good in my book."

"Awwww, Day." Thyri reached for Dayana's freehand and squeezed it tight. "Thank you. I really do appreciate you so much."

"And if you even think about making anyone but me your maid of honor then I promise you I'm fucking you up and her together. On sight, hoe."

"Dayana! I can't with you."

It was a Saturday night and Thyri was glad to be out with Dayana. They'd decided to come to one of their favorite hookah lounges in the city for food, drinks, and hookah of course. It was always great spending time with her best friend and tonight was no different as the girls kept each other company, sharing all the updates of their busy lives.

Thyri had confirmed her feelings for Killian to Dayana. Feelings she knew were growing stronger each day the more time she spent with him. There was no point denying the truth to herself. She was in love with him and falling more in love with him every single day. Dayana had confirmed that things with her and Ethan were getting much better. His insecurities about her tattooing male clients had disappeared and he'd become a lot more supportive with her career.

Thyri was glad to know that things were going great in her

relationship and her best friend's relationship. They were both experiencing happiness with the men that they loved and it was a fact that had her heart leaping with joy.

Thyri and Dayana continued to enjoy their night together, smoked hookah and drank cocktails. The lounge they were in tonight had started off fairly quiet but now that it was getting later into the night, more people had occupied the lounge. It was a large, spaced lounge with upholstered cream velvet booths and white marble tables.

Thyri and Dayana were deep in their conversation about taking a vacation together sometime next year when the sudden call of Thyri's name had her whipping her head around to see...

"Soraya?"

"Fancy seeing you here tonight," she said before looking over at Dayana. "Hey, Dayana."

"Hey," Dayana coolly greeted her.

"I hope you're having fun tonight."

"We are," Thyri replied. "I hope you are too."

"I am," Soraya confirmed with a smile. "Enjoy the rest of your night, ladies."

Thyri returned her smile and watched as Soraya walked away from their table, heading back to wherever it was that she'd come from. Thyri didn't even notice that she was in the function and now that she knew that Soraya was here, she felt a weird sensation form in her heart. She'd now noticed where Soraya was seated across the room with her friend and had a clear view of her.

"Atlanta really is a small ass city," Thyri voiced with a sigh as she looked away from Soraya and her friend.

"It sure is... that bitch knows damn well she don't give a fuck about us enjoying the rest of our night."

Thyri chortled.

"Dayana, be nice."

"Nah, fuck that bitch. Remember that nasty comment I told you she said to me about me not being the one in her way? Basically insinuating that you were in her way?" Thyri nodded, remembering the day that Dayana had called her, filling her in on what Soraya had said to her. "That hoe only apologized to you about Grenada because Killian made her, not because she wanted to. Wack ass hoe. Can't believe I actually used to like her ass."

After Thyri had told Dayana about what had went down in Grenada, Dayana wasn't impressed by Soraya's behavior and already started feeling some type of way towards her. Then the day that Soraya had made the *"You're not the one that got in my way,"* comment to Dayana, Dayana told Thyri and decided from that day onwards that she didn't fuck with Soraya anymore.

Thyri didn't have a problem with Soraya anymore and thought that they'd put the issues of Grenada to bed but clearly she'd thought wrong. It was what it was though. Soraya wasn't important to Thyri and she really wasn't about to stress about her.

Thyri and Dayana continued to talk, drink and vibe to the upbeat tunes being played in the background. Minutes later, Dayana voiced her disapproval.

"I swear to God if she looks this way like that one more time it's about to be a fucking problem."

"Day."

"What? She's the one that's been sending dirty looks this way. I told you that bitch ain't right."

Thyri had indeed noticed Soraya sending dirty looks their way but she'd tried to shake it off as best as she could, focused on having a good time with her girl.

"Just ignore her. She's clearly the only one with the problem." Thyri lifted her wrist to stare down at the silver face of her watch. "Damn, is that really the time?"

It was eleven-thirty p.m. and Thyri was shocked that time had flown by so fast.

"Time really does fly by when you're having fun," Dayana commented. "You ready to go, boo?"

"Yeah."

"Of course you are. You're ready to go home to your mannnnn," Dayana sang, sticking her tongue out which made Thyri blush and giggle.

Dayana told no lies because Thyri was indeed ready to go home to her man. Killian had no idea of her plans to surprise him tonight because in his mind after her date night with Dayana she'd be heading home. But the liquor that was in Thyri's system had her feeling very nice and she was more than ready to go home to her man.

The girls had already split their bill an hour ago so all they had to do was grab their things and head out. But before leaving, Thyri needed to use the restrooms so Dayana followed her there.

Thyri rushed into the first empty cubicle she laid eyes on and shut the door before pulling her panties down to pee.

"Girl, you and your weak ass bladder."

"Don't be a hater, Day!" Thyri laughed.

The sound of the restroom door opening was heard just as Thyri flushed.

"Is there a problem, Dayana?"

Thyri froze at the sound of an unexpected voice.

"I don't know you tell me, Soraya. You're the one that's been sending dirty looks to me and Thyri all night."

"Only because you started it."

"Started what? Quit lying. You came up to our table with your fake nice act and expected us to buy it. Get the fuck outta here."

"I wasn't being fake but I can see that you definitely have been.

426

We see each other almost every day at work and you ain't never had this same energy, Dayana."

"That's because I wasn't tryna lose my job cursing your dumb ass the fuck out."

"So your fake ass really has a problem with me."

"Oh there's definitely a problem, hoe."

Thyri tore the cubicle's door open after hearing Dayana's confirmation of there being a problem.

She first laid eyes on her best friend standing at the far end of the restrooms, by the sink whereas Soraya and her female friend stood on the other end close to the exit.

"Dayana, just chill," Thyri tried to coach her but it was no use because Dayana had been set off by Soraya following them into the restroom, like a cheetah stalking out its prey.

"Hell no, I ain't gonna fucking chill. She's been looking at us crazy all night and I'm not letting it slide anymore."

Dayana set her eyes directly on Soraya as she said, "Just admit that you're jealous of Killian and Thyri."

"Jealous?" Soraya's laughter filled the room. "What's there to be jealous of? I've already had him, sweetheart." Soraya's pearly whites flashed in a smile. "Plenty of times."

A knot formed in Thyri's stomach.

"You're jealous that he chose her over you and don't think I didn't hear what you said that day at the shop. You're mad cause Thyri got in your way and took a spot you could never have."

"Why I would I be mad about a spot she's not gonna have for long?" Soraya countered with a smirk. "Every woman in Atlanta knows that Killian's not a one woman man. He fucks whoever, whenever he likes."

"He's not fucking anyone but me thank you very much," Thyri finally intervened, crossing her arms across her chest. "So stop worrying about shit that doesn't concern you."

"Have fun dreaming that you'll be the only one by his side for long... lemme guess..." Soraya placed a hand to her chin as she pretended to be deep in thought. "He painted you too, huh?"

Thyri's heart skipped several beats at Soraya's rhetorical question.

"And now that's gassed you up into thinking he's going to marry you one day." Soraya cackled. "News flash, darling, Killian paints all the bitches he fucks. It's his thing."

What the hell? Thyri couldn't believe what she was hearing right now. *She's lying. She has to be lying.*

"So don't get comfy. He'll ditch you and move onto the next new bomber pussy soon enough."

"You jealous little bitch!" Dayana shrieked, charging at Soraya but the second she charged at her was the same second that Soraya's friend grabbed her and dashed her to the side.

Then they started going at it and Thyri's fists tightened as she went to defend her best friend.

"Oh no you don't."

Thyri's arm was yanked and she was pulled back, stopping her from helping Dayana beat up Soraya's friend. "Your ass is mine, bitch."

Pow!

The hard hit of a punch landed on Thyri's face and she stumbled backwards.

Did this bitch just really hit me?

"Damn that felt good." Soraya laughed. "Been meaning to give you that since you cockblocked me in Grenada. You made me miss out on getting the vacation dick I deserved."

Thyri quickly squared up and ran up on Soraya, jabbing her fist towards her face.

Pow! Pow! Pow!

Punch after punch Thyri landed on Soraya's face, releasing all the anger she felt at what Soraya had said about Killian.

Pow! Pow! Pow!

Soraya stumbled backwards, almost losing balance and falling to the floor but she kept her stance. She lifted a hand to her nose, feeling blood trickling down her nose and cursed when she saw the blood on her fingers. Soraya didn't hesitate to charge at Thyri, rushing into her as she grabbed her body and sent them both crashing to the ground.

Thyri immediately went into defense mode, hitting and scratching at Soraya wherever she could as they were on the ground. She'd been meaning to fuck Soraya up since Grenada and though she'd let bygones be bygones, all bets were off.

Thyri climbed on top of Soraya, jabbing punches continuously on her face and pulling on her hair, trying to yank her hair extensions out. Soraya had a leave out hairstyle and Thyri had every intention of fucking it up.

She pulled out one hair extension, grinning happily and eagerly pulling out another one. But a sudden sharpness poked into her side, causing Thyri to scream out in pain. The sharpness was pulled out of her, only worsening her cries and a hard punch into her stomach knocked her to the ground. The sharpness returned, this time in her thigh and the fiery slices of pain that shot through her were unbearable.

The next few minutes were a blur. One tragic blur. Thyri's hair was pulled and her head forced up as Soraya dragged her across the bathroom floor to the nearest sink. Then her head and face were continuously bashed into the sink. Hit after hit after hit after hit came pounding on her face. Then she felt kicks on her stomach and her back too.

It got to a point where Thyri became numb, no longer feeling the mind shattering pain because she was falling in and out of consciousness. She could not think straight or see straight. Everything had become blurry.

"Get the hell away from her! You bitch!"

"She deserves this shit. Punk ass hoe."

Thyri heard a ringing noise in her head and inky black dots formed in her blurry sight.

"Killian was never yours to have, you stupid little thief. Let this be a lesson for getting in my way," were the last words she heard before the darkness came in and stole her away.

Chapter Thirty-Four

"**G**ive me her address."

"Even if I do that, you won't find her, Truth. You know she's not there."

"I'm not asking you, Killian! I'm telling you. Give me her fucking address!"

"Tru..."

"No, don't fucking touch me, Tanai! Did you not see what the fuck she did to our sister's face? The stab wounds? I don't care if she's not home! I'm still going over there!"

"To do what, Tru?" Tanai asked.

"I can't fuck her up yet so I'm fucking up her shit for the time being but I promise you when I catch that bitch, it's on!"

Truth began pacing back and forth, boiling with so much rage that she felt like she was about to explode.

"Attacking my sister, *my sister!* I'm gonna kill her! There's no other option, she has to die! She clearly doesn't know what family she's fucked with!"

Tanai sighed as she watched her sister walk back and forth in the middle of the hospital waiting room they were all in.

The past twenty four hours had been hell on earth.

Tanai remembered exactly where she was when she'd gotten the call. She'd been sitting in the spa like bathtub of her en-suite bathroom with a glass of Chateau Margaux by her side.

Being couped up in the house all day had provided Tanai with a solace that she'd been needing. Usually on Saturdays she'd be stuck by her hubby's side, willing to do whatever he wanted them to do but because of the rift between them she was keeping her distance away from him until further notice.

Kason had been giving her space as she wanted and had left their house early this morning to head to the office. He never went into work on the weekend unless it was an emergency but because he was giving his wife space, he felt like he had no choice but to head to work. Besides, Trinity's location was still something he was dying to know and he could find out instant updates about her from his men by going into the office.

*Evening time had come and all Tanai wanted was a bath before putting her soul to rest for the night. So here she now was, deep in her tub, her eyes shut, her glass sealed to her lips and her Beats By Dre headphones glued to her ears as Adele sang all about **Rolling In The Deep.***

Never in a million years would Tanai have guessed that her marriage would turn this sour. A part of her wished she could just act like nothing was wrong and act like she hadn't seen that video. It was just a little coke, right? It wasn't that deep, right? She was blowing this whole situation out of proportion, right? She should just forget what he'd done and move on.

But she couldn't. She just couldn't bring her mind to forget. She couldn't bring herself to erase the pain she'd felt seeing him do the one act that had taken one of her best friends.

Tanai knew she loved Kason. How could she not love him? In the short amount of time they'd been boyfriend and girlfriend, travelling across the globe together, she'd taken one look into his eyes and known that her heart was no longer hers. It was his and his alone.

Tanai felt tears prick her eyes as she thought about how much she missed Kason. She missed being in his arms, she missed feeling his lips against hers and she definitely missed feeling his lips on her most sensitive spot. Not falling asleep with him right by her side had been complete agony. How she'd done it? She had no clue.

The first tear escaped and her eyes popped open, seeing the bubbles her body was submerged in. Her head slowly lifted and she was startled by the sienna brown eyes that were fixed on her. Her tears became endless, falling one after the other and betraying her commitment to not showing weakness.

He rushed over to her from where he stood by the closed door and got on his knees once by the edge of the bath. She saw his lips move but couldn't hear a sound from him because all she could hear were Adele's powerful vocals. Her headphones slid off her ears, allowing her to hear his speech.

"Nai, baby, please..."

He placed her rose gold headphones to the floor before bringing his hands to the side of her face and making her stare at him.

"Enough of this. I'm begging you." He leaned in, planting a soft peck to her mouth. "I need you to forgive me." He pecked her again. "I need my Nugget back."

He kissed on her wet cheeks, only causing more tears to fall from her eyes at how affectionate he was being. Then his lips meshed with hers and she found herself undone.

Completely undone.

God, she'd missed this. She'd missed him kissing her in ways only he could. She'd missed him taking control, using his tongue to take her breath away and bringing her to her knees. A moan slipped out from her lips when his kiss got deeper, needier, and nastier.

Kason dropped his hands from her face only to push them into the water and grab hold of her waist. She tensed at his sudden touch.

"Ka... Kason."

He began lifting her out of the water while their lips remained locked but Tanai reached for his hands and pushed them away.

"Kason, stop," she said after tearing his hands from her body.

"Nai, please," he groaned, placing his hands back on her body. "I need you."

She gazed into his hooded eyes, reading the pain burning within them.

He leaned closer, pressing his forehead to hers as he let out a deep breath.

"I need you, Tanai," he whispered. "I need to hold you... to kiss you... to taste you."

Heat rushed through her at his words.

"Please."

Tanai felt her muscles relax and she sighed, knowing she could no longer fight off her feelings for her husband. She wanted and needed him just as bad as he wanted and needed her.

Her lips parted just as she started talking but the sound of her iPhone ringing cut her off. Both their eyes drifted to her phone sitting on the tub's edge. The caller ID read Dayana and Tanai was reminded about Thyri texting her earlier during the day telling her about how she was spending her Saturday night with Dayana.

Tanai rarely spoke to Dayana so her name popping up right now on her screen was baffling to Tanai. She lifted her hand out the water, bringing a finger to her screen and tapping the green answer button. She clicked the audio icon, placing her phone on speaker as she said, "Hey, Daya—"

"Tanai!" she frantically yelled, not letting Tanai get a word in.

434

"Please come quickly! Thyri's hurt!" Dayana's sobs filled the line. *"She's hurt real bad, Tanai!"*

That was all it took for Tanai to jump out the bath, rushing to grab her towel without even caring about the fact that she could slip and fall.

Twenty four hours later and Tanai was still in pure shock at what had went down last night. When she arrived at the hospital to find her sister, she found Dayana in the waiting room with unkempt hair, rips in her top and a few bruises on her face.

It took Dayana ten minutes to explain what had gone down. They were the longest ten minutes of Tanai's life that she would never be able to forget because of the way she trembled with fury as she heard what had been done to Thyri.

Tanai wasn't a fighter but she had never wanted to fight someone as bad as she wanted to fight Soraya. As a matter of fact, she didn't want to fight Soraya. She wanted to kill her.

Laying eyes on her unconscious sister made Tanai feel like she'd been stabbed in the heart.

Thyri's face was battered. *Everywhere.*

She had two black eyes, a busted lip, cuts all over her face, severe swelling on her face and bruising. The doctor in charge of Thyri's care had told her family about the small stab wounds they'd found in the right side of Thyri's abdomen and her left thigh. Thyri was almost unrecognizable and Tanai could not believe this had happened to her sister.

"This still isn't making any fucking sense. Why the hell would she attack Thyri like this? Thyri told us that she apologized to her about Grenada and the issue was solved," Tanai announced and got up from her seat, causing Kason's hand that had been resting on her lap to fall. "Unless there's something you're not telling us, Killian."

"And what exactly is that supposed to mean?" He shot her a

venomous look that instantly made Kason frown. "I haven't touched that bitch since I met Thyri."

When he'd gotten the call from Dayana about Thyri's attack, Killian had nothing but murder on his mind. For what Soraya had done she deserved to suffer in the worse way possible and Killian was more than willing to make that happen.

"She attacked Thyri because of you," Truth chimed in. "Why the hell would she do that if you haven't been fucking her?"

"Because she's a jealous, stupid bit—"

"Ahem."

A throat clearing made everyone turn around to see a short gray haired European man standing a short distance away from them in the waiting room.

Killian, Tanai and Truth rushed over to him whereas Kadiri and Kason leaped out of their seats to follow them.

"Dr. Rivera," Tanai called out his name as she came to stand in front of him. "How is she?"

"Better." He nodded, lifting a finger to push his glasses closer to his face. "We've cleaned all her wounds and bandaged them up. The swelling has gone down too."

"Oh thank God," Tanai whispered, feeling a hand grab hers and feeling her heart ease at Kason's hold on her.

"She's well rested and she's ready to see you all now."

Truth didn't hesitate in running past Dr. Rivera and racing towards Thyri's room. Tanai bolted after her and Killian decided to hold back so Thyri could see her sisters first. As bad as he wanted to see her, he knew that her sisters had the right to see her first.

Dr. Rivera gave the three tall men a respectful nod before walking away from them with his clipboard tucked in his armpit. The Miller men had already spoken to Dr. Rivera in private, making sure that he knew not to call law enforcement about his new patient. It wasn't something they wanted to be challenged on and Dr. Rivera recognized that from their tones and expressions. He agreed, getting a sense that these persuasive, dominant men were going to handle the situation themselves and there was nothing he could do to stop them.

"I can't believe this is happening," Kadiri announced, in a pissed tone. "Why the hell would Soraya do this shit, Kill?"

"I don't know!" he bellowed, throwing his hands in the air.

Both Kadiri and Kason gave him a wide eyed stare.

"I don't fucking know! And I really wish everyone would stop asking me that shit!"

"You need to calm dow—"

"Don't tell me to calm down," he spat, glaring at Kason. "You saw what the fuck she did to Thyri's face! How the hell do you expect me to calm down, nigga? My girl has two black eyes because of that bitch!"

Killian moved to the nearest wall and jabbed his fist against it.

"I'm gonna kill her!" He punched the wall again and again and again.

People who were on the other side of the waiting room shifted in their seats and flinched at the stranger punching the wall.

"Killian, stop!" Kason grabbed his brother's arm and attempted to pull him away from the wall but Killian's larger biceps gave him the advantage to remain rooted in his spot. "You're angry and you have every right to be, but this is not how we act."

He grabbed Killian's fists, stopping him from lifting them once again.

"Not in fucking public," he hissed.

Killian's breaths were quick and jagged as his eyes blazed into Kason's.

"Relax," Kason coached in a calm tone before lowering his

volume to say, "You will handle her. *We* will handle her. The right way."

That was all Killian needed to hear in order to calm himself down.

Footsteps were heard drawing near to them and the brothers turned to the right to see Truth walking to them with a serious expression.

"Killian."

Killian quickly stepped away from Kason.

"She wants to see you."

There was something about the way she'd spoken to him that left a bitter taste in Killian's mouth but he decided not to dwell on it and took quick, focused strides to Thyri's room.

He arrived in the open doorway of her room to see the back of Tanai's head as she hugged her sister. Then Tanai straightened up and left Thyri's side, allowing Killian's heart to break as he focused in on his Bubba's face.

She had a bandage wrapped around her face, a plaster on her nose and an IV drip attached to her hand. He'd been too busy staring at her to notice that Tanai had walked past him and left the two of them alone.

"Thyri," he croaked out.

Thyri's emotions were unreadable but when she spoke up, that's when he realized that things between them were... *strained.*

"I hope you're happy," she said, her voice low and raspy.

"Happy? Thyri, why would I be happy about you being hurt?"

"Two women fighting over you... isn't that every man's dream?"

That certainly wasn't his dream. It never had been.

"Thyri, I'm so sorry she did this. I promise you I'm gonna fin—"

"There's nothing for you to fix," she retorted. "Please don't come near me, Killian."

He stopped walking towards her bed side, feeling his throat close up at her cold, condescending tone.

"You can't fix this. She attacked me because of you. She never got over Grenada. She never got over the fact that you decided to mess with me instead of her."

"And I promise you, Thyri, she's not getting away with this shit."

"She's already gotten away with it, Killian! Look at my face! Look at where the hell I am!"

"Thyri... I'm so—"

"I never should have messed with you. I never should have left Chosen for you."

A chill went through him and he looked at her like she'd suddenly grown two heads. His hands dropped to his side to form clenched fists of tension.

"Are you fucking serious right now, Thyri?"

"Dead serious."

"No you can't be." A hollow, callous chuckle left his lips, making goosebumps rise on her skin. "Because I know you're not dumb enough to play with me like this."

"I'm no—"

"I know you haven't suddenly developed amnesia and forgotten what I told you in Grenada. You are mine and I am yours."

"No I don't believe you're mine because *mine* wouldn't have had a woman from his past attack me like this! *Mine* wouldn't have a thing for painting all the women he fucks!"

"What?" His brows dipped as he squinted at her. "Thyri, what are you talking about?"

"Now look at who's acting dumb. You know exactly what I'm talking about, Killian."

But he didn't and he shook his head 'no' as he took a couple steps closer to her bed.

"I told you not to come near to me, Killian, so don't!"

He stopped walking, not wanting to get her anymore worked up. She was supposed to be recovering not stressing.

Silence sprinkled the room with its dust as their eyes remained locked. Killian could see the resentment in her eyes and he hated it. But there was nothing he hated more than the next sentence that dropped from her lips.

"Please leave my room, Killian."

He did a double take, thinking that he'd misheard her.

"I don't want you here," she explained. "So get out."

"I'm not leaving."

"Then I'll simply call security who will get you out of here."

No... she wouldn't, he thought but the look in her eyes told him *yes she would.*

"Leave, Killian."

Her final order was enough to make sorrow shred his insides and instead of trying to fight her wish, he decided to grant her it.

"And don't bother coming back," she said as he turned around to face the door.

His jaw clenched and he felt the urge to turn around to challenge her words but he decided against it. Thyri's muscles relaxed once Killian walked out her room without looking back.

She had lashed out at him because she was hurt and she had every right to be hurt after what Soraya had done to her last night. Every part of her ached because of the physical abuse she'd faced and she couldn't help but blame Killian for her current predicament.

This is all his fault, Thyri. You're in this situation because of him. You're hurt, Thyri and it's all his fault.

It was at this exact moment that Thyri remembered Chosen's words. Tears gleamed in her eyes as his voice filled her mind.

He hurts people, Thyri, and pretty soon he'll hurt you.

Chapter Thirty-Five

Monday morning had arrived the next day and neither Tanai nor Truth had any plans to go to work. Thyri was their main focus from here on out. After dropping Alana off at pre-school, Truth texted Tanai, telling her that she would be at Thyri's house in a few hours. She just needed to do a few things at home then she would be on her way.

Thyri had been discharged from the hospital yesterday and was now back at home. Tanai had made it her priority to ensure that Thyri got into her home safely. She'd had her driver, Saber, assist with taking Thyri home and although Kason offered his assistance, Tanai wanted to take care of her sister without his help. Besides, even though they'd had a mini reconciliation that night in their bathroom, the air was still quite tense between them. She still wanted her space from Kason despite how much she loved, wanted, and needed him.

She'd stayed the night at Thyri's house. Helping her sister with any and everything she needed help with. Thyri's body was still healing and she wasn't back to her normal self yet which is why

Tanai was devoted to ensuring her sister's road to recovery was one hundred percent stress free.

Truth was devoted too but she was a mother who needed to balance her devotion between her sister and daughter which Tanai understood completely. She was fine with taking most of the responsibility when taking care of Thyri for the next few weeks while Truth helped whenever she could.

Theresa, their mother figure, had come to see Thyri yesterday at the hospital. She was heartbroken to see one of the women she considered to be a daughter, hurt. Thyri assured her that she was doing better and would be back on the mend very soon.

Tanai had a private conversation with Theresa about their business affairs. Since Tanai and Truth had made the joint decision to look after Thyri for the next few weeks, they needed Theresa to hold down the fort at their company and take care of the business until further notice. Theresa agreed without hesitation. Those were her girls and she'd do anything for them in a heartbeat.

One-thirty p.m. came around and Truth had arrived at Thyri's house. Thyri was currently napping while Truth and Tanai were in her kitchen, preparing one of her favorite meals, shrimp tacos.

"Nai..."

The call of her name made her look up from the sizzling shrimp in the silver pan below her.

"What's up, sis?" she asked as she watched Truth chop lettuce.

"Let me ask you something."

Truth kept her eyes trained on the silver knife she moved across the chopping board.

"This is all hypothetical by the way."

"Okay, shoot."

"If you and Kason were on the brink of divorce..."

Tanai's heartbeat sped up and she was suddenly reminded that her sisters had no clue about what was going on in her marriage. She hadn't told either of them about Kason's sex tapes.

"And you were a few weeks away from signing the papers. Would you be mad if you found that he'd taken an interest in someone that you know?"

"Depends on who it is that I know," she replied. "If it's just a woman that I know of, then that's got nothing to do with me."

"But what if it's someone you considered a friend... not a super close friend but someone you were just starting to get to know better."

"Oh I'd be mad," Tanai admitted with a scowl. "Big mad."

Truth felt guilt rip through her heart. She kept silent and continued to chop through the lettuce.

"Truth."

Her head lifted and she met the pretty face of her sister.

"What's going on?" Tanai's left brow arched.

"Nothing."

Then a frown formed on Tanai's lips.

"Nothing," Truth repeated.

Unfortunately, her sister knew Truth better than she knew herself and knew when she was lying.

"Truth, just tell m—"

Ringing filled the atmosphere and Tanai looked down at the counter where her phone sat. The caller ID was a number she didn't recognize so she chose to ignore it, hitting the decline button before turning back to Truth.

"Truth, tell me what's going o—"

The ringing noise filled the space again and Tanai sighed, picking up her phone and staring hard at the number she didn't recognize. Reluctance crossed Tanai's features and Truth decided to speak up.

"You should probably pick that up, sis," Truth advised. "It might be important."

Tanai continued to stare at her phone's screen for a couple more seconds before giving in and answering the call.

"Hello?"

"Tanai... I see you finally decided to answer my call."

She knew that voice... *right?* The person's face wasn't coming to her mind straight away but she'd definitely heard that voice somewhere before.

"I'm sorry... who is this?"

"Don't tell me you forgotten me already, beautiful."

A face suddenly came to mind and her eyes widened.

"Sebastian?"

She turned around, her back now facing Truth.

"How did you get my number?"

"I have my ways," he replied, chuckling lightly. "Anything I want in this life I get Tanai... and honestly, I really want you."

Her lips parted but no sound came out. She couldn't bring herself to say a word.

"I know I've caught you off guard with this call but I just couldn't keep denying myself what I've known from the second I laid eyes on you at the gala."

Has he lost his mind and forgotten who I'm married to?

"Just give me one date, Tanai. One date to prove to you why I'm the man for you and if you don't want anything to do with me after that date then I promise you I won't contact you again."

"Sebastian, I'm mar—"

"Married to a man that's making you unhappy with his promiscuous past? Yeah I know."

What? How the hell does he know that?

"One date, Tanai. That's all I want."

Shock, confusion, and shame all coursed through her veins.

"And I'm not taking no for an answer," he affirmed. "You deserve to be treated like a queen, Tanai Wright and I intend to do that and so much more."

She remained speechless, especially because of the choice he'd made to call her by her maiden name and not her marital one.

"I'll text you a date and time sometime during the week. All you have to do is say yes. If that date and time doesn't work then we'll figure something out."

"Sebastian, I—"

"I'm not taking no for an answer, beautiful. Don't forget that," he concluded before ending their call.

He smiled to himself as he brought his phone back to his line of gaze and searched through his call log for his next important call. The call was picked up after the second ring.

"Hello?... Yes, she picked up... nope, I didn't give her the option to decline... oh don't you worry she'll be mine... by the time I'm done with her your son won't need to worry about her anymore... and she I will be making a sex tape of our own... yes of course... that marriage will be over in no time, just like you want... I'll keep you posted... speak to you soon."

Sebastian then ended the call and turned around to face the floor to ceiling window of his office. A smile began to grow on his lips as he thought about that fact that soon Tanai Wright would be his.

Chapter Thirty-Six

uilt.

It wasn't an emotion that Truth experienced often because what exactly did she have to feel guilty about? She was a great mother to her three year old, a great sister to Thyri and Tanai and a great friend... well a great friend to all except Kiana.

Truth hadn't planned for things to change so suddenly between her and Kadiri but they had. In the beginning they hated each other and Truth was sure things would remain that way until Kadiri had stepped up as a father figure to Alana. He'd treated Truth's daughter like his own and had gone out of his way for her in ways that he didn't have to.

That doesn't mean you needed to fall asleep on his chest, Tru, or cuddle with him or let him touch you in ways that would make Kiana want to kill you for messing with her boyfriend.

Truth ran a hand down her face, feeling her frustrations mount because of the situation she'd placed herself in. The whole situation was messy and she hated messy.

Truth stared at the mirror in front of her, taking her appearance in one last time before walking away from her sink to leave her bathroom.

"You're gonna be a boss just like boss baby when you're older, Lani. Gonna have all these niggas at your beck and call too, trying to wine and dine you but I'm gonna be waiting with my Glock ready to hunt down anyone that tries to hurt you."

"Glowck? Wass that?"

"That's slang for gun, baby girl. The gun I'm gonna use to kill all those foo—"

"Ahem!"

Alana and Kadiri's heads turned to see Truth walking into the living room. Truth shot Kadiri an unimpressed look and he smirked before reaching into the mini popcorn box that sat on Alana's lap.

The image of them sitting on the sofa with Alana resting against his chest while they watched The Boss Baby movie together was a very sweet one. But what wasn't sweet was Truth hearing Kadiri talk to her baby about guns. He was so reckless with his mouth sometimes that you never knew what wild thing he was about to say next.

It had been four days since Thyri's attack and she was a doing a lot better each day. Tanai had been sleeping over at her home for the past couple days and Truth had been going over whenever she dropped Alana off at pre-school. Despite Thyri being on the road to recovery, she was still very much scarred physically, mentally, and emotionally, by what Soraya had done to her and because of those scars, she refused to see or talk to Killian. Even when he came around her apartment last night, Thyri told Tanai not to let him in. She didn't want to see him and Truth didn't blame her. He'd definitely had a part to play in Thyri being attacked and Truth sided completely with her sister when she said that she didn't want to see him. She lowkey wished she could adopt the same energy as Thyri and not have to see Kadiri but he'd shown up this evening with gifts for Alana and once Alana heard his deep voice outside their front door, she ran out to greet him. Truth knew there was no way she could turn him away now that his Lani had caught wind of his presence.

Truth and Kadiri hadn't laid eyes on one another since Sunday when they'd been at the hospital for Thyri. At the hospital, she refused to look at him or offer him any words. She didn't want to look at him because every time she did, she was reminded of how attracted she was to him. She was reminded of that night they'd shared in her bed... with his hands on her body... his fingers deep inside her... her hands on his body... and his lips on hers. A night that couldn't happen again.

She knew what they'd done was wrong. She'd be a fool trying to deny it. She was a trifling ass friend to Kiana and she knew she needed to put an end to whatever the hell was going on between her and Kadiri.

Tonight.

"So what bedtime story are we reading tonight, Lani?"

"I don't wuanna sleep!"

"Come on, Lani. You know what time it is."

"I not tired!"

"So why was your ass falling asleep on my shoulder during Boss Baby, huh?"

"I didn't!"

"Quit capping, Alana. You know I saw your ass."

"I don't wuanna sleep! I don't wuanna sleep! I don't wuanna sleep!"

"We can do this all night, sweetheart, I don't mind. It's bedtime and you know it... oh so now you using Mr. Snuggles to hit me? A'ight cool, I guess he belongs to me now and you won't mind sleeping without him."

"Noooooo! My Mr. Snuggles. Gimmie!"

"You should have thought about that before you used him to hit me, Lani. He's mine now."

Truth couldn't help but smile as she stood outside Alana's bedroom, listening to Alana fight Kadiri on the topic of her going to sleep. Hearing Kadiri mention how she'd used her favorite toy, Mr. Snuggles, to hit him made her chuckle quietly. It was sometimes a struggle to get Alana to sleep especially if she'd been having too much fun being awake but Kadiri was becoming more of a pro at getting her to sleep. He was such a great father figure to Alana, an even better one than her real father who didn't even know of Kadiri's existence.

Truth thought that Alana would have brought him up in conversations with Jodell but she hadn't because Jodell hadn't said anything to her about Kadiri. She knew what type of baby daddy she had – one with a jealous streak – and if he knew of Kadiri's hold on Alana, he would definitely let Truth know his disapproval about another man being close with *his seed*.

Truth appreciated all the things that Kadiri had done for Alana and how great of a father he was. Her appreciation is what broke her heart even more because of what she needed to do tonight.

"And just like that, the queen is out like a light."

Kadiri gently closed Alana's room door behind him and came to stand in front of it with a grin spreading across his lips.

That grin was almost enough to make Truth say:

Fuck Kiana. He doesn't like her! He clearly likes me.

But she knew better.

She let her gaze linger on his face, admiring all the features of this irresistible man.

Those cognac eyes that always seemed to be staring into her soul, those juicy looking pink lips that she'd had the honor of feeling against he—

Focus, Truth. This is important.

"Kadiri... we need to talk."

They were the five words that he really wasn't trying to hear right now. So he chose to ignore them as he sauntered over to her.

She went quiet as she watched him walk over to her, realizing that he wanted to take a seat. She shifted to the far end of the loveseat so he would have enough space to sit down. He sat down and looked over at her.

"You can't com... Kadiri!"

One swift motion was all it took for Kadiri to pull her across the couch and lift her up to sit on his lap.

"Kadiri..." She sighed as he wrapped his arms around her and rested his head in the crook of her neck. "We can't do this."

He continued to ignore her, planting kisses on her flesh that were starting to drive her insane.

"Kadiri, please... don't."

She could no longer think straight with the way he had his arms around her, holding her tight and keeping her close to him. She could no longer think straight with the way those pillow soft lips of his were seducing her.

"Kadiri, no," she protested, reaching for his tatted arms, and trying to peel them from her body. The more she tried, the more he held onto her tighter.

"Tell me this doesn't feel right and I'll stop, Tru."

"Kadiri, please."

"No, tell me this..." He pressed another kiss to her skin at the same time he reached for her right breast, squeezing her flesh tighter. "Doesn't feel good..." His kisses and squeezes continued. "And I'll stop."

God... why is he doing this to me?

Truth helplessly sighed, feeling her most intimate spot come alive the more he kissed and teased her.

"Kadiri..." She turned to gaze into his eyes, reading the lust within them. "You have a girlfriend."

"She's not important right now," he countered, teasing her hard nipple with his thumb.

"She's my friend, Kadi!"

"And?"

"Kadiri." A look of disbelief washed over her face. "You and I can't do this. You know we can't."

"We're doin—"

"And I can't have you coming over here anymore," she interrupted him. "I won't stop you from seeing Alana but you'll have to see her outside this house."

"I'm not going to stop putting my daughter to sleep, Truth."

"Kadiri, you can'—"

"And I'm not going to stop falling asleep with my baby mama in my arms," he affirmed, lifting his hand from her boob, and wrapping it around her throat.

"Come here," he ordered, pulling her face closer to his.

"Kadiri."

"You're talking too much, Tru. Come here now."

Before Truth knew it, his lips crashed to hers and she was like putty in his hands, giving into his kiss. She felt her juices gush out of her as his slow, sensual kiss began. He took his time with her, giving her the chance to realize that he had no plans to go anywhere and make her realize that from here on out – she belonged to him.

His tongue found its way to its new home – her mouth – which he skillfully explored like a treasure hunter searching for his precious gold. And in Kadiri's mind, she was gold, *his* gold, and he had no intentions of letting his gold go.

Truth's moans seeped out between their mouths as Kadiri's kiss made her pussy throb and every part of her flooded with heat. She could feel his bulge poking her butt as it grew bigger by the second. She began to rotate her hips and grind on his erection, causing groans to drop from his lips.

The blood rushing constantly to his dick was surely about to kill him if he didn't do something about it and Truth felt the exact same way with how swollen her yoni had gotten.

He released her throat only to place both hands back on her waist. Truth's hands went to his neck, keeping him close as she followed his lead and felt him push her down to the couch.

Their hands then went to each other's clothing and they rushed to strip each other from their garments. Their mouths refused to stay away from each other for too long as they quickly lifted their tops over their heads and focused right back on kissing.

When her bra's hook was freed, Truth was finally able to release a breath again as Kadiri tore his lips away from hers to lower his head.

"Kadiri."

Her moan was instant when he latched his mouth to her left nipple and as he worked his magic, Truth stroked his head of waves, feeling like she was in paradise. Her teeth sunk into her lips and she looked up at the ceiling as lust blinded her from all common sense. There was no going back now and she knew it. She wanted Kadiri Mill—

Knock! Knock!

Truth froze and her heart raced at the sudden knocking on her front door. Kadiri pulled his lips from her nipple and lifted his gaze. Confusion stained his handsome face as he looked down at her.

"Who is that?" he asked in a low tone.

"I don't know," she whispered, her eyes now trained on her front door behind his head.

"Just ignore i—"

Knock! Knock!

"Truth... I know it's late but I need to see you," Jodell's voice came sounding from the other side, making her groan internally. "I'm done with this co-parenting shit, man. I need my family back. I need you back."

Knock! Knock!

"Open up."

Truth sighed and let her eyes fall back on Kadiri who remained in the middle of her thighs. He now wore a blank look that didn't allow her to read his emotions.

"It's Alana's daddy," she explained quietly. "Jo—"

"Jodell," he answered for her, shooting shockwaves down her spine.

"Wait... How do you... how do you know his name?"

"'Cause I recognize that nigga's voice," he retorted, lifting his body from hers. "He works for me."

"Wha—"

Knock! Knock!

"Truth, let me in! I know you ain't got some wack ass nigga in the crib where my daughter lays her head. Let me in before I break this damn door down, girl."

Chapter Thirty-Seven

"I feel like this is all my fault. I'm so sorry, TT."

"Girl, don't be silly. This isn't your fault."

"If I'd just ignored the bitch rather than giving into her dirty looks then she never would've approached us in that bathroom... we would've never been ambushed."

"Trust me, Day, this isn't your fault. She'd been plotting on me from the jump since Grenada. She just found the perfect opportunity to carry out her plans. If anyone's to blame, it's Killian."

"Killian?"

"Yes, Killian. He's the one that created the whole triangle in the first place. He's the one that messed with her in the past and he's the one that she was fighting me over. It's his fault and I don't want anything to do with him right now."

"But girl... didn't you tell me that you're in love with him?"

Thyri shrugged.

"You can't ignore the man you love forever."

"The man I love wouldn't have ever put me in this position.

Why am I the one suffering at the hands of a woman scorned? Scorned by his actions."

Dayana sighed.

"That bitch is lucky she hasn't shown her face at the shop because I would've given her the beat down she deserved with no hesitation."

"Day..." A smile graced Thyri's lips.

"Nah I'm serious! She's also lucky she had her friend right by her side that night to fight me. What a fucked up individual. It's like she had that shit planned down to the T. Fucking psycho."

Dayana reached for Thyri's hands and held them tight.

"I'm so sorry, Thyri. You didn't deserve all that."

"It's fine... I'm done thinking about it. I just want to move on."

"Agreed... but you can't ignore Killian forever, TT."

"I just don't want or need to see him. I had my face bashed into a sink multiple times and my skin cut into. I'm good on seeing the man responsible for all that."

"Okay, babe. I get it. You're angry and you have every right to be... just don't be mad at your man for too long, you still need to talk to him."

Dayana leaned closer to her best friend and hugged her tight.

"But for now you're stuck with talking to me. I'm here for you always, Thyri."

"Thank you, Dayana. You're such a great best friend. Thank you for coming to check on me and making me soup."

"You welcome, boo. You know I got you. Always."

Dayana spent the rest of the day with Thyri, watching Netflix and talking away about any and everything.

Well not everything.

At eight-thirty p.m., Dayana said her goodbyes and left Thyri's apartment. She'd had fun spending the day with Thyri and keeping her company but it was time to head home to her man.

Twenty minutes later, Dayana pulled up to her apartment building and parked her Tesla in her apartment's private parking. Within ten minutes, she was inside her building, on her floor and standing outside her door with her key in hand.

She let herself in and shut the door behind her, smiling as she heard that familiar neo soul instrumental playing in the background.

Ding!

The sound of her phone chiming made her bring her phone out of her red Telfar bag as she strolled to her bedroom.

No need to keep thanking me. Thank you for the 150k! I'd gladly beat that bitch's ass for free but being laced with some bread to beat her ass was worth it.

Dayana smiled as she read the text from an unknown number.

Those stab wounds were a great extra touch, she replied. *You really fucked her ass up.*

Ding!

Unknown: *The pleasure was all mine.*

Unknown: *I'll let you know once I'm settled in Houston.*

Dayana: *Alrightie boo.*

Dayana looked up from her phone once she arrived in the doorway of her bedroom. Her head lifted to meet the mahogany eyes of the one man she couldn't get enough of.

"How was she?"

Sadly, he was stuck on someone else that wasn't her. But she wasn't complaining about that, as long as she got what she deserved from him then she didn't care about his obsession with another woman.

"Fine," she replied, stepping into her bedroom, and walking over to where he sat on the edge of her bed.

"You know what you need to do next, right?"

"Yes." She dropped her bag beside him and nodded, assuring him of her obedience. "I do... get her to start thinking about you again. I got it."

"Good." He placed a hand to her waist, drawing her nearer to him. "You've been so good to me, D."

His back met the mattress as she climbed on top of him.

"I know."

"Oh you know, huh?"

She nodded, smirking down at him.

"I also know you're about to be good to me, Chosen..."

His brow arched in a teasing manner.

"By giving me what I deserve."

He groaned when he felt her hand cup his dick through his shorts. A smirk graced his lips.

"Oh, I'm definitely about to give you what you deserve."

She crashed her lips to his and the two began to kiss like they'd been starved of one another for years. The truth was they weren't starved of one another. They'd been sleeping together on and off for the past two years.

The day that Dayana had missed Thyri's tattoo appointment, she'd been in Vegas with Chosen. Her mother had never gotten in a car accident, that was all one big lie she'd made to use as her excuse for leaving Atlanta. She'd missed Thyri's tattoo appointment because she was too preoccupied with fucking Chosen. That day, Dayana had told Thyri that she was "waiting to board her flight now and won't be back in the city for another five hours" when in reality she was in the middle of getting her pussy eaten by Chosen. She made him pause so she could talk to Thyri on the phone without releasing any accidental moans. Chosen had convinced her to miss her flight so they could fuck around some more and promised to buy her the next flight out, which he did.

Her "boyfriend" Ethan that she kept mentioning to Thyri, didn't exist. Ethan had been a one night stand from two years ago that Dayana had and she pretended that she was in a relationship with him to have something to talk about with Thyri. If they were both in a relationship, Thyri would feel more open in sharing what was going on in her relationship and Dayana wanted to know everything that was happening with Chosen. Anytime Chosen and Thyri had a fight, she would know about it and use it to her advantage to get Chosen in her bed. While Thyri at him were at war, she'd be his peace, providing him with the solace he needed. And even when they were fine, Dayana would still be there for Chosen with open arms, open legs, and an open mouth.

She was sleeping with her best friend's man and she felt no guilt towards it. She didn't love Chosen. All she wanted was what he could provide. Amazing sex and fat checks. Thyri could deal with the headache he came with emotionally which is why she felt no remorse coming up with the idea for Soraya to beat Thyri up so that Thyri would feel hatred towards Killian and ultimately end up back with Chosen. It had all been her idea. She'd noticed Soraya's dismay towards Killian and Thyri's relationship, a relationship she could never compete with, and Dayana knew how bad Chosen wanted Thyri back. She knew Soraya would be willing to hurt Thyri for the right price and Chosen had money to cough up so it was a win-win situation.

Her and Soraya had set the whole thing up. From the night they'd have Soraya fight her to the hookah bar they'd all meet at. She'd told Soraya all she needed to know to make Thyri jealous enough to want to fight her and it'd all worked out. Telling Soraya to tell Thyri that Killian had painted her too had been a very nice touch that made Dayana laugh every time she thought about it.

Now Soraya was out the city, 150k richer, starting over in a new city with Chosen's bread and Chosen was working his way back into Thyri's arms with Dayana's help. After realizing that she'd lost Killian, Soraya was starting to consider moving out of Atlanta and Dayana's proposition had provided her with all the incentive she needed. She was initially surprised that Dayana was happy to set her friend up but after Dayana explained that they weren't really friends and that Thyri deserved to get her ass beat for stealing Killian from Soraya, Soraya no longer cared. She'd hurt Thyri with no regrets and would do it again in a heartbeat if she needed to. Her only concern right now was staying out of Atlanta so that she wouldn't run into Killian.

Things would soon be back to normal once Chosen and Thyri were back together and Dayana would be happy remaining his side chick, providing him with a refuge that Thyri could never provide.

A Note From Miss Jen:

Thank you so much for reading my novel! It truly means the world to me. I hope you enjoyed reading part one of 'Real Love From A Real One'. I hope you enjoyed reading about The Miller Brothers & The Wright Sisters. What a crazy bunch, right? Part two will be out very soon! Make sure you're in my readers group, subscribed to my mailing list and following my Instagram to find out the exact release date.

Please head over to my official website, where you'll be able to find out about me and find more of my novels:
www.missjenesequa.com

You can also join my mailing list via: www.missjenesequa.com/sign-up

Make sure you join my private readers group (Jen's Tribe) on Facebook to stay in touch with me and my upcoming releases:
www.facebook.com/groups/missjensreaders

Follow me on Instagram: www.instagram.com/miss.jenesequa

I've also created Apple Music and Spotify playlists for the book which you can check out here: www.missjenesequa.com/playlists

Signed paperbacks & merchandise are available at: www. jenesequatreasure.com

Once again, thank you very much for reading! Please let me know what you thought by leaving a review/rating on Amazon. I'd love to know what you thought about my novel.

Love
From,
Jen xo

Miss Jenesequa's Novels

Sex Ain't Better Than Love: A Complete Novel
Down For My Baller: A Complete Novel
Bad For My Thug 1 & 2 & 3
The Thug & The Kingpin's Daughter 1 & 2
Loving My Miami Boss 1 & 2 & 3
Giving All My Love To A Brooklyn Street King 1 & 2
He's A Savage But He Loves Me Like No Other 1 & 2 & 3
Bad For My Gangsta: A Complete Novel
The Purest Love for The Coldest Thug 1 & 2 & 3
The Purest Love for The Coldest Thug: A Christmas Novella
My Hood King Gave Me A Love Like No Other 1 & 2 & 3
My Bad Boy Gave Me A Love Like No Other: A Complete
Novella
The Thug That Secured Her Heart 1 & 2 & 3
She Softened Up The Hood In Him 1 & 2 & 3 & 4
You're Mine: Chosen By A Miami King: A Complete Novel
A Love That Melted A Capo's Cold Heart: A Complete Novel
Real Love From A Real One

Made in the USA
Monee, IL
06 November 2021

81559756R00277